For My Family

Acknowledgments

Barry Fishler deserves all due credit for the title. Jo Anne Vaughn and Mike Bateman read the rough drafts for me. Max Campanella looked over the gun stuff and took me shooting. Brian Whitehead kept calling me, demanding blood—I hope this satisfies him. In 2005, Jean Hortman read the ARC of the first book in less than two hours at a party and since then has poured out fountains of encouragement and sanity checks, for which I'm eternally grateful.

As usual, my editor Jaime Levine made this a better book. Thanks also to Ashley Grayson and Company, for herding cats, or Kitty, as it were.

kitty
AND THE
SILVER BULLET

*Also by Carrie Vaughn
from Gollancz*

Kitty and the Midnight Hour
Kitty Goes to Washington
Kitty Takes a Holiday
Kitty and the Silver Bullet
Kitty and the Dead Man's Hand
Kitty Raises Hell
Kitty's House of Horrors
Kitty Goes to War

kitty
AND THE
SILVER BULLET
Carrie Vaughn

Copyright © Carrie Vaughn 2008
All rights reserved

The right of Carrie Vaughn to be identified as the author
of this work has been asserted by her in accordance with
the Copyright, Designs and Patents Act 1988.

First published in Great Britain in 2008
by Gollancz
An imprint of the Orion Publishing Group
Orion House, 5 Upper St Martin's Lane,
London WC2H 9EA
An Hachette UK Company

This edition published in Great Britain in 2011
by Gollancz

10 9 8 7 6 5 4 3 2 1

A CIP catalogue record for this book
is available from the British Library

ISBN 978 0 575 10065 7

Printed and bound in the UK by CPI Mackays,
Chatham, Kent

The Orion Publishing Group's policy is to use papers
that are natural, renewable and recyclable products and
made from wood grown in sustainable forests. The logging
and manufacturing processes are expected to conform to the
to environmental regulations of the country of origin.

MORAY COUNCIL LIBRARIES & INFO.SERVICES	
20 31 75 76	
Askews & Holts	
F	

www.carrie vaughn.com
www.orionbooks.co.uk

The Playlist

Billie Holiday, "They Can't Take That Away From Me"

Shonen Knife, "Milky Way"

Pretenders, "Talk of the Town"

The Clash, "Clash City Rockers"

Creedence Clearwater Revival, "Commotion"

Stephen "Tintin" Duffy, "Kiss Me"

Sinead O'Connor, "You Do Something to Me"

Peggy Lee, "Fever"

Front 242, "The Untold"

The Dresden Dolls, "Missed Me"

The Supremes, "Where Did Our Love Go"

The Beatles, "Hey Bulldog"

Depeche Mode, "Home"

I hated the smell of this place: concrete and institutional. Antiseptic. But all the cleaning in the world couldn't cover up the unhappiness, the sourness, the faint smell of urine. The anger.

The guard at the door of the visiting room pointed me and Ben to empty chairs at a table on one side of a glass partition. The room held half a dozen cubicles like this. Only a phone line would connect us to the other side.

I was shaking. I didn't like coming here. Well, I did, and I didn't. I wanted to see him, but even being here as a visitor made me feel trapped. The Wolf side didn't handle it very well. Ben squeezed my hand under the table.

"You okay?" he said. Ben had been coming here once a week to see Cormac. I didn't come quite as often—once a month, for five months now. I'd never get used to this. In fact, it seemed to get harder every time, not easier. I was so tense, just being here exhausted me.

"I think so," I said. "But this place makes me nervous."

"Don't let him see you upset," he whispered. "We're supposed to be supportive."

"I know. Sorry." I held his hand with both of mine and tried to stop the trembling. I was supposed to be the strong one. I was supposed to be the one who helped Ben keep it together, not the other way around.

On the other side of the glass, a guard led out a man wearing an orange prison jumpsuit. His light brown hair was cut shorter than it used to be, which made his face seem more gaunt. I tried to convince myself that he wasn't thinner. His mustache was the same as always. So was his stoic frown.

My smile felt stiff and fake. Cormac would know it was fake. Had to be cheerful, couldn't let him see me upset.

He was handcuffed. When he picked up the phone to talk to us, he had to hold both hands up to his face. Ben held our phone between us. Leaning close, we could both hear.

"Hey," Ben said.

"Hey." Cormac smiled. Broke my heart, him smiling like that behind the glass. "Thanks for coming."

"How you doing?"

Cormac shrugged. "Hanging in there. No worries."

He was here on felony manslaughter charges. He'd killed to save my life, and now he was serving time for it. I owed him a huge debt, which hung on me like lead weights.

It could have been worse. The only way we could all sit here smiling at each other was thinking of how much worse it had almost been. One or all of us dead, Cormac in here for life—

He didn't seem to begrudge me the debt. Right from the start, he'd approached the prison sentence as doing penance, just like he was supposed to. Just another obstacle to overcome, another river to cross.

Ben handled this better than I did. "You need anything? Besides a cake with a file baked in?"

"No. Just more of the same."

I'd been ordering books for him. It had started out as a joke after I'd accused him of being illiterate. Then it turned earnest. Reading kept his mind off being trapped. Kept him from going crazy.

"Any requests?" I said, and Ben tipped the mouthpiece so he could hear me.

Cormac shook his head. "I'm not picky. Whatever you think is good." I had a list of classics I was feeding him. But no Dostoyevsky.

We had an hour for small talk. Very small talk. I couldn't say I'm sorry, because then I'd get upset. Leave on a happy note. Ben and I wanted to make sure Cormac got out of here in one piece, or at least not any more damaged than he was when he went in.

"Would you believe some of the guys listen to your show?" Cormac said.

"Really? That's kind of weird."

"I tell them you're not that mean in person. I'm ruining your reputation."

"Great," I said, smirking. "Thanks." Ben chuckled.

"You two look good," Cormac said, leaning back in his chair. "You look good together." His smile turned satisfied, almost. Comforted.

He'd told us both to look after each other. Like he couldn't trust either of us to take care of ourselves, but together we'd be okay. He was probably right. Ben and I had cobbled together our little pack of two, and we were doing okay. But it still felt like we were missing something. He was sitting across from us, on the other side of the glass. And we were all pretending like everything was okay.

A guard loomed behind Cormac. Time's up.

"I'll see you next week," Ben said.

Cormac said, to me specifically, "Thanks for coming. Everyone in here's ugly as shit. It's nice to see a pretty face once in a while."

Which broke my heart again. There had to be more I could do than sit here and be a pretty face, however pretty I could possibly be with my pale skin, blond hair tied in a short, scruffy ponytail, and eyes on the verge of crying. I wanted to touch the glass, but that would have been such a cliché and hopeless gesture.

He put the phone back, stood, and was gone. He always walked away without turning to look, and we always stayed to watch him go until he was out of sight.

Ben put his hand on my shoulder, urging me away. Hand in hand, in silence, we left the prison gates and emerged into too-bright summer sun and a baking parking lot. Quietly we slipped into the car, Ben in the driver's seat. Then the blowup happened.

He closed the door, settled for a moment, then hit the steering wheel with a closed fist. Then again, and again, throwing his whole body into it. The car rocked. I just watched.

After a moment, he slouched back. He gripped the steering wheel, bracing himself. "I hate this. I hate that he's in there, and there's nothing I can do."

He blamed himself as much as I blamed myself. If I hadn't needed saving, if Ben had found the right legal out— and there was Cormac, accepting it all without complaint. He and Cormac were cousins. They'd grown up together, looked out for each other, and now they were helpless.

I touched his forearm and squeezed, like I could push out the tension. He sighed.

"Let's get out of here," I said.

* * *

Friday night, time to party.

"Good evening, and welcome to *The Midnight Hour*. I'm Kitty Norville, your ever-cheerful hostess. Tonight it's all vampires, and all calls. I want to hear from you about those mysterious bloodsuckers of the night. Questions, problems, nothing's off-limits. Tell me a story I've never heard before. It's getting pretty tough to scare me these days, but I'd like you to try. Or even better—let's see if someone out there can give me a little hope. I've had one of those days."

I was such a lucky girl. After doing this show for two years, my monitor still lit up with calls. My listeners had been waiting with their fingers on the speed-dial button. One of these days, I'd ask for calls and the phones would come up silent. Then I'd have to retire for sure. But this wasn't that night.

"Our first call this evening comes from...Maledar...Maledar? Is that right?"

"Yes, it is." The light male voice managed to drip with pretension.

"Your parents actually named you Maledar."

"No." He sounded pouty. "That's the name I chose for myself. I'm preparing for my new identity. My new life."

Inwardly, I groaned. A wannabe. Even more pretentious than the real thing. "Am I to understand it, then, that you want to become a vampire?"

"Of course. Someday. When I'm older."

It clicked then—the voice, the name, the utter cheese of it all. "Wait a minute—how old are you? You're supposed to be eighteen to call in." The kid had lied to my screener. Fifteen, I bet. And to his credit smart enough to know how much it would suck to get frozen at age fifteen for all eternity.

"I'm ageless," he said breathily. "Ageless as the *grave*."

"Okay, this is *not* the kinderbat poetry hour. You'll want—oh, I don't know—public access television for that."

The pause was ominous. Then, "Whoa, what a wicked cool idea."

Dear God, what have I done? Hurry, move on quick before I get into more trouble. "I don't know what your question was, but you're leaving now. Bye. Please, somebody with sense call me so we can discuss Byron or something. Next caller, hello."

"I knew him, you know." This was a suave male voice, coolly assured. The real thing. An older vampire showing off his hard-earned ennui.

"Knew who?"

"Lord Byron, of course."

"*Really*," I drawled. "You know, there are about as many vampires who say they knew Byron as there are reincarnation freaks who say they were Cleopatra in a past life. Which would mean Byron had, like, *hundreds* of obnoxious simpering twits trailing after him. When he really only had Keats and Shelley."

The guy huffed. "How very droll."

"I'm sorry, you just hit one of my buttons, you know?"

"You've never considered that perhaps one of those vampires who say they knew Byron might be right?"

"Okay, fine. You chilled with Byron. You want to tell me what he was like? Him and the others? Hey, maybe you can answer a question for me—that other guy who was there the night they told the ghost stories and Mary

Shelley came up with *Frankenstein,* the one whose name I can never remember—"

"Polidori."

"Uh, yeah. Him." Oh crap, what if this guy really had known Byron? Was I going to sound like a royal idiot? "I always wondered why he never amounted to anything."

"He was what we call a hanger-on. Mary was the really clever one."

I grinned. "I always thought so. Now, I don't think you called just to talk about the Romantic poets. What's on your mind?"

"Destiny."

"Right, the *big* question. Like, why are we here, what's the point to life, that sort of thing?"

"I'm curious to hear what you think about it."

I pouted. "That's my line."

"Are you going to tell me?"

I sighed loudly to make sure the sound carried into the mike. "All right. I'll bite. Here's what I think, with the caveat that I may be wrong. I think we're here to make the world a better place than we found it. I think we don't always deserve the cards that we're dealt, good or bad. But we are judged by how we play the cards we're dealt. Those of us with a bum deal that makes it harder to do good—we just have to work a little more is all. There's no destiny. There's just muddling through without doing too much damage."

Most of the time I even believed that.

"Hmm, that's very nice," the vampire said, coy and condescending.

"All right. I *know* you're just trying to bait me. Why don't you come out and say what you want to say."

"You talk about us, vampires and lycanthropes, like we're afflicted. Like we have a handicap. And if your goal is to *pass* as human, to *blend in* with society, then I suppose it is a handicap. But have you ever thought that *we* are the chosen ones? Fate marked us, and we became what we are. We are superior, chosen by destiny, and one day we will rule the world. The Families know this. They are grooming us, the masters of the night, to be the masters of everything. We're the top of the food chain. One day humanity will see the truth of it."

By this time, I'd heard a dozen versions of this shtick. Fortunately, vampires only ever *talked* about taking over the world.

When they stopped talking about it, I'd start to worry.

"Why are you telling me this?"

"I want you to know the truth."

"Well, thank you for the public service announcement. I'm cutting you off now, you've had a little too much ego tonight. Next call—ooh, I think I might have a debate for us here. Hello, Jake? You're on the air. What do you have for me?"

"Um, Kitty? Oh, wow. I mean—hi."

"Hi. So you have a response to our esteemed vampire caller."

"Oh, do I ever. That guy is so full of'"—he paused amusingly to censor himself—"crap. I mean, I really want to know where I can get in on some of this vampire world domination action. 'Cause I'm a vampire and I'm stuck working the night shift at a Speedy Mart. *I'm* not the top of any food chain."

"You're not part of a Family?"

Jake chuckled. "If it weren't for your show I wouldn't even know about Families."

This was the part of my show that freaked me out a little. There were people out there for whom I was their only source of information, who used me as a lifeline. It felt like a burden. I had to sound encouraging to someone who'd been dealt a truly shitty hand: working the night shift at Speedy Mart for all eternity.

I said, "I know this is personal, but I take it that you were made a vampire under violent circumstances, against your will."

"Got that right. And if destiny had anything to do with it, I'd sure like to know why."

"I wish I had an answer for you, Jake. You got one of the bad cards. But since you and I both know there's no destiny involved, you have a choice on what to do about it."

"I really just wanted to tell the other side of the story. My side. That guy wasn't speaking for all vampires. Thanks for listening."

"That's what I'm here for. I'm going to move on to the next call now, okay? Good luck to you, Jake."

And so it goes.

I heard from men, women, vampires, humans, human servants of vampires, people who were funny, sad, lost, and angry. The problems ranged from silly to terrifying. I heard stories of people trapped in lives they hadn't expected, couldn't escape from. A lot of the time I didn't know what to tell them. I was totally inadequate to dispense advice—I could barely take care of myself. Early on, though, I'd learned that a lot of times people just needed to vent, and they needed someone to listen. People were desperate for conversation, and many of them didn't have anyone to talk to.

Talking about it made a thing—a problem, a weakness, a fear, a hope—more solid, and easier to confront. Easier to control.

I would do well to remember that in my own life.

"I've got time for one more call. Becky, you're on the air."

"Hi, Kitty," said a woman who sounded like she was on edge. "This isn't about vampires. I hope that's all right. It's important, I think."

At the end of the show, it didn't much matter. "What's the problem?" I didn't doubt that she had a problem. I recognized that tone. The screener had put in "domestic abuse" as the topic.

"I'm a werewolf, I'm part of a pack, and I'm worried. There's a new wolf. She's really young, really vulnerable, and the alpha male—he's taking advantage of her. But it's worse than that because he's beating up on her. This goes way beyond the dominance and submissive crap. The thing is, she won't leave. I've tried to talk her into going away, but she refuses. She won't leave him. I don't know what to do. How can I make her see that she doesn't have to put up with this? That she shouldn't? She won't stand up for herself."

The story sounded way too familiar. My first three years of being a werewolf, I'd been on the bottom rung, completely submissive to an alpha who was borderline abusive. But the pack meant protection, and I didn't want to leave. A time came when I had to choose between the pack and my own life—my show, my goals, my future. And I picked me. I'd never looked back.

Despite my experience, I didn't know what to tell her.

I said, "You should be given some credit for wanting to help. But sometimes that isn't enough. As hard as this sounds, there isn't much you can do if this person isn't willing to take that step for herself. I'm sorry."

"But—" she said, and sighed. "I know. I know you're right. I just thought there might be a trick to it."

"You can be a friend to her, Becky. Keep talking to her. And maybe you could lead by example. Maybe you should both leave town." I wasn't all that hot on the pack structure. My bias showed.

"That's hard to do," she said. "I'm safe here. But I can stand up for myself. She can't."

"Then all you can do is look out for her the best you can. Good luck to you, Becky."

You can't save everyone. I'd learned that.

I lightened my tone to wrap up. "All right, my friends, we're about out of time. How quickly it goes when we're having fun. I'll be counting the hours 'til next week. In the meantime, a bit of shameless self-promotion: don't forget that my book, *Underneath the Skin*—that's right *my* book, written by me, all about stuff I want to talk about—will be on sale in a few weeks. Like you weren't getting enough of me already. Stay safe out there. This is Kitty Norville, voice of the night."

Cue credits, with wolf howl—my own wolf howl, recorded especially for the show.

I was exhausted. Sometimes doing a show left me so buzzed that I couldn't sleep until morning. Not tonight. I couldn't wait to get home and crash. I felt like I'd been awake for days.

After chatting with the producer and finishing some paperwork, I headed outside. In his car, idling by the curb, Ben was waiting to pick me up. I hopped in on the passenger side, leaned over for a quick kiss, and smiled. Now this was a lovely way to end the night.

"How did it go?" Ben asked on the drive home. We were renting a place in Pueblo, a hundred miles or so south of Denver.

I pulled the elastic off my ponytail, shaking out my hair and scratching my head. I wanted a shower. "Great. It was a good night. But it really wore me out."

"You okay?"

I was always worn-out, lately. A condition of success was what I told myself. "Yeah," I said with a sigh and closed my eyes. I could feel Ben in the seat next to me, a comforting presence.

Ben and I never decided to be involved in a relationship. We'd fallen into the role of committed lovers by accident. Which was to say, both of us being werewolves, our wolf sides had bonded immediately and formed a pack. Our pack of two, I called it. A mated pair. This made it sound like our wolf sides and our human sides were two different beings, separate, distinct. But our human sides hadn't resisted the impulse. It had been easy, falling into each other's lives like this. Ben and I had been friends before he'd become a werewolf. Given time and opportunity, maybe we'd have become something more. I'd never know, now. Most of the time, I could ignore that niggling worm of doubt that hinted that this wasn't right. That this had somehow happened against my will. Ben was a good man, and I was lucky to have him in my life. We looked out for each other. But sometimes our relationship seemed a little bit like being in limbo. We were just along for the ride.

I slept like a rock and woke up nauseous. I'd been working too hard, I told myself. I hadn't had enough to eat the day before, but I couldn't bring myself to eat anything for breakfast. This morning, this day, was the day of the full moon. We had to drive, get out of town to someplace where we could Change in safety. Our safety, and everyone else's.

"You okay? You're looking a little green around the gills," Ben said as we packed the car. Usually on full moon days, I was the one asking him if he was okay. He was still a new wolf, still learning to control himself. I studied him; he seemed a little pale, a little tense. He had this habit of distracting himself from his troubles by worrying over me.

"Just a little off," I said. "Not ready for tonight for some reason."

He gave a grim smile. He was starting to understand.

Our territory was in the foothills of southern Colorado. Three hours of driving brought us to a remote national forest area. No camping allowed out here, no stray hikers to worry about. We'd be isolated.

We arrived and sat in the car.

"You're still looking off," Ben said again.

"I'm fine."

"Are you sure? You don't—" He paused, pursing his lips, clearly uncomfortable. "You don't smell right."

I stared at him. "I don't *smell* right?"

"I don't know, I can't explain it. You just smell off. Never mind."

Great. Now I smelled *off*. I grumbled, "I'm just tired."

"Even now?"

Now, full moon night, was when the other halves of our beings had their time. The wolves got to run, and they tore to the surface with all the power of the wild creatures they were. It felt like getting drunk, like being high, and however much we said we hated it, we couldn't wait to run out there and Change. The Change drew us.

I felt sluggish.

"I'm okay," I said. "Let's get this over with."

We left the car and hiked into wilderness.

Ben was getting good at controlling his wolf. This was his fifth full moon. He could make it from the car to the woods without losing it and sprouting claws. Almost, he could hide any sign that he was about to shift. But I could tell: his heart rate was too fast, and he was sweating.

We had a den, a sheltered place to keep us out of sight, warm and safe. We stripped and stashed our clothes: shirts, jeans, and shoes. The moon was rising, bright enough to cast shadows through the woods.

Ben looked out into those trees, his breath fogging a little in the cool air. I moved around him, touched his arm, slid my hand across his shoulders. He was pale in the moonlight. His skin was hot; he shivered under my touch. He turned and bent his head to me, kissed my ear, my neck, nuzzling. I pressed myself against him. Naked in the woods, bathed in moonlight, every nerve charged with feeling—this was Wolf's time. I began to see him through Wolf's eyes, fierce and full of life.

He breathed by my ear, "You first this time. I want to watch you."

I smelled him: skin and sweat, pheromones, desire, need. "You'll be okay?"

"I think so."

I'd always waited, making sure Ben was okay while he shifted. Comforted him. He probably didn't need supervising—it was for my own peace of mind. Our wolves called to each other—they wanted to shift together. Could he keep it together while watching me?

Maybe he just wanted to see if he *could* keep it together.

"Okay," I said softly. I kissed him; he kissed back hungrily, but I pulled away—teasing. I couldn't help it. It was her, the Wolf, daring him to chase her. She felt his need and stoked the fire.

I backed away, step by slow step. I was so hot, had so much energy tied up in a knot in my gut I could have screamed. It scratched at my skin, fighting to get out. All I had to do was breathe out, let go, and it would tear out of me. I held Ben's gaze. He crouched, his hands clenched into fists, his breathing coming too fast. But his gaze was steady.

All at once I released it, bent my head, doubled over, and as the veil slipped my vision blackened.

Shakes out her fur, and every hair is charged, sparking. Coils her muscles, ready to run—she trots in place, a spring and a jump, raises her head, and meets the gaze of the one she travels with, the pale figure watching her with wide eyes.

Here is her mate—still on two legs. She gives a little whine, a short bark, calling to him.

"God, look at you. You're amazing."

She trots forward, nudges him. He reaches for her, rubbing the not-paws along her coat. The stroking is both odd and pleasurable. She squirms away, whines again— now, it's time, come now—

And so he does, doubling over, groaning, and the sound changes, becomes less wrong and more right, until it is a howl, and she joins in, filling the woods with their song. He gasps a little, still not used to his legs and fur and voice. Still a pup, but stronger every time. All her hopes and desire and power go out to him—they rule these woods together. She greets him, licks him, nips him, lets him do the same to her, they writhe around each other, a tangle of fur and muscled bodies.

Then he launches into the forest. It's a surprise—he leads the chase this time. She has to scramble to keep up. They hunt, nose to the ground, following the zigzag patterns of their prey.

He's the one who finds the deer, a small one but large enough to feast on, upwind so it hasn't sensed them. Together they pause. Can they do it? They've never hunted anything so large together. He is eager, he's tasted blood, has hunted it, and the lust of it fills him because before anything else they are hunters. He makes a frustrated whine, because she hesitates. He wants to leap at it, tear into its haunches, bring it down. Together they can, one at its haunches, one at its throat. She knows this, can see the image in her mind. His limbs are trembling, he wants so badly to chase it down.

But she holds back.

Then it's gone. Raising its head, twitching its ears, it senses something that makes it run, leaping around trees and bushes. Too much work to chase it down now.

He shakes himself, scratches the dirt in frustration, pins his ears at her. She snaps at him and trots away, in search of some easier creature that she can catch with little effort.

In a moment he follows, because they're pack, and they hunt together. Rabbit instead of deer, but blood is blood in the end.

chapter 2

I didn't feel good.

I never felt great after a full moon night, but that not feeling good was like a hangover after a party. You suffered and didn't complain, because you'd had your fun and this was the price. Rather, the Wolf had her fun and left me to deal with the consequences.

But right now, I really didn't feel good. I felt sick, which was weird, because I hadn't been sick since becoming a werewolf. The same thing that made me a werewolf made me immune. Indestructible, almost. I curled up on my side, holding my stomach, which churned with cramps. No, it wasn't my stomach, it was lower than that. Deeper. Like menstrual cramps, but I'd never had them this bad. My insides felt like they were grinding themselves up.

"What's wrong?" Ben shifted behind me, where he'd been nestled asleep. He propped himself on an elbow and kissed my shoulder.

I must have let out a groan or something. "I don't feel good."

"What is it?"

"I don't know. Cramps or something."

"They always this bad?"

"Ben, we've living together for five months, you should know the answer to that." He glared, unamused. I shook my head. "No, never."

"What else could it be?" He was sitting up now, his hand on my arm, frowning worriedly at me.

"I don't know." That came out with a definite whine.

"Should you go to a hospital or something?"

"I never have to go to the hospital."

"Kitty, what if this is serious? You've been tired and sick for weeks."

"It's just cramps. What else could it be?"

"I have no idea what it could be—cancer? You accidentally swallowed a butcher knife last night? I don't know."

"Werewolves don't get cancer."

"Kitty." He bowed his head. "Never mind, do what you think is best."

"You think I should go to a doctor."

"Can you even sit up right now?"

I didn't want to think about sitting up, I hurt that much. Which meant maybe he was right.

"I don't have health insurance. Werewolves don't need health insurance." I reached for his hand; he took it, held it. He gave me that exasperated look he always did when I was being stubborn.

"One checkup won't break the bank."

"But what if something's really wrong?"

"You said it yourself—werewolves don't get sick."

"Then I don't have to go to the doctor."

We glared. He looked away first—deferring to the more

experienced. A submissive wolf. He dug my clothes out of the hole we'd stashed them in and threw them at me.

"Let's get moving, then see how you feel."

"Ben?"

"Hm?"

I held his arm, pulled on it, drew him close. Kissed him, and was happy when he smiled. "Let's go."

Back at home, I returned my mother's weekly Sunday phone call. Every Sunday she called, like clockwork. She'd known I was out for the full moon, but she'd left a message anyway. "Call back when you can, let me know everything's okay." She tried to be supportive in her own way. She'd convinced herself that my being a werewolf was like joining a club that did some vaguely dangerous and thrilling activity, like rock climbing.

"Hi, Mom."

"Hi, Kitty. How was your weekend?"

Oh, I turned into a wolf, killed something, woke up naked in the middle of the woods, went home, and brushed my teeth a half-dozen times to get the taste of blood out of my mouth. "It was okay. I haven't been feeling too great, I think something's stressing me out."

"Any idea what?"

"Maybe it's the book coming out. I'm worried how it's going to do."

"It'll be fine—I've read it, it's a really good book. People will love it."

"You're my mother, you're supposed to say that."

"Of course I am," she said happily.

And who could argue with that? "Ben thinks I should go to the doctor."

"It certainly couldn't hurt. It might make you feel better if they can tell you that nothing's wrong."

And if something *was* wrong? What was the local general practitioner going to know about lycanthropy anyway?

"Nothing's wrong," I insisted.

"Of course not," she said. "Nothing's ever wrong until it is." Her tone had become serious.

"What's that supposed to mean?"

She paused, like she was trying to decide what to say. Then she sighed. "It means it's better to be safe than sorry."

"Mom, is something wrong?" The conversation had gone a bit weird.

"Oh, no, not really. I just think Ben's right is all."

I couldn't win. I was besieged. "Okay. I'll think about it."

She changed the subject. "When are we going to meet this Ben character of yours?"

She knew I was living with Ben; I couldn't keep him a secret. She'd expressed a great deal of worry that, out of the blue, I'd apparently shacked up with my lawyer. I didn't tell her he'd become a werewolf in the meantime.

"I don't know, Mom. Maybe Christmas?"

"Kitty. That's months off. That's most of the year off."

"You aren't even ecstatic that I'm bringing up the possibility of coming home for Christmas this year?"

"I'll admit, that would be nice."

"I'll talk it over with Ben. Maybe we can work something out for this summer."

She seemed to be happy with the compromise, because she changed the subject, moving on to the topic of family,

Dad and my sister and her brood, like our typical calls. The whole thing was comforting. No matter what I did or what happened to me, Mom was always there with her phone calls.

After I'd hung up Ben said, "I'm still not ready to meet your family."

"You'll notice I didn't commit us to anything."

"I'm just saying."

I almost argued. I could have said all sorts of things, needled him, picked at that sore spot until it festered: why not, what's wrong with my family, you just don't want to admit that we're in a relationship, and so on. I started to say these things, just to see what his reaction would be.

But I let it go, because I wasn't ready for that argument any more than Ben was ready to meet my family.

I started bleeding that afternoon. I should have been relieved—my period, that's all it was. But it was late, there was too much, and something about it wasn't right. So I went to the doctor on Monday.

The nurse drew blood. The doctor wanted a urine sample. She wanted me to strip and sit on the examination table in a flimsy paper shirt. Then she poked, prodded, all the rest of it. In the five or so years since the last time I'd been in a doctor's office, I hadn't missed it, not once, not at all. The place had a weird smell. Everything was disinfected to within an inch of its life, but the antiseptic only covered up an underlying odor of illness telling me that sick people passed through here all day long.

I sat there for an hour, waiting. When the nurse poked

her head in and said I could get dressed, I nearly sprang off the table.

"Is Dr. Luce coming back? Did she say anything?"

"She'll be with you in just a minute."

The door closed, and I dressed quickly. A knock came a moment later. It cracked open before I said anything, and Dr. Luce, a busy middle-aged woman, short, with graying hair and a fancy multicolored patterned lab coat, hustled in.

"Good, you're dressed. If you'd take a seat there?"

She took the chair at the desk, I sat in the one right next to it. My stomach was jumping with anxiety. She wasn't smiling. If nothing was wrong, she'd be smiling. She glanced at my hands, which were kneading the fabric of my jeans, then met my gaze.

"Kitty, did you know you were pregnant?"

I froze, mouth open. That wasn't what I thought she would say. In retrospect, I should have expected it. All the signs were there: the exhaustion, the nausea, which was how everyone said it started. But that didn't apply to *me,* apparently. For some reason I couldn't process the question. She waited patiently, but my mouth was too dry to speak. I had to swallow a couple of times.

"No. I mean—no. Were? *Were* pregnant?"

"You've had a miscarriage. I'm very sorry."

"Oh," was all I could manage.

She launched into the prognosis. "You're fine. You're going to be fine, I'll say that first off. I'm not surprised you didn't know, you were probably only three or four weeks along based on the hormone levels. You'll experience cramping for a few more days; I can give you a prescription for that. This is actually fairly common..." And so on. I wished Ben were here. I very much wished Ben were here to hold my hand.

"I recommend waiting several months before trying again."

"I wasn't trying this time," I blurted.

She pursed her lips. "Then I recommend taking extra care with protection for the next few months."

Protection, hah. Mornings after a full moon, with the Wolf still so close to the surface, filling me, curled up with Ben, protection wasn't exactly the first thing on my mind. In fact, that was probably when it had happened—last full moon. I was embarrassed to admit that I didn't know enough about my own cycle, my own plumbing, and the whole process to know if that was when it could have happened.

"Doctor, you saw my record. My…" Um, what should I call it? "My preexisting condition. What impact does that have on any of this?"

"Yes, the lycanthropy. I'm afraid I have no experience with that—it hasn't made its way to the literature yet. I don't even know where to go to find out. Do you have any contacts? Anyone you could ask?"

"Yeah, I think I do. Thanks."

I accepted all her advice and the prescription form in a daze. She kept asking if I had any questions, and I couldn't think of any. I should have had questions, lots of questions. But the whole world had gone fuzzy, like I was looking at it through a filter.

I made it to my car and found my cell phone.

After two rings I heard, "Hello, Dr. Shumacher."

Dr. Elizabeth Shumacher was the new head of the Center for the Study of Paranatural Biology, the government research branch that really ought to start sending out bullctins to people like Dr. Luce. But really, how often did any doctor expect to see someone like me show up in their waiting room?

"Hi, Doctor, it's Kitty Norville."

"Oh! Hi, Kitty, how are you?" She sounded cheerful and genuinely happy to hear from me—unlike her predecessor, who had always acted like he was starring in a spy drama.

"Okay. I have a question: What do you know about lycanthropes and pregnancy?"

"Not a whole lot. The research hasn't gotten that far. Everything I have on file is anecdotal."

"What do the anecdotes say?"

"Well, everyone I've talked to, everything I've heard or read, says that female lycanthropes don't get pregnant."

"No, that can't—"

"Rather I should say they don't stay pregnant. They can conceive, but the embryo doesn't survive shape-shifting. They miscarry every time. My guess is a female lycanthrope may become pregnant many times and never realize it, since she'll never be more than a couple of weeks along before she has to shift. If the timing is right she might be as much as a month along. But I'm guessing that's rare."

Holy shit. I leaned back in the seat, holding my forehead, feeling ill all over again. Feverish, I wanted to throw up. I rolled down the window and let in clear air.

Dr. Shumacher kept talking in the manner of a scientist who's launched in on a topic she finds utterly fascinating, without much thought about her audience's reaction. "It makes sense, if you think about it. The mutation has to reproduce via infection because biological reproduction is impossible. This is probably true of vampirism as well. The same mechanism in vampirism that stops aging prevents the cellular growth required for biological reproduction. Formulating a theory along these lines is pretty high on my list…"

She must have known something was wrong when I stayed quiet for so long. She said, "Kitty—why are you asking this? Has something happened?"

"It's about a friend," I said blithely, transparently. She'd guess the truth. "I'm asking for a friend."

Why didn't I know this? Why had this never come up before? Why hadn't Meg—the alpha female of my old pack, who'd held my hand when I was new, then driven me out when I wasn't—told me any of this? Had she known?

Why didn't any of us talk to each other? Warn each other?

"You'll call me if you need anything, yes? You're my primary informant, you know," she said, concerned. I couldn't tell her. I didn't feel like talking about it.

"Yeah, yeah. I'll call. Thanks." I moved like a robot to put away the phone.

I held my stomach. Why had I never thought of this before? Why had I never considered? I hadn't wanted kids. I didn't want to be pregnant. This shouldn't matter. Then why did I feel gutted? I hadn't known, so it shouldn't mean anything. But it did, and the shock of that was one shock too many.

Ben came home from a courtroom appearance late that afternoon. He found me sitting in the kitchen, the lights out, working on my third beer. I hadn't filled Dr. Luce's prescription. Alcohol seemed to work just fine; I was starting to feel very, very relaxed.

He set his briefcase on the floor and pulled up the chair across from me. "What happened?"

I took a deep breath. I'd been rehearsing this carefully. My brain was hazy, though, and it came out weird. Obliquely. I spoke too slowly to make sure the words came out right. I must have sounded nuts.

"Have you ever had the experience of not knowing you wanted something until someone told you you couldn't have it?"

"I don't know. I've always kind of wanted a Porsche. Can I have one?" His attempt at a smile faded.

I closed my eyes and shook my head. "This is different. This is...it's screwing with me and I don't know what to think."

"Kitty. Stop talking around it. Tell me what's wrong."

Mine. His. It had been both of ours. "The doctor said I had a miscarriage. I called Shumacher at the Center, and she told me lycanthropes always have miscarriages. That shape-shifting and pregnancy...it doesn't survive. I thought—I guess I assumed that if I wanted to have kids someday, it wouldn't be a problem. I just assumed. I never even asked. But I can't. And I didn't think I'd be this upset about it. I'm sorry, I'm not making any sense." I took a swig of beer and turned away to hide my face.

He didn't say anything. I couldn't guess what he was thinking. Wasn't sure I wanted to know. So I didn't look at him. I tried to block out the world, so I wouldn't have to process anything that wasn't in my own head.

Then he moved. Slipped out of his chair and knelt next

to mine. Put his arms around me, held me against him, lay my head on his shoulder, and murmured, "Shh."

He knew I was crying before I felt it myself. He saw it coming, but I didn't know it until I was sobbing onto his shoulder and kneading the shirt across his back with stiff fingers.

After I'd cried myself out, we migrated to the sofa, where I lay curled up against him, snuggled in his arms.

"Did you know you were pregnant?"

"No. I should have known. Should I have known? You think I'd know something like that."

"I don't know anything about it."

"I'm kind of glad I didn't know. What if I'd known, gotten used to the idea, maybe even gotten excited, and then—" I shook my head. "Does that sound weird?"

"I don't know. What would sound normal?"

"This happens all the time, people go through this all the time. Why is it so... What about you? Do you want kids?" I twisted around so I could see him better.

He waited a long time before he said, "No."

"Then you're glad it turned out this way."

"Kitty, no, it's not like that." He blew out a frustrated sigh. "A year ago it never would have occurred to me that it was even a possibility. That I'd be living with someone and that the issue would even come up. I might have changed my mind. I don't know."

Neither did I. A common phrase, lately.

I snuggled closer. "I feel like someone's taken something away from me. It makes me angry."

We must have stayed there for hours. I was intensely grateful. I didn't know how I expected him to react. I wouldn't have blamed him if he'd run screaming. But I needed to be close to him, and he stayed.

I'd started to fall asleep—it must have been close to midnight—when the doorbell rang. The freaking doorbell.

"Who the hell is it at this hour?" Ben said, grumpy.

"Vampire?" I muttered.

He gave me the smirking *you can't be serious* look. Neither one of us moved. We couldn't be expected to answer the door at midnight.

But the bell rang again, longer, like our visitor was leaning on the button.

Ben groaned. "It's an emergency. Has to be."

"Light's on. Can't pretend we're asleep."

Making a production out of it, he extricated himself from my grip and stood. "You stay, I'll check on it."

I didn't argue.

A full minute later I heard from the front door, "Kitty? It's for you."

I had no idea who it could be. I didn't know anyone in Pueblo beside Ben.

I trudged to the front door. Ben gripped the handle of the open door and looked back at me. And there, on the other side of the threshold, stood Rick. The vampire.

I needed to stop making flippant remarks like that.

"Oh my God. Rick."

"Hi, Kitty." His height was average and his features pale, vaguely aristocratic, like a figure from an old painting. That may also have been the way he carried himself—straight-backed, self-possessed. Nothing would ever make him lose his temper. His dark hair was brushed back from his face and just touched his shoulders. He wore dark slacks, a well-pressed shirt, smart shoes—and an overcoat, in summer.

Rick was an odd duck. He was affiliated with Arturo, the Master vampire of Denver, but he also maintained a degree of independence. I wasn't sure what he did for Arturo, or what he got out of the association. I wasn't exactly an expert on vampire internal politics. I did know he was at least a couple hundred years old, and he'd been in the region for much of that time. He had some great Old West stories. In the past, we'd done favors for each other, passing along useful information. Neither of us was as territorial as others of our kind.

"What are you doing here?"

"It's a long story. May I come in?" He gestured at the threshold.

I had to invite him in. He looked at me, waiting, and I stared back, stupefied.

Ben inched closer to me and said to my ear, privately, "He smells dead."

"Yeah," I whispered back. "That's how vampires smell."

"It's weird." He glared sidelong at Rick.

The vampire waited quietly. I couldn't decide what to do.

"Do you trust him?" Ben said. Ben and Cormac had been vampire hunting together. We'd never really discussed how Ben felt about vampires, but I knew he didn't think well of them in general.

"I wouldn't be here if it wasn't important," Rick said.

Rick had never given me a reason to be suspicious of him. I thought of him as one of the good guys. He'd done me favors. Still, I couldn't help but feel like I was going to regret this.

"Come on in," I said with a sigh, and stepped aside. Rick stepped across the threshold, hands stuck in the pockets of his overcoat.

I snuck a glimpse out at the curb. I wanted to see what kind of car a vampire would drive. Fully in character, I spotted a BMW convertible, silver and zippy. No way anyone in this neighborhood drove that car.

I gave a low whistle. "Nice."

"Thanks," Rick said.

Turning back inside, I closed the door. "I'd offer you something to drink, but, well—no way. No offense."

"That's all right. I had a drink before I came."

Ben shook his head, scowling. To me he said, "I hate vampires."

Rick wore an amused smile. "Kitty, it's been a while. How are you?"

"Now's not really a good time to ask that. I'm kind of drunk." And sick. Sick at heart. "Um, this is my friend, Ben. Ben, Rick."

"Ben O'Farrell, isn't it?" Rick said.

Ben's back tightened, his shoulders bunching like hackles rising. A response to danger. He looked hard at Rick. "Have we met?"

"No. But you have an entry in the same file Arturo keeps on that bounty hunter, Cormac. It doesn't say anything about you being a werewolf."

I thought for a minute Ben was going to jump him, the way every muscle in his body seemed to quiver. I resisted an urge to grab him and hold him back. But I had to admit, I was also creeped out that Arturo was keeping files on

Cormac and God knew who else. Me, most definitely. Couldn't help but wonder what it looked like.

Trying to exude calm, I touched Ben's arm.

"You going to take that information back to him?" Ben asked.

"No," he said.

"Rick—how did you find me?"

"Matt gave me your address."

Matt, the engineer from KNOB, my old radio station. "Okay, now did he give it to you, or did you, let's see, how do I put this . . . persuade him to give it to you?"

"He, ah, might have taken a little persuading." He actually smiled at that.

I rolled my eyes. I was sure Matt was fine. Rick probably hadn't needed to do more than look him in the eyes and work a little of his vampire mojo on him. If I asked Matt, he wouldn't remember what had happened.

"Can we sit down somewhere?" Rick said.

We retreated to the living room. Ben and I sat on the sofa, and Rick found a chair to pull across from us. He sat, then leaned forward, elbows on knees. He seemed casual, almost friendly, at odds with the usual vampire sense of sophistication. Most vampires liked to be the coolest thing in the room. Rick usually didn't bother with the pretension. The BMW notwithstanding.

He hesitated, studying me and Ben both, sizing us up. I didn't look straight back at him. Didn't meet that hypnotic gaze.

"I need your help," he said.

I couldn't guess what he could possibly need from me that would drag him all the way out here from Denver.

"What kind of help do you need that you couldn't just call?"

He said, "I'm going to move against Arturo. I'm looking for backing."

He surprised me into staring back at him. He wanted to stage a coup and take over Denver? I hadn't thought he had that kind of ambition in him. Hell, he'd told me he didn't have that kind of ambition. Something had changed, obviously.

"Why?"

From an inside pocket of his overcoat, he drew out a folded piece of paper—a newspaper article. After unfolding it, he offered it to me. It showed a front-page story about a series of attacks that had taken place at a downtown nightclub. No one had been killed, but at least three people had been taken to the hospital with severe bite wounds. The victims claimed vampires had attacked them—though the vampires must have been pretty sloppy if the people even remembered being attacked. According to the article, the authorities were skeptical, but in this day and age they were considering all options. The article also included a quote from the CDC assuring people that a simple bite from a vampire would not infect them with vampirism. That didn't stop people from freaking out.

The fact that Rick was showing me this suggested it really had been vampires.

"I'm afraid he's losing control."

Part of a city's Master's job was to keep things like this from happening. Keep the city's vampires under control. If they weren't controlled, people could die. When people died, the authorities got interested, and vampires didn't want that kind of attention if they expected to maintain their little empires.

"There's more," Rick continued. "If he's perceived as weak by outsiders, others could move in to take control. He's in danger of losing his authority. If he seeks help from outside, he's in danger of losing his autonomy entirely."

"Other Masters are moving in? Besides you?"

"It's complicated. But I don't want to see control of the region fall into the wrong hands."

"And your hands are the right ones?"

He presented those hands in a gesture of offering.

My gut feeling liked Rick. But I didn't know much more about him than that. Not enough to feel confident that his hands were the right ones. But I trusted him more than I trusted Arturo. Arturo hated my show and had tried to have me killed to get me to stop. Just on that basis I'd rather have Rick in charge.

"What am I supposed to do?"

"The Denver werewolves will side with Arturo. Arturo has Carl and Meg's allegiance." Carl and Meg, the alpha pair that headed the Denver pack. Not my favorite people in the world by a long shot. In fact, I'd be happy if I never heard their names again.

I did not like where this was going.

Rick said, "If you could take over the pack—"

"No," I said.

"You're strong enough. Especially with help." He glanced at Ben suggestively. Like he thought we would make a good alpha pair.

This was crazy.

"No. No way. I lost that fight. I'm in exile, and you know what? I like being in exile. I don't want to go back.

They can keep the damn pack. I'm sorry, Rick, but you're going to have to find another way to get the werewolves on your side."

"The situation's changed since you left. Degenerated. How long have you been gone, six months?"

"Eight. Nine, maybe."

"Three more from your pack have died in that time. Carl and Meg killed them. You and T. J. stirred up the rest of the pack, and those two are barely maintaining control. It's unhealthy, Kitty. It's on the verge of anarchy. It needs help to make it safe for its members again."

I couldn't save the world. I couldn't solve everyone's problems. I was barely keeping my own life together.

"What makes you think I could do that?"

"Because you almost did it eight months ago. You've grown stronger since then. I can tell just by looking at you."

"No."

Ben took my hand, squeezed it. His turn to comfort me, now. He said, "Kitty's right, this isn't the best time to talk about this."

"I'm sorry, but I'm running out of time," he said. "The city is running out of time. Some vampires don't care about control."

I shook my head. "Rick, I can't save everyone. The thing is, I like being a rogue. I like being on my own. I like not having to worry about a pissy alpha looking over my shoulder all the time, or worrying what a dozen other werewolves are doing behind my back. I get to have my own life."

"Your own life—with your mate."

Pack of two. I kept forgetting. "That's right."

"What would it take to bring you back to Denver?" Rick said.

I glared. "Nothing will bring me back to Denver. I'm sorry."

"Well. Thanks for your honesty." He stood and shook out his coat.

I walked him to the door, with Ben lurking behind us, trying to be menacing and unobtrusive at the same time. It made him look surly.

To Rick I said, "It's awfully trusting of you, telling me what you're planning. There's a lot of people in Denver who'd like to know about it."

"If you were on good terms with any of them, I might be worried." He smiled a crooked smile. "You're trusting enough to invite me into your home. I'm returning the favor."

I wouldn't have thought twice about inviting a friend into my home. But Rick gave the action gravity. In his world, one couldn't take such invitations for granted. I wondered: Had he expected me to say no? Would he have turned around and driven away if I hadn't offered the invitation? Had he only told me his plans after I passed that test?

"When's it happening?" I asked, testing this new trust we'd apparently established.

He shrugged. "I'm still marshaling forces. Soon."

"How do I find out how it all turns out?"

"Come to Denver in a month or so. See if anyone tries to kill you." That smile again.

"I hate you people. I hate this crap."

"Then stay in Pueblo." With a sarcastic edge he added, "I'm positive no one will bother you here."

That was some kind of dig, I was sure.

He was halfway down the walk to his car when I leaned out the doorway. "Rick? Good luck."

He glanced at me over his shoulder, buried his hands in his pockets, and continued on.

Ben came up behind me, body to body, and put his hand on my hip. "I don't have to tell you that guy made me nervous, do I?"

"Yeah, well, let's hope you never meet the guy he's trying to replace."

"That's the guy with a file on Cormac."

"Denver's Master vamp."

"I didn't know Denver even rated a Master vampire. You've met him? What's he like?"

"Let's just say Rick has his work cut out for him."

I squirmed out of his embrace just enough to close the door, then pulled myself back into his arms. The beer hit me all at once, and I was about to fall asleep on my feet. I tugged at his shirt and hoped my voice wasn't too slurred. "Let's go to bed."

The getting drunk worked, because I fell asleep without thinking of babies, miscarriages, blood, vampire wars, or much of anything at all.

My cell phone, sitting on the bedstand, rang. I jerked awake, feeling like someone had hit a gong over my face. Then the headache struck. I groaned and burrowed under the pillow.

"Are you getting that?" Ben sounded annoyed.

"What time is it?"

"Early."

And the damn phone kept ringing. I grabbed it and checked caller ID. My parents' number showed on the display. It was Tuesday, not Sunday, Mom wouldn't be calling if it wasn't Sunday. Unless something was wrong.

I pressed the talk key. "Hello?"

"Kitty?" My father answered.

I sat up. Something *was* wrong. I loved my dad, and we got along great—at least since I'd moved out on my own. But he never called me. A sudden wave of gooseflesh covered my arms.

"Dad, hi."

Ben propped himself on his elbow, watching me, his brow creased with concern. He'd probably sensed something in my voice, and in the way my whole body went rigid.

"Can you come up here today? This morning?"

"What is it? What's wrong?"

"Your mother's checking into the hospital."

"What?" My voice came out too high-pitched. "Why, what for?" Ben's hand moved to my leg, a comforting pressure.

"Did she tell you she went in for a mammogram last week?"

"No. Wait a minute—how long has she known about this?" She'd known something was wrong during our phone call on Sunday and didn't tell me. My eyes stung, suddenly, painfully.

Dad took a deep breath—a calming breath, preparing for exposition. It couldn't have been that bad, I told myself. If Dad could be calm, nothing could be that wrong.

"She went in because she found a lump," he said. "It

could be nothing, it could be benign. They'll remove it and run the tests. She'll only stay there overnight. It's perfectly routine."

Was he trying to convince me, or himself?

Dad continued. "She didn't want me to tell you. She said she didn't want to be a bother just in case it turns out to be nothing. But I think it would mean a lot to her if you could be here."

If not for her, then for him. Maybe the weight of fear and uncertainty would be easier to bear if there were more of us to carry it.

"Yeah, sure I'll be there. What time? Where?" I took the phone to the next room in a search of pen and paper. Found it, scribbled down Dad's instructions. Repeated them all back. Mundane details kept the brain numb.

"Sorry about waking you," he said. "I wouldn't have called if I didn't think it was important."

"No, it's fine, I'm glad you called. Dad—how are you doing?"

"It's going to be fine. We'll go in and get this taken care of, and everything'll be fine." He spoke with an edge of desperation. He said the words as if he thought speech would make them fact.

"That didn't really answer my question."

After a pause, he said, "I'm holding up. Mom's the important one right now."

"Yeah. I'm coming up. I'm leaving right now."

"See you soon."

We hung up. I set down the phone and returned to the bedroom. I started pawing through the closet for clothes. My hands were shaking.

"Kitty?" Ben said, watching me from the bed.

"I have to go to Denver. I have to go right now."

"Just like that? Exile over?"

"Ben—it's my mother."

"I know, I heard."

I thought about taking a shower, to wake myself up. No, too long. Clothes—jeans, T-shirt. No, something nicer. Blouse. I dressed quickly. Put my hair up.

Ben dressed as well. He followed me to the front of the house, watched me scoop up my bag, rush around looking for shoes—then he took my car keys out of my hand.

"I'm driving," he said.

"You don't have to go."

"Kitty—you're a wreck. I'm driving."

I started crying. Ben held me. It only lasted a minute, then I pulled myself together. No time to panic. No time for despair.

In ten minutes we were heading north.

chapter 3

Fighting with morning traffic, it took us three hours to get to Denver. Ben knew where the hospital was and drove us straight there. "I'm not just a lawyer," he'd explained, grinning. "I'm an ambulance-chasing lawyer."

Good thing he came along. The parking garage was packed, but he patiently wound our way up each level until we found a spot. Then I couldn't figure out what button to push on the elevator to get us to the hospital lobby, and once in the lobby I stood at the end of intersecting corridors and froze, uncertain where to go. Ben steered me in the right direction each time, finally pointing me to an information desk.

I held my stomach, which still hurt. Cramps still gnawed at me. My insides emptying themselves out. *I* was still sick.

"Don't say anything," I said, walking close to Ben. "Don't tell them about it. The miscarriage, I mean."

"Okay."

I leaned on the information desk. "I'm here to see Gail Norville, she was supposed to check in this morning."

The receptionist took way too long to type in the name and search in her database. Almost, I was ready to believe that it had all been a mistake. Mom wasn't really sick, she wasn't here at all, it was a big misunderstanding, and I'd get to throttle Dad over it later.

"Here she is," the receptionist said brightly. "In the outpatient ward, she's scheduled for surgery in an hour, but right now she's in room 207, one floor up, then turn right."

I was already away from the desk and on the move toward the elevator. Ben said, "Thank you," behind me.

The elevator moved too slowly. I wanted to growl at it. Ben and I stood together, side by side, arms touching. The touch calmed me a little. At the very least, it kept me from screaming.

One floor up, the elevator opened into a standard institutional corridor: off-white floor and walls, faintly humming fluorescent lights, doors and hallways branching off. I saw people moving, things happening, but only focused on the numbers above the doors. Turn right, 201, 203 . . .

The door to room 207 stood open. I had no idea what I'd find inside. I crept in, shoulders bunched up, so tense I thought I'd break.

Everybody was there—my whole immediate family. Mom, Dad, big sister Cheryl, her husband Mark, their two kids. Mom lay in bed, wearing a cloth hospital gown. The bed was cranked up so she was sitting up, and she had my sixteen-month-old nephew Jeffy in her lap, entertaining him with a stuffed tiger. Three-and-a-half-year-old Nicky was with her father, sitting in a chair in the back. She was red-eyed, face squished up, crying and unhappy, like she could sense that the grown-ups were upset but couldn't understand why—only that something was wrong. Mark was trying to distract her. Cheryl sat in a chair next to the bed, hovering over Jeffy, and my father, Jim Norville, hovered over her.

"Hi."

Everyone looked at me. For a moment, the smiles stopped being so forced.

"Kitty!" Mom said, laughing.

I practically fell on top of her in my rush to hug her, however awkwardly, with me leaning over her and her pushing off from the bed. "You're here, you're really here!" she mumbled into my hair.

"Why didn't you tell me? You should have told me," I muttered at her.

"That's exactly what your sister said," she answered.

"Mom!"

She shrugged, unapologetic.

Jeffy blinked at us, kind of blankly, and batted the tiger. We regarded each other. "Um, he's gotten bigger, hasn't he?" He was barely sitting up by himself the last time I saw him.

"Well, duh," Cheryl said, grinning at me.

I had to hug everyone then, moving around the bed to get to my sister and Dad.

"Thanks for coming," he whispered.

"Had to," I said.

I waved at Mark and Nicky. Mark waved back, and Nicky stared. My arrival seemed to disrupt her blubbering, and now she seemed as blankly fascinated by the new arrival as her brother. She hadn't doubled in size like Jeffy had—I actually recognized her from our last visit. But she clearly didn't remember me. I wasn't enough a part of her life for her to remember.

Kids. Dammit. Those two were as close as I was ever going to get.

No tears, not here. I stood back and took a good look at my family. My first family. We looked like a family—all of us relatively athletic, fit, like some kind of country club advertisement. Mom and Dad met on their college tennis team and still played a couple times a week. Dad's brown hair was going a rather distinguished gray. The girls all had the blond hair, though Mom's had almost turned the color of ash.

For a moment, Mom didn't look like Mom. She hadn't put on makeup, her chin-length hair was straight, unstyled, and the hospital gown left her looking lumpy, untailored. Mom was an extremely put-together woman. This version of her was unmistakably ill. She had no overt symptoms. She smiled easily enough. But the anxiety was there, in the tension of her jaw and hands.

Dad saw Ben first. Ben had slipped in quietly and leaned against the wall by the door. Dad's gaze drew everyone else's attention.

Well, I hadn't quite planned this to happen this way. Nothing to do but plunge ahead.

"This is Ben," I said. I went to grab him and pull him forward, guiding him by the elbow. I pointed and introduced. "Ben, this is my mom and dad—Gail and Jim. Cheryl, married to Mark over there, and the rug rats are Jeffy and Nicky."

"Hello, Ben," Mom said with a rich smile and insufferable smugness. "It's so good to finally meet you in person."

Ben very politely shook hands with my parents. "Mrs. Norville, Mr. Norville."

"God, this is so high school," I muttered, suddenly feeling sixteen years old. Weren't things like introducing your significant other to your parents supposed to get easier?

"Please, call me Gail," Mom purred, looking pleased as anything.

The room was almost cheerful, the walls painted rose, the blanket on the bed a happy yellow. They'd tried to add some brightness to the institutional setting. But it still smelled like a hospital. And Mom was still sick.

"What's going on? What's happening?" I said.

Mom brushed it all away. "I'll be fine. One way or the other, I'll be fine. The biopsy might even come back negative, and I'll have nothing to worry about. But even if it is malignant—I'll have a little radiation therapy, and it'll all be gone. I won't even have to stop working. It's all going to be fine."

She was the only one in the room who was smiling. I looked at my dad. I had never seen that expression on his face. I hadn't seen that expression on anyone's face. He was anguished in a way that was more than trying not to cry—he never cried. It was like he was watching the world fall apart, and he believed he was the one who had to hold it together. I assumed he'd talked to Mom's doctor, that he knew everything Mom did about the situation. For some reason, he didn't share her sunny proclamation of the outcome. Surely it was too early to be glum. Wasn't it too early to expect the worst? Even if she really did have breast cancer?

Right now, Mom wanted us all to be as cheerful as she was. Wanted us all to believe that everything was going to be okay. Maybe she was right. A little surgery, a little radiation. Cancer wasn't an automatic death sentence. Thousands of women survived this. Mom would be one of them.

Before they wheeled her off for the surgery, Mom squeezed my hand. "If I had known all it would take to get you to come home was getting cancer, I'd have done it sooner."

Sick or no, I could have slapped her for that. "Don't joke like that, Mom."

She had the good grace to look abashed. "I'm sorry, you're right. It's just so good to see you. You're not going to run off again, are you?"

I shook my head. "I'll be right here when you wake up."

"Good."

And that was that. The surgeon had a very soothing demeanor. When he said this was all routine, nothing to worry about, I started to believe it. We waited in one of those generic hospital waiting rooms, with plastic chairs and out-of-date magazines fanned out on the tables. Fake plants and pictures of flowers continued the atmosphere of forced cheerfulness. Ben was very patient, sitting with me the whole time. Dad asked him dad-type questions about work: So, son, what is it you do for a living? Ben managed to answer without bringing up any of the more sordid tales from his practice. Like Cormac, for example. Dad made small talk about his banking job. And there were always the kids to distract us. They turned out to be very useful for that. I watched them reading—pretending to read—their board books and flinging their stuffed toys. Ben watched me watching them, and we didn't say a word.

* * *

Mom sailed through the surgery without a hitch. The surgeon was sure he'd removed the whole lump—nobody had said tumor yet—but the test results wouldn't be in for a week. So now we waited.

After the surgery, Ben and I went home—a new home this time, at least for me. He had a second-story condo north of the Cherry Creek area. In his absence, it had gone a bit stale. Mothballed. I hadn't let him come here himself, not with the chance that Carl might find Ben and hunt him down as an invading rogue.

It was a bachelor pad, with little in the way of decoration. The living room had a cushy leather couch and a flat-screen TV. An old coffee table had books, magazines, and file folders piled on it. Half the room was an office: a desk in the corner was covered with work except for an empty space about the size of a laptop computer. There was a balcony off the living room. The kitchen was small, and the single bedroom was in the back. I had an urge to go snooping through all the cupboards and closets, to uncover his secrets.

"It didn't burn down," he said, closing the door behind him. "I'm almost shocked."

"How long have you lived here?"

"Four years maybe. I liked the place, the price was right." Moving over to the glass door to the balcony, he looked out over his view of the city, a carpet of treetops and stretch of buildings. He took a deep breath and exhaled. "It's good to be back. I've missed it."

To tell the truth, I'd missed Denver, too. My favorite restaurants, my old stomping grounds, the line of mountains to the west. But I couldn't enjoy being back. Too many worries.

I dropped my bag and sat on the sofa. Clasped my hands together and looked around, nervous. Exile over, just like that. I'd been displaced for months, since I left Denver. Now I was back, and I still felt displaced. I was a guest in a strange house.

Ben continued. "I guess we should go for groceries. I had my mom clear out all the food when she looked in on things for me. At least the fridge won't smell like sour milk."

Barely listening, I leaned back, holding my head. What was I going to do? I'd have thought I'd be used to my life falling apart by now. It seemed to happen so often.

He slumped onto the sofa next to me. "You want to check out the bedroom?" He had an obnoxious lilt to his brow.

"I bet you say that to all the girls," I said.

"I can tell you're not impressed by the place."

"It's not that. I'm just not sure what to do next."

"I suggested the bedroom—"

I groaned in mock anguish and curled against him, cuddling there, looking for comfort. "I half expect Carl and Meg to break through the door."

"Are they really that bad? You told me all the shit they did, but still. Are you sure you're not building them up in your mind, making it worse?"

I stared at him. "Trust me, I'm not making it worse. They killed my best friend." Carl, murderer, rapist, and Meg the raging bitch egging him on. Match made in hell.

Ben played with my hair, and I settled down, relaxing to his touch. This was his place, it smelled like him, and I felt safe. Mostly safe. I sighed again.

"I'm not sure what to be more freaked out about," I said. "My mom, or me, or the pack. Or Rick. God, if Rick finds out I'm here he'll take it the wrong way."

"How's he going to find out you're here? Denver's huge, no one's going to know you're here."

"Oh, Ben, you're so cute when you're being clueless."

"And you're cute when you're being paranoid."

"It's not paranoia—"

"When they're really out to get you, I know. Remember what you told me, when I freaked out and sat there whining about not knowing what to do?"

"No, what?" Whining, just like he said.

"Get back to work. The cure for everything."

My old radio station, my old home base, KNOB, was in Denver. Maybe I could go back. I'd love to see Matt, Ozzie, and the whole gang.

"Everybody would know to find me there," I said.

"So don't tell anyone you're there. You think they're going to post a watch on the front door?"

"Maybe."

"Fine, I give up. Hide out here the whole time. But if you start climbing the walls, I'm kicking you out."

I lasted a whole day before I left Ben's condo. He didn't have to kick me out. The next day was Friday, and I had the show to do. I couldn't let a little thing like paranoia—however justified—keep me away.

The KNOB building hadn't changed. It was a seventies brick pile, three stories, tucked away on a side street. If it didn't have the grove of antennae on the roof, it could have been anything.

I slunked through the front door, the prodigal daughter returned.

I didn't recognize the woman at the receptionist's desk. She was my age, wore glasses, and was poring earnestly over some kind of paperwork. She didn't look up, and I didn't know what to do. Should I just walk in, as if I still worked here? Had they given my office to someone else?

In keeping with my general mood, I snuck past her and took the stairs to the next floor. Avoidance was always a good strategy. Second floor was offices, third floor was studios and libraries. I had an urge to go all the way up, to take in the atmosphere and smells of the place. I wanted to find my favorite squishy chair and give it a spin. I'd spent a lot of time here, first as an intern, then as a regular DJ before I started the show. This was where it all started. I was too young to be feeling this nostalgic.

Maybe that was why I avoided the third-floor studios and went to the second floor to find Ozzie, the station manager and my boss. I should have called first. I should have given him some warning.

I really ought to stop second-guessing myself.

Creeping like an intruder, I listened for voices, trying to guess who was here and where Ozzie might be. Maybe I hadn't been gone all that long. Some of the same flyers were up on the bulletin board, the same notices to please clean your crap out of the fridge in the break room and to sign up for the employee picnic.

"Kitty!"

Matt—young, stocky, his black hair in a ponytail—appeared around the corner at the end of the hallway. He ran the show for me, first live and then remotely when I had to go on the road.

I grinned wide and squealed just a little. "Matt!"

We ran into each other and hugged. Ah, I was home.

Matt talked a mile a minute. "What are you doing here? I didn't know you were back, why didn't you call? Hey—we're all set up for the show to broadcast in Pueblo, are we going to have to move everything back here or are you just dropping by or what?"

We separated, and I hemmed and hawed, sheepish. "I'm back, I guess. It was kind of sudden. Is that okay? Is there a problem?"

"There shouldn't be—"

"Kitty!"

And there was Ozzie, coming around the same corner Matt had. Ozzie was an aging hippy type, thinning pony-tail, and—geez, he'd grown a beard. Wild.

"Hi, Ozzie."

He swept me up in a hug that lifted me off the floor. Even after everything that had happened, all the publicity, I didn't feel like a werewolf here. This was the only place I was a DJ first and a lycanthrope second. It felt great.

"What are you doing here?" he said, a familiar scowl on his face. He was the kind of manager who got grouchy when things didn't go as planned. "I thought you weren't coming back. We turned your office into a storage closet."

That answered that question.

"Change of plans. Sorry I didn't call, it was kind of last minute." Very last minute. Had it really only been two days since Dad called with the news about Mom? "Is it a problem? Can we do tomorrow's show here?"

"Yeah, sure, of course. Matt?" Matt gave a shrug that Ozzie took to mean yes. "No problem. So what brought you back? Is everything okay?"

I made a decision. Here in this space, everything was okay. All problems stayed outside, and this was home.

"Everything's fine," I said and smiled.

I crept through the next week like I was moving through a minefield—careful where I stepped, waiting for an inevitable explosion. I settled into a kind of routine, albeit a stressful one. Mostly, the stress came from waiting for the phone call about Mom's biopsy. The one that said whether she had cancer, and if so what kind and how bad, and where did things go from there. Ben and I went back to Pueblo briefly to collect a few belongings and the other car. The move to Denver was starting to feel permanent, even though I kept thinking if the test came back negative, I would flee town again.

I avoided downtown and the northwest foothills where the pack mostly ran. Anyplace where anyone supernatural hung out that I knew of, I avoided. I didn't go out much. KNOB, Ben's place, Mom and Dad's in Aurora. That was it. I caught up on a lot of reading.

Ozzie didn't clean out the supply closet formerly known as my office, but he gave me a new one, an equally cozy hole in the wall that had been waiting for a new marketing assistant that hadn't been hired yet. The place rapidly devolved into a state of messiness that made it look like I'd been working there for months. Newspapers and magazines piled at a corner of the desk, piles of letters and e-mails—I had to deal with it directly now, instead of having someone else filter it—and a radio tuned to KNOB. It felt like I never left.

Right down to the phone ringing more than I wanted it to. And it still made me jump out of my skin. It was my cell this time.

"Hi, this is Kitty," I managed to answer in a friendly enough tone.

"Well, it's the famous werewolf Kitty Norville," said a cynical female voice.

I knew that voice. I put a fake smile into my tone. "Detective Hardin. Hello."

Detective Jessi Hardin had gotten caught up in a spate of werewolf killings that happened before I left Denver. She was unusual in that I had told her a werewolf was involved, and she'd believed me, before anyone else even acknowledged the existence of werewolves. She was ahead of the curve. I liked her, except she was always calling me and asking difficult questions. I was her go-to person for cases involving the supernatural.

"A question for you: Are you keeping up with things back in Denver?"

She didn't know I was back. She'd called my cell; I could be anywhere. It felt like a tiny victory. Keeping my head down seemed to be working. Now if I could just keep from letting it slip that I *was* back in Denver. Then she'd start coming to see me in person, to show me bodies that had died gruesomely.

I remembered Rick's newspaper article. "I heard about the nightclub vampire attacks. Have they got you looking into that?"

"Only on the side. The attackers were vampires, and

we've got descriptions. We're staking out the most likely clubs—in a manner of speaking. But I've had a different problem thrown at me."

"Oh?"

"I've just been made the head of the Paranatural Unit of the Denver PD." Her voice was wry, like this was a big, ironic joke. "I'm getting to write the law enforcement book on this stuff."

"Great. Congratulations. I think. So tell me, if the cops have to lock up a werewolf on the night of a full moon, what do they do?"

"Paint the bars with silver."

Damn, she was good. "And what about a life sentence for a vampire?"

"That one we haven't quite worked out. I'm kind of in favor of giving the vampire a cell with a nice southern exposure."

And *this* was the person writing the book on paranormal law enforcement? "Detective, not that this isn't pleasant, but do you need something from me?"

"Can't fool you."

"I sensed it with my keen animal instincts."

She actually chuckled. "Right. This whole legend about vampires and mirrors. That their reflections don't appear. How much of that is true and how much is bogus?"

I shrugged, even though she couldn't see it. The uncertainty carried into my voice. "I don't know, I haven't really had a chance to test it."

I should have. I should have been more observant. I'd met plenty of vampires, but at the moment I couldn't remember any relevant details, like a reflection in a glass door or a distorted image in a piece of fine china. No doubt about it, vampires were weird, and powerful in ways they didn't reveal to anyone. Had I simply failed to notice their reflective properties, or was there something about them that drew the eye, the attention, away?

"Why do you ask?" I said.

"I have to ask myself some questions: If they really don't show up in mirrors, do they show up on film? Is there something about the way they reflect light, or bend light, that keeps them from appearing in mirrors that would affect how they appear on film?"

"I don't know. I could ask around for you."

"I'd appreciate it. I have surveillance camera footage from a convenience store robbery that happened downtown a couple days ago. It got handed to me because something about it isn't right. You can see the perpetrators, right there by the register, collecting the cash. But they're not really there. It's like they're ghosts, or afterimages. A double exposure, maybe. The clerk, the other customers, everyone else in the image is clear, except for these two blurs. And on top of that, none of the witnesses remembers what they look like. The clerk remembers being robbed, but she can't describe the thieves, can't remember what they said, if they held a gun on her, or what. It sounds fishy to me."

It was certainly an interesting bit of speculation, though I hadn't ever heard of a vampire robbing anything. Most of them preferred to make their money with long-term investments. "I can't recall ever seeing a photo of a vampire. But I never really asked."

"Any lead will help. The department's resident skeptics are suggesting that 'vampire' really means 'I have no fucking clue.' I'd love to prove them wrong."

"So if I see a couple of vampires carrying bags of cash, I should call you."

"You got it."

She signed off, and I was grateful that she hadn't asked when I was coming back to Denver, or asked to send me copies of the images from the surveillance footage so I could give her my opinion. I'd half expected her to.

That wasn't the only call I had that day. Oh no, they always came in droves.

The next call came to the office phone, forwarded to me from KNOB's main line. The answering voice was confident and saccharine—someone in show business. I recognized that tone. "Hi, Kitty Norville? My name's Judy Jones, do you have a minute?"

"Sure. What've you got?"

"I'm a publicist here in New York City, and I have a client who I think you'd love to have on your show, if you'll let me arrange it."

I got calls like this all the time. My show didn't have a huge audience, but for some people it had the right audience, which was more important. A quick interview on my show meant great free publicity for them.

I could always say no. My next question was the obvious one. "Who's your client?"

"Have you heard of Mercedes Cook?"

"Yeah. She's a legend on Broadway. Been playing leading roles for like forty years. Why do you think she's a good fit for my show?"

Jones's voice took on a tone of amusement, like she was telling a joke and wasn't going to reveal the punch line. "Ms. Norville, I'm going to have to ask you to keep the rest of this conversation in strict confidence. Can you do that?"

Could I keep a secret? I always answered that question the same way. "Sure. What's this all about?"

"People are starting to ask questions about Ms. Cook's career. As you said, she's been playing leads for forty years. *Romantic* leads. She hasn't aged a day since her first spot on the chorus line in the sixties."

A chill crept up my spine. I hadn't thought of it. I wouldn't have thought of it. I'd have written it off to plastic surgery or a great makeup job. I'd have figured Mercedes Cook was one of those lucky people who hit twenty-five and didn't seem to age for the next couple of decades. But if that was so, Judy Jones wouldn't have been calling me.

I'd never been in the same room with Mercedes Cook to smell her, to be able to tell if she wasn't quite human.

"Go on," I said.

"After all this publicity about the paranormal over the last year, which you might be aware of—" Uh, yeah, did she think? "People are starting to ask the right questions about Ms. Cook and her remarkable career. The bottom line is we'd prefer to make this announcement on our own terms rather than have some reporter splash this all over the nightly news. What could be more perfect, Ms. Norville? America's first celebrity werewolf conducts a live interview with America's first celebrity vampire."

Perfect, indeed. One of the country's most beloved stars of one of its most beloved institutions—a vampire? Oh, the conservative witch hunters were going to have a field day with this. She totally hadn't been on my list—my potential vampire list that included every celebrity who looked younger than plastic surgery could explain.

And I couldn't tell anyone. Jones was smart—she'd given me a very good reason to keep the secret. I had to, if

I wanted to get the exclusive story. Breaking this kind of news on my show? Ha! This was too cool.

I took a breath and tried to sound nonchalant. "That's quite intriguing, Ms. Jones. I think I can make the time to have Ms. Cook on for an interview." I acted like I was poking through a calendar. "Yes, I'm sure I can fit her in. When is she available?"

"Is this week too soon? She'll be in Denver for her concert tour."

"This week is fine."

"I can arrange for her to come to your studio for an interview. I'm assuming that would be convenient?"

"Yes, yes, of course. I'll make sure we're set up on this end."

"That's great. Would you like tickets for her concert?"

Why the hell not? "That would be great. Thanks."

"I'll be in touch."

She clicked off, and I had my show for the week all set up. Belatedly, I realized I had admitted that I was in Denver. But surely the publicist couldn't reveal that to anyone who would cause trouble.

After the show, I'd have to call Detective Hardin and tell her that Mercedes Cook had hundreds of publicity photos and several videos of her musicals. Vampires did appear on film, and something else had robbed that store.

chapter 4

Judy Jones reserved tickets for me for the Thursday night concert. Not only that, but I had an invitation to visit Mercedes Cook afterward, with a backstage pass. I was starting to feel like some kind of big deal myself. This was all to butter me up so I'd give a flattering interview. We'd see about that.

I had two tickets, and I wanted a date. Ben didn't want to go.

"That really isn't my kind of thing," he said, working at his desk the day before the concert.

"Have you ever even been to a show like this? World-class singer, world-class concert hall, it'll knock your socks off."

He spared a brief glance over his shoulder. "I'm really not all that into music."

Oh, now he tells me. "Ben, I started my adult life as a radio DJ. You can't live with me and not be into music. Are you saying that all the times I blast The Clash while making dinner you haven't been into it?"

"To be honest, I mostly tune it out."

How the hell do you tune out The Clash? Turned all the way up? Once again I reminded myself that Ben and I were together by accident. Did we even know each other, really?

"Ben, I'd really like to go to this. Together."

He leaned back in his chair and sighed. Still wouldn't look at me. "Can't you get someone else to go? Maybe your sister."

Uh, no. Not the same. "You know how you keep saying that we've never been on a real date?" We were living together, sleeping together. We were practically married. We'd skipped clean over the whole dating thing and went straight into settled. I wanted to change that. "Can this be it?"

Finally, he turned, stared at me in a way that was almost a wolf challenge—asking for a fight or offering to give one. Then, he gave a sly half smile.

"Are you asking mc out?" he said.

"Yeah, I am."

"Well, okay then."

I turned my gaze to the ceiling, as if that would tell me how his brain worked. "You're really obnoxious, you know that?"

He was still grinning when he turned back to his desk.

I convinced Ben to dress up—suit, tie, the works. I knew he could pull out the *GQ* polish for important courtroom appearances and high-level meetings. The rest of the time, not so much. But we were having a night on the town, and I wanted to go all out. Who knew when we'd ever do anything like this again?

He finished dressing while I was in the shower, and I hurried because I didn't want to be that stereotype of the woman who takes forever to get ready while the guy is in the living room glancing at his watch. Hair dried and up, makeup on, earrings, necklace, little black dress, and strappy heels. I was probably way overdressed, but I didn't care. The dress was a clingy silk number with spaghetti straps, sexy without being trampy. I'd only worn it once before—it had given me good luck then. I contorted in order to see myself in the narrow full-length mirror, making sure the skirt was all smoothed out, that a few wisps of hair were artfully· arranged around my face—and rearranged, and arranged again—and that everything was in order.

"Kitty, we'd probably better—" Ben's steps approached just as I bent over to adjust a strap on my shoe one more time. "Wow."

He stopped in the doorway. He stared. I straightened and stared back. The look in his eyes—I found myself blushing in places I didn't know I could blush.

For his part, Ben was wearing his best courtroom suit, charcoal gray, perfectly tailored, with a rust-colored tie. The lines were smooth, giving him a slim, fit appearance, an image of power and privilege. His hair was a touch too long to lay slicked back, so it flopped over his forehead, with a rakish, mischievous air. Put a pair of Ray•Bans on him, he'd be downright scary. Dreamily scary.

"Wow yourself," I said. I resisted an urge to lick my lips, but I did gulp a little.

"You, ah, clean up pretty well." His voice seemed a bit subdued, and he'd started fidgeting with his cuff links.

"You, too." I didn't have cuff links to fidget with, so I laced my fingers together behind my back. The blushing was getting worse. My whole body was turning red, I was sure of it. Did he have any idea just how...how *amazing* he looked?

"Can I kiss you?" he said, kind of offhand, as if we hadn't kissed a hundred times before and the thought had just occurred to him.

In reply, I took a slow step toward him, and another. Before I knew it, he touched my face and brought our lips together. The kiss was hot, hungry. I held him and pulled myself close to him. His hands slipped down my back, one of them moving farther, cupping my bottom. Just a thin layer of silk lay between us. And still, we kissed.

We finally pulled apart to catch our breaths.

"I suppose we should do this sort of thing more often," he said.

"Yeah," I said, whispering, a little shaky. All of a sudden, I didn't want to go to the concert. I was still holding on to him.

He ducked his gaze. "I was going to say—we'd probably better get going. We'll be late."

"Yeah." We still didn't move.

Then, at almost the same moment, we started giggling. I pressed my face to his shoulder to stop myself, and he hugged me, and the intensity of whatever had just happened went away. Mostly, it went away.

I said, grinning, "Hey, wanna go on a date with me?"

"Absolutely."

We looked like a million bucks. Stalking arm in arm, we crossed the courtyard of the Denver Center for the Performing Arts, a collection of theaters in the heart of downtown, to the doors of the concert hall. We turned heads, the two of us. Like we were in a commercial for diamond jewelry or a music video. Sure, we were way overdressed compared to a lot of the crowd—why did some Coloradoans think it was okay to wear jeans to a symphony concert?—and it made us stand out, but in the kind of way that the stares told me that they all wished they could be us. My grin felt silly, but I felt better when I glanced at Ben and saw the same grin on him. The alpha pair indeed.

I even almost forgot that I was supposed to be in hiding. I kept telling myself that none of the Denver wolves would be here, lycanthropes avoided crowds like this and the vampires didn't hang out here. I'd be fine, just fine. I didn't wilt in the middle of the crowd. I felt on top of the world.

We collected our tickets from Will Call, were ushered to our seats, and settled in as the orchestra was tuning up. The lights went down, the conductor appeared, and the orchestra launched into an overture.

Then she appeared, entering stage right.

Mercedes Cook had ivory skin and brick red hair, the rich color and sheen of silk, rippling past her shoulders. A midnight blue, shimmering gown clung to her slim figure. Her limbs were slender, her face aristocratic, like that of a Greek statue. I couldn't tell her height from where we sat, about halfway back in the orchestra section. She seemed to fill the stage. She seemed bigger than life.

I was close enough that the hall's air-conditioning system carried her scent to me—the cold, clean scent of a vampire. If I hadn't been warned, I'd have been shocked. She moved with such energy, such vibrancy. A consummate performer, she had a spark in her gaze.

I could guess her story: she'd always aspired to the stage. A talented performer, vampirism wasn't going to halt her ambitions. Maybe she even sought out the vampirism, or encountered the opportunity and grabbed it as a chance to hold on to that elusive advantage of youth and beauty. She'd been on stage since the sixties, when her official biography set the start of her career. Maybe she'd even been around longer, a vaudeville performer or singer in the twenties and thirties who disappeared and changed her identity to start a career on Broadway. That would take a bit of research and digging. I was hoping I could get the scoop from Mercedes herself.

Vampires didn't need to breathe. Their blood was borrowed, and their hearts didn't beat. They existed in a kind of stasis, never decaying, and never experiencing the cellular processes of life. But they used their lungs, inhaling air in order to speak. And to sing.

Mercedes's vocal cords didn't suffer at all from her being a vampire. She was a belter, yet her mezzo voice rang like a bell. She sang show tunes and torch songs. Fast, jazzy pieces and slow, bluesy pieces. Some I recognized, some I didn't. Every one of them had me at the edge of my seat. She owned that stage, and she needed the full orchestra to keep up with her. Nothing else possibly could.

She spotted me. From the stage, she looked right at me, caught my gaze, and she knew who I was, could tell what I was from forty feet away. Her smile thinned, her eyes narrowed into a sultry gaze, almost but not quite winking at me. Then she turned, and it was all part of the song, all part of the act. Every person in the audience probably imagined she was looking right at them.

Part of me didn't trust her talent. Vampires had . . . something. Energy, power, presence. They were seductive, they spent decades practicing being seductive. More than that, some of them could entrance you with a look. Hypnotize you. You'd follow them anywhere without knowing what was happening. They lured their prey to them.

She might have been casting that spell over the whole audience. Ben's jaw was open.

She gave two encores, then the lights came up, and it was over. I shook my head, like I was trying to clear a fog from my mind. The spell was fading. I reached over to close Ben's mouth for him. He blinked, also spellbound.

"She's impressive," he said.

"Want to meet her? I've got a backstage pass."

"Are you kidding?"

"Perks of the job, baby."

"Did—was I imagining it? Is she really—"

"Yeah. That's why I'm here. Come on."

I grabbed his hand and pulled him into the aisle. Back in the lobby, I followed my nose to a side corridor that led to a plain-looking door. We slipped through it to the chaos of back stage. Cables and lighting fixtures decorated shadowy concrete walls. Velvet drapes hung from a ceiling that was lost in darkness. The whole thing was, strangely, both cozy and industrial. Musicians carried instrument cases from the brightly lit stage.

I didn't spot anyone who looked official. At most rock and pop music concerts, a whole barrage of staff and bouncer types would have stopped us from getting this far. I'd marshaled my speeches that would get me past them to see Mercedes. But no one paid attention to me here. I was almost relieved when I spotted someone dressed all in black and wearing a headset. Even then, I had to intercept her.

"Can you help me? I was invited to visit with Ms. Cook after the show, do you know where I can find her?"

Just like that, the techie showed Ben and me to a back hallway where the dressing rooms were.

"Well?" I asked Ben. "Ready for this?"

He shrugged. "It's your show."

"Remember, she's a vampire. Totally creepy. Don't let her seduce you."

"Hey," he said, indignant, and I knocked.

"Come in," said Mercedes Cook in her rich mezzo.

I opened the door inward. As I did, the stunning redhead seated at a long, brightly lit makeup table turned to me. She'd put a black silk robe over her gown. Her face was perfectly made-up, if thickly for the benefit of the stage. Cosmetics masked the usual pale vampire complexion. She looked alive, more so than any vampire I'd ever met. And her image showed in the mirror, perfectly clear.

Vases of flowers covered the table and spilled onto the floor nearby, giving the room a tropical, heady atmosphere.

"You must be Kitty Norville," she said.

I offered my hand to shake, and she did, smiling indulgently. Her grip was cool. I gestured over my shoulder. "This is my friend, Ben."

"Great show, Ms. Cook," Ben said diplomatically. He stayed a step behind me, ready to let me make my own mess.

"Thank you very much," she said, flashing a brilliant smile. "Please, come in, have a seat. I think there are a couple of extra chairs here." We found the chairs, and I scooted mine close to her, like we were a couple of old friends.

I rarely had a chance to prep for an interview like this, meeting the subject beforehand and getting a feel for how they'll respond to my questions. In moments, Mercedes put me at ease. Already I could feel that she was going to give a great interview.

"Thanks so much for the tickets. We had a great time."

"I'm glad. I had a good audience tonight, but I always wonder. Maybe they're just being polite."

Friendly, endearing—she didn't even talk like a vampire. Maybe she was young—for a vampire—and hadn't yet acquired the arrogance of centuries. I started to ask, then thought I should save it for tomorrow's interview.

"If you're up for taking calls during the interview tomorrow, you'll get to ask your fans directly."

"I'm looking forward to it. I've done lots of interviews, but never anything like this." That smile glittered. Not a hint of fang showed. She genuinely seemed happy about the interview. "I want to thank you for giving me this chance. Once I decided to tell the world what I am, I had to decide how to do it. Being on your show seemed like such a fun alternative to a stuffy press conference."

I was *sought after*. My show had *credibility*. I could have burst with pride.

I tried to stay grounded. "Going public will change everything. No one will ever look at you the same. This could end your career."

"Or raise it to an entirely new level. Going public certainly hasn't hurt your career."

"I can't argue with that. But most of the time I feel like I'm madly treading water just to keep from going under."

She laughed, a musical sound—of course. "Oh, that doesn't have anything to do with being a werewolf. That's life."

She had a point. I just smiled. "I won't be offended if you decide to back out of the interview."

"Don't worry, Kitty. I'm not exactly an innocent young thing in this business. It's my choice to go public, and I know what I'm doing."

These kinds of interviews involved a bit of give and take. We were both after publicity, but ideally we wouldn't sound self-serving. We wanted to be entertaining. I wanted the whole thing to sound like a pleasant conversation. And at the same time I wanted to get as much information as I possibly could.

My smile turned sly. "Just how 'not young' are you, if you don't mind me asking?"

"Why is that the first thing anyone wants to know about you when they find out you're a vampire?" Her gaze became hooded, her smile mysterious.

Ah well, it was worth a try. "Morbid curiosity, I think. Can I ask if you belong to a Family? Do you have a Master or someone you had to argue with about this?"

"No Family. I'm the Master of my own little world. I like it that way."

"Amen," I said. "I figure in the interview we'll get the big news out of the way, I'll ask a few questions, then open the lines for calls. Sound good?"

"Fabulous."

"Then I'll see you at the station at eleven tomorrow night. You have my number? You'll call me if you need anything?"

"I'll be fine, thank you," she said, another laugh hiding in her voice. "Thanks again for agreeing to do this."

"My pleasure."

We shook hands, she and Ben smiled at each other, and we made our way out of the theater. I was almost skipping, I felt so good.

I chatted at Ben. "This is going to be great. She's so cool, she so doesn't act like a vampire. Most of them are total snobs, and I was thinking snob and Broadway star to boot, she'll be terrible. But she was totally decent. My audience'll love her."

An amused smile touched Ben's lips. "Maybe it's because she's been passing as human. She's like you—you spend enough time acting human, you seem more human."

"Hmm. You may have something there." I mentally wrote it down for the interview tomorrow. I could use it to launch a whole discussion. Oh, I was so looking forward to this.

"It's nice to finally see you in a good mood," Ben said.

I was in a good mood, wasn't I? Grinning, I hugged his arm. "How long do you suppose I can make it last?"

"You'll have to find a way to stay distracted, so you're not worrying about anything."

Even mentioning worries darkened the edges of my thoughts. Stay distracted. Just like he said. I pulled his arm over my shoulders and pressed myself close, so we walked body to body. "And how do you suggest I do that?"

He stopped and cupped my face to kiss me, a long, sensual caress of lips, filled with heat and longing. My scalp flushed and my toes curled.

I pulled back and smiled. "That's a start," I said.

We went straight home, and Ben made sure I stayed distracted for a good long time.

Another Friday night arrived, right on schedule.

I sent one of the interns—one who loved show tunes and would be awed by her presence—to the KNOB lobby to wait for Mercedes Cook and escort her to the studio.

Ten minutes ahead of schedule, Mercedes swept into the studio, gracious and scintillating. I was heartened that it didn't seem to be an act. Maybe she was like this all the time. She wore a black camisole, matching cardigan, and a long, sweeping skirt with sandals—comfortable and perfect for summer, while still managing to display the height of fashion and panache. Her hair was tied back in a bun, and beaded earrings dangled from her ears. I'd never possess that much flair if I lived a thousand years.

I greeted her and introduced her to Matt, then showed her to her seat. The intern scampered into the booth to watch. Even Matt seemed a little awestruck.

"Here's your headphones, your mike—" She adjusted the mike herself and threw me an amused glance—she'd done this before after all. She could take care of herself.

"Thirty seconds, Kitty," Matt called from the booth.

"You ready for this?" I said to the singer. I for one was thrilled. This was the same studio where I'd announced on the air, for the whole country to hear, that I was a werewolf. This was perfect. Kismet.

"More than ready," Mercedes said, seeming just as excited as I felt. She perched at the edge of her seat, leaning on the armrest. I couldn't tell if her poise came from her being a supernaturally self-possessed vampire, or a world-class performer. She blurred the lines.

"Then here we go." Matt counted down, and routine took over. The opening chords of CCR's "Bad Moon Rising" played, but faded quickly to be replaced by a recording of Mercedes Cook singing Cole Porter.

"Good evening, faithful listeners, this is Kitty Norville here with *The Midnight Hour,* the show that isn't afraid of the dark or the creatures who live there. Tonight I have a very special guest with me, someone who in her own way is well acquainted with the night, Broadway legend Mercedes Cook. She's been a leading lady on the Great White Way for forty years now and shows no signs of slowing down. Mercedes, welcome."

"Thank you, Kitty. I'm happy to be here."

We'd agreed beforehand not to mess around, just get straight to the purpose of her being here, then deal with the fallout. Away we went.

"Mercedes, I've had a lot of people asking me why I invited you onto the show. Of course I have a huge respect for Broadway theater, but musicals aren't my usual topic of discussion. Would you like to tell our listeners why you're here?"

"Well, it's because I'm a vampire. I thought it was time people knew that."

Straight to the point, calm and collected—of course she was, she was a professional actress. I had goose bumps. Through the booth window, Matt was shaking his head, with an expression like he was whistling low. The intern's jaw had dropped.

"All right," I said. "Remember, folks, you heard it here first. I might as well ask the two questions everyone wants to know about vampires: First, how old are you?"

"Oh, don't you know it isn't polite to ask a girl her age?"

"That never stops me. Not even a little hint?"

"What if I said I got my start in vaudeville?"

Ha! I'd guessed right! "Oh, that would be *cool*. Now that you're out of the vampire closet, any chance you'll release some photos? Let us know what acts you were part of? Any secret recordings folks can dig out of their attics?"

"I don't know, I never really thought about it. I ought

to see what I can come up with. Now, you said there were two questions. What's the other?"

"How did you become a vampire?"

She got this sly look, and the expression carried into the tone of her voice. She knew how to be cagey and charming at the same time. "That's almost as bad as the first."

"Did you choose to become a vampire?"

"Yes, I did."

"Did you do it for your career? Did you want to stay young for the sake of your career?"

"Not precisely. It was more complicated than that— these things always are, aren't they? I wouldn't want any young actresses listening to think that vampirism is a viable way to boost her career. In the end, there are a lot of drawbacks. I remember when I was asked to sing in the Macy's Thanksgiving Day Parade, and I couldn't explain why I had to say no. I've made vampirism work for me because I wanted it to."

"Along those lines, you have what I'm sure lots of actresses wish they could have—eternal youth. But do you ever regret that you won't get to play some of the great roles for older women, like in *Hello, Dolly!* or *Arsenic and Old Lace*?"

"That's exactly one of the drawbacks. I do regret it sometimes. It would be ironic if I ever decided to try for a part like that and had to wear of ton of makeup to look old."

A vampire with a sense of humor. I loved it.

"What do you think will happen to your career now? Now that you've said you're a vampire, how will things change?"

Mercedes said, "I'm taking a risk. I'm gambling that my reputation as an actress and singer will outweigh my identity as a vampire. It's a test, really."

"Are you also maybe betting that audiences will want to come see you because you're a vampire?"

"Maybe," she said.

"Has being a vampire helped you in other ways? You'll stay young-looking, but what about stage presence? Your ability to connect with an audience? I saw your show, and I have to say it was almost supernatural."

"Thank you, I think. But you're talking about the powers vampires are reported to have. The mind control, that sort of thing." She said it wryly, like it was a joke, an urban legend that had no basis in reality.

"That's right."

"I was an actress and singer before I became a vampire. I really hope my talent is my own."

That didn't really answer the question, which shouldn't have surprised me. "Well, Mercedes, are you ready to talk to a few listeners?"

"Sure, that sounds like fun."

The board was all lit up—like the lights of Broadway. Ha.

"Hello, Frankie, you're on the air. What would you like to ask Ms. Cook?"

"Oh, my God, I knew it! I just knew it! You had to be a vampire, you haven't changed a bit in forty years."

"You've been a fan for a long time, then?" Mercedes said, a laugh behind her voice.

"No—I mean, I haven't even been *alive* that long!"

I butted in. "Wow, Frankie, you really know how to make a girl feel special."

"You know what I mean. What I really want to say—it was only a matter of time, with so many actors and actresses these days who seem ageless. It can't all be plastic surgery. I want to ask Mercedes if she knows any other celebrities who might be vampires."

"It's not my place to reveal such information. I'd certainly have hated it if anyone else revealed my nature before I was ready."

"Not even any guesses?"

I interrupted. "I do have to wonder if coming out as a vampire will be the next cool thing. I'll let you know if I hear anything. Next caller, hello."

"Ms. Cook, I've been a fan of yours for *ages*. You must have such a unique perspective. How has musical theater changed over the course of your career? You've seen the whole history of it. You could probably write a book."

"What an interesting idea, maybe I will."

I had a lot more musical theater fans among my audience than I would have expected, and I was thrilled to no end that they asked intelligent questions. Mercedes never seemed bored. A few numbskulls called in demanding to know how to become vampires. Mercedes politely used my line—that this wasn't a lifestyle she advocated. We were here to talk about problems and issues, not to advertise. The whole thing managed to stay pretty light—right up until the end.

"All right, I think we've got time for one or two more. Next caller, hello."

The caller had a low male voice, like he was speaking close to the phone and didn't want to be overheard. "Mercedes. I can't help but wonder what you get out of this revelation. I know vampires, and I know you—at least by reputation. And everything you do has a purpose."

It hadn't occurred to me until that moment that her reputation among vampires might be as something other than a great Broadway actress.

I said, "You seem to be talking about a different Mercedes Cook than the one sitting with me in the studio."

"Perhaps I am. Remember, she didn't start out as the person with you now. She's probably reinvented herself a dozen times over the decades."

"And you know this how?"

The line clicked off.

Mercedes and I exchanged a glance—she artfully arched her brow, shrugged a little, as if to say she didn't have any idea what that was all about.

"We're back to the age question," I said. "You're still not going to tell me, are you?"

"No, I'm afraid not."

"To that mystery caller, I'd like to say, I can see exactly what Mercedes gets out of revealing her nature. It's the same thing I got. A lot of crazy publicity."

Putting a purr in her voice she added, "And maybe I thought it was time vampirism had as pretty a public face as the one Kitty's given lycanthropy."

I blushed. That kind of compliment could keep me going for weeks. "It looks like that's all the time we have tonight, folks. Thank you to everyone who called in with your great questions, and a very big thanks to you, Mercedes."

"You're very welcome, Kitty."

"Good luck with the new direction in your career. Until next week, I'm Kitty Norville, voice of the night."

After the interview, Mercedes signed a CD for the intern and shook hands with Matt. I walked her down to the lobby myself. I hated for the evening to end. I wasn't an actress or musician like Mercedes, but I knew about the rush of being "on" for a couple of hours and trying to come down from that high of giving a good show. I felt like running around the block a few times.

Instead, I gushed at her. "Thanks so much. I think that was one of my best interviews ever."

"Mine, too," she said. "It's hard to believe it's over. Cat's out of the bag, as they say. I hardly know what to do with myself."

"I know exactly what you mean."

She graced me with that brilliant smile. "I'm staying on in Denver a few more days. Come have a drink with me tomorrow evening at the Brown Palace. Bring that nice gentleman of yours."

"Are you talking a drink at the bar, or something else?" Always double-check what a drink meant when vampires were involved.

She laughed. "Figure of speech. The drinking will be conventional."

The Brown Palace—fanciest digs in Denver. When else was I going to have an excuse to hang out there for an evening? Not to mention, I wanted to learn as much as I could from Mercedes while I had the chance. The interview had been good, but there was always more. Like that age thing, for starters.

"Great. We'll be there," I said.

"Wonderful. Ask at the desk, they'll send you up to my suite. I'll tell them you're coming."

"Cool. Thanks."

We went outside into the quiet dark of a late, late night. Mercedes paused and took in a breath of the chill air. This was her element, and she smiled, seeming to revel in it. A career as a Broadway star was perfect for her; I imagined her leaving through the stage door and taking a breath like that after every show. Not for the oxygen, but for the atmosphere—the smells, the sharpness of it.

Her limo was waiting. I didn't think a limo had ever been on this street before. Seeing it here was surreal. The chauffeur opened the door, and she waved at me as she climbed inside.

Basking in the glow of sweet success, I watched her drive away.

The next day, Ben went to Cañon City to check on Cormac. The trip would take most of the day, but he assured me he'd be back in time for drinks at the Brown Palace. He might get down with this whole dating thing yet.

I called Hardin. Now that the news had broken, I could explain that yes, vampires did show up on film: Mercedes had appeared in thousands of publicity photos over the course of her career, as well as a dozen video recordings of her performances in various musicals. And she'd certainly appeared in her dressing-room mirror. Hardin didn't sound particularly pleased when I told her. Apparently, she'd been looking forward to pinning this on one of the undead. "I have a dream," she told me, "of someday watching someone be given a hundred-plus-year prison sentence and actually being able to serve out the whole damn thing." Her passion on the subject was almost admirable. Frightening, but admirable.

After that, I fielded calls and answered messages. Mercedes wasn't giving any interviews today, so I was the next best thing, and lots of reporters from most of the major papers and news magazines wanted to talk to me about last night's show: How had I learned about the actress's vampirism, what impact did I think the revelation was going to have on her career, and so on. I was happy my show could still generate some buzz. I even managed to work in some plugs for my own forthcoming book. Publicity was a wonderful thing.

Then I went to Cheryl's for lunch with her and Mom. Girls day in, Cheryl called it.

I was late. She'd moved right before I left Denver and I hadn't been to the new place yet. I made a couple of wrong turns. The place was in Highlands Ranch, pretty swank to my eyes. Then again, I'd spent most of my adult life in one-room apartments and wasn't really one to judge. Cute tract housing, a bit too pastel a shade of blue. The trees were all new, thin, and tied down with wires.

All smiles, Cheryl, Jeffy propped on her hip, let me in. She'd locked her golden retriever in the backyard, but I could hear it barking. I couldn't get within twenty feet of the dog without it freaking out. It could tell what I was and didn't like me at all.

She said, "Sorry, I'm still getting ready, come on to the kitchen." She led me through the spacious front room to a sunny kitchen.

"Mom's not here yet?"

When she looked back at me, she winced slightly, her smile turning apologetic. "I told her to come an hour later. I thought maybe we should talk, you know—alone. About her."

My first thought, aside from the gut-stabbing reminder that Mom might be seriously ill, was, *Oh God, it's started.* The late-night talks where we figured out what to do with old Mom and Dad, now that they're getting on in years. We used to joke about it, how they'd better treat us right because we'd be picking their nursing home. I didn't think I'd have to face this for real for another twenty years. No, thirty years.

Stubborn, I said, "Oh yeah, and she isn't going to guess that we're up to something when she gets here on time and sees that I'm actually early."

Cheryl set Jeffy down in a playpen, where he immediately found something plastic and colorful to bang against the bottom. She straightened and ran her hands through her hair, pulling strands out of the ponytail. All at once, she looked ten years older. She looked tired. Of course she looked tired, she was a mother.

"I know, I know," she said. "I just thought it would be better if we could plan—"

"Scheme behind Mom's back, you mean?"

"Okay. Yeah. It was stupid. I'm sorry."

I leaned on the counter. Couldn't help but smile. "When we were kids I always thought I'd be the one to settle down, house in the suburbs, two point five kids, and that you'd do something crazy like sing in a rock band or something. Now look at us."

Cheryl had almost been a punk in high school. She'd missed the height of the old school real deal by a few years, but she listened to the music and wore the surplus army jacket and combat boots. Lost more safety pins than most people see in a lifetime. Four years younger, I'd worshipped the ground she walked on and borrowed all her tapes, locking in my musical tastes forever. Halfway through college, she'd grown out of it. Finished a degree in computer science and did the IT management thing. Met Mark and became a suburban statistic. Mostly she'd grown out of it. I occasionally caught her wearing a Ramones T-shirt, as if to say, *I wasn't always like this*.

Today, her T-shirt was plain blue, faded from many washings, like her jeans.

"It's funny how meeting Mr. Right can change your perspective."

"I guess so."

"This Ben guy—is he Mr. Right?"

I wished I knew the answer to that. I shrugged. "Who knows."

She said, a sly and knowing lilt to her voice, "There's still time. You may still get sucked into that suburban two point five kids thing."

My expression froze into a polite smile. I didn't want to tell her. I wasn't ready to tell her about the kids thing. We had more important things to talk about.

"So what about Mom?" I said.

"What are we going to do?"

"It's not really up to us, is it? She's a big girl."

Cheryl started pacing. "I know, but she's going to need help, we're going to have to help her, if she has to have more surgery and chemotherapy we're going to have to look after her, aren't we?"

"I think you're jumping the gun here. Why don't we wait until we know how serious it is before we start freaking out."

"So we can make important decisions *while* we're freaking out?"

"Bridges, Cheryl. We'll cross them when we get to them."

"We have to be ready for the worst, we have to be ready to help."

"We will be," I said. "We totally will be, whatever it takes."

"Then you're staying? That means you'll be around,

you won't go zipping off across the country at the drop of a hat, without telling anyone." She didn't ask this casually; she leaned in, glaring with a kind of desperation, almost but not quite jabbing her finger at me.

This wasn't about Mom at all, I realized.

"Cheryl, what are you asking? You want to make sure that if Mom needs help it won't all be you? Is that it?"

We stayed like that, staring at each other. It was almost wolfish.

The door opened, and Mom's voice called, "Hello, Cheryl? Kitty? Is that your car out there?"

How could she sound so damned cheerful? She ought to be mentally curled up and quivering like the rest of us.

All smiles, Cheryl went out to meet her, our conversation forgotten. "Hi, Mom! We're in here!"

Jeffy was on his feet, leaning on the edge of the playpen, talking at me, but I couldn't understand a word he was saying. I regarded him a moment and said, "She's still crazy after all these years, isn't she?"

Nicky had stopped Mom—Grandma—in the living room, and the two of them were gushing at each other about toys when Cheryl and I arrived. Now the whole house was filled with hugs and greetings. It was all very girly and domestic. Mom seemed to have recovered from the surgery. And why wouldn't she? Perfectly routine, everyone kept saying. As if the words "perfect" and "surgery" belonged in the same sentence. She was sore, though she tried to hide it. She managed to hug us without using her right arm. If she was nervous about waiting for the results, she hid that as well.

Cheryl had sandwiches waiting in the kitchen, and we settled down to eat. Nicky peeled the crusts off hers. Mom helped her.

The whole time, Mom talked about nothing in particular, filling the silence so the unspoken worry couldn't be mentioned. Cheryl kept glancing at me, her expression prompting me, like she wanted me to say something. Wanted me to ask Mom if she needed help. But I wasn't going to bring up anything. She was the oldest, that was her job. I didn't care if I *was* the self-help guru in the family.

When she got the test results, Mom wouldn't even have to tell us. I didn't know why Cheryl was so worried about helping her—the more I thought about it, the more I thought Mom wouldn't want our help. She'd get through as much of this as she could all by herself.

That was what I'd have done. At least, I'd have tried.

For this afternoon, at least, I pretended that nothing was wrong and enjoyed the day with my mom and sister. The last time we'd done a girls' day like this, Nicky had been a squirming baby.

I was the one who broke up the party, since I had to get home and get ready for this evening. I said good-bye to the kids—Nicky seemed to remember me from the hospital—and hugged Cheryl while trying to transmit *don't worry* vibes. I couldn't tell if it worked. Then Mom and I hugged, careful of her right side.

"You'll let me know if you need anything, right? If there's anything I can do to help?"

She pulled back and gave me a wry look. "You never let me help you, why should I be any different?"

Called that one, didn't I? "Because...I don't know. I just wanted you to know you could call me."

"I know. Thank you, dear." Smiling, she kissed my cheek, and that was that.

chapter 5

The Brown Palace was a downtown icon. Built during the gold rush days when Denver was filled with nouveau riche who wanted a taste of high society, it was a landmark and a status symbol. Presidents stayed here. *Really* posh. I'd have expected nothing less from Mercedes.

The clerk at the front desk directed me to Mercedes's suite. I dragged Ben to the elevator. He'd been waiting in the lobby, hands shoved in his trouser pockets, gazing around at the artwork, fireplaces, stained glass, and foliage. He wore a jacket but no tie. Edging more toward scruff than polish, but he still looked great. For my part, I wore a skirt, dress shirt, and heels. Felt pretty good, even though it wouldn't measure up to whatever Mercedes was wearing.

"You're sure about this?" he said as we went down the hallway. He'd been muttering about walking into the spider's parlor.

"Why wouldn't I be?"

"I don't trust vampires."

"And how many vampires do you actually know? That you didn't stake?"

"I haven't staked that many vampires."

I stopped and stared at him. I'd been joking. I'd known he'd sometimes helped Cormac on vampire hunting jobs, before Cormac went to jail. But we'd never talked about it. "How many have you staked?"

After a pause, he said, "Two. That's it."

"That's enough, don't you think?"

"And I helped with four of Cormac's."

"Exactly how many has Cormac staked?"

He just smiled.

Those guys drove me crazy. I huffed and stalked on ahead. He'd caught up by the time I knocked on the door to the suite.

From within, Mercedes called, "It's unlocked, come in!"

I opened the door and stepped into a spacious sitting room, furnished with big, velvety armchairs and chaises, grouped around a fireplace and mahogany coffee table. Rich carpets and crystal lamps gave the place a warm, opulent atmosphere.

Directly across the room, Rick stood from a brocade-upholstered chair. He was suave and polished as ever, but held himself tautly, like he was nervous. His hands clenched at his sides, but his face was neutral.

"Shit!" I glared at him, frozen.

"That's quite the greeting. I assume you two know each other?" Reclined on an antique sofa, Mercedes regarded me calmly.

I should have known, I should have expected. She couldn't be here without drawing the attention of the local vampires. I was so focused on her I forgot about the big picture. I even forgot about looking after my own ass. Closing my eyes, I took a deep breath to try to collect myself.

Then I studied Mercedes Cook. She wore a smoke-colored, slinky dress made of a lacy fabric that seemed modern and antique at the same time.

"Uh, yeah," was all I could manage. My secrecy was well and truly blown, it looked like. I wondered who else knew I was back in Denver?

Rick recovered from what I took to be shock—clearly he'd been as surprised to see me as I was to see him. Which meant that for some reason Mercedes hadn't told him I was coming. But what was *he* doing here?

Regaining his usual calm, he returned to his seat. "Back in Denver, I see." Flat statement.

I could argue, make excuses, play dumb. Or play it straight. Really, this was none of his damn business. "Looks like it," I said, smiling as amiably as I could manage.

"Interesting," was all he said. No why or how or when.

"How long have you two known each other?" I asked. They exchanged one of those glances that suggested a long association—the suppressed smiles and questioning looks in the eyes. Trying to decide how much to tell, whether to tell anything at all.

Mercedes took the initiative. "Oh, we've known each other quite some time, haven't we?"

"Come on, you're vampires," I said. "What does that mean? A decade, or a century or three?"

"You and Rick are friends," Mercedes said. "Do you know how old he is?"

I studied Rick, who remained impassive. Were we friends? I wasn't sure I'd go that far. I knew him without knowing anything about him. I felt like I'd stumbled into some kind of game, or long-running joke. "Two fifty," I said. Meaning two hundred fifty years.

Mercedes glanced at him, her smile widening. "Oh, my, we are keeping secrets here, aren't we?"

I blinked. "How old is he? How far off am I?"

"I told you, Kitty, it's not polite to talk about age." She smoothed out her already perfect skirt and changed the subject. "At some point I suppose I'll pay my respects to Arturo. Are you friends with him as well?"

I frowned. "I know him. "I'd really appreciate it if you didn't tell him I'm back in Denver."

"Sounds like there's a story behind that," she said. No assurances that she'd keep my secret. I had to reassess my impression of her completely. I'd taken her at face value—she came across as a young, vibrant, successful performer. That was a persona, the one she wanted me to see—and to be fair, that was exactly what she was. An actress. And I'd fallen for it. Underneath was something else, manipulative and dark. Vampire. Ben was right—again. He stood close to me, our arms touching.

"It's really not that interesting. If I'm interrupting, I can leave."

"Oh, no, please," Mercedes said, looking genuinely put out. But I didn't trust the expression. I didn't trust her anymore—and she knew it. I could see it in her glittering eyes. She'd played me and been happy to do so.

I should have walked out of there right then.

"Come and sit with us. Rick was telling me about the situation here, among our kinds. I'd like to hear your opinion as well." She gestured at chairs near Rick.

I looked at Ben. He said, "It's your call."

They were vampires, but I didn't think they were going to hurt us. Not here, anyway. We went to sit, while I tried to calm my racing nerves. The coffee table held a bottle of wine already uncorked, and four glasses poured and waiting. I chose one and took a sip. By then I needed a drink.

Four glasses. But vampires didn't drink wine.

A knock sounded on the door.

"Ah, that should be my other guests." Mercedes leaned back and donned a smile.

Other guests. I looked at Rick, to see his reaction; he frowned and straightened to the edge of his seat. He hadn't expected anyone else either.

I set my glass of wine on the table and braced.

The handle turned. The door opened inward, as if in slow motion. I could smell them before I saw them, I could hear them breathe, and I recognized the beats of their hearts. All my senses were pushed to their limits, waiting. I knew it all, I knew everything, I knew before the door opened all the way and they walked into the room.

Carl and Meg. Arm-in-arm, looking sullen.

I stood and stumbled back, knocking over my chair. My body felt like fog, drifting, melting away. I wasn't here, I couldn't be here, I couldn't move. Every pore burned. I wanted to vomit, but was too shocked.

Carl saw me and turned animal. He didn't shift, but his wolf came to the fore. It was amazing to watch. Our gazes met, and he lunged. His back bowed, his arms bent, his fingers locked into claw shapes, all in preparation of charging me. His lips rippled back in a snarl as he bared his teeth. A growl burred deep in his throat. The sound pinged a memory in my hind brain, turning my limbs to ash.

Arturo, who'd entered behind the couple, caught Carl as he took his first step toward me. The alpha werewolf lunged, and Arturo—svelte, blasé Arturo, Denver's Master vampire—dropped him where he stood by grabbing his arm, putting a hand on his neck, and squeezing. Carl arced his neck, gasped a breath, and stepped back, arresting his lunge. Arturo didn't even appear strained.

"Margaret, you, too! Stop!" Arturo's voice lashed, and Meg, Carl's mate, cowered, lurking on Carl's other side, kneading his arm like she might pull it off.

Arturo glared at us. Only ten feet separated us. I didn't remember moving, but Rick stood on one side of me, Ben on the other, and both had death grips on my arms, holding me back while I struggled against them. My throat was sore—from growling. Without being conscious of it, I'd matched Carl's lunge. I'd been ready to meet him head-on and fight, right here in the elegant suite.

Rick slipped in front of me, blocking my view. "Calm, Kitty. Stay calm," he whispered.

Fight him, fight him, get out of here, fight, run, escape—

Wolf swam at the front of my mind, pure instinct driving me.

I shut my eyes tight and gasped a breath that sounded like a sob. Took another, steadier breath, and stomped on the Wolf, tamped her down tight. Deep breath, keep it together. Focused on Ben's touch on my arm, his warm, safe scent in my nose.

Carl struggled briefly against Arturo's grip, and I wanted to scream.

"Ah," Mercedes said in her sugary, stage-diva voice. "*That's* why you left Denver."

Bitch. "You knew. You set this up." My voice still growled.

She shrugged, just a bit. "I wanted to see for myself."

"Let me go. Please let Ben and me go," I said softly,

well aware that Carl and Meg stood between us and the door, that we'd have to get past them to escape.

Mercedes didn't speak, and the tableau didn't change. We stood like statues, waiting for someone to cough. For someone to break.

"You're playing games," I said, my panic rising.

"Oh, no, this isn't a game, this is politics. Rough politics," she said.

Arturo, bless his undead heart, sounded as irate as I felt. "Mercedes, she's right. You're playing games, and keeping leashes on a pack of werewolves is not how I'd planned on spending my evening. Meg!"

The alpha female—nemesis, rival, chief bitch of my nightmares—had crept around her mate. Carefully, she stood in front of Carl and held herself straight. She didn't attack, didn't make the least sign of aggression. She just studied me. Me and Ben both. Ben's shoulders tensed, like hackles rising.

Meg had long, straight black hair, deeply tanned skin, unidentifiably ethnic features. She had a wild and exotic look about her, and a slim and powerful build. She was dressed for an evening downtown—a rust-colored blouse, dark slacks, high-heeled sandals, jewelry. I'd been used to seeing her in the outdoors, in a T-shirt and jeans. Carl, wearing shirt and slacks, hadn't changed much—he was tall, six-five or so, and broad to match, all muscles and quivering temper. You didn't challenge Carl. You just didn't.

Unless you were my best friend T.J. T.J. had challenged, and Carl had killed him for it.

For the moment Meg had taken up her old role of instigator. She'd poke and prod until I lashed out, then let Carl take me down. Now Ben, the newcomer, the unknown in the room from her perspective, occupied her attention. She took a long moment to stare at him. I willed Ben to stay calm, to stay quiet. I didn't want him reacting—either aggressively or submissively. I didn't want him to give her any points by admitting, however inadvertently, that she was stronger.

When Meg spoke to me, it was like glass shattering. "You really did it. You went and made yourself a mate so you could come back here and take over."

Gah, same old Meg. Some things never changed, and my next few breaths were calmer. "No, Meg. That's what *you* would have done."

Carl said, "I told you not to come back. I told you I'd kill you."

I argued. Maybe they'd see reason. Maybe they'd be reasonable. "I'm not here to make trouble, I promise I don't want any trouble. My mom's sick, Carl. I had to come back, just until she's better." I'd slipped into the old pattern, groveling before him, begging, head bowed, slouching. I'd fought hard so I wouldn't have to do that anymore. T. J. died so I wouldn't have to do that. I consciously straightened my back, straining against tense muscles. Made myself as tall as I could. Didn't tremble. I met Carl's gaze. Didn't quite offer a challenge, but I had to face him as an equal. No—I had to believe I was better.

"If you don't want trouble then who is he?" Carl nodded at Ben.

Ben stood close enough, just behind my shoulder, that I could feel his body heat. He hadn't cowered before Carl's and Meg's bluster. I sensed some tension, some anxiety in him. But his back was straight, and his gaze steady. I was glad to have him at my side.

"He's a friend. He's only here because of me. You can leave him alone."

Carl didn't like him. He didn't like the presence of a competent, self-assured male who didn't owe him loyalty. Ben could stand there without flinching and Carl would take it as a challenge.

But Ben didn't just stand there. Oh, no.

"So you're Carl," Ben said, taking a couple of slow steps forward and studiously looking Carl up and down. "I thought you'd be taller."

I mentally slapped my forehead. But I had to admit, Ben always knew just what to say.

Snarling, Carl sprang forward, hands outstretched, fingers clawed. I braced, preparing to dodge, then run like hell. Ben, damn him, didn't flinch at all because he must have guessed what was coming next.

Again, Arturo stopped Carl. In a flash of movement, he grabbed Carl's arm and twisted it, using the bigger man's momentum to divert him and drop him to his knees. His breaths heaving, Carl struggled, his eyes gleaming with animal ferocity, ready to rip out of the vampire's grip. But with his hand on Carl's shoulder, Arturo only had to squeeze once to quiet him. I didn't know where the strength came from—Arturo seemed to exert no effort.

Arturo said, "Let it go."

"They're a threat—"

"They've made no challenge. Let it go, Carl."

Carl knelt there for a moment, panting, then shrugged away from Arturo's grip.

Mercedes said, "This is utterly fascinating." She continued to play the gracious hostess. "Come, sit. I've already poured the wine. To let it breathe."

I had backed toward the wall, keeping hold of Ben's sleeve, letting Rick stand between us and the others. "I'll stay right here, thanks," I murmured.

Carl started to move forward, but Arturo stepped in front of him. "No, you two are staying right there. I won't have you dogs messing up the carpet."

Arturo never lost his composure, his offhand manner and focused gaze. His apparent age was late twenties, but he had the weight of centuries behind his eyes. He had golden hair pulled back in a short tail, and an aristocratic face.

He and Rick exchanged a look, and I couldn't read it. The two were close in age—both apparent and actual, from what I could gather. Age meant power among vampires, and the two should have been rivals, but they'd coexisted in some kind of alliance for years. Arturo was the Master in Denver, but Rick had some amount of autonomy within that territory.

Did Arturo suspect that Rick wanted to change the situation?

For now, they only seemed to want to coordinate their efforts at keeping the wolves under control.

Mercedes sat back and observed the drama she'd orchestrated. "Hmm, maybe the situation here isn't as chaotic as I'd been led to believe. You boys seem to have things well in hand."

"No thanks to you," Arturo spat in his refined accent. "What's your business here, Mercedes? Is it anything more than poking a stick in the burrow to see what strikes?"

"Isn't that enough?" she said.

"More than enough," he said, wearing a tight smile. "How long will you be here?"

"Oh, a few more days. Maybe a week. Or two." She lifted her hand and studied her fingernails, a contrived gesture worthy of the stage.

This was Arturo's territory as far as vampires were concerned, and he controlled it the same way Carl controlled it among the werewolves. He could tell her to leave. He could make threats and carry them out. So why didn't he? What was her power here?

"Don't look so put out," she said to Arturo. "I'm only here out of curiosity. I heard some rumblings and I thought I'd come and make some observations."

Arturo's gaze narrowed, sizing her up. "For whom? Who are you working for these days, Mercedes?"

The question chilled me.

Everyone looked at her. But she was used to being the center of attention and didn't wilt.

"I'm scheduled to start rehearsals next month for a revival of *Anything Goes*. I suppose you could say I'll be working for the production company."

Arturo rolled his eyes and turned away.

Mercedes said, "If you tell me straight out, well and truly, that all is calm here, that the rumors that your Family is unstable are unfounded, I'll smile sweetly and believe you. I can see that the wolves have some problems, but don't they always? Tell me, Arturo, that you are the Master here and that you have no rivals."

Arturo glanced at Rick. I would have wilted under that glance. For his part, Rick didn't flinch. He met it square and didn't say a word.

"I am the Master here, and I have no rivals," Arturo

said—to Rick. Not to Mercedes. She observed the subtlety with a lilt to her perfectly plucked brow.

Oh, this was going to get ugly.

I raised my hand. "Since you obviously don't think too much of us, can we leave? Please?"

"Kitty," Mercedes said. "You and your mate carry yourselves like alphas. Two alpha pairs can't live within the same territory. It can't be done, you know it."

I looked away to hide my smile. "See, I think it can. I've seen some interesting things since I left. I've seen two dozen lycanthropes packed into a room, with none of them fighting. If they all agree to it, they can get along. Carl, I promise you, I don't want this territory. I'll stay out of your way if you just leave Ben and me alone. I've always been straight with you."

He grimaced. "Just you being here is a threat to my authority."

No, your incompetence is a threat to your authority. I didn't say it. What I did say wasn't much better. "Can you just for a minute *try* to act like a rational human being?"

On cue, he growled.

Rick gave me a look over his shoulder. "You're provoking him."

I couldn't help it. "Sorry."

Mercedes sighed dramatically. Could she sigh any other way? "I can see we won't have any kind of civilized conversation with all of you here. Kitty, you're right, you and yours should probably leave. Thank you for coming, especially since the circumstances were a bit...staged. You—" She pointed at the trio by the door. "You will let them leave."

Who was she to command us all like that? I suddenly didn't want to go, just to be contrary.

"Rick, will you escort Kitty and Ben out? Thank you."

In a strange choreography, Arturo steered Carl and Meg away from the door, while Rick cleared a path for me and Ben. Herding werewolves. It was almost laughable.

I paused for a look back. Mercedes sat like a queen on her sofa, a totally different woman than the one I'd met two days ago. I didn't know who she was. Carl, standing off to the side, still looked like he wanted to jump out of his skin to get me. The gratifying sight of Meg hiding behind him didn't even make me feel better.

"Thanks for the drinks," I said with pure sarcasm. Then I got the hell out. Rick followed us into the hall and closed the door. With that sound, a weight lifted. I slumped back against the wall and sighed. Ben watched patiently—far too calmly in my opinion. I resisted an urge to fall into his arms and start blubbering.

"I hate him," I muttered, wiping away a few stray, stressed tears. "I hate him so much."

"Let's go," Rick said. "The more distance between you the better."

I grilled him as we rode the elevator to the lobby. "So. When I asked if there was another Master moving in and you said 'not exactly,' were you talking about her?" He grimaced, which was all the answer I needed. "What did you tell her? Did you have any idea what she was going to do in there?"

"Um...not exactly," he said softly. His face was taut, strained. He was worried, and that made me worried. "I went to her for information. Maybe even to find out which of us she'd support. Our conversation never got that far."

"Who is she really?"

"The Master vampires have always known she's a vampire. She's moved as an envoy between the cities for decades. As a performer, she travels freely, and by tradition vampires like her have immunity, even outside the protection of the Families. In a sense, she's a member of all the Families. And none of them. The system helps keep the peace. But it's also started wars. If I were smart I'd walk away. Leave town and find someplace else, like I've always done before."

"Why don't you?"

"Because sooner or later, I'm going to have to make a stand. I like it here. I like the people." He looked squarely at me. "Seems as good a place and time as any."

We'd reached the lobby by that time, and stopped near the front doors, shifting out of the doorman's hearing.

"What does 'sooner or later' really mean to a vampire?"

He said, "It means not thinking about the future. It means there is no future. There's only now, and what you can protect now. Sooner or later is always now."

"Protect. From what?"

"Predators," he said. "She's sizing us up. She'll take the news to the other Families. It isn't like it was a hundred years ago, when Arturo settled here. There are no new cities to build. A vampire who wants to be a Master has to become one by force. Or guile. If word gets out that Denver is unstable, others will come. Scavengers. If I wanted to be really sinister, I'd say that someone sent Mercedes here to stir things up. To make the situation unstable. More unstable, that is."

"How long has she been doing this? How old is she?"

"God knows. I should get back to it." He turned back to the elevators. Ben took my arm and drew me away, out the hotel's front doors.

"Well, that was fun," he said with false brightness.

"You see what we're dealing with?" I marched along the sidewalk, quickly putting distance between me and that place. We'd parked in a lot a couple of blocks up the street. I couldn't get there fast enough.

"Sure. There were a lot of really insecure people in that room."

I almost laughed, except I suddenly felt like I was going to throw up. Spent adrenaline. "Yeah. Did you have to provoke him like that?" I said. I could still see the look on Carl's face.

"He's a bully. I love bullies. They have such big, shiny red buttons to push."

He was such a lawyer.

"Didn't he make you at all nervous? The wolf side, I mean. Didn't he make you want to either grovel or crawl out of your skin?"

"Yeah, but you were with me so I felt okay. I feel okay when you're around."

I could have hugged him for that. But it was too much responsibility. I didn't want to be alpha, not even of a pack of two. "That's flattering. Most of the time I feel like I'm falling apart."

"But you haven't actually fallen." His smile was tight, anxious. Using humor to combat the fear.

"You're insufferable, you know that?" I held his arm, both gaining and giving comfort with the touch.

It didn't entirely help.

"Oh, my God. I'm fucked. I am so fucked." I started

shivering when the cool evening air got to my sweaty skin. Or it could have been the churning in my gut. I walked faster, as if I could flee my own reaction.

Ben kept up, stayed alongside me, watching me. "I've never seen you like this. It's kind of freaking me out."

I stopped and doubled over, clutching my stomach.

Run. We can run. Get away, out of his territory, far away—

"Kitty." Ben put his hand on my back, a comforting pressure. "Keep it together."

Anyone passing by would have probably tsked at the scene, maybe smiled in amusement—some chick drank too much at the bars, and her attentive boyfriend was looking after her. How cute. My Wolf was right on the surface, though, fighting. Carl brought her out and I couldn't put her back.

"Kitty."

I concentrated on Ben's voice, his touch, human skin against human skin. His palm slid across my shirt. Focusing on my spine, I straightened—stay upright, vertical backbone, not horizontal, not like Wolf. I took deep, careful breaths.

Ben took off his suit jacket and put it over my shoulders. I clung to it tightly, snuggling into its warmth. His arm across my back, we walked on, close together, our bodies touching. Our pack of two.

"If he finds you alone, he'll kill you, won't he?" he said.

"I think so."

We'd traveled another block before he said, "Right. Just as long as I know where we all stand."

Then, finally, I did laugh.

chapter 6

I felt betrayed, and I couldn't even say by whom. Not by Rick—he'd seemed as much a victim of the evening as anyone. Then again, some of it was him; he must have talked about me to Mercedes. Gave away pieces of my history that put me in danger. I wanted to be angry at Arturo, but he'd probably saved my hide back there. Carl and Meg—of course, I'd felt betrayed by them a long time ago.

Mercedes Cook. Now, there was a character. She was up to something. She'd set that little game in motion. Put the pieces into play to see what would happen.

Really, I had no one to blame but myself for walking into the trap.

"Kitty, can you come here a minute?" Ben called to me from the kitchen, leaning over the counter that overlooked the living room. I left the desk and computer to sit on the bar stool, where he indicated.

We stayed like that for a long minute, looking across the counter at one another. Now what? What had I done wrong?

I was about to say something when he put a gun on the counter between us. It made a clunking noise, a sound of finality. It was chillingly black.

I stared at it. Guns were Cormac's thing. Having the gun here, without Cormac, was just... wrong.

"What's this?" My voice seemed small.

"Nine-millimeter Glock semiautomatic, weapon of choice of law enforcement officers everywhere. Compact, light, has some kick because of that, but it's worth the trade. It can still do a fair bit of damage."

Dread fell like a weight over me.

He continued. "We're not strong enough to take on Carl and Meg hand-to-hand. We need other advantages."

Like hell. "Ben, no, I've never touched a gun in my life—"

"That's why I'm taking you to a range where you can practice."

"No. No no no. It's cheating. We're supposed to use claws and teeth. Survival of the fittest—"

"Law of the jungle crap?" he said. "You don't think they'd cheat given half a chance?"

As a matter of fact, they had cheated. T.J. had agreed to walk away when Carl killed him. I just didn't want to have to use a gun.

"Do it for me," he said. "It'll make me feel better. If you run into that guy alone, I want to know that you can drop him where he stands."

I couldn't believe it. I couldn't believe it had come to this.

When I got my voice back I said, "Is this one of Cormac's?" For a minute it felt like the bounty hunter was with us in spirit.

Ben shook his head. "Did you think he was the only one with a concealed weapons permit?" His smile turned sly.

Well. You learn something new every day. Even about the guy you're sleeping with.

The shooting range was in a low concrete building north of town, in the suburbs. It might have been any business, and I'd have probably overlooked the unobtrusive sign, black print on white, announcing GUNS, AMMO, RANGE. SEVEN DAYS A WEEK.

Inside, the place smelled like Cormac. Rather, Cormac smelled like a gun shop, if I had ever known what a gun shop smelled like. Gun oil, metal, burned powder. That said something about Cormac.

Ben picked up a couple boxes of bullets, headsets for ear protection, and safety glasses from the guy at the counter. Boy, there were a lot of guns locked up behind the glass case under that counter. They all looked dark and angry.

At the back of the shop, past the double metal doors, came the sound of gunfire. Two guns, I thought, firing slightly out of synch. One was faster than the other.

His hand on my back, Ben steered me toward that door.

The back room was straight out of a police drama— various booths opened into a long hallway. Targets hung on lines in the back. The people in the two occupied booths ignored us.

Ben was all business and got straight to work.

"First off, here's the reason so many accidental shootings happen with semiautomatics." He clicked a latch, and the clip dropped out of the gun's grip. Then he slid back a release, revealing the bullet still in the chamber. "Losing the clip doesn't mean the thing's empty."

He tipped the gun, knocking the bullet into his hand. Closed the release. "Now it's safe." He pointed to the target, pulled the trigger a couple of times, and nothing happened.

"Rule number one, never point a gun—empty, loaded, whatever—unless you plan on firing it. If you point it at a person, it means you want to kill them." He slipped the spare bullet back in the clip, put the clip back in the gun, pulled back the slide, chambered the round. Live and loaded. Rock and roll. Shit.

"Rule number two, if you need to kill someone, make sure the thing's loaded." He grinned.

"You've been hanging out with Cormac too long," I said.

"Yeah, well," he said, and left it at that.

"Who taught you all this? Rule number one, rule number two." He handled the weapon like he'd been doing this his whole life. Maybe he had. He'd grown up on a ranch on the northern Front Range.

"My father."

"Your freaky militia father who's in jail?" Yes, my boyfriend had quite the history. Two of his three closest relatives were doing time.

"Yep." He smiled. He handed me safety equipment. "Put these on."

How the hell did I ever get mixed up with him? I was a nice girl from the suburbs. I put on the glasses and earphones, which mostly muffled my hearing, but I could still hear him as he instructed.

Hold it like this, sight along these two points on the barrel, don't jerk at the trigger—squeeze slowly as you exhale. He fired, then fired again. The gun exploded with noise.

I flinched. Nothing good ever happened when I heard that sound. I was glad of the ear protection in this enclosed concrete space. We looked across to the target—he'd made two little holes off center, within the black circle.

"Now, you try." He handed the thing to me.

I took it like it was alive and had teeth. Sighing, Ben stood behind me, cupped his hands around mine, and guided them into place, showing me how to hold the thing: right hand on the grip, left hand underneath, steadying it. Our bodies pressed close together.

Okay, this part was kind of sexy.

"Don't brace your arms," he said by my ear. "Relax. Now, breathe out, tighten the trigger—"

Supersensitive, it felt like it only moved a millimeter before it clicked and the gun jumped in my hand. Boom, loud as an explosion, I felt it in my bones. My whole arm tingled. My heart was beating fast for no good reason.

"Hey, I think you actually hit the target." He pointed to a white tear on the edge of the paper, far outside the circle of black.

"I don't think I was even aiming." I furrowed my brow at the weapon.

"I couldn't tell," he said sarcastically. "Try again."

He reminded me to aim along the sights, but he didn't guide me this time. I was on my own. I fired. It still made my arms tingle, but I was ready for it this time. Again, I hit the target, but not the black circle.

"Again." So I did, again and again and again. Went through four clips, fifteen rounds each, so that I was standing in a mess of brass casings. I got used to the noise, got used to the way the shots rattled my arms. And that was the point.

By the last clip I hit the black circle every single shot. I regarded my handiwork with grudging admiration. I didn't want to feel proud about this.

Ben crossed his arms and nodded, seemingly satisfied. "Now pop the clip. Check the chamber, make sure it's empty."

I did, dutifully, like I was some kind of army trainee.

"Now, don't you feel better?" he said.

"No. Can we go now?"

Back in the car, I asked, "You're not going to make me carry a gun around with me all the time, are you?"

"Not yet. Have to get you a permit first."

I just couldn't win.

I spent that week at work handling the fallout from Friday's show and introducing America's first celebrity vampire. Bitterly, now that I was dealing with a manipulative player rather than a genial actress. Although a couple of calls from the agents of people who wanted to be the *second* celebrity vampire were awfully intriguing... I sensed a reality TV show in the making.

I didn't have the license or the gun when I got shanghaied in the parking lot outside work.

If you want to make yourself hard to find, you're supposed to vary your route between work and home. Leave at unpredictable times. Make your schedule unpredictable. Get a P.O. box, hide your home address. Get an unlisted phone number.

But everyone could find me at KNOB. They were waiting for me after dark.

"Hi, honey. Love your show."

I heard her and smelled her at the same time, my nostrils widening as soon as I stepped outside and took in the night air. She was cold, she had no heartbeat—undead. Vampire. She leaned on the wall right outside the door, arms crossed. Her thick brown hair was tied in a wild ponytail, her skin was porcelain pale and smooth. She wore a black lace camisole, leather pants, and high-heeled black boots. And sunglasses. Her red lips smiled.

She wasn't one of the locals. The vampires in Arturo's clan had more style and less punk-ass stereotype.

"Who the hell are you?" I said, quiet and wary.

"She's with me." The guy just appeared, behind me, leaning on the other side of the door. He had the same pale skin, spiky black hair, and sunglasses. Leather jacket, T-shirt, jeans. That same wicked, predatorial smile.

Fuck.

I walked forward, like I could pretend they weren't there. A second later, they stood beside me again, and each one had a grip on my arms.

I sighed. "What do you want?"

They both grinned, having too much fun with their game.

"We want to talk," the guy said.

"I'm listening."

"Not here," he said.

Of course not. Side by side, holding me tight, they steered me to a black SUV parked around the corner. Strangely, rather than panic I felt an odd sort of fatalism settle over me, like I finally had too much to deal with. I didn't have any anxiety left to muster. Maybe they weren't planning on killing me. Maybe they'd started a fan club and just wanted me to give a little talk to the gang. Maybe they were going to lock me in a shipping crate and sell me into slavery.

See, whatever it was, I just couldn't think of how bad it could possibly get. My imagination failed me.

I made a token effort to escape. I braced my arms and dropped my weight back—and was shocked when I actually broke out of their grips. Blinking, I looked at them looking back at me. Then the Wolf took over and ran. I turned and launched myself in the same step, dashing down the sidewalk.

Seemingly without moving, without effort, they grabbed hold of me again. I didn't even sense them moving. In one breath I was running, and in the next I jerked back, flailing like a fish on a line. They hauled me back toward the SUV. I managed to get my feet under me, so I wasn't completely dragged.

"Cute," the woman said. "Real cute. Though I can't blame you for trying."

"Thanks," I muttered.

She went around to the passenger side, the guy shoved me in through the driver's side, and they pinned me between them as they climbed in.

"Don't worry," she said. "This'll be fun."

Yeah, right. They both looked to be in their twenties. They seemed young, as vampires went. They were having too much fun with it.

They didn't blindfold me. They didn't care if I knew where we were going, which boded both well and ill. Maybe they really did just want to talk. But if they were planning on killing me, it wouldn't matter if I knew where we were going.

I put on an air of bravado. "You guys are from the eighties, aren't you?"

She giggled and put her arm across my shoulders, pressing far too close to me for comfort. Goose bumps broke out over my arms. She said, "That's exactly what he said you'd say."

"Who? Who said I'd say that?"

Nothing. The guy grinned, and she kept stifling giggles.

I slumped back against the seat and eyed him in the review mirror. Except he wasn't there. Leaning forward suddenly, I checked the side mirror—I should have seen him there, but I only saw the back of the seat, bathed in shadow. But the mirror thing was bunk. I'd seen it.

"What are you doing?" the woman asked, watching me crane my neck, trying to look at a different angle.

Sounding more panicked than I wanted, I said, "Do you guys cast reflections in mirrors or not?"

She grabbed the rearview mirror and tilted it toward herself—and I caught a glimpse of her, right there in the mirror, in all her poofy-haired glory.

Then he took hold of it and turned it toward him. And I didn't see anything. Maybe an extra shadow. He did it quickly, then moved the mirror back to its original position, like he'd only been adjusting it.

"You mean it turns on and off?" My voice was a tad shrill.

"It's all tricks of the light," he said. The woman only smiled.

Oh, great. What *couldn't* vampires do? I sat back and stayed very still and quiet for the rest of the trip.

After a half an hour of driving, we ended up south of the freeway, near Broadway, behind a one-story, windowless, warehouse-type building. The area was all steel and concrete, desolate at this time of night. I could scream, and it wouldn't do any good.

She dragged me out of her side of the car. Her grip was firm—no breaking out of it this time, especially when he joined her.

Inside the warehouse, the space was lit by emergency lighting, dim circles around the perimeter, leaving much of the place in shadows. On top of that, crates and boxes formed walls and canyons, dozens of pallets wrapped in plastic and waiting shipment. This was a working warehouse, beside whatever hideout these guys were using it for.

I smelled people. Beings, rather. Both vampires and lycanthropes were here, and the scent crowded together so I couldn't tell how many there were. The shadows hid them well, but I sensed them there, watching. I kept close to the door. Maybe I could run, if they gave me a chance.

A low growl echoed, and something animal and musky approached. It was canine, but not wolf, and it had a distinctive...something else. A touch of human. I backed toward the door, my shoulders bunched up.

The thing moved into the light, and I'd never seen anything like it. As large as a Great Dane—bigger, even—it stepped lightly on slender legs. Its body was sleek, its coloring mottled—red, white, yellow, and black splotches decorating it, like it had had a run-in with a paint set. It had a boxy, doglike face and huge, desert-dwelling ears that focused on me like satellite dishes.

I couldn't help but stare at it, which it took as a challenge, lowering its head, straightening its tail like a rudder, and growling.

"Hush, Dack. Be still." A voice spoke from the darkness, and the creature looked toward it, flattening its ears and dropping its tail.

The leader was here, and I knew his voice. Rick gave the animal a quick scratch behind the ears as he approached us, emerging from shadows.

"Rick, you bastard! What the hell's this about?"

The animal started growling again, and I backed up. Again, Rick shushed it, murmuring gently. His power was subtle, but indisputable.

When he entered into view, so did his army. They came into the light, just enough so I could see them—so they could see me, size me up. Seven lycanthropes and two more vampires, beside the ones who'd ambushed me. One of the vampires was a woman. So was one of the lycanthropes—and she wasn't a wolf. I couldn't tell what variety she was. A diverse and terrifying group, they all looked tough, and they all frowned. Some of them carried weapons—guns, knives. I wouldn't want to meet any of them in a dark alley.

I swallowed back my fear. "So. Am I here to be threatened or recruited?"

Rick said, "I wanted to show you how vulnerable you are. You need me as much as I need you."

"And how exactly is facing off with Carl and Meg supposed to make me *less* vulnerable?"

He had the decency not to answer that.

"Rick, I want to go home, and I want you to take me. Not Sid and Nancy over here."

"Charlie and Violet," he said. "Their names are Charlie

and Violet." The pair of vampires leaned against a nearby wall. I swore the woman, Violet, was smacking a piece of chewing gum. Charlie smiled enough to show fang and gave a wiggle of his fingers.

I nodded toward the strange, leggy creature. "And what is that thing?"

"African wild dog, lycanthropic variety. Dack and I are old friends."

The animal—person, I forced myself to acknowledge, since I'd sensed it from the first—didn't appear any more friendly after the introduction. I kept my distance. Rick whispered to him, and the dog turned and trotted away, close to the wall of the building. Walking the perimeter, keeping guard.

Motley didn't begin to describe this group.

Then he introduced me to all of them, the nine others, as if I would remember their names. As if knowing their names would give me some stake in the outcome of this confrontation. One of them, the woman lycanthrope of unknown variety, flashed a smile and said, "I love your show."

What else could I do but mutter, "Thanks." Then I stepped close to Rick and said softly, "It's going to take more than this to get rid of Arturo."

"Yes. It's going to take the city's werewolves supporting me," Rick said.

"No. Even if I thought I could take on Carl and Meg, even if I took over the pack, I wouldn't do it and then turn my wolves into cannon fodder for your little war."

"And that is exactly why you should lead the city's wolves, and not Carl. Carl wouldn't hesitate to use them as cannon fodder."

"You're trying to turn this back on me, to appeal to my

sense of duty. It's not going to work. Just this once I'm going to be selfish and stay the hell out of it."

"You'll have to do what you think is right, of course."

"Oh, no you don't! You're not going to guilt me into this."

"Wow," said Violet. "You were right, Rick. She is kinda jumpy."

"Kitty, let's take a walk," Rick said, nodding toward the door.

Charlie stepped forward, frowning. "You sure it's safe?"

"It'll be fine," he said. He opened the door and gestured me outside. Dutifully, I exited.

I was happy enough to be outside the close, stuffy air of the warehouse, and the smells and stares of beings who didn't much care for me. Were-African wild dog? If I hadn't actually seen him...I wondered what he was like as a human.

Rick guided our walk along the wall, staying in the shadows and out of the streetlights. He kept his gaze forward, like he wasn't at all concerned. We reached the corner of the building, and he still didn't say anything. I couldn't say that I knew him all that well, but he seemed unusually pensive. Lost in thought.

"They don't trust you," he said finally. "They think I'm making a mistake, trying to recruit you. I thought if they met you, they'd change their minds."

"Rick, I've got my own worries right now. I've got too much to lose to...to fight someone else's war."

"I thought maybe you'd be interested in revenge."

I shook my head. "I put too much distance between me and them to want revenge anymore."

"T. J. would have sided with me without any doubts."

"Don't you dare use him as a pawn in this," I said, my voice rough. "He doesn't deserve that." Even though Rick was right.

"I'm sorry." His voice was muted.

We walked a few more paces, until the silence was too much.

"Charlie and Violet," I said. "Where'd you pick up those two?"

He actually smiled, an offhand amused smile. "Charlie was turned about forty-five years ago by a West Coast vampire of my acquaintance—a bit power hungry, a bit mad. I helped Charlie escape from his Family. About thirty years ago, he met Violet and turned her himself. They decided they were made for each other, and I can't say I disagree. They've operated independently since then. They seem to have a lot of fun being petty outlaws—it tends to make the Families twitch."

"So they're not from the eighties."

"They got a bit stalled there, didn't they? Charlie owes me a favor, so he came."

The others probably all had stories like that. Rick had helped them, now they answered his call. But would they be enough to confront Arturo?

"Is that everyone you have? Are others coming?"

"I could use more," he said. "I ought to have more to face Arturo."

"You're talking like this is going to be a war. Like you and Arturo have armies. Is that what this is going to be? Vampires and werewolves battling in the streets of Denver? That can't happen. I'll tell the police—I have a contact with them."

"This has been going on for hundreds of years under the noses of mundane authorities. No one will notice."

He was right. People like us were killed all the time and no one much noticed. Through most of history there'd been a curtain drawn over our world.

"That's changing. The Denver PD has a Paranatural Unit, did you know that? If bodies start turning up, they'll notice. Look at how the newspaper played those nightclub attacks. You can't operate under the old assumptions."

He studied me sidelong. "What's your story? You're on edge, even more paranoid than usual. It's more than your mother's illness, isn't it?"

I almost told him. It was on the edge of my tongue. I hadn't told anyone but Ben, and for a moment I thought that if I told Rick about the miscarriage, it would explain everything. He'd leave me alone.   .

I ought to be milking it for all the pity I could.

"Rick, it's all I can do to take care of myself right now. I can't help you." I didn't want to get involved. I couldn't get involved.

He nodded, lips pursed thoughtfully. "I'm going to move soon. I have to do this before Mercedes leaves town. She has to spread the word that a new, stronger Master is in control here, and that Denver is off-limits."

"What's the deal with her? How is it she has both you and Arturo cowering?"

He smiled, a wry and bitter expression. "A Master vampire is a Master only as long as other vampires recognize him as such. Arturo will be desperate to prove that he's still in charge. And she has the power to decide that he isn't. When she moves along on her concert tour, the news of that will spread."

"So she's the vampire gossip mill and everyone tries to get on her good side? It can't be that simple. What happens if she decides to nudge things along in one direction or another?"

"Maybe we'll find out. Kitty, I know you have pressing concerns, but if Carl and Arturo win, you won't be able to stay to help your mother. You'll be in danger, and you see how easy it is to get to you."

"You're trying to scare me. I've already been scared. It's a lot harder to terrify me these days."

"I imagine so. Just remember, fear is good. Fear is a survival mechanism."

"And a tool used to manipulate others. Rick, I need to get back."

"All right." We turned the corner to where his slick BMW was parked.

We drove the whole way back to KNOB without saying a word. He stopped in the parking lot next to my hatchback and let me out without argument. He didn't have to do that. Carl or Arturo would have kept me locked up, just to show who had the power.

It occurred to me that Rick was one of the good guys.

"Thanks," I said, climbing out of the car.

"Just a minute. Take this." He reached over and offered me a slip of paper. It had a phone number written on it.

"This yours?" I said, and he nodded. "In case I change my mind?"

"Or if you need my help."

I couldn't decide if the gesture was out of optimism or pity. I stuck the number in my pocket. "Rick. How old are you?"

He shook his head, quirking a smile. "I'm not going to answer that."

"If I keep asking, you might one of these days."

"I admire your persistence, Kitty."

I almost laughed. "At least somebody does. Good luck, Rick."

"I'm thinking I'll need it."

I closed the passenger door and he drove away, and I wondered if I'd ever see him again.

When my cell phone rang the next day, I checked the caller ID and my heart caught in my throat. It was Dad.

"Hi, Dad? What is it?"

Like I was afraid he would, he said, "The test results came in." His voice was serious, tired. Bad news, I was ready for bad news. "It's positive. Malignant. She's going in this afternoon to talk to the doctor."

"Do I need to come over? Do you want me to come over? What can I do?"

Nothing. Nothing but sit here and worry.

"I'm going with her to the doctor, but if you could come over for dinner, I think it'd be good. I think it would help."

"Really?"

He sighed. "I don't know. This happens to people every day—but it feels like we're the first people in the universe to have to deal with it. Does that make any sense?"

"Yeah, it does. You want me to pick something up? Chinese? Pizza? Just so no one has to cook."

"Sure, that sounds great. How about six?"

"I'll be there. Thanks for calling, Dad."

"See you soon."

I clicked off the phone and started crying.

Ben had a new case to work on and begged off for the evening. Cheryl had also bowed out of dinner. One of the kids had caught a cold, Mark was working late, they didn't want to be a bother. A dozen excuses. But I wondered: *Now* who was shirking her filial duties?

I arrived at my folks' place with a bag full of take-out Chinese and a cheerful disposition.

Mom took the bag from me as I asked, "What did the doctor say? What's happening?" I didn't even say hello first. She was back to her put-together self, her fashionable blouse and slacks, with the right amount of jewelry and makeup. But she seemed harried.

"Let's eat first," she said. She wasn't smiling.

Dad came in from the kitchen and hugged me—something he never did, not right away like this. His face was pale, and he wasn't smiling either. Silently, the three of us put out plates, spooned out rice and stir fry, and settled in to it.

This was the most stressful meal I'd ever eaten. Not that I could honestly say I ate anything.

"How's work?" Dad asked finally, falling back on the standard question.

I blathered on, determined to keep the grim silence from falling again. It had definitely been an exciting weekend, even after leaving out all the stuff about Carl and Meg, vampire politics, learning how to shoot, and instead sticking to the upcoming book release and how great it was that I could break a story like Mercedes Cook being a vampire. Running my mouth also meant I mostly moved my food around on the plate without really eating. Mom and Dad did the same. At this rate, the leftovers would last a week.

Mom pushed her plate away first, and Dad and I gratefully followed suit.

"Jim, would you clean up, please? Kitty and I can go have our talk."

In reply, he kissed her cheek—a communications shorthand after thirty-five years of comfortable marriage—and collected plates. Mom took my hand and led me to the living room. We sat side by side on the sofa.

"Okay," I said, trying to be brave. "How bad is it?"

"It's a little worse than we thought. They didn't remove all the cancer, it turns out. It's invasive."

"What does that mean?" And how could she be this calm?

She shrugged stoically. "It means things are a little more serious is all. I'll need more surgery. They want to remove lymph nodes for testing. If it, spread I may need chemotherapy as well as radiation. I'll be a little sicker for a little longer. The prognosis is good, it's still good." Her smile went tight and strained. The power of positive thinking and all that. You had to be positive. "They're recommending aggressive treatment, and they want to start right away. That would mean more surgery in a week or so."

I choked on the words. "That soon? Isn't there something else, another way—"

"We'll see. I'm going to get a second opinion. But

really, the lump was there, the spot on the mammogram is there, only an idiot would claim that nothing was wrong."

She turned her gaze to the ceiling; her eyes were shining. "You know what's strange? I'm not even thinking about myself right now. I'm thinking about you girls, my darling girls. My Aunt Patty died of this, and now I have it, so it obviously runs in the family and if you and Cheryl ever get this I'll be so...so...*upset.*" Like she couldn't think of anything stronger to feel than that.

"Mom." I held her hand in both of mine, squeezed until she looked at me. "Don't worry about me. I won't get it. I can't get it. I'm a werewolf, werewolves don't get sick. They don't get cancer."

I froze, because a terrible, insidious worm of a thought started in the back of my brain. A vicious, hopeful thought.

My mind was in a panic, I couldn't speak. Mom didn't seem to notice. She touched my cheek and rested her hand on my shoulder.

"You know, I look at you and I can't even tell? I still don't believe it most of the time. You're not a monster, I don't care what *Time* magazine says." The glint in her eye laughed silently at the joke.

I smiled back. I forced my limbs to relax. I acted normal. As normal as I ever could.

I didn't say, *I could bite you, Mom. I could cure you.*

chapter 7

A clock was ticking just behind my back. The noise of approaching doom was always right behind me, like Captain Hook's crocodile. I could never turn around fast enough to actually see it. But it was always there, and I knew that soon the alarm would go off. The ringing of it would break me. Mom's surgery, Rick's war, my career, my own rebellious body—something was going to start ringing soon. Then it would blow up, like a time bomb.

I was exhausted, waiting for the explosion.

"So then I said to him, look, I don't care if it *is* a full moon tonight, *I* want to go to the Coldplay concert and *you're* going to take me. You're just going to have to turn into a wolf some other night. And you know what he says to me? He says—"

This caller was why I didn't counsel people in person. If she'd been sitting here I'd have throttled her. "Let me guess. He says, 'Baby, I don't have a choice.'"

"Well, yeah, except for the baby part."

"Let me ask you a question, Mia. What have you done for him lately?"

The pause lasted a beat. Then, "What do you mean?"

"I mean have you ever done anything nice for your boyfriend?"

Mia gave an unattractive snort. "Why should I? He's lucky to have me."

"Oh, honey, I used to beat up girls like you in grade school. Look, I'm as sympathetic about inattentive boyfriends as the next girl, but when he said he didn't have a choice about turning into a wolf—he *meant* it. He's supposed to be able to look to his girlfriend for support, right? 'Cause you know, this whole relationship thing works both ways, give and take and all that. And what do you do? Ask him to do the one thing he can't. Could you *be* any more insensitive? Wait, don't answer that. Of course you could. But I'm thinking he's the crazy one for putting up with your crap."

"You can't talk to me like—"

"Listen. You have so many problems with this boyfriend of yours, here's my advice. Break up with him. You'd be doing him a favor."

"But I *like* dating a werewolf. It's *cool*."

"You can't have it both ways." I clicked off the line, because really, that conversation couldn't go anywhere else. "You like fur so much, buy a poodle. Except I wouldn't wish you on a poodle even. Damn, I'm cranky tonight. Let's see, where do we go from here. Stan, you're on the air."

"Hi, Kitty. Thanks for taking my call. Can you answer a question for me?"

"I'll give it a shot." I tried to learn everything about him from the sound of his voice: male, indeterminate age. He wasn't overly emotional: frustrated, depressed, sad, or angry. He was neutral, interested. His question could be about anything.

"A lot of people call in to your show wanting to know about vampires and werewolves like they admire them. Like they want to *be* them. But these are monsters we're talking about—they're not saints. They're not something to aspire to. Even if it is a disease, like you say, why would anyone *want* a disease like that? I don't understand. Can you explain what people see in the whole thing?" His question sounded genuine. It didn't sound like a put-on.

I was sort of in his camp at the moment.

"I don't know, Stan. Different people see different things in it, I think. Some see glamour. Or power. They feel helpless, and these identities are a way not to feel helpless. The thing is, people who aren't vampires and werewolves aren't looking at the reality of it. Often they only see the stories, the lore, the mystique. They're basing their feelings on what they *think* those lives must be like. They don't see the dark side. Or if they do, they paint it in glamorous colors as well. It's exciting, it's dangerous. It's an adventure. Maybe that's it."

"Maybe?" He sounded skeptical.

"You have to remember, I never wanted to be a werewolf. I never thought twice about it until I landed in the middle of it. Frankly, I still fail to see the appeal. But I will admit there are people who do. Maybe it's a simple case of the grass always being greener on the other side of the fence."

"You mean if they have crummy lives, they think it might actually be better if they were a vampire?"

"People are funny that way, aren't they? I'll tell you what: I'll throw this one out to the listeners. Give me a call. Tell me why you want to be a vampire or a werewolf. Educate me."

I went straight down the line, taking one call after another. Men, women, young, old, vampires, werewolves, and everything in between. Some of them hated life, some of them loved it.

"It's the power. I want to have that kind of power." I heard that over and over again.

"I just don't feel like I fit in my skin. I—I don't think I was meant to be human. But I see wolves... and it feels like coming home. Does that sound strange? It sounds strange to me. I've never talked about it with anyone before."

"I want to live forever."

"I want to be immortal."

"I'm afraid of dying."

"It hurts. If I was something else, maybe it wouldn't hurt. At least not as much."

"I want to live."

"I want to kill."

And finally, from a man who said he was a werewolf, "Here's the thing, Kitty. I didn't *like* being human. What is there to being human? You wake up every day, work your ass off just so you can barely put a roof over your head and food in your stomach. If you're lucky you get a minivan and a trip to Disneyland for the kids. This life, our life—all that becomes secondary." He gave a laugh. "It doesn't matter anymore. It's a simpler life. There's a whole other set of priorities guiding you."

"Blood," I said. "Control."

"Magic," he said.

"The ultimate in escapism."

"That's right," he said, like it was a good thing.

"Okay, thanks for sharing."

On the other side of the booth window, Matt pointed to his wrist and mouthed the word "thirty." Thirty seconds to wrap up the show. I rubbed my face; I was ready for the escape. "I don't know if any of this answers Stan's question. My feeling is there is no one right answer. The people who choose this life, and the people who would like to, all have their own reasons. I'll insert my standard disclaimer here: forget any romantic notions you have about vampires and werewolves. They're diseases. They're not easy to live with. They change your life. And you can't go back afterward if you change your mind. This is Kitty Norville, voice of the night."

Run credits.

"You okay in there?" Matt asked.

"Do I look that bad?"

"You've looked better."

"I've been better," I said, and managed a smile. This was one of those times, one of those moments where everything seemed to pile up, and I didn't have a choice but to keep clawing my way up and over the obstacles. Just get through it. I *liked* being human. I was willing to put up with those particular struggles in exchange for the benefits of being human. Like chocolate and cable TV. Like having my own radio show.

We wrapped up. More than ready to get home, I grabbed my things and headed for the station lobby, then outside. Since the other night when I met Charlie and Violet, I always paused in the doorway to take in the scent of the parking lot and street. If something was waiting to pounce on me, I'd spot it. Then I could go back inside and call for help. Rick had done what he'd intended—scared me. Put me on my guard. But I wondered how long I'd have to go tiptoeing around my own life.

The thing was, tonight, I hesitated in the doorway, and knew something waited out there. I caught a scent of lycanthrope, a musky smell where there should have only been people, cars, and concrete.

I should have panicked, but I didn't. While I might have expected the scent to belong to Carl or Meg, it didn't. I sensed a hint of Carl—someone from his pack, then, but someone I didn't know. So maybe Carl sent one of his thugs after me. But I didn't smell aggression. I didn't feel like I was being hunted. Stepping softly, I moved along the wall to the edge of the building, following my nose. Someone was definitely here, watching me. Spying, maybe.

I had almost reached the corner when I said, "Who's there?"

I heard rustling, like someone scooted away from the corner. I slipped around and discovered a young woman pressed against the wall. She was thin, very young, with short blond hair. She wore a black baby doll T-shirt and faded jeans. She couldn't have been more than about nineteen or twenty and looked especially pale in the shadowed, nighttime lighting outside the building.

"Hi," she said and ducked her gaze away from me, a sign that she didn't want trouble. Her shoulders slumped, and I could imagine a tail between her legs.

I stood quietly and smelled her: sweating, frightened, and wolfish. And one of Carl's. If he knew she was here...I couldn't imagine that he knew she was here. If he'd wanted to pass along a message, he wouldn't have sent her—small and cowering.

I avoided staring at her, but it was hard not to. I wasn't sure I knew what to do with this.

"What are you doing here?" I said.

"Becky said I should come talk to you."

"Becky." I drew a blank for a moment, then remembered a Becky among Carl's wolves. Standoffish, another one that I'd avoided because she'd been tougher than me.

Then I remembered another Becky, the werewolf who'd called into the show a couple of weeks ago about a submissive in her pack who needed help. It hadn't occurred to me she'd been talking about Carl's pack.

I gave her half a smile. "You couldn't just call in like everyone else?" I thought I was being funny, but she looked down, frowning. She inched away; any minute, she'd bolt.

We were in the open here, which made me uncomfortable. Just because she hadn't been Carl didn't mean Carl couldn't sneak up on us. He might even be looking for her. Made me nervous.

Backing off, I said, "You want to come inside and talk? We'll stay in the lobby. I'll leave the door unlocked."

After a moment, she nodded. She still wouldn't look at me. I turned and walked away, made sure not to look back, but I could hear her following.

The security guy at the front desk waved at me as I returned to the lobby, and paid attention when the woman followed me in. She glanced around and wouldn't leave the vicinity of the front door.

"Everything's okay. I'm just going to borrow a couple of chairs," I told him, grabbing a couple of the plastic chairs from the wall. If she needed help, I didn't want to scare her off, and that meant leaving her an escape route. I didn't want to corner an already frightened wolf.

She was trying not to look scared. She kept pushing her shoulders back, trying to straighten up, and her frown had almost become a snarl.

I put the chairs by the door. We could talk out of anyone's earshot. "Sit."

And she did, just like that. Completely obedient. I bet Carl loved it.

I sat more slowly. "What's your name?"

"Jenny."

"And what's Becky want you to talk to me about?"

"I shouldn't be here," she said. "I shouldn't have come." She glanced at the door, as if expecting monsters.

"Can you try for a minute to forget about the whole werewolf thing? We're just a couple of people having a chat. I can't talk to you if you're scared of me."

She closed her eyes, took a breath, and that seemed to steady her. Her wolf lingered, though. It probably never really went away for her, and always guided her responses.

"Becky wants me to get away from Carl. She wants me to leave town. You did it, and if I talk to you, I might be able to, too."

"It's really not as hard as it seems."

"But I don't want to." She started crying, quiet tears slipping down her face. I found a clean tissue in my bag and handed it to her. "He takes care of me, I owe everything to him, he's a part of me, I can't leave that."

Then why are you crying? I wanted to ask. I let her talk.

"He's not an angel," she went on. "I know that. But he

can't help it, he—" She stumbled to a stop. Her rhetoric amazed me. Did she even realize what she was saying?

She was young and pretty. Carl treated the women in his pack like they were part of his own personal harem. I knew firsthand what he did to the young and pretty ones. He wasn't above smacking them around.

"The thing about being a werewolf," I said. "The bruises heal quickly. No one ever sees them. Makes it easier to just roll over and take it, doesn't it?"

Finally, she looked at me, really looked at me, with astonished human eyes. I understood, and that surprised her.

"This is why Becky said I should talk to you," she said. I nodded.

"Jenny, do you mind if I ask how you were infected? How you became a werewolf? You haven't been one long, have you?"

Slouching miserably in the chair, she looked away. Didn't say no outright, so I gave her time to collect herself.

Finally she said, "I met him at a club a few months ago. Carl, I mean. He was nice. I liked him, you know? He paid a lot of attention to me. I took him home and all."

I listened, my brow furrowed in thought. This didn't sound like Carl. Carl, picking up girls in clubs? And what did Meg have to say about this? I could guess that Meg had lost a lot of points with him during that last fight, the one that drove me out of Denver. She'd made a bid for his position as pack alpha, lost, and then groveled at his feet to beg his forgiveness. He'd given it, but he'd probably lord it over her to the end of time. He could step out on her and she wouldn't be able to say anything. That was all I could figure.

"We went out a couple more times. And then he told me. He told me what he was. I—I didn't believe him at first. I know werewolves are real, I saw you on TV that time, read the news stories. But I didn't think I'd ever actually meet one. I thought it was some crazy new come-on, that he was trying to impress me. I thought maybe he was crazy. But I played along, to see what would happen. I told him if he was really a werewolf he should show me. He wouldn't, not at first. He just talked about it, a little more each time. He made it sound really cool, really great. Like it made you powerful, and the sex was amazing, that you could smell and see and feel things a human never could. He made it sound like a good thing. And I finally said yeah, okay, I'll do it. He was so happy when I said yes, I really thought he was in love with me, I really thought he wanted us to be together. I didn't know about Meg or the pack or anything. After, when he brought me to them, Meg said he'd just wanted a new pup."

My heart jumped to my throat. I sat back and stared at the ceiling, taking a moment to catch my breath. Jenny was young, blond, waiflike—like I had been when I joined the pack, a naive girl caught by a monster on a mountain trailhead, turned by accident. Carl hadn't been the one to turn me into this thing, but he'd taken an interest in me after. Kept me under his paw, so to speak. Everyone knew I was his. Apparently, after I left the pack, Carl found a replacement.

I'd kill him. I'd fucking kill him myself the next time I saw him.

Right now, I had to pretend like I was doing the show, on the phone with some poor distraught girl. I wasn't used to seeing the face in front of me, seeing the tears. I wanted to keep staring at the ceiling. But I didn't.

"You know what I'm going to say, don't you? There's absolutely no reason to stay with him. Abuse is still abuse, and just because you're both werewolves doesn't justify a damned thing. You don't have to stand up to him—just get in a car and *leave*."

"But I'd just run into the same problem somewhere else. That's what Carl says, no matter where I go there'll be other…other people like us, and that they'll kill me. He'll protect me, he says he will—"

"Carl doesn't know everything. There are places you can go," I said. "Places where the other wolves won't hurt you, where there aren't wolves at all. I'll make some calls, I'll set something up."

"Kitty, I can't. I don't have a car, I don't have a job, I don't have any money—"

"Carl supports you, doesn't he? He said, don't work. Don't do anything. I'll take care of you, I'll protect you, just do what I say and you'll have it all."

Again, she nodded. He'd made that same offer to me. I'd clung to my humanity instead. I'd had the radio station and my show to pull me through, to give me something else to live for. Jenny didn't have that, obviously.

She almost seemed angry now. "It's easy for you to tell me to get out. You stood up to him. You and T. J."

"You never even knew T. J."

"No. But the others still talk about him, when Carl and Meg aren't around. They say he's the only one who ever stood up to him."

Like he was some kind of fucking folk hero. I wanted

to scream at her. We'd failed. T.J. had died, and I'd run like a coward. We were nothing to base a revolution on.

If I'd stayed with Carl, I'd be dead. It was that simple. Carl would have killed me months ago, because I couldn't have kept rolling over on my back for him. How long before that happened to Jenny?

I made a decision.

"Jenny, if you want to get out, I'll help you. I'll find a place for you to go and make sure you get there in one piece. But you have to want it, and you have to figure out what to do next. Before you met Carl, what did you want? Were you going to school, was there a job you liked, anything? If you want to get away from Carl, you need to learn to take care of yourself. You have to get a job, support yourself, learn to control the lycanthropy without him looking out for you. Do you understand?"

She thought for a long moment, staring out the window, letting tears fall, wiping them away with the tissue. Then she shook her head. "But I love him. And I know he loves me, I just know it. He's so good to me the rest of the time, when he isn't—" She choked on the rest of the sentence. As well she should.

I couldn't blame her, no matter how much I wanted to, because I'd been in the same place, once upon a time. What was it about guys like Carl that made girls like us throw ourselves at their feet?

Digging in my things, I found a business card. "Here's my phone number. Call me, okay? When you decide you're ready, call me."

She took the card, clutching it in both hands. She seemed a little dazed, staring at it like she didn't quite know what it was. When I stood, so did she. I held the door open for her.

"When Carl smells me on you, you're going to have to come up with a good explanation. And he'd better not find that card."

She paled a little, and we went out to the parking lot.

"Do you need a ride somewhere?" I asked.

"No. I think I'll be okay. I just need to think."

"Yeah, you do. Be careful, okay?"

She looked at me. It wasn't a wolf's challenging stare. Rather, it was intense and studious. Like she was trying to guess what I'd do next—a subordinate watching her leader for a sign. She was making me nervous.

"You're not at all like Carl and Meg," she said.

I had to smile. "I think that's the nicest thing anyone's ever said to me."

She walked away, ducking to the back of the building and leaving by the alley.

I started for home, but I only drove a couple of miles before my cell phone rang. It was Jenny saying, "Can you come get me?"

Ben was waiting in the living room of the condo, sitting on the sofa, reading a magazine. When I opened the door, he set the magazine aside and crossed his arms. He was wearing sweats and a T-shirt, looking ready for bed. Only the living-room lamp was on, and the place seemed dark.

I pulled Jenny in with me and shut the door quickly. Glancing sidelong at Ben, she huddled near the wall, arms crossed, slouching.

Ben said, "This is keeping your head low? Avoiding confrontation?"

"What was I supposed to do?" I touched her shoulder, trying to peel her off the wall. "Jenny, this is Ben. He's one of the good guys."

"Gee, thanks," Ben muttered wryly.

"Ben, this is Jenny."

"Hi," he said. She managed a brief smile.

"Jenny, you need anything? Will you be okay while I make some calls?"

She shook her head. "It smells wrong, it's not like pack in here."

"Different pack. Different territory." I hadn't thought of Ben's condo as territory before—this tiny little pocket of Denver that didn't belong to Carl. I liked the image.

"It's weird."

"You don't have to stay." And when she went back to Carl, she'd smell like me. She'd smell like a different pack, and Carl would know. God knew what he'd do about it.

"No, no—I'll stay. I need to figure things out."

"That's the spirit. Do you want to see if maybe you can get some sleep? Things might look better in the morning."

"You can have the sofa," Ben said, patting the leather cushion next to him. "It's a great napping sofa. I'll get some blankets."

"That okay?" I asked her.

"It's up to you," she said.

"No, see, that's exactly the kind of thing you have to get over. If you're going to do this, you have to make some decisions. Otherwise, you'll let anyone who happens to come along walk all over you."

She looked away. "Yeah. Okay."

Ben gave her blankets and a pillow, and Jenny curled

up on the sofa, hugging a blanket around her, and fell asleep in seconds, like this was the first real, relaxed sleep she'd had in weeks. Months, maybe.

We retreated to the bedroom.

Ben sat on the bed and watched me pace back and forth while I talked.

"I shouldn't be doing this. This is ridiculous. I can't protect her. I should never have brought her here."

"You realize you look like an animal in a cage?"

That always happened when I was nervous. I sat down with a huff.

"The pack's not any of my business. Not anymore. Why am I even getting involved?"

His lips curled in a half grin, like he wasn't convinced by my arguments. Like he was about to say something snarky. "You've just given a dozen reasons why you shouldn't have brought her here. So why did you?"

I shrugged. "It felt like the right thing to do? The wolf side wants to keep her safe." I whined and squeezed my hands over my head, like I could push some sense into my brain. "You'd think after this long the wolf side would stop surprising me."

"She's like you were, isn't she?"

I wanted to argue. I couldn't possibly have been that bad, that helpless. Honestly, though, I remembered. Those early weeks, my first time meeting the pack, surrounded by wolves, I'd only wanted to know what I had to do to keep from getting hurt, from making them angry. I'd been the most submissive one in the room, to keep Carl happy, to make sure he protected me.

"Yeah. And if it weren't for the show and T. J. and leaving,

I'd still be like that. She said that's why Carl turned her. He wanted someone like that again."

"Jesus." For a long moment we sat quietly, letting the doom settle over us. Then he said, "I want you to take the gun. Keep it with you. We'll worry about the permit later."

"Ben—"

"He'll come after you, sooner or later. You have to be able to stop him. And don't just keep it in the glove box in the car. Get a purse, carry it with you."

I drew a deep, frustrated breath. "Guns aren't always the answer."

"Not always. Sometimes, they are." He offered a galling smile.

"Who's the alpha wolf here?"

"Don't packs usually have two alphas?"

He was getting cheeky. I kind of liked it. I squeezed his hand and kissed him. "Thanks. I have to go make some calls."

Jenny slept for ten hours. The next day, she had the look of a fugitive—sunken eyes, permanent frown. But she held herself a little straighter, and she wasn't crying.

I knew of a couple of places where lycanthropes lived and didn't have packs. There were werewolves there who'd look after her. They could help her find a job, get her on her feet. I'd waited until morning to call them, but I made one call before dawn. I knew at least one vampire who could find a place in her household for a wayward cub.

I'd developed this network of friends without even realizing it. Ahmed, an amiable old werewolf, and Alette, a surprisingly humane vampire, in Washington, D.C., both offered to take her in, if I could get her out there. Ahmed gave me a couple of more names, lycanthropes in Los Angeles and Seattle who would help her, if she wanted to go there instead. He said that problems like this came up fairly often, but a few people had found a way to deal with it. Battered lycanthrope shelters. Who'd have guessed?

At last, here was a problem I could fix. Here was someone I could well and truly help. When Jenny woke up around lunchtime, I presented her with a page full of names and phone numbers.

"Do you want to go to Seattle, L.A., or Washington, D.C.?"

She looked at the page wearily. "What?"

I tried to sound kind. "If you don't want Carl to be able to get to you, you have to leave town. I have contacts. The ones in D.C., I know them and trust them. They gave me these other contacts, so they're good. You can go, and you won't be alone. The people there are friends, they'll help you."

She stared at the table, and at the glass of orange juice that was all she'd wanted for her late breakfast. The finality of it must have sounded startling. I couldn't imagine what was going on in her head, with so much to think about.

"It's what I did," I said. "I left. Things'll be easier— they'll seem clearer when Carl isn't around."

She swallowed, and still her voice cracked. "This woman in Washington, the vampire—you said she's nice?"

"Yeah, she is. Maybe a little snooty, but aren't they all? She likes taking care of people."

"I think I'd like to go there," Jenny said. "To stay with her."

Alette was female, and wasn't a werewolf. I wasn't surprised Jenny made that choice. "Then we'll get it all set up. See? It's easy."

She sniffed, and I was afraid she'd start crying again. I didn't want her to start crying again. She was going to get me started. But she smiled, for the first time she smiled, a thin and shy expression.

"Thanks," she said. "Everything people say about you—Becky said you'd help."

"I'm happy to," I said, and I was. It felt like winning, and I didn't have to fight anyone, and no one had to die.

Over the next few days, we set everything up. In that time, I wouldn't let her leave the condo, and I wouldn't leave her alone. Ben or I stayed with her the whole time. Usually me. Ben made her nervous, and I couldn't blame her. I was constantly looking out the window, checking the streets, jumping whenever the phone rang. I expected Carl to show up any minute. He didn't.

Ben cleaned a couple of handguns and wore gloves while he loaded them with silver bullets.

I bought Jenny's plane ticket, gave her some extra clothes, and put her on the phone with Alette so the two could get acquainted. Jenny's expression was constantly numb, almost shocky, like she'd survived a disaster. She'd given herself over to strangers and had succumbed to fatalism. For my part, I wouldn't be happy until she was on the plane and away.

The best I could do was walk her to security. We lingered at the end of the line snaking its way to the metal detectors and X-ray machines.

"You have my phone number. Call me if you need anything, anything at all. If it doesn't work with Alette, we'll find something else. You have a lot of choices, okay? Everything'll look better when you get to a new place."

I wanted her to be happy and excited, but she still looked terrified. "I've never been this scared. Not even the first time I shifted."

"It's going to be okay."

"But I think I miss Carl. Is that weird?"

How I could I convince her that she was doing the right thing? "Part of you always will. I still do sometimes." Though the Carl I missed—the strong, protective Carl, the sex, the feeling of being adored—had faded to a very faint shadow. I mostly remembered Carl the domineering, Carl the angry. "But you have a right to your own life. You don't belong to him."

She nodded, her expression was still uncertain.

"Call me when you get there, okay?" I said. "Make sure you meet Ahmed. He runs this bar, it's amazing—"

"I know. You've told me about it ten times now." She flashed a smile. It made her face light up. I could see why Carl had zeroed in on her. It just added fuel to the fire, though, seeing how completely he'd managed to bury her personality.

"Yeah. I have to admit, I think I'm kind of jealous. You get to start out on this great adventure."

"It feels like stepping off a cliff."

"Kind of does, doesn't it? You just have to remember your parachute."

We hugged. It was a human gesture, not a wolf one. She had to be able to draw on the human side—the side that knew she could live without Carl—if she was going to get through this.

I watched her disappear down the escalator leading to the trains that ran to the concourse. You needed a ticket to go any farther. I took that as a consolation. No one who could hurt her knew she was here. No one could get to her. She was safe now.

"Mission accomplished?" Ben said when I got home.

"Yeah." He met me at the door, and I folded myself in his arms. "I need a hug." He obliged.

"What's Carl going to do when he finds out?"

I mumbled into Ben's shoulder. "Nothing he can do. Not if he doesn't know she got help. As far as he's concerned, she just left. And there's nothing he can do about it."

I almost wanted to call him myself and shout the words at him.

There's nothing you can do about it, you bastard.

chapter 8

Mom had a surgery date: Friday, barring unexpected test results or complications in the meantime. The doctors were calling it a "reexcision" and kept saying it was routine, but that was just to make us feel better. They were still cutting chunks out of my mom. I wanted to stop it if I could. But there were no good solutions, any way you looked at it.

After sending Jenny off, I had a free evening and spent it with Mom, working up the courage to mention lycanthropy. It was a crazy, stupid idea—I couldn't suggest that my own mother take up this life. I'd have to take care of her the way I'd taken care of Ben when he'd been infected last winter. That had been hard enough, watching him struggle with the changes to his body, what the pain did to him, knowing what he was going through and being unable to make it any easier. I couldn't imagine Mom in that situation.

But if it was a choice between going through that and losing her entirely, it wasn't a choice at all. I had to talk to her about it before the surgery.

We sat at the kitchen table and ate ice cream out of the carton. She'd handed me the spoon as soon as I walked in the door. "Life is short," she said. "I'm going to be completely decadent this week. To think, all those years I was worried about my weight. If I'd known I might lose it all in a heartbeat, I'd have eaten more ice cream."

"Mom, don't talk like that," I said halfheartedly.

She gestured for me to dig into the bucket. Rocky Road. The whole kitchen smelled like rich chocolate. "I'm entitled to a little grim humor."

"It sounds like you're giving up."

"Oh, no," she said around a mouthful of ice cream. She shook her head. "Not at all. Trust me, I won't give up. I've got too many reasons to stick around." She sounded tough, like an Amazon or a Valkyrie, with a tone of fight in her voice that she usually only revealed when she talked about her tennis matches. I was proud of her. She'd survive this. She'd survive anything. She took another bite and continued. "Nicky and Jeffy—those are two big reasons right there. I can't wait to see what they're going to turn into. Can you? And you—don't think that just because Cheryl has kids you're off the hook. I'm going to stick around and see what your kids are going to turn into."

I started crying. Couldn't help it. I didn't want to cry; I wanted to be strong. But I did, my face turned away.

Mom set down her spoon and stared at me, looking shocked. "Kitty? Oh, don't do that. It's too soon for that." She went and retrieved a box of tissues from the kitchen counter.

I should have told her straight off when it happened. Too late now. I tried to speak, but my throat had closed up. The words wouldn't come. I grabbed a whole handful of tissues and tried to pull myself together. Patiently, she waited, sitting across from me on the edge of her seat, like she was restraining herself from coming over and gathering me in her arms. But I wasn't four and this wasn't a skinned knee, so she waited. Finally, I got it out.

"It's not that." Not yet, anyway. "I had a miscarriage." Had to get it out all at once, somehow, around the blubbering. I wished I could say it without crying. "A couple of weeks ago. I didn't even know I was pregnant."

"Oh, honey, I'm sorry."

"I didn't want to say anything, because we were all worried about you. You were more important."

"You should have said something."

"I know. But—there's more. It's the lycanthropy, the shape-shifting—it'll cause a miscarriage every time. I can't have kids at all. And I didn't think I'd care, I didn't think it would matter, but I do, it does—"

Then, she came over and put her arms around me. We stayed like that a long time, hugging. She kept saying, "It's okay, it'll be okay." And I marveled that she could even say that, with everything that had happened to us.

As much as I might want to turn four years old again and have my mother take care of me, I couldn't. And I couldn't keep this up all night. My eyes hurt. My whole face hurt. I pulled away to grab a new handful of tissues.

"I just wanted a normal life," I said, my voice thick. "I always thought I was going to have a normal life."

Smiling a wise, knowing smile, Mom brushed a wet strand of hair out of my face. "Nobody gets a normal life. You think it's normal, then something like this happens. You find a lump. You get bitten by something out in the woods. And you think, 'Why me?' But the universe says, 'Why not you?' And I think about how very lucky we've all been. I've been married to my best friend for thirty-five years. My beautiful girls are making their way in the world. Most people don't have it this good."

"So something was bound to come along and wreck it, is that what you're saying?"

She shook her head. "It's not wrecked. I'm very lucky to have this life. I think that luck'll hold for a little while longer. I can handle a lump or two. And you—you've held on this long, Kitty. You've been through so much. I can't imagine anything keeping you down for long. We'll be fine, we're all going to be fine."

It was a mantra of pure faith.

She kept on with the ice cream, and I switched to hot cocoa. My insides needed warming, and my throat needed melting.

I couldn't not say it any longer. If I was going to make one revelation tonight, I might as well make them all. I'd stopped crying and felt a little less wrung-out. I gripped my mug and made a start of it.

"Mom, I have to ask you something. You may not like it, but I have to say it and I want you to think about it, seriously, before you blow me off. Lycanthropy—it does something. Like what I told you—I'll never get cancer, I'll never get sick. If you were infected, if you were bitten right now—it would cure you. It's a trade-off, I know. The lycanthropy, it's hard to deal with. But... it would cure you. You wouldn't have to go through this surgery." She could keep her body intact.

She let her gaze fall to the table, to where her hands lay folded over one another. "What exactly are you saying?"

As if I hadn't already spelled it out. "I can cure you. I think I can cure you." It was insane, but it was also a shred of hope. That hope burned in me.

"By turning me into a werewolf," she said, her voice gone flat.

"Yes. I haven't really thought out the mechanics of it, but I'm sure—"

She held her hand in a calming gesture, and I stopped. "Do you know that this is a cure? Have you tried it? Do you know anyone who's tried it?"

No, but I didn't want to say that. "I'll have Dr. Shumacher talk to you. The data's still a little fuzzy because it was secret for so long, but she has the case files—"

Again, Mom stopped me.

"The surgery's scheduled for Friday. It's all settled."

"You can change your mind. You have a few days to think about it."

For a moment, she looked like she was going to argue. She wore a familiar, pensive expression. Like I was about to do something stupid and she was going to let me, so I'd learn a lesson. I was trying to save her, and I was the one who felt like an idiot.

"I'll think about it," she said finally.

I wanted Mom intact, healthy, strong. I knew this would work. I *knew* it.

"I'll come see you Friday. Okay? Call me if you need anything." *If you want me to do it. If you change your mind.*

"I'd like that."

"I love you." It came out desperate, like I wasn't going to have another chance to tell her.

"I love you too."

We hugged. She felt small in my embrace. For the first time in my life, she felt frail.

Dad walked me to my car. We went slowly, enjoying the warm evening.

"How do you think she's holding up?" he said.

I shrugged. "I was about to ask you. I have no idea if she's really being that positive or just putting on a brave face."

He chuckled. "You'd think I'd be able to tell the difference, wouldn't you?"

"Dad, I may have said something that upset her. I think that lycanthropy might cure it. The cancer, I mean."

He leaned against my car and gazed up the street, not really looking at anything. "I can't claim to know too much about it, but that sounds like a cure that's not a whole lot better than the disease."

I gazed heavenward. I was only trying to help. "I know, I know. But—if things get bad, if the doctors can't do anything..."

He shook his head. "We haven't gotten there yet. It's going to be fine. Everything's going to be fine."

My eyes were stinging then. "Okay. I'll see you later, 'kay?"

We hugged, and he watched me drive away.

On the way home, my cell phone rang.

"Kitty, it's Tom." Tom was one of vampire Mistress Alette's people. Chauffeur, valet, human servant—and a grandson many generations down the line. Part of her family in every sense of the word.

"Hey, what's up? Did Jenny get in okay?"

"That's why I'm calling. Her flight came in, but she wasn't on it."

The question had been rote; I'd asked it fully expecting a

positive response. No alternative was possible. My stomach froze.

"What do you mean she wasn't on it?"

"The airline says she didn't check in at the gate. She never got onto the plane. We can't find her."

"I walked her to security myself. She couldn't have not gotten on that plane. Maybe the airline made a mistake."

"I suppose it's possible. Does she have a phone?"

"No, she doesn't. There has to be an explanation. Maybe I gave you the wrong flight number."

"I'll make another pass through the airport. Maybe give Ahmed a call." Ahmed was the closest thing the D.C. lycanthropes had to a leader. She might have found her way to him. I had to hope something like that had happened, that she'd made it to D.C. and just missed Tom somehow.

"I'll try to find something out on this end." And what happened if she hadn't gotten on the plane? Why wouldn't she have gotten on the plane? "Let me know as soon as you find out anything."

"Will do." He clicked off.

There had to be a good explanation. I went home and made some phone calls.

The airline showed that Jenny had been issued a boarding pass, but she hadn't checked in at boarding. Her seat was empty when the plane took off. Had she maybe changed flights? Changed time or destination? The reservation person said there'd been no change to her ticket after the boarding pass had been issued. It was like she'd disappeared. I talked to airport security. They said they'd check surveillance camera footage, to find out what had happened. If someone had come after her. That was my biggest fear. Somehow, some way, Carl had found out and gotten to her. It wasn't just possible, it would be easy. But I'd have hoped that Jenny would have enough confidence, enough strength, to scream if he tried to take her.

I called Hardin and tried to report Jenny as missing. But she hadn't been gone long enough. Unless I had any ideas about where to look for her, or who might have information, the police couldn't help. "Carl," I said. "He'll know something." I told her how to find him.

"I'll see what I can do," she said, but her tone wasn't encouraging.

I'd been at it for hours, sitting at the kitchen table with a phone book, trying to think of more people to call. Ben came in, dressed for bed.

"Kitty. Stop. There's nothing else you can do."

"There has to be."

"You can get some sleep."

"No, she's out there, she's in trouble."

"Maybe—maybe she changed her mind." I stared at him, bleary-eyed. He sighed. "Maybe she decided not to go to D.C. Maybe she found another way out and thought it was better if no one knew where she was going."

Maybe. It was possible. "Do you really believe that?"

He gave a fatalistic shrug. "I don't know. But there's nothing I can do about it."

"You're not even trying." I rubbed my forehead. He was right, I should get some sleep. Go to bed at least. Didn't think I'd be able to sleep.

He touched my shoulder. It was meant to be a comforting

gesture, but I was so tense, I flinched. He took a step back, hand raised defensively.

"You okay?" he said.

"I just want to keep trying. There has to be something else I can do."

Ben started to say something, but turned and went back to the room instead.

I joined him an hour or so later, finally putting the phone away, shutting out the lights. Giving up. "Ben?"

He didn't react. Already asleep, his breathing was deep and steady. I climbed into bed next to him, secretly hoping he would wake up and hold me. But he didn't.

When I arrived at KNOB the next day, I had a visitor waiting in the lobby for me.

I walked through the door, and she stood from a lobby chair, crossed her arms, and regarded me with an irritated frown. She wore rumpled slacks and a jacket, with a blouse open at the collar. Well-worn business wear. A real working woman. Her dark hair was pulled into a short ponytail.

"Detective Hardin," I said, unable to sound happy about seeing her. "Hi."

"Nice to see you, too," she said wryly. "Why didn't you tell me you were back in town?"

"I've been trying to keep my head down."

"Not doing a very good job."

"Tell me about it," I muttered under my breath. "Had any luck with your robbers?"

"Not yet. I've had to put that aside for now. Another

case has come up. I'd like you to look at something." She pulled an attaché case off the chair.

"It's not autopsy photos, is it? Because I'm not really in the mood for autopsy photos."

I'd meant it as a joke. In our last set of encounters, Hardin kept asking me to look at bodies and tell her if a werewolf had ripped open their torsos and torn them to pieces.

But her expression didn't change. She frowned, expectant and impatient. "Crime scene photos. Homicide."

Damn.

"Is there someplace we can talk in private?" she finished.

"Do I have to?" I almost whined.

At least her smile was sympathetic. "I'll owe you a favor. Never underestimate the power of a cop owing you favors."

Fine. Whatever. "Upstairs conference room."

I led the way, surreptitiously glancing over my shoulder at her. I could feel her studying me, as a prickling up and down my spine. I made the trip as short as I could, and she got right to work, pulling a handful of five-by-seven photos from her case and spreading them on the table. Ten of them lined up.

Each one showed a face, some of them merely spattered with blood, some of them drenched, so that their hair was red and plastered to their skin. Some of them showed slashes across cheeks and throats—claw marks. A couple had jagged wounds, pieces of flesh torn and hanging. Teeth marks. All of them had their eyes closed. My gut twisted.

"We got a 911 call at around 3:00 A.M. from a warehouse south of downtown," Detective Hardin explained. "This is what we found when we got there. We traced the 911 call to a mobile phone dropped just inside the building. It might have belonged to one of the victims. We couldn't get prints off it. All the victims were inside. All of them showed signs

of struggle, like there'd been a fight. A really nasty fight—
no weapons, all hand-to-hand. Or claw and fang to hand.
All ten victims tested positive for lycanthropy. Do you
know any of these people? Can you identify them?"

These were Rick's lycanthropes. Despite the blood, I
recognized them. No sign of the confident pack he'd gathered looked out at me now. I touched the pictures, lining
them up.

"We also found three sets of what might also be remains,
but there's not much there. Some ashes. I think they might
have been vampires. There's no way to ID them."

Only seven of these were Rick's. Two others were wolves
from Carl's pack. Tough guys who didn't mind fights. Both
had been wolves for over a decade. One of them worked as
a bouncer in Denver. Now they were dead.

The tenth photo was Jenny. Her throat had been torn
out. I couldn't see her neck, only a pulped mess. She was
wearing the shirt she'd had on yesterday. Blond hair made
a tangled, bloody frame around her. Her face was only
speckled with blood and seemed incongruously relaxed,
almost peaceful. She'd found another way to escape.

"You do know them," Hardin said.

I'd lifted Jenny's photo and couldn't turn away from it.
I couldn't feel what my face was doing, what expression
Hardin saw on me. I only knew that I couldn't talk. My
throat had shut tight, my voice had died.

"Kitty?" the detective prompted.

"She wasn't supposed to be here," I said, forcing it out.
The effort made my voice taut to the breaking point. "She
was supposed to be on an airplane. She's the one I told
you about last night." She was supposed to be free now.

Gently, Hardin drew the photo from my hand and put

it back with the others. "That one's odd. Her time of death came about seven hours earlier than the others. Her body was left there. She didn't die with them."

No, Carl had killed her before and then dumped her with the rest. I had to assume it was Carl. He might have had help with the rest, but he'd killed Jenny all by himself. But how had he found her? How had she let him find her? How had he stolen her past airport security?

The implication of the rest of the photos only settled on me slowly, the shock wave after the initial blast of seeing Jenny dead: Rick's coup had failed. One of those piles of ash might be him. I had no way of knowing if he'd died. I might never know. Seven lycanthropes, three vampires—that was almost everyone.

"Are they all wolves?" I'd never seen Rick's henchman Dack as a human. I couldn't know if one of these was him. "Was there any other kind of lycanthrope?"

"The tests aren't that good. I can tell you lycanthrope or not. Not which flavor. Yet."

"What happened?" I said softly, though I could already guess. I already knew.

"These seven died from wounds inflicted by other lycanthropes They practically had their hearts ripped out." She grouped five of the photos together, the ones with the worst of the blood and mess. A lycanthrope could survive a lot of damage, but not that. "These three, the bites are smaller, human-sized, and the victims died of blood loss. Vampire, I assume. I have to make some calls to verify that. What I don't know: Were they part of the same pack, or were they from two different packs having a conflict? Do vampires ever get involved in this sort of thing? What can you tell me about this?"

This wasn't just about the vampire and werewolf territories anymore; a third one had gotten involved: the law enforcement jurisdiction. How would she treat this sort of thing going on in her territory? I didn't want her involved. She and her people couldn't handle it. Unless she could, of course. She was open-minded about this. She had educated herself. She had silver bullets.

Maybe I didn't want to see what would happen if she took on this mess and *was* able to handle it.

"Detective, if I tell you, you have to promise to stay out of it. To keep your people out of it."

"I can't promise that," she said, shaking her head, clearly offended. "I've got murder victims, I've got higher-ups breathing down my neck. What am I supposed to tell them? The werewolves are just getting a little feisty?"

"This isn't like anything you've ever dealt with before. You have to believe me." What could I tell her that would convince her to back off? Nothing. Absolutely nothing. That was what made her a good cop.

I didn't want the cops involved. This whole thing would turn into us against them against them. I didn't want another front to worry about. I didn't want Arturo to decide that Hardin was a rival as well. I didn't want him to put her in danger.

"Kitty, I want to understand this. I need your help if I'm going to understand it."

Then again, maybe she would be on my side. Maybe she could help me find out what had happened to Rick. Maybe she had the solution: throw them all in jail.

I wanted to run. I had this sudden, overriding instinct to *just run*.

"There's a war on," I said.

A beat. "You're kidding."

"No, I'm not. It's over territory, over who gets to call themselves the Master vampire of the city."

"Denver has a Master vampire," she said flatly, disbelieving. Why didn't anyone think Denver was important enough for a Master vampire? Inferiority complex?

"Yeah. But it could all be over now." They were all dead. We were all dead... I grouped the photos: Rick's seven, Carl's two, and Jenny, off by herself. "These... they were working for the challenger's faction. These two are local. Jenny shouldn't have been there at all. I can't explain it."

"The lycanthropes work for the vampires?"

"Sometimes, yeah."

"Which faction do you belong to?"

I shook my head in vehement denial. "I'm staying out of it. I tried to stay out of it." I'd only sided with Jenny.

"They were strangers in town," Hardin said. "So this challenger brought them in to confront the local Master and local wolves, who fought back."

"That's right." Hardin was sharp.

"Then all I have to do is go to this Master vampire and charge him with instigating a dozen murders."

I almost laughed, but my voice turned rough. "Do you really think it'd be that easy? Look what he did to them." What he'd do to me, if he found me... And Ben. Had they found Ben? I had to call Ben. We had to get out of here. "You don't know what they're like, what I've seen them do—"

"Kitty, let me ask you a couple of questions. Just yes or no. Don't try to explain it to me. Okay?"

"Uh... yes?"

"Master vampires—if I understand the concept correctly, they claim certain cities as their territories. They have or create flunkies, other vampires, sometimes human servants, to do their bidding. Is that right?"

"Yes."

"And if another vampire—with his own flunkies— moves into the city and wants to become Master of it, they fight. This war you're talking about."

I nodded.

"Right. You know what I'm going to do? I'm going to treat this like any other gang operating in my jurisdiction. This is gang-related violence. And if there's a gang war going on on my turf, I'm going to crack down. And you can pass that along to any vampires you happen to chat with, okay?"

I nodded. I loved Detective Hardin, really I did. She was an awesome, kick-ass woman cop. Didn't take any crap, didn't put up with any nonsense. I didn't want to end up on her bad side.

"Great. I'm glad we've had this little chat. You have my number in case you have any other bits of enlightenment for me?"

"Yes."

"Good. Because I don't care what they are, or who they think they're Master of, nobody gets away with this in my city."

She gathered her photos and left. I'd half expected to be arrested, to be questioned about how much I knew— to be forced to lead them to Arturo at gunpoint. I knew where he kept his lair.

But she let me go because she was going to tail me. She was going to have people watch to see who I talked to, who tried to contact me, and they'd follow those threads until they had someone they could charge.

I almost ran after her and begged to be taken into protective custody. Surely no one could get to me if I was locked in a jail cell. But then I'd have no place to run.

I called Ben on my way home. Every ring he didn't pick up terrified me. I was too late. They'd gotten him, Carl had tracked us and I was next—

"Yeah?" Ben finally answered.

I stumbled over the words in my hurry to speak. "Ben, we have to get out of town. We have to leave right now, we can't stay, we—"

"Kitty, whoa. Slow down. What happened?"

"She's dead. I don't know how Carl got to her but he did, and Hardin showed up at work with the photos and he'll know we helped her. He's probably looking for us right now."

He didn't have to ask who was dead. "But you took her to the airport. How did he get to her? How did he get her away from there to kill her?"

"I don't know! It doesn't matter now. It's all over."

"Where are you?"

"On my way home."

"We'll talk when you get here. Stay calm, okay? Keep it together."

He'd picked up my catch phrase, the thing I told myself when Wolf came too close to the surface, when her instincts started to override reason.

I nodded, which wouldn't reassure him on the other end of the phone. "Okay. I'll be okay." No, I wouldn't.

"I'll see you soon."

"Okay," I said, and we both hung up.

Nobody tried to kill me between the parking lot and the door of Ben's condo. It seemed like a miracle.

He was sitting on the sofa, waiting for me, looking far too calm. I wanted him to have guns on the coffee table. We had to circle the wagons, defend the Alamo.

We regarded each other in a moment that felt anticlimactic. Where was the panic? The hysteria?

He said, very calmly, "What happened?"

I heaved a frustrated sigh. "There's no time, I'll explain while we drive. We have to leave now."

I went to the bedroom, found a duffel bag, and started shoving clothes into it. I didn't care what clothes—a handful of underwear, some shirts, some jeans. Pack it up, jump in the car, and go.

"What are you doing?" Ben said softly, patiently, like a parent with a kid throwing a temper tantrum. Waiting me out.

"Leaving. Rick made his move and lost. He's probably dead. Jenny is dead, I couldn't save her, Carl got to her somehow. And he'll kill me, and you, and there's nothing we can do."

"Kitty—it's not your fault Carl got to her. You tried. You did what you could."

"I can't fight him. I can't even instigate a little civil disobedience."

Closet to bed, a few more clothes. Couldn't get the zipper closed, so I pulled something out and threw it aside. Had to get my toothbrush in there.

"You'd leave while your mom's sick? Abandon her too?"

She'd understand. If I explained that staying here was going to get me killed, she'd want me to leave. I didn't answer. I turned my back to him, moving to grab my bag.

He tried again. "What if there was a way to stand up to them without fighting. There's got to be a way to compromise—"

"That's the lawyer in you talking. These people don't understand law, or compromise, or talking. There's no plea bargains here. It's all violence and hate." My throat was tight, my voice thick. "You don't know what they're like, you don't know, you haven't seen the worst of it, I've tried to keep you safe from that and here I am dragging you into it—"

"Don't worry about me. I can look out for myself."

"No, Ben, you can't! You don't understand, you haven't seen what he's like, what he can do. You think all were-wolves are like me, but they're not, most of them are fucking *insane*—"

"Like you? Like me?"

He was being far too rational. "You know what I mean."

"All I know is you're starting to smell more like a wolf than a human and if you don't sit down and pull it together you're going to lose it."

Didn't have time for that. This was a time to let Wolf's instincts guide me. We were in an enemy's territory, we couldn't fight, so there was only one thing to do. I had to make him understand that. "Come with me, Ben. You have to."

He hesitated, and I could see the wheels working in his mind, as he edited his own speech. Thought of one thing to say, then rejected it.

"I'm staying," he said finally. "Do whatever the hell you want, but I'm not running." He walked out of the room.

Funny thing was, that pause gave me a chance to catch my breath, and to realize that he was right. That had been the Wolf freaking out, and she was right on the surface, blurring my vision. I wasn't thinking straight.

I sat on the bed and stuck my head between my knees, drawing in long breaths. Keeping it together.

I called after him, hating how plaintive my voice sounded. I didn't want to have to beg. "Ben, we can't stay here. They'll kill us."

He reappeared in the doorway, not looking any more amenable or sympathetic. We might manage our own little civil war right here.

"No, they won't," he said. "You say I haven't seen the worst of it, but you don't know anything about what I have or haven't seen. And I *can* take care of myself, no matter what your alpha attitude says about it. We've got weapons. If we make a stand, they'll leave us alone. I'm willing to make that stand even if you're not. This is where I live. I'm not going to go running away to Pueblo just because you're chicken and you've got your tail between your legs. And I *hate* that that isn't just a metaphor anymore." He ran his hands through his hair. He was breathing hard, and smelled a little more wolf than human.

I wasn't keeping it together. I wasn't listening to reason. The pack of two was breaking up. No, it wasn't, this was just a pause, a hiccup.

"Are we a pack or not?" I said.

Softly, he said, "I don't know."

It was something of an epiphany, that the instinct to run was stronger than the need to stay with him. To defend him. As he said, he could look out for himself. He had guns on his side.

Bag over my shoulder, I stalked out.

chapter 9

I drove south. I'd done this before. Run away, abandoning my family, KNOB, everything. I had to ask myself: What was so important, what was so traumatic, that it was worth giving up all that?

Nothing, came the obvious answer, clear as a bell. Nothing was worth giving up all that. In those terms, facing Carl was a small price to pay to keep my life. Either way, I risked losing everything.

Maybe that was why I found myself turning off the interstate at Highway 50, going west toward Cañon City. I went to the prison, went through their security routine, and waited in that stark, stinking room for Cormac to emerge. I didn't bother trying to be cheerful, not this time.

I didn't have anyone else to talk to.

Clad in his orange jumpsuit, his expression neutral, he sat and picked up the intercom phone. Belatedly, I did the same. Even then, we only stared at each other for a long moment. He was clean, healthy-looking, his hair and mustache freshly trimmed. He looked rested, even. This was what keeping out of trouble did for him.

"Hi," I said.

"I wasn't expecting you," he said. "What's wrong?"

I almost laughed. My first impulse was to deny that anything was wrong, but that would have been a raging lie. I glanced away, wondering how bad I really looked.

"Is it that obvious?"

"Yeah," he said.

"Every time we come to visit, Ben makes a big deal about being upbeat. We have to be cheerful, to help keep your spirits up. But I really need to talk."

"Don't worry about me. Talk, if you need to."

"I don't know where to start."

"Ben told me about the miscarriage. I'm sorry."

For a flash, I was angry at Ben for saying anything. But I guess he had to tell someone, and Cormac was his friend. Truth be told, Cormac's statement had startled me. That a remorseless killer like him was capable of that kind of sensitivity, to even register what something like that might do to me. I knew I'd done the right thing, coming here to talk to him. He was my friend, too, even considering the killer part.

"Thanks. But that isn't the worst of it," I said. "My mom is really sick. And the situation in Denver just exploded. I tried to stay out of it, honest I did—"

Cormac ducked his face to hide a grin.

"Hey, don't laugh."

"Kitty, when have you ever been able to stay out of anything?"

I glared. "You should have met me back when I was quiet and unassuming. I used to be a nice girl."

Cormac had the good grace not to respond to that. "Tell me the situation."

I did, my voice hushed, not sure who might be listening

in, not sure if what I was saying would even make sense to someone listening in. The description sounded like a war, a nasty guerrilla war where both sides occupied the same territory and no clear lines of engagement existed. Attacks came at any moment, treachery was the norm, and both sides fought with their own sense of righteousness.

"I wish you could come to the rescue this time," I said, smiling weakly. "I don't know what to do."

"You have two choices: You leave Denver. Or you fight to win."

"We can't win, they're too strong. I've already left—"

"And how long before you go back the next time? You won't stay away. That's why you need to win. So you don't have to keep running. And Ben won't leave, so you need to go back and cover his ass."

I leaned my head on my hand. He wasn't telling me anything I didn't already know. I just had to hear it. And it wasn't anything Ben hadn't already said. But I expected to hear it from Cormac. Cormac was the one who talked like that. I still had this attitude that I was supposed to be protecting Ben. Maybe I should have listened to him.

"Right, fine, okay. But I don't know how to fight a war."

"Then don't fight one. Not straight out, not like this Rick guy's been doing. You're going to have to do this down and dirty. Draw them out. Split them up. Get them looking over their shoulders at every little shadow, then move in to clean up. I could do the whole thing myself with enough planning."

"I don't think I have a lot of time for this."

"Then you'll have to move fast."

Carl was only as strong as the whole pack. And the pack was weak, at least according to Rick. I couldn't gauge Arturo's relationship with his followers as easily. Rick had tried to catch Arturo off guard. But he'd also wanted to go after them in a straight fight, army to army. We couldn't do that. We had to use our strengths as outsiders. Not dependent on the system. Not invested in the system. We couldn't go in and replace Carl and Arturo. We had to bust the whole deal up and start from scratch.

Assuming Rick was dead, I'd have to go after Arturo myself. Or convince him that Denver was better off with me in charge of the werewolves. Compromise with Arturo? Maybe I could do it.

Cormac continued. "Remember, you're hunting predators. With them, it's all about territory. You take their territory, you take their power. When you draw them out, you can't leave them standing. Are you ready to do that?"

I nodded quickly, not wanting to think about that part just yet. "Rick tried it and failed. They got him at his base. He didn't have a chance to bring the fight to them."

"Then he's got a leak," Cormac said. "Someone fed the bad guys his plans, and they knew exactly where and when to find him."

That was so simple I almost cried. But all Rick's people were handpicked, Rick wouldn't have brought them in if he couldn't trust them. Maybe there was a spy on the outside. Someone who could move freely, collect information without anyone realizing she was doing it. Mercedes Cook?

In spite of myself, I was starting to make a plan.

Cormac spoke softly, adding to the clandestine feel of the conversation. "You'll have to keep this quiet. Avoid the cops. They just mess everything up." Cormac would know all about that. He'd saved me and five others by shooting dead the creature that threatened us. But when it was all over, the police only saw a dead woman and Cormac standing over her with a smoking rifle.

I winced. "The cops are already involved. You remember Detective Hardin?"

"Shit." Make that a yes.

"But still..." The wheels were turning. I had to think about what advantages I had and how I could use them. "She wants to treat this as a gang war. She wants these guys as badly as I do. If I can use her to do some of the dirty work"—like, shooting people—"that'll leave me in the clear."

"That's a tricky gamble to make."

"Yeah." But I could make it work. I started to think I could make it work.

"Do you still have the Jeep?" Cormac said. "Does Ben have it?"

"Yeah, it's at his mom's place."

"Go get it. Pop the hood. On the inside edge, on the left, there's one of those magnetic boxes for spare keys. The key in it is for a storage unit at a place on 287, south of Longmont. Ben knows where."

"Storage unit—storing what?"

"Stuff you might be able to use."

"Cormac—"

"I'd go in and clean up the town myself if I could. But I can't, so I want to make sure you have the tools for it."

Cormac had his own personal armory in a rented storage locker. He never ceased to amaze me.

"Ben took me to a range. Taught me to shoot."

"Good," he said.

"I don't want to be a part of this kind of life," I said.

"Sometimes you don't have a choice," he said. "When you're the only one around who can make a stand, you don't have a choice. Not if you want to be able to sleep at night."

I wasn't thinking of doing this because I wanted to, or because I thought it'd be fun. I was doing this for Jenny, for Ben, for myself, to keep those of us left alive safe. I was doing this for T. J. It was what he'd have done.

Cormac was much better suited for a world where wars happened.

"Can you sleep at night, Cormac?"

"Most of the time. When I'm not thinking about you." He grimaced. "I shouldn't have said that. Sorry."

"No," I said softly. "I'm sorry."

His voice was low, drawn from a dark place. "Sometimes, I wonder what would have happened if I'd shot him. After he was bitten. If I'd killed him like he wanted me to. And then, what if I came to see you. To tell you what happened. You'd be all sympathetic. You'd tell me how sorry you were, you'd start crying, I'd hold you, and then—"

"Cormac, stop. Stop it. You don't actually wish…" I couldn't even say it. Cormac and Ben were like brothers, he couldn't wish Ben dead.

"No," he said. "Only sometimes."

"That's psychotic."

"'Sociopathic' is what the prison psychologist wrote down."

"Geez, Cormac—"

"No, never mind. It's all just thinking." He glanced away, hiding his expression. "I don't think it would have worked out. At the end of the day… it just wouldn't."

That little mischievous bit of my brain reared her catty head. I narrowed my gaze and said, "But it might have been fun finding out."

"Yeah," he said, smiling.

For this moment at least, and maybe for a few future ones, things were all right between us. I'd come to him for help, and he'd given it, and we'd made a few confessions and cracked a few jokes in the meantime. Just like friends are supposed to.

He said, "You look after yourself. Look after Ben. Remember, you're hunting predators. It's different than deer and rabbits. Predators get angry, not scared. You know that."

Then the visit was over. The guard led him away, and I fled the prison.

Back on the road, I hit the interstate and headed north, back to Denver.

As I drove, the first thing I did was call Detective Hardin. She owed me a favor, and if this worked right, she wouldn't even know she was paying me back.

"It's me," I said when she answered her phone.

"Please tell me you've got something for me."

"I do, but you're not going to like it." Or even believe it, for that matter. But Hardin had demonstrated a great capacity for believing the unbelievable.

"I rarely do," she said.

"Mercedes Cook. You heard about her, right?"

"The singer. You had her on your show a week or so ago, announced that she was a vampire."

"She's in the middle of it. She's not the Master or the challenger, but she's been egging them both on. You might not want to confront her directly. Vampires can be kind of manipulative."

"I'll keep that in mind. Is she still in town? Do you know where she's staying?"

"She was staying at the Brown Palace. I don't know if she's still there. She's in the middle of a concert tour, so she should be pretty easy to find wherever she is."

"Thanks. I knew if I gave you a day to think about it, you'd come around."

"Yeah," I said. "That's exactly what happened."

It was suppertime when I got back to Ben's place. I hadn't looked at my watch in hours. I'd spent the whole drive back thinking. Planning.

No police cars waited in the parking lot, no crime scene tape wrapped the building. If Carl and Arturo had moved against us—or rather moved against Ben since I'd abandoned him—it hadn't been here.

Maybe, I hoped, they hadn't known where to find Ben. And if I was really lucky, Ben hadn't gone looking for them. I went in, almost expecting the place to be trashed, with signs of a massive struggle, and Ben dead, torn to bits all over the living room. If I had found that, I would have taken the gun with its silver bullets and gone after Carl myself. It wouldn't have mattered if Meg and the rest of the pack slaughtered me after, as long as I was able to shoot him first. I braced myself for what I would have to do if I found Ben dead.

But the condo was fine. Ben was at the dining-room table, eating some sort of carryout food straight from the carton. He didn't seem particularly surprised to see me.

In fact, he glanced at his watch. Humorlessly, he said, "Back already? It hasn't even been twelve hours. I figured it'd take at least twenty-four to grow your spine back."

Ben was perfectly all right. Why had I even worried? But there was a semiautomatic pistol sitting on the table next to him.

I didn't look, didn't say a word. Didn't even stop. I did not need that kind of crap right now.

I went straight back to the bedroom and looked for the pair of jeans I'd been wearing the last time I saw Rick, when he gave me that phone number that I'd shoved in my pocket. If I was lucky, it hadn't gone through the wash yet.

As it happened, I'd put the jeans in the duffel bag I'd taken on my short-lived retreat. I should have done this first thing, right after Hardin's visit, before ever leaving town. Rick was probably dead, but I had to try. Maybe he'd escaped.

It was twilight; the sun had set. I dialed, and the phone rang, and rang. The certainty that Rick had been one of those piles of vampiric remains that Hardin had found settled on me, the weight of doom clenching in my gut. I wasn't surprised, but I was sad.

Then, the phone clicked on. "Yes?"

It was Rick.

"Oh my God, you're alive!"

"So to speak. Kitty—are you all right?"

I didn't know. I didn't want to talk about me. "Detective Hardin came to see me this morning. She had pictures from the warehouse. Arturo and Carl hit your place, didn't they? What happened?"

"They surprised us," he said simply. I could imagine him shrugging. "It was a slaughter. A few of us were able to escape—Dack dragged me out of there himself. Charlie and Violet made it out. Impeccable survival instincts in those two. But...that's all. All I've been able to contact."

"Hardin has ten dead lycanthropes and three dead vampires."

"Damn," he whispered. "That's everyone. And some of theirs."

"Rick, have you considered that someone gave Arturo your location and the timing of your attack?"

"Of course I have," he said. "Mercedes maybe. Or one of Arturo's people followed us. I wasn't careful enough. Obviously." He sounded anguished.

"We have to talk. Where can we meet?"

After a pause, he said, "It's too late for that, Kitty. It's over. I made my move and lost."

I wasn't going to let him get away with that. "And what now? You run away? Like I did? I thought you were doing this out of a sense of righteousness, not for power. You don't want Arturo running this town."

"The cost has already been too high."

"Rick. Please. Just talk to me, face-to-face."

"What made you change your mind?"

"Hardin has ten dead lycanthropes. Only seven of them were yours. Two were Carl's. The tenth was mine."

"Oh, no. Ben—"

"Ben's fine. This was someone else. I'll explain later. Tell me where and when."

He gave me the name of a bar on Colfax. The time: midnight.

As I ended the call, I looked up to find Ben standing in the doorway. "Do you want me to go with you?"

"Only if you want to," I said. I wouldn't look at him.

"I want to."

"Okay. I have another errand to run before then. I'll come back to pick you up." I was already headed for the door. I had to keep moving, letting the adrenaline push me forward. Otherwise, I'd melt.

But I managed to turn to him before I left and said, "Thanks."

Next, I wanted to find out what happened to Jenny. Why had she left the airport when she was just an hour away from being free forever? Then how had Carl found her, and why had he seen her as enough of an enemy to tear her throat out?

I used to be part of that pack. I expected that I still knew most of its members, and that I still knew how to find a few of them. But I couldn't be sure of trusting any of them. That approaching any of them wouldn't get Carl on my tail.

Before I left, I checked the glove box. Yes, Ben's gun with its silver bullets was still there. Ben was so utterly practical, and I was still mad at him. I slammed closed the glove box and hoped I wouldn't need the gun, thereby proving him right *again*.

I knew Shaun from my days in the pack. He kept to himself mostly, and that was why I looked for him first. Like most werewolves, he was part of a pack for safety, for the protection of numbers, the reassurance of a regular territory to run in on full moon nights. He didn't make trouble, he paid proper respect to the alphas, and thereby maintained an equilibrium. He wasn't one of the ones so blindingly loyal to Carl that he'd fight and die for him. I was counting on that—and counting that I could run fast enough if I'd judged wrong.

Conversely, I had to hope that even though he was a loner, he knew enough about the pack to tell me what had happened to Jenny.

Back in the old days—only a year ago, I had to remind myself that I'd left the pack less than a year ago—Shaun had worked at a trendy bar and café in Lodo, near the baseball stadium, as a cook, usually during the late shift. Funny, how many lycanthropes liked working late. First, I called to ask if he was still working there. He was, and in fact had been promoted to the head of his shift. The guy had some ambition, it seemed. I showed up at the place a little after the evening rush and made my way to the back entrance. An open doorway in the back alley led to a clean, white work area and kitchen. A busboy dropped a bag of trash in a nearby dumpster, and voices, rattling dishes, and the sound of spraying water drifted out, a counterpoint to the sounds of traffic nearby. The smell of rich food and wonderful spices overpowered the city smells entirely, wafting out on the hot air spilling from the kitchen. The comforting scent made me smile.

"Hey," I called to the kid as he turned to go back inside.

"Yeah?" He was surly, wary, bent on his task, and probably not used to seeing blond chicks wandering out back.

"Can you tell Shaun someone's out here to talk to him?"

"He know you?"

"Tell him it's Kitty." I decided to be honest. If Shaun didn't want to come talk to me, I'd march inside and talk to him instead.

The busboy nodded and went back in, leaving me to scuff my sneakers on the asphalt for several minutes. I didn't want to go in there. I'd prefer doing this outside, in the open. Neutral territory—plenty of escape routes.

I shouldn't be doing this. Leaving town was a perfectly viable option.

A young man of average height and solid build appeared in the doorway, leaning on the jamb, arms crossed, shoulders hunched. The watchful, defensive posture suggested he wasn't going to start a fight—but he wasn't going to give ground, either. He had short, dark hair, and coffee-and-cream skin, wore a chef's white smock over his shirt and jeans, and had the wild, fur-under-the-skin scent of a lycanthrope. Someone who didn't know what to look for would never see it in him.

"Hi, Shaun," I said, hoping I sounded friendly and non-threatening. "How are you?"

"What are you doing here?" he said by way of greeting. Didn't bother trying to sound friendly, and I couldn't blame him.

"Tell me about Jenny."

Shaking his head, Shaun looked away. "I can't talk to you. Carl is pissed off. I've never seen him as pissed off as he is at you." And that was saying something. A lot of things pissed Carl off.

"Not as pissed off as he's going to be," I said, donning a terrible sweet smile.

Shaun had pulled himself from the doorway and started to walk back inside, but my words stopped him. Slowly, he looked back over his shoulder. His body was taut with fear, uncertainty—the stiff shoulders, the clenched fists. Ready to run, ready to fight if cornered. I recognized the stance because I'd felt it myself so many times. He studied me, his dark eyes shining.

"You're going to do it," he said. "You're going to take him down."

Not "you're going to challenge him," or "you're going to try to take him." He said "you are." Like he believed I could. That sent a charge through me, a brush of static that made my hair rise. He thought I was stronger—maybe I could get him to side with me. Maybe.

"Right now, I just want to know what happened to Jenny. I put her on a plane. She was supposed to be on a plane and away from Carl. How did he get to her?"

His stance changed. Some of the caution slipped, replaced by...something. I couldn't read the new tension that creased his features. Could it be grief? I waited for him to collect himself.

When he finally spoke, his voice was soft and hesitant.

"She called him from the waiting area. I think she chickened out. She talked a lot about getting away, when he wasn't around. But it was like talking about winning the lottery. Nobody believes it, you don't believe it yourself. Then she'd turn around in the same breath and say how much she loved him. How she wouldn't want to hurt him. Like it didn't matter how much he hurt her." His expression turned bitter. "When she disappeared, I was happy. I thought she'd really done it, gotten away from him, left town. I didn't care how, I didn't care where, just that she was away. But she called him, and Carl talked her out of it. Pulled out all that 'we're a pack, we're family, I need you' shit. He still had a hold on her. I can't really blame her—it's hard walking away. You know that."

I shook my head. "It isn't hard. The hard part is knowing that if I'd done it sooner, T. J. might still be alive."

"Yeah."

"She called him. He picked her up at the airport. He took her—where? To their house?" Meg and Carl had a

house west of town, against the foothills, with easy access
to wilderness for running on full moon nights.

"They didn't get that far," Shaun said. Quickly he
added, "I wasn't there. I heard about it later. I'd have tried
to stop him if I'd been there. But I've been staying away
from him. He's wrapped up in some of Arturo's shit right
now, and I don't want to have anything to do with that."

"There were some other lycanthropes in town," I said.
"Strangers. Carl sent the pack after them. He left Jenny
with the rest of the bodies. He must have picked her up at
the airport knowing he was going to kill her."

"You know him as well as I do. You tell me."

"You knew what he'd do, and you didn't even try to
stop him."

"What did you expect me to do?" he shouted.

I didn't flinch, because his anger wasn't directed at
me. Not that it mattered, because I was angry enough at
myself. I'd been so close. She'd been so close. How could
she have waited by the curb, how could she have gotten
into his car, knowing him the way she must have known
him? Knowing that he wouldn't *not* hurt her, at the very
least? Knowing that he was capable of killing her.

I blamed it on the stupid security rules that meant I
couldn't walk her to the airplane without buying a ticket
myself. I should have known that it wasn't enough to see
her walk through that metal detector. I shouldn't have
breathed that sigh of relief until I'd gotten Alette's call
that she'd arrived safely. Why was I so goddamned *trusting*? I could imagine what Carl had said to her: *You need
me, I can take care of you, you're just a pup, you're too
weak to be on your own, let me come get you, I'll save you*

from yourself. He'd have worn her down until there was nothing left. No confidence, no purpose—no self.

And part of her loved him despite everything. Of course she'd call him. Of course she'd start to doubt, without someone telling her everything she had to gain by leaving him. I leaned against the soot-stained brick wall of the alley, wiped my eyes, and sniffed back tears. It didn't help. I felt battered and exhausted.

"At least you tried," Shaun said. "It's more than anyone else did." He glanced away—bearing his own part of the shame.

"You couldn't stand up to Carl any more than she could," I said. "T. J. was the only one."

"I liked T. J." He gave a little shrug and a sad smile. "Everybody liked T. J. He was the best of us. After he . . . you know. There didn't seem to be much point in standing up to Carl."

There had to be a way to do this with brains instead of brawn. I hadn't gotten this far on my less-than-brute strength.

I looked at Shaun—then tried to look into him. Looked at him like I could see everything: his mind, his soul, his fears. A wolf's stare. "If I need you. If I call on you—will you come? When I put together a plan, will you stand with me?"

His indecision was plain. He shuffled his feet, looked skyward, and winced, squinting into the streetlight. Didn't want to answer. Didn't look at me. I didn't want to push him—I was asking a lot of him: to break rank, to possibly put his life on the line. But I didn't have time to wait.

"Shaun?" I spoke with an edge. I had to mean it. I had to sound like I knew what I was doing.

He took a deep breath, then he looked at me. "If it's a good plan," he said. "Yes."

I felt a little bit stronger.

"Thank you," I said. "I'll let you know when."

I walked away without looking back. Turning my back on him was a sign of trust, and a sign of power. Wolf's sign.

Now, about that plan...

As Ben and I drove to meet Rick, Hardin called back. I hadn't expected her to have anything so soon. She quickly dashed my hopes for progress.

"Cook checked out of the Brown Palace on Monday," she said. "By all accounts, she's left town."

On the one hand, I was relieved. She wouldn't be around to mess things up anymore. On the other hand, we couldn't learn anything more from her.

Hardin continued. "Funny thing, though. All her concerts for the week have been postponed."

"She could be anywhere, then."

"I've got someone going over the hotel's security tapes from the last week. Maybe we can track down a few of her associates. See if anything links her to the warehouse or this Master vampire of yours."

It seemed like little enough to go on, but I wasn't going to complain. "Thanks, Detective."

"Something I can't figure out," she said. I braced for a difficult question until I realized a laugh hid behind her voice. "Am I doing you a favor with all this or are you doing me one?"

"Maybe we'll just call this one a wash," I said.

She clicked off.

Rick had picked what must have been the seediest dive available on East Colfax. When I told Ben the address, he'd done a double take.

"You are not going there," he said.

"How do you even know about this place?"

"If I told you how many assault cases come out of that bar, you'd faint."

"And how many of those have you defended?"

"Enough to know we have no business being there." Ben might have been a few steps up the moral and social ladder from Cormac, but that still left him a few steps down from normal. *Many* steps down from normal.

"Rick'll look after us."

"Like he looked after the rest of his people?"

"You don't have to come if you feel that way."

"You're not going there alone."

His vehemence gave me a warm feeling, even in the midst of the argument. *He likes me . . .* We hadn't stopped the catty back-and-forth for days, it seemed like. We were learning each other's sore spots, and we were both the kind of people who would pry at those spots. I didn't know how to stop.

The place was in an old brick storefront, and it didn't have a sign. If you didn't know it was here, you didn't belong. That kind of place. I felt like I'd stepped into a gangster movie, and that didn't comfort me at all. Bars covered the windows. The entrance even had a set of bars on a storm door. A weedy lot next door served as a parking lot, which was full of a mix of old model beaters and shiny new pickups. A few Harleys occupied the sidewalk in front. No sign of Rick's BMW. But Rick was too smart to bring that car. Or maybe it had already been stolen.

This wasn't a setting I'd ever imagine finding Rick in. This wasn't the kind of place I'd expect to find any vampire in. They tended to prefer sophisticated, elegant. They didn't spend centuries practicing their charm and accumulating their power so they could hang out in places like this.

Ben insisted on entering first, pulling me in behind him while he scanned inside. My eyesight adjusted to the gloom, while my nose worked. The place reeked. Alcohol, mostly stale beer. Working-class sweat. Tobacco and harder drugs. Meth, maybe, not because I recognized it but because it was a smell I *didn't* recognize, and that was one I hadn't encountered. And more—the vomit may have been scraped off the floor, but the smell was still there. I didn't imagine health inspectors ventured near here too often. I tried to breathe through my mouth.

A loud TV over the bar to the left showed a baseball game. Rickety tables and chairs filled the rest of the tiny space. The floor was concrete. Most of the tables were occupied, and a crowd lined the bar, chatting, laughing, and watching the game. A group sat in a corner, watching the TV and sharing a couple pitchers of beer. Another group was playing darts in the back. The bartender was stealing a glance at the game while he wiped down the counter. Maybe this place wasn't so bad, even if it did seem like rock-bottom. Even gangsters needed to chill out sometimes.

One of the hunched figures at the bar was Rick, transformed. The Rick I knew wouldn't have fit in here. He'd have gotten hostile, sideways looks from everybody here, and he probably would have been mugged on his way out. But Rick was smart, and he knew this.

This Rick hadn't washed his hair in a couple of days, and it hung limp and slightly greasy. He wore a worn-out flannel shirt over a plain black T, frayed jeans, and work boots. He looked like someone who'd spent all day working at an unpleasant construction site, the kind where workers got paid under the table. Listlessly, he watched the game and gripped a mug of beer in both hands.

If I hadn't scented the undead chill of vampire, I'd never have spotted him.

I approached, and Ben followed a step behind—taking my back. He was close enough for me to elbow his ribs the minute he said something snide. Rick glanced over his shoulder as I reached him.

"See," he said, "I knew if you met me here, you'd be serious."

"You're a bastard for bringing her here," Ben said.

Rick quirked a smile at me. "I think he likes you."

This was impossible. *They* were impossible. "Are we going to talk or just bitch at each other?"

"There's a table." Rick nodded and made to get up.

"Ah, since you're not going to be using that, I'll take it." I took charge of his beer. Rick didn't argue, and Ben rolled his eyes.

The table was already occupied by a tall blond man, burly and scowling. Both his skin and his hair looked sunbaked. He leaned back against the wall and had a view of the whole place. Rick was standing next to him before he looked up and smiled. It was a hard-edged, cold smile. I didn't think he could smile any other way.

"I think you've met Dack," Rick said.

He did, in fact, have the same scent as the creature in the warehouse. I could almost see the spindly, big-eared dog-thing behind his eyes. Both his incarnations had a watchful air.

"Hi," I said, trying not to sound nervous. "Nice to see, ah, the rest of you."

He smirked. "'Ullo." Even in the single word, an unidentifiable accent came through.

"You want to keep an eye out?" Rick said, taking his own seat.

"Can do." Dack pushed off from the wall and stood, his movements slow and deliberate. Like he had a powerful body and used it sparingly. Without another word he picked up his beer and moved to take Rick's seat at the bar. He was also dressed in denim and flannel. Unless they'd been watching, people might not notice the two had switched places.

Rick gestured for me and Ben to join him.

"Can you trust him?" I asked Rick. The lycanthrope seemed to be watching the game, unconcerned. I wondered if he could hear us from here.

"I do," Rick said. "Though I suppose I have reasons not to. He's saved my life a couple of times now. I've saved his. That has to count for something."

I understood those kinds of calculations. "Where's he from?"

"South Africa. I've known him for fifteen years, Kitty. Longer than I've known you."

"That's not the only criteria for trusting someone."

"But it's a good one for knowing someone."

"Somebody had to have sold you out, Rick. Can you trust Charlie and Violet?"

"Can I trust you? You knew where we were. It's a very short list of people who did."

"But why would I tell anyone?" I said, almost shrilly. "What reason would I have?"

"For protection. Maybe you made a deal with Arturo or Mercedes. I don't know, you tell me."

Great. We were all paranoid now. And I couldn't even blame him for questioning me. I took a deep breath and tried to sound reasonable and not like a traitor. "I didn't know when you were planning on moving. I didn't know enough to be able to sell you out. You're the one who came to me. Don't go putting me on the spot now."

He glanced away.

I sighed. "Rick, if you don't think I can help you, if you don't trust me, tell me now so I can get the hell out of here."

He studied me—and I met his gaze square on, vampire mojo or no. If it would give him some kind of reassurance, it was worth the risk.

And if I didn't trust him not to pull one over on me, I had no business being here in the first place. The logic of it was simple.

He looked away first. "Let's move on."

Ben had brought along today's paper. A story on the front page related the gruesome discovery of ten mauled bodies in an industrial warehouse. The first paragraph of the story included mention of the involvement of Hardin's Paranatural Unit in the investigation, and the following conclusion that vampires, or werewolves, or some combination of the above were involved. The rest of the article didn't reveal too many details. Hardin had given me more information at her briefing this morning. Hard to believe it was only this morning. The editorial pages contained a long rant about the danger paranormal elements obviously presented to the public, bringing up the spate of alleged vampire assaults at downtown nightclubs last month, and demanding to know when the authorities were going to do something about containing the menace. Never mind that all the victims had also been paranormal, and the paranormal hadn't presented such an obvious menace *before* this slaughter.

Before this, no one outside the paranormal community ever heard about slaughters like this. People went missing, that was it.

"Why didn't Arturo clean up the mess?" I asked Rick. "He's Denver's Master. I'd have thought he'd want this covered up. He wouldn't want the attention."

"You're right, but Dack called 911 just before we escaped," he said. That solved that mystery. "Arturo's people didn't have time to do anything before the police showed up."

"That must have driven him crazy," I said.

"Not that it does us any good. Whether he got rid of the bodies or not, my people are still dead." He rubbed a hand over his face.

"Oh, but it does do us some good," I said. "Because now we have Detective Hardin on our side."

"You look like someone who has a plan," he said.

"I do."

The three of us sat close, heads bent, in what seemed to me to be an obvious conspiracy. I told them what Cormac and I had discussed—paraphrasing, while talking about territories and predators, drawing them out, and making them panic.

I didn't mention the bounty hunter; nonetheless, Ben spotted me. "That sounds like one of Cormac's plans. You went to talk to Cormac."

"I hadn't planned on it," I said. "It just sort of happened."

"There's someone who could be very useful right now," Rick said.

"If you can postpone your revolution for another four years or so, he might be available," Ben said, cutting.

"Afraid not," Rick replied.

"We have to get Carl and Arturo at the same time," I said. "Whatever we do, we have to get to them both, so they can't help each other."

"That was my plan the last time. Now we have to do it with fewer people and them fully warned. I'm ready to give the whole thing up as lost."

"And where will you go? What Master is going to let you stay in their city knowing you tried to pull a coup in Denver and failed?"

He didn't answer, which was all the answer I needed. Vampires preferred cities because of the larger feeding pool, and for the greater anonymity. I couldn't picture Rick fending for himself in rural America.

"I've survived this long. I'll find a way."

"No. We'll draw them out. We don't strike at them— we strike near them. They'll have to respond, and that's when we get them."

Ben said, "They'll respond. Do you know what that means? They'll strike at what's visible. That's you, Kitty."

"Then we know right where they'll be." My smile felt maniacal.

"No. Because they won't go after you directly. They'll do exactly the same thing—they'll strike *near* you." He spoke with vehemence, his words pointed. Like I wasn't hearing him.

"I'm not very good at this strategy thing, Ben. What are you saying?"

"Your family," Rick said. "They'll strike at your family."

Ben added, "Your parents, your sister, her kids."

Stupidly, I blinked at him. "They wouldn't."

"Look what Carl did to Jenny. He would," Ben said. "Are you ready to play that game? Are you ready to use your family as bait?"

I rubbed my face, which had suddenly flushed hot, and tangled my fingers in my hair. Fighting for myself was one thing, even fighting for revenge was one thing. Ben put this in such stark terms, and he was right. Yes, Carl and Arturo would target my family. They were easy enough to find, in the phone book and everything. And yes, if I continued on, I'd be knowingly putting them in danger. Knowing that Carl and Arturo would go after them meant I was using them as bait. I was scum for even thinking of it.

But I did it anyway.

The words that came out of my mouth next didn't feel like mine. I couldn't feel myself speak anymore. "Then at least we'll know where they'll hit next. We know where Carl and Arturo will be, and we can be ready for them. We'll keep a watch on my folks, on Cheryl. We'll move them. We can protect them. If we can protect them, it'll work."

"It's a risk," Rick said.

My eyes weren't even focused anymore. "We have to get them before they can hurt anyone. We'll get to them before they get to me." My family. They wouldn't even know what was happening, I couldn't explain all this to them. I could just hear what Cheryl would say if she knew. *How dare you even think of this!* If anything happened to Nicky and Jeffy... And Mom would be in the hospital tomorrow. I should call her.

"I think we can do it," Ben said. "I think we can protect your family and take care of those two."

"You do?" I said hopefully. His gaze looked as maniacal as mine felt. We both knew that Carl really did need to go. Utterly and completely. We both believed it was worth the risk.

Rick said, "If I can get Arturo alone, without any of his minions, without the lycanthropes backing him, I can take care of him and the rest of the vampires."

"Then I'll have to take care of Carl—"

"Can you?" he said. "I saw you with him. He's still your alpha, on some level. You still believe he's stronger than you."

That made me mad. I didn't even want to consider that he might be right. I wanted to growl. Ben touched my hand.

"Rick. I can do it," I said. "Are you with us?"

Rick's hands, resting on the table, clenched into fists, and his glare turned inward, to thoughts I couldn't guess at. He had the look of a predator all right, one that was cornered and growing dangerous. "If you're willing to risk everything for this, how can I refuse?"

"We still need a plan," Ben said with a smile.

I was stronger than Carl. I had to believe that. What could I do that Carl couldn't? What did I have that Carl didn't? When I thought about it in those terms, the answer was easy. Simple, really. Been staring me in the face the whole time.

What did I have that Carl, and Arturo for that matter, didn't? *The Midnight Hour.*

chapter 10

I called Mom in the morning. She didn't answer her phone. Dad didn't answer his. They'd already left for the hospital I was guessing. Mom never gave me an answer to my question. No—that was the answer. She hadn't changed her mind. She wouldn't let me save her. We'd have to trust the doctors and modern medical science to do it.

To tell the truth, I was glad. And if science didn't work, if the surgery didn't remove it all, well ... I could ask her again. And again ...

I left a message apologizing for not being there. She'd want the whole family there as they wheeled her into surgery. She'd be disappointed. But right now I felt like the best way I could protect my family was by staying away from them.

We had a plan, but had to wait to put it in motion, and it was killing me. The show wasn't until Friday night. I had to make it all the way through Friday, first. We had a lot to do to get ready.

And if we were on the move, Carl couldn't find us.

Ben and I drove to Longmont to take a look at Cormac's storage unit.

The Jeep was parked at Ben's mother's house, a bungalow near downtown, one of those cute little houses built in the thirties, all brick and tiny rooms, with a porch in front and a shed out back.

"I still haven't met your mom," I said as we walked around back to the end of the driveway.

"She's at work now. Let's get this over with, I don't want to explain to her why we're getting into Cormac's Jeep."

I couldn't blame him. Cormac hunted vampires and werewolves because that was what his father—Ben's mother's brother—had done, and their father before him. It ran in the family. Ben's mother knew enough to guess what kind of trouble we'd gotten involved in. Ben hadn't yet told her that he'd been infected with lycanthropy, that he'd become one of the family's enemies. I wasn't sure she knew that we'd shacked up together.

It was all just as well.

The key was right where Cormac said it would be, and Ben knew the storage place it went with. Cormac had rented a small unit, the size of a walk-in closet. This was somehow comforting. I'd been afraid that Cormac needed a warehouse to contain his arsenal.

"Yeah, this'll definitely be useful," Ben said after stepping into the closet and turning on the light. "I think some of it's my dad's. Cormac moved it off the ranch when it looked like the Feds were going to haul him in."

Ben's father—Cormac's uncle—had been active in a militia in the nineties. He was now serving time for illegal weapons possession and conspiracy charges. Ben hadn't spoken to him in almost a decade.

Most of the stash was organized, stacked neatly on

shelves, rifle cases on the bottom, other boxes and metal cases higher up, boxes of bullets, and I didn't have to look to know that many of them were silver. In the back, longer weapons lay propped in a corner: javelins, spears—even some of those tips gleamed silver. Several crossbows of various shapes and strengths lay on another shelf. Cormac could kill anything, almost any way he wanted to with this stuff. He must have been gathering the collection for years. Or maybe he'd inherited it. The wood on some of the pieces seemed well varnished and smelled of age.

Ben brought an empty box from the car and started putting items into it. He opened cases, chose or rejected individual weapons based on no criteria I could name. Then he packed several boxes of ammunition and covered a pair of the crossbows with a tarp before bringing them into the light and loading them into the trunk.

"Point of no return," I said softly.

"Hm?"

"Is this going to work? What if I get everyone killed?"

"Second thoughts?" he said, leaning on the doorway.

"It's got to be done. I don't know how else to do it."

Ben gave my arm a comforting squeeze. I was too startled to respond.

It had been my idea to go to the shooting range next and get some more practice. I had a feeling I needed all the practice in the world, and it still wouldn't be enough. We spent an hour shooting, burning through several boxes of plain ammunition.

I was starting to understand the attraction of shooting things. Mostly it was the noise. Even with the earphones, each shot burst like an explosion in my head. The noise traveled through my bones. It rattled loose everything else, the worries, anxieties, fears. All that remained was the noise and the punctured target a couple dozen yards away. I was getting better. All the shots hit the paper now. Most hit the center of the black target.

Ben and I didn't say a word to each other.

Back at the car, Ben put on gloves and reloaded the clips with silver bullets.

"Where does Cormac get those?" I asked. "Is there some kind of mail order catalog? A web site?"

"There's a guy in Laramie who makes them," Ben said. "Been doing it for years."

"Everybody get them from this guy?"

"No. Other people make them. There's a community out there—Cormac's not the only one who does what he does."

I should have known that, but it was still a sobering thought. Shining a light into this shadow world didn't illuminate much of anything. It only made more shadows. Darker shadows. All this time, all these miles, I was still ignorant.

"Community, huh? Is there a union? Conventions?"

He just smiled.

I picked one of the silver bullets from the box and held it in my bare hand. Instantly, it started to itch, and a rash developed, splotchy red. I kept it in my palm, letting it burn.

"What are you doing?" Ben said.

I didn't know. Letting the pain grow, I stared at the shining capsule in my hand. It gleamed, brighter than the ones we'd spent on paper targets, like a bit of frozen mercury or a piece of jewelry, beautiful almost. Like magic.

This little thing could kill me. And I held it, inert. Like playing with fire.

Ben picked it off my hand and slid it into the clip. I rubbed my hand on my jeans. Slowly, the pain and the rash faded.

"Maybe we won't have to shoot anyone," I said. "Maybe they'll just leave. Maybe I can convince them to leave town, leave us alone."

Ben took a long pause before saying, "Maybe."

"I don't want to have to shoot anyone, Ben."

Another long pause. "Then it's a good thing Dack and I are around." He packed the guns into the trunk and went to the driver's scat.

"This'll work," I said as we drove away.

"Yeah," Ben said.

Neither one of us sounded sure.

Finally, it was time.

Rick settled into the chair in the studio. He looked distinctly nervous, his gaze unsettled, his skin too pale, even for a vampire. I wanted this all to be over just to see Rick back to normal. I was used to seeing him confident and even amiable.

At least he was back to the suave Rick I was used to, all polish and expensive clothing.

"I'm only here because I have nothing to lose," he said.

"Oh, don't sound so glum. This'll be fun!"

Matt back in the booth didn't look so sure. Rick also looked skeptical.

"Humor me a little longer," I said. "Then it'll be all over."

"I leave it to you. You're the professional." He put on the headphones, glaring at me. "I have a small request, though. You need to call me Ricardo."

"That your real name?"

"It's a Master's name."

And that was another thing about vampires: Why did they have such a problem with nicknames? "Whatever you say."

Nothing more than sheer, pigheaded enthusiasm was carrying me along at this point. Show business, baby. Matt counted down, and the music cued up.

"Good night, everyone, and welcome to *The Midnight Hour.* It's vampires again tonight. It might sound like I've been doing a lot of shows on vampires lately, but that's just the way it goes. There seem to be a lot of them around at the moment. This time it's vampire politics. Like any other community, they have their leaders, their followers, their structures, their organizations—and their problems. Here to help us talk about vampires' wily ways and notions is a very special guest: Denver's own Master vampire, Ricardo."

This was going to piss a lot of people off. Kind of like kicking a wasp's nest.

"Hi, Ricardo, how are you this fine evening?"

"I'm just wonderful," he said, gritting his teeth but managing to sound honest. The microphone would hear honest, at least. "It's an honor to be on your show."

"Thank you, that's great to hear," I said. "I was starting to think most vampires put up with me because they think I'm cute and harmless."

"Oh, I wouldn't accuse you of that."

"Wait—which one?" He just smiled. "Right, moving on. Tonight I'd like to delve into some of the secrets, the hows and whys. The questions that never see the light of day, so to speak. But first, do you think you'll get in trouble for answering such questions? For breaking the code of secrecy?"

"Oh, probably. One thing or another will get me in trouble."

"So being a vampire is dangerous stuff."

"Yes. Usually. People assume immortality comes with vampirism. But you'd be surprised how much work the immortality takes. The old vampires are dangerous because they know what it takes to survive."

"Take note of that all you wannabes out there. So, Ricardo—how did you become the Master of Denver?"

"Finesse," he said, his face perfectly straight. "Sometimes it's just a matter of walking in and saying, 'Here I am.'"

Oh my God, I loved it. "Is that how such transitions usually take place?"

"Usually they're quite violent. Vampires are territorial. Taking another vampire's territory isn't something to be done lightly. But I firmly believe this territory is better off in my hands than my predecessor's."

This sounded like a political campaign, which was exactly the right description, I supposed. Except the tactics threatened to get much more vicious.

"Better off? How?"

"Safer."

"For vampires—"

"For everyone."

"Wait a minute, I may not know much, but I know

vampires keep to themselves. Most of the fine citizens of Denver have never interacted with a vampire and wouldn't know one if they met one. How does a city's Master vampire keep the city safe for everyone?" I knew the answer; this was for the benefit of my listeners.

"Because when a Master vampire can't control his followers, the rest of the city's vampires, then no one is safe from them. They will hunt indiscriminately, uncontrolled. They'll kill. Most people never notice vampires because they're kept in check. They don't kill for blood. When that control is gone..." He left the statement hanging ominously. "It's the same with werewolves, you know that."

The system—alphas commanding their packs, Masters controlling the vampires—had been handed down for centuries. Most of our kinds knew they had to stay hidden to survive, to avoid the mob with torches and pitchforks scenario. Occasionally, though, we had rogues who lacked common sense. We had to police ourselves. The system was archaic, born in the days of monarchs and empires. It showed, even in someone relatively down to earth like Rick.

"I do, and we'll maybe get to that later in the show. But here's a question for you: Do you think maybe the system is outdated?" That caught him off guard. He narrowed his gaze at me. I said, "I don't expect you to tell me your age—I haven't yet gotten a vampire to admit his age—but tell me this: were you born in a country with a king? An absolute monarch, in the days when that actually meant something more than getting chased by paparazzi."

Cautiously, he said, "Yes."

I filled in a few holes. He'd been born in Europe, at least a couple hundred years ago. With a name like Ricardo, that probably meant Spain. Lots of holes remained, like when he'd become a vampire, when he'd come to America, and—the eternal question—how old was he *really*?

"Then does Denver even need a Master, or do you think the system is outdated?" I honestly wanted to know, and I had no idea what he was going to say.

"I thought you were supposed to be making me look good."

"I decided to go for heavy-hitting philosophy instead."

He took what I threw at him in stride, with a narrow gaze and nary a beat missed. "I think we already answered that question. You've met some of the vampires in question, and I don't think you'd really want them to have free run of the city."

It was hard to tell the difference from my end. They all seemed arrogant and selfish. They all wanted you to know they could own you if they chose to, if they didn't have someone like Arturo holding them back.

"You've got a point," I said.

Rick continued. "The system isn't absolute. The Master isn't an absolute monarch. The relationship works both ways—it's based on a more ancient, feudal form than anything most modern people are used to dealing with. Vampires put themselves under control of a Master. In return, the Master owes them protection. And if a Master can no longer provide his followers that safety—that's when the system falls apart."

"And you're saying Denver's old Master couldn't provide that protection for his followers."

"Yes, I am."

"Let's open the line for calls now and see what other

secrets we can pry from Ricardo. Hello, Amanda, you're on the air."

"Hi, Kitty, thanks for taking my call!"

"No problem."

"And Ricardo, oh, my God, this is such an honor." I'd warned Rick about the hero worship. Even after all these calls, it was a bit perplexing.

"What's your question, Amanda?" I said.

"Ricardo—are you, like, hot?"

Rick blinked and looked at me with an expression that said *help?* I just grinned. I was the master here, and I had absolute power. I wanted to see him sweat it out. Do vampires sweat? Why didn't anyone ever ask if vampires sweat?

"Would you mind explaining the question a bit more?" Rick said, very diplomatically. I applauded him silently.

"I've seen all these movies and stuff, and the vampires in them, they're just so good-looking. So I just wondered if it was like that in real life. Are all Master vampires totally irresistibly good-looking?"

At last, Rick was smiling. He might even have been blushing a little. "I'm afraid I don't feel qualified to, ah, pass comment on my own appearance. Kitty—you want to offer an opinion?"

"He's not bad. He's got a little of that tall-dark-hand-some thing going."

"Thank you. Too kind," he said, with plenty of sarcasm.

"Just keep in mind, Amanda, what vampires really want is your blood, and the way a lot of them get that is by looking as attractive as they possibly can. They use hot-ness as a lure. They're like those deep-sea fish with the tentacle lights."

Rick raised an eyebrow at me and mouthed the words *tentacle lights*?

"Anyway, moving on, next call please—"

And so it went. I had to shove the plan to the back of my mind and concentrate on the show. I wanted every show to be the best it possibly could, and having Rick on was something I'd wanted to do right from the start. That part of it, I enjoyed immensely.

After the first hour, I started to worry, because I'd expected a reaction by now. I had my cell phone ready. Dack was keeping watch at my parents' house, Ben at my mom's hospital room, and Charlie and Violet were watching Cheryl's place. They had instructions to call 911 if anything was about to go down. This was an emergency, wasn't it? I figured a bunch of wailing sirens would at least make the bad guys pause. That was all we needed— a pause during which we could evacuate.

My cell phone stayed quiet. What was happening outside the studio? Dare I ask?

Then it came. The first hornet left the nest, stinger all ready to go.

Matt cut in over my headset. "Kitty, line three's up."

That was the private line, in case someone had to get through the rest of the phone chatter to talk to me. Only a few people knew the number. But I had a good idea who this one was.

I punched the line. "Hello," I said carefully.

"Katherine, I have no idea what you think you're doing, but you will pay for this. Do you understand me? I would have left you alone but you've chosen sides and now—"

Bingo! Bait taken. Now time to set the hook. I switched

the phone line over to live. "Hello, Arturo! Thanks for calling. You're on the air here at *The Midnight Hour*."

"Oh, no," he said. "No you don't. I won't be a party to this." His fury made his accent thicker. It lost some of its aristocratic edge, making me wonder: What had Arturo been before he'd become a vampire?

"I've got Ricardo here," I said. "Wanna talk to him?"

"Rick," Arturo said darkly, "this will win you nothing, you know that."

"Think of it as an opening salvo," Rick said.

I sat back to watch the fireworks.

"You weren't able to take over when you had an army at your back. What makes you think you can do it using a *radio show*?"

"Because you weren't this angry when I had an army," Rick said.

"You'll regret taking this fight into the open."

"I'm not the one who left a warehouse full of bodies for the police."

"*Katherine* will regret taking this fight into the open."

"She understands the risks as well." Rick and I exchanged a glance, of understanding and resolve. I felt like we were soldiers on the same battlefield. *Once more unto the breach, dear friends...*

"I don't think she does," Arturo said, his tone sharp. I could imagine him spitting as he spoke. "You haven't told her all that the Masters do. Yes, we control the vampires, yes we keep order. But you haven't told her everything, have you? You haven't told her about the stakes, about what else is out there, hungry for these cities—" Rick looked uncomfortable, and I knew Arturo was right. Rick hadn't told me everything. The rant reached a fever pitch.

"When Denver falls because you couldn't hold them back—"

"Why are you so sure I won't be able to protect this city?" Rick countered.

"What the hell are you guys talking about?" I interrupted, dumbstruck. "Hold *what* back?"

They both fell silent. Oh, this was the big story. This was the secret lives of vampires coming to light for all to see. "What are you afraid of?" I prompted. "What are vampires afraid of?"

"Losing control," Rick said softly.

"Control," I said. "Is that it? Like, freaking out, going nuts, singing show tunes, that sort of control?"

"Vampires are about control," Rick said.

"Power," Arturo added. "What kind, and who controls it."

"I have news for you, guys. That's what everyone's about. Most people only aspire to having the power to control their own little lives, but there it is. The only difference is how completely enamored vampires are of their own perceived importance."

Rick started to interrupt. "Kitty—"

"You, too, Rick! You're not exempt from this. You may be better than most but you're still sitting here talking about how *you* know what's right and *you* know what's best. Well I'm sorry, but you're going to have to start taking the rest of us into account!" Whoa, that rant had been building for a while. I managed not to apologize for it; it needed to be said.

A pause hung for a moment—dead air. My thoughts had scattered, and I quickly marshaled them to try to follow my diatribe with something clever.

But Arturo spoke first. "Rick. You do not have the resolve to play this part. You want a salvo, I will show you a salvo."

He hung up.

That was when I noticed Matt waving over the board, pointing at his watch. I hadn't been watching the time, and I'd almost missed the end of the show.

I talked fast. "Right. I have about twenty seconds to explain what just happened. I'm not sure I can, except to say that yes, Ricardo here's a friend of mine and he's got some rivals out there. Any of you looking to vampirism to solve your problems, keep that in mind. You'll only trade one set for another. Stay safe out there and I'll return next week. This is Kitty Norville, voice of the night."

The on-air sign dimmed, and I could see Matt's sigh of relief from here.

"You're right, of course," Rick said quietly. "We've spent centuries ruling our worlds at the expense of others. It's a hard habit to break."

I tried to make my smile friendly. "Nice of you to say so. But we'll have to discuss the political philosophy of the whole thing later. Remember, that was only phase one."

Matt came in from the booth. "Kitty, what's going on?"

Rick and I were already on our way out the door. "I'll let you know when it's all over."

"I don't like the sound of that."

"Good. You shouldn't. Matt—do me a favor and if anything weird starts happening around here, you see any people who don't look right, anyone who shouldn't be here, or if anyone turns up missing unexpectedly, call 911. Don't wait, don't hesitate. Just call."

"Kitty, what the hell—"

"I'm sorry. I can't explain. I'll see you later." I hoped. My heartbeat felt like a jackhammer in my chest. Carl and Meg wouldn't have to lift a claw to kill me. Stress would do it just fine.

We left the studio with about four hours until dawn and waited in front of the building. Not much time for what I wanted to do. Ben was already waiting in the parking lot. Shaun pulled up in his car right on schedule, just after the show, like I told him to. My pack was growing, I thought with trepidation.

We'd ruffled Arturo's feathers, now it was time to ruffle Carl's. I had to keep moving, plowing ahead as fast as I could, before I had second thoughts. It wasn't too late to back out of the whole thing, was it? As Ben and Shaun approached, I said, "Hi, guys."

They eyed each other warily, and their gestures were uncanny. Their wolves were speaking in their sideways glances, the way they avoided staring at each other directly, the way they made sure not to approach each other, but to approach me in parallel, not coming near each other. They were sizing each other up without offering a challenge. Did they even realize they were doing it?

I made myself relax, to keep the tension in the air from spiking any more than it already had. I needed these two to cooperate. To trust each other. I needed them to be a pack, even though they'd never met each other.

"Ben, this is Shaun. Shaun, Ben." They didn't offer to shake hands. Just nodded in acknowledgment, keeping their gazes down, maintaining an easy distance between them. Their noses were working, though, their nostrils flaring.

"He's yours?" Shaun said, and I heard an unspoken

question in his tone: *He's your mate, your alpha, and I must defer to him as well?*

"That's right," I said. He nodded, then moved a step back, giving Ben precedence. Making way.

God, this was weird.

"All right," I said. "Let's get a move on."

"Kitty, good hunting," Rick said, moving off to his BMW. He was going to the hospital to keep watch over my mom, at least until dawn. "And be careful."

"You, too."

The three of us piled into my car.

"Where we headed?" Shaun finally asked as I turned onto Highway 6 toward Golden. I hadn't told him the details. I just said I needed a warm body for an expedition. He'd been trusting enough not to ask any more questions.

"We're going to the Park and Ride on 93. We'll drop the car off and head into the hills. Then we start marking territory."

"You're kidding," Shaun said.

"Gives a whole new meaning to the phrase 'pissing contest,'" Ben said, grinning.

Shaun whistled low. "Carl's going to hate this."

"That's the idea. It's not a full moon, so he won't be out. None of the pack'll be out. He won't know what we've done until he steps out of the house tomorrow morning and takes a big breath of air." I didn't want to be anywhere near him at that moment. If we did it right, he'd smell it on the air: foreignness, invasion, another pack moving in. He'd smell *us*.

"I've never done anything like this before. It sounds like fun," Ben said. I couldn't tell if he was joking. And I felt terrible, because even though he'd met Carl and Meg, he really had no idea what I was getting him into. He might have helped Cormac hunt vampires and werewolves on occasion, but he'd never had to fight for dominance as one of them. His battles were usually in courtrooms, where people followed rules.

Flying by the seat of my pants didn't begin to cover this.

"You're crazy," Shaun muttered. "We are so dead. We're so gonna die."

Ben looked at him over the car seat. "Then why are you even here?"

"We're not going to die," I said. "We'll keep moving. We won't stop long enough for them to be able to find us."

Shaun wouldn't let up. "That's fine for you to say as a human. But are you going to remember that great plan as a wolf? How am I going to remember it?"

"I'll remind you," I said, low enough for it to be taken as a growl. That and a quick glance in the rearview mirror made him settle down. He actually cringed a bit.

A girl could get a big head over that kind of power. Not now, though. I had a job to do.

"Shaun, if you're not sure about this, you don't have to do it. I'll let you out, take you back, whatever."

"No, I'm sure. I'm just nervous. That's all."

He might have said scared and it would have been as true.

"I know. Just keep thinking about the big picture. This is supposed to make everything better in the long run. This is supposed to keep people like Jenny from getting killed."

"Yeah, I know."

Ben put his hand on my thigh—a touch of comfort. I hadn't realized how tense I was until I twitched at the pressure. But his touch transmitted calm. Stay calm. This'll work.

We arrived all too quickly. Quicker than I thought we would. No traffic at 2:00 A.M. Maybe that was it.

"We can still change our minds," I said after I shut the engine off.

"You're the alpha," Ben said. "Isn't that what you keep saying? It's not up to us."

"Ben—" It came out as a whine.

"Are you guys married?" Shaun said. "'Cause you sound married."

I leaned my forehead on the steering wheel and groaned. "How did my life turn into this?" I didn't even want to see how Ben was taking the comment.

Shaun quickly said, "No, it's in a good way. Way better than Carl and Meg."

"What do they sound like when they argue?" I said.

"They don't argue. They don't even talk to each other. Compared to them, you guys are Ozzie and Harriet."

Ben patted my arm. "Come on, dear. When this is all over, we can go home and you can make me a martini and fetch my slippers."

We climbed out of the car. "Oh, no. I don't think so."

Ben glanced at Shaun. "See? No Ozzie and Harriet here."

Shaun shook his head, and I had a sneaking suspicion he wanted to laugh.

A ridge of hills and ravines ran north and west from here, leading up to the Flatirons, roughly marking the western edge of Carl's territory. He and his wolves ranged farther into the mountains on occasion. But the foothills and plains along this stretch were their favorite stomping grounds. Kicking the wasp nest. Yeah.

Wolf coiled inside me, like my insides were pacing even though I wasn't. For once, we agreed on something. She was as pissed off at Carl as I was. Carl was breaking trust with his wolves; he'd killed wolves under his protection. He wasn't a good alpha, and we had to do something about that.

I walked up the side of the hill, beginning the trek into wilderness. I sensed rather than saw Ben and Shaun hesitate, then follow. Even if one of them had spoken, had called to me, I didn't think I could answer. Not with human words. I was entering Wolf's world.

First thing was to find a den. I found one where stands of pine trees started growing, up in the hills near Coal Creek Canyon. Trees stood over a sheltered hollow. It couldn't be seen at all from down slope. We could stash our clothes and have a safe place to come and sleep it off. And it was relatively near the car for that fast getaway come morning.

I started stripping, pulling off my shirt. Shaun did the same. Ben watched us.

"This is weird," Ben said. "Doing this in front of a stranger. It's like having sex with the curtains open."

He didn't have any experience with a real pack, where naked wasn't sexual, it was just natural. He'd only ever Changed when it was the two of us. And yeah, curled up together the next morning, sex was usually involved. I couldn't blame him for making the connection. But I did anyway.

"Would you get your mind out of the gutter?"

"Can we trust him?" Suddenly he sounded serious.

And he was right. This was war, and there were spies. I only knew Shaun as someone from my old life who didn't like Carl.

"You can trust me," Shaun said, his shirt off, his jeans unzipped, half undressed. "I trust her." He gave me that look that a subordinate gives his alpha. That focused gaze, waiting to be told what to do, when to jump.

I hadn't done anything to earn that trust. Not yet. I didn't deserve it. I hadn't been able to save Jenny. I nodded to him, all the acknowledgment I was able to give.

He finished undressing, and a sheen of sweat covered his skin. His hands were shifting already, thickening, and his back hunched. Ben saw it; he'd clenched his own hands into fists, and his hair was damp. He was close, too.

"Ben." I touched his hand, and it uncurled to grasp mine. I drew close to him. "I need you, okay? I need your help. I can't do this by myself."

"You seem to be doing just fine." His cheek brushed mine. His other hand caressed my back. God, I wanted him. I wanted to ditch this whole thing and run into the woods with him.

We kissed, and the touch was hot, tense, desperate. A last kiss before battle.

"Later," I whispered, hoping he'd been thinking the same thing. He nodded.

Nearby, Shaun gave a grunt—or what had been Shaun gave a grunt. In his place, a dark and silvery wolf shook out his fur and turned to us with gleaming eyes. His tail was low, questioning.

Ben was trembling, holding in his own wolf. I started unbuttoning his shirt. "Come on. It's time."

We got most of his clothes off before he fell, kicking

off his pants as he shifted, bones melting and skin sliding, the other form bursting out of him, swallowing him. He didn't make a sound, kept it all in and just let it happen. Flowing like water was how I thought of it. His wolf was rusty gray, turning to cream on his nose and belly. The two wolves approached each other, heads low, sniffing. Ben growled and Shaun ducked, clamping his tail between his legs. That was all it took. Pack order established. Ben was alpha male. Weirdly, I was proud of him.

I looked at my two wolves. When I knelt, they came to me, rubbed against me, smelling me, and I stroked them. "Thank you for believing in me," I said, and maybe they understood and maybe they didn't. But Ben wagged his tail once.

Go go go—

And Wolf was right, I couldn't hold it any longer.

This is war.

This is battle, this is chaos, this is breaking taboos, edging into the territory of another pack. Seeking out this alien scent, letting it surround her—the nearness of danger makes all her hair stand on end, and a growl is ready to break loose in her throat.

And yet, she seeks it out, and the danger thrills her. She knows: We are stronger, we will win, we must.

She has a pack. A small one, but hers, and they follow, her mate and the other at her flanks. With their ground-eating strides—sometimes trotting, sometimes loping—they cover miles of ground on plain and hill. All the while, at junctures and borders, they mark. At the reeking places where the other pack has marked they especially linger.

There is joy in this as well, and she stops her followers to play, leaping at each other, snapping, yipping. Her mate finds a rabbit and they eat. Then they range again, mindful of the battle.

She feels the dawn approach rather than notes any sign of it—the lightening of the sky, the first songs of birds. Just as the urgency of war drove them for the few hours of night, the same urgency tells her they must be away from here by daylight. They must sleep, so she leads them back to their den. The three of them settle down, curled up nose to tail, touching, safe in each other's company.

I woke up in a strange place, with strange pressures around me. I lay on my side, on dry grass with pine boughs overhanging. Ben was in front of me, his head against my chest, one arm over my waist, the other tucked between us. He was snoring a little—it was awfully cute. Another body pressed close against my back, breathing deeply in sleep. Shaun lay against me, back to back.

A pack. Waking up in a dog pile of naked bodies, safe and comforted by their warmth. I'd forgotten what it was like. I wanted to revel in the feeling for hours.

But we weren't safe. We were in enemy territory, and we'd set a urinary time bomb that would be going off any minute now.

I elbowed Shaun and shook Ben. "Come on. We have to get going. Up up up, guys."

Ben groaned and took a firm grip on my arms, holding me in place while he sidled closer to me. His eyes were closed, and I couldn't tell if he was awake. Then he started necking me, working his way to my ear, where he started nibbling.

He sure knew which buttons to push. I just about melted. "Ben...this...this isn't—" Oh, come on, a little voice said...This was just *fine*. Make that a big voice.

Oh, no. There were so many reasons why this wasn't the time or place for this. "Ben. Wait." I pulled away and took his face in my hands. Finally, he opened his eyes. Then glanced over my shoulder, to where Shaun was sitting up and watching us.

"Don't stop on my account," he said with a laugh behind his leer.

Ben gave me a look—smirking and clearly annoyed. "I didn't sign up for this," he said, nodding at Shaun.

"You didn't sign up for any of this." I kissed his forehead.

"Ozzie and Harriet," Shaun said, shaking his head again.

I glared. "Let's get out of here."

Shaun was smiling, seeming far more content with the world than he had a right to be. "It's good to have you back, Kitty. Back and all grown up."

I thought about what I must have looked like through his eyes: I'd been weak. I'd felt small, vulnerable, at everyone's mercy. Then I disappeared for months and came back waging war. And this made him happy? He must have seen something I'd missed.

"Thanks," I said and held my hand to him. He clasped it, securing a bond of pack, of friendship. I was ready to pull both of them into a group hug, no matter how much Ben grumbled about it.

But Ben was looking out, across the hill, through the trees. "Someone's coming."

Shit. Too late. We'd waited too long.

"Who?" I whispered. The three of us had straightened, lifting our faces to the air, smelling—three wolves in human form, alert and wary, all senses firing.

Shaun said, "She's coming from upwind. She wants us to know she's here."

She. Meg, I thought in a panic. I took a deep breath, catching the smell that Shaun had found. Human and wild—lycanthrope, yes. And female. But it wasn't Meg. I'd recognize Meg. Her scent lived in my nightmares.

Meg wouldn't give us any warning. She'd pounce, and she wouldn't be alone. This was one person, and Shaun was right; she was giving us a good long approach. We waited, still and quiet, until she emerged from the trees. She was average height and build, with an edge: sharp features, wiry limbs. Her auburn hair was short, brushing around her ears. She wore a tank top and shorts, and she might have been anyone out for a morning stroll, but for the look in her eyes: hooded, anxious. Her jaw was set, and her shoulders tense, a bit like rising hackles.

"Becky," I said.

She was another one of Carl's, a couple years older than me both in chronological age and in time as a lycanthrope. She was tough, maintaining a spot in the middle to upper end of the pack hierarchy. She was one of the ones who thrived in this life. My first thought: I had underestimated him. Carl had expected something like this and sent a patrol. He was ready for us, and we'd been caught. We'd lost. Sitting here in the great outdoors, naked, along with the two men, I couldn't help but feel like I'd been caught at something illicit. That made me blush, and the blushing made me angry.

But then, she'd been the one who tried to help Jenny. What was she doing here now?

"What are you going to tell Carl?" I said. "You going to run back and tell him we're right here, easy pickings? Is that what he sent you out here to find?"

She shook her head, and her voice was low. "He didn't send me. I came out here for a walk. To think. I do that sometimes. Then I smelled you and followed you here."

I was taken aback. "Carl doesn't know we're here?"

"Oh, he will. You guys were busy last night." A smile flickered, and she looked away. To the wolves, that was a gesture of peace, of submission. It heartened me.

"You're going to tell him."

"No," she said. She licked her lips. Gaze downcast, she said, "I want to join you. Take me with you."

chapter 11

We'd goaded our rivals, with this bright idea of luring them into the open. They'd be angry, unprepared, and—I hoped—they'd get stupid. It looked nice on paper. At least it would have if I had written any of it down.

In the meantime, the four of us grabbed breakfast. I now had a pack of four. How had that happened?

Over coffee, Shaun told me what had been happening with the pack. "You remember Gabe?"

"The bike courier from Boulder, right? Thirty something. Ran marathons."

"Right. He was the first one. After T.J., Carl flipped. Kept thinking others would try it. That we were all questioning his authority. He had to slap everyone down to prove his point. Most of us rolled over and took it. You know how it is. But Gabe...Gabe thought he could talk to Carl. Reason with him. Appeal to the human side. But Carl..." Shaun shrugged, looked away, to collect himself. "Carl went too far. Gabe listened to your show, you know. Didn't tell you. Didn't dare tell Carl. But he really liked what you had to say. About being human. I think... I guess he thought he had to try."

Great. Now I could lay him on my conscience, too. Made me question all over again if I was ready for this.

"And it's kept happening. Carl makes examples, keeps throwing his dominance at us. And we keep questioning him. I'd like to have my own place someday. Start my own restaurant or bar or something. But Carl's made threats. Says he'll make sure the place sinks. He doesn't want anyone but him in charge of anything. I can't make a move with him in the picture. I don't want him trying to shut me down like he tried to do with you." He nodded at me. "Then he starts dragging us into Arturo's turf war, not even thinking twice about getting us all killed. I'm not sure he even sees people anymore when he looks at us."

Rick had said it had gotten bad for the werewolves here. This was the first chance I'd had to really talk to them.

"Jenny wasn't strong," I said. "She wasn't confronting him. Did he just lose it or what?"

Becky nodded. "It's like he can't control himself anymore, and Meg isn't any help, she's right there with him. God, Jenny. I thought if I could get her away from him, she'd be safe. I thought if anyone could convince her, you could, Kitty. I should have looked out for her better, if we had all just looked out for her—" Shaun rested a hand on Becky's arm, quieting her.

I hadn't realized how much T. J. had been a buffer between me and Carl. How much his presence had saved me from some of Carl's ire. Another debt I owed him, that I could never repay. Jenny hadn't had someone like T. J. looking out for her.

From the first, Rick had told me that the pack wasn't

healthy. A pack needed balance. Checks and buffers. Everyone needed to take part, to share in the responsibility. Carl had cowed everyone, and subsequently, had collected all the power. He couldn't carry it all by himself.

She continued. "It's like we've been waiting for something to give, waiting for something to break, to shake things up. We've just been waiting for a chance to bring him down."

"And you think that chance is me," I said.

"It'd better be," Shaun said. "Or we're all dead."

Frustrated, I said, "Why are you guys putting so much faith in me?"

Becky didn't even have to think about it. "We all saw what happened to you in Washington, D.C. And you came through. You're strong. I've been listening to your show. I can hear it in your voice. You're a natural leader. We've been waiting for someone to follow."

I wasn't ready for this. I just wanted to get rid of Carl, I didn't want to take over the whole pack. Right?

I took a deep breath. This was one of those moments where everything might change. I felt the tracks of my life curve in a new direction. "If you guys believe that, then you need to believe that I can't do it by myself. I need your help."

Becky ducked her gaze. "It'll come down to a fight. We'll have to fight, we know that."

I shook my head. "Not if I can help it. I'm not that good in a fight. I'm happier using wit and guile." I braced, waiting for a snappy remark from Ben. He only raised an eyebrow. In respect of his refraining from commenting, I refrained from kicking him under the table.

"Here's what I'd like you to do," I said. "Call up everyone

from the pack you think you can talk into leaving. Or at least into not standing with Carl when the time comes. We need allies, and you know the pack better than I do now. The more defectors we can get before a fight, the better off we'll be."

Shaun grinned. "I'd love to see Carl standing there all alone, when he thinks he has a ton of backup."

"I don't want everyone to leave right away," I said. "Once they leave, they can't go back. But if they stay, they might be able to let us know what he's up to."

"Or give him a false sense of security," Ben added.

"They'd have to be really careful," Shaun said. "Carl and Meg would both pick up on it if they thought someone was turning on them."

"Then maybe it'd be better for them to just leave. I don't want anyone to get killed because of me. Anyone else."

"Don't worry about us," Shaun said.

"We're going to need help before it even gets to Carl and Meg," Ben said. "We're expecting them to go after alternate targets. We'll need help—"

"Alternate targets?" Becky said, her brow furrowed.

"Probably Kitty's family. We have to make sure they don't get hurt."

Becky set her jaw, and Shaun nodded with new resolve. *The pack will grow, we will win this war.* Wolf was sure of it.

"Thank you," I said. "Have you guys had enough sleep? Are you okay with keeping watch today?"

"We'll be fine. Don't worry about us," Shaun said.

I dropped Shaun and Becky off at the KNOB parking lot. "We'll call if we see anything," he said, before leaving. They left together in Shaun's car.

Almost, it felt like a plan. Ben and I headed back to the freeway.

Some research into wolf behavior—wild wolves, not the lycanthropic variety—suggests that the alphas of a pack aren't necessarily the strongest, biggest, and toughest wolves, contrary to conventional belief. Instead, the leaders were sometimes the wolves best able to keep peace. They were the most diplomatic, the ones most able to negotiate compromise and organize the pack into the most efficient unit for hunting prey and raising young. The alphas were the ones who were best able to keep more members of the pack alive.

This was a theory I chose to embrace. Carl was undoubtedly the strongest, toughest wolf in this pack. But the pack wasn't healthy. He wasn't keeping his members alive.

I had to believe I could do better.

We had one more stop before we could go home. We met up with Dack at the bar on Colfax. Or rather the parking lot of the bar, since this time of day the place was closed. It looked plain and derelict in the morning light.

He was alone, driving the SUV that Charlie and Violet had been driving last week. When we arrived, he was leaning against the hood, arms crossed, staring out at the world through a pair of aviator sunglasses. He looked tough and worldly.

"What's the story?" I asked, getting out of the car.

He shrugged and spoke in his round South African lilt.

"Nothing to tell. Nothing happened. The vampires are bedded down for the day, your family's all right."

My nerves trembled with relief. "Thank you, Dack," I said. "Thanks for watching out for me."

He almost sounded amused. "No problem. What's next, then?"

"Waiting. See who jumps first. Keep your phone on, be ready to move when something happens. Maybe you should get some sleep for now."

"Plenty of time for that later," he said.

He started to get back in the car, but I stopped him. "Dack?"

"Yeah?"

I collected stories. That was how I kept doing the show week after week. There were always new stories to tell, each one stranger than the one before it.

"African wild dog?" I said. "You want to tell me where that came from?"

His smile went crooked. "Don't know. I've only met one other. The one who turned me."

"Where is he?"

"I killed him."

Ah. Right. That wasn't really a surprise. "So you're the only one?"

"Only one that I know of. Haven't really gone looking for others."

"And you met Rick how?"

He grinned. "Rick said you were a nosy one."

"I talk too much. That's my superpower. I still want to know why the world's only were-African wild dog is here working for Rick."

Dack had hired muscle written all over him: the well-built frame, the wary stance, the attitude of bullheaded confidence. I recognized it from Cormac. This was a guy you'd want watching your back. If you could trust him.

"Vampires are strong," he said. "It's a good thing, having a vampire owe you a favor. You want to be with the strongest."

"And that's Rick?"

He just smiled.

"Well then," I said. "On to the rest of the plan, then."

With that, we zoomed off in our respective cars and charged up our cell phones. I began to think this might turn out all right.

On the drive home, I dozed and kept jerking awake, waiting for a phone call to tell me something had happened, Carl or Arturo or someone under their orders had struck. When the phone finally did ring, I slept through it. I only woke up because Ben stopped the car.

"I wonder what they're waiting for," he said, speaking into my phone. I couldn't hear the voice on the other end of the line. It wouldn't be Rick, not during full daylight. After listening a moment, he said, "We're going to get some sleep. Call if anything changes."

He looked at me. Bleary-eyed, I stared back at him. "That was Shaun. No sign of anything."

"Where is he?"

"Keeping an eye on your sister's place. Your dad's at the hospital, and I figure their security can look after your folks during daylight hours."

That made sense, not to mention the place would be busy during the day. I hoped Arturo and Carl were still sane enough not to want to draw too much public attention to this.

I ought to go. I told Mom I'd go see her. But I couldn't, not in the middle of this. I didn't want to bring more trouble down on them.

"Cheryl's going to start wondering why strange cars keep parking outside her house."

"I bet she doesn't even notice." He handed my phone back to me.

Moving at half speed, I climbed out of the car. "Ben? Why are you doing this? You keep saying you didn't sign up for this like you don't want to be here, but then..." I trailed off, not sure what I meant. He'd turned out to be good at this, leaping to the fore, keeping me going. What would I have done if it had just been me?

I'd have run away.

"We're pack," he said. "Isn't that what you're always saying? We have to stick together."

That would always be an acceptable answer. That would always be there to fall back on. I wasn't satisfied with that answer anymore.

"Will that be enough to keep you and me together?"

"I hope so." He walked away.

Slowly, I followed, letting my brain run down so I wouldn't have to think anymore.

Arturo and his vampires couldn't move until nightfall. Carl probably wouldn't make a move until he did, which might have been why he hadn't come looking for me. Maybe they wouldn't strike at all. As the silence drew on, as the calls from my lookouts didn't come, I didn't start to hope. I'd become too cynical for that. Too many blows had undermined my safe little life.

I was trying to nap on the sofa when the call came. I lunged for my phone on the coffee table.

"Yes? What is it?"

"It's Becky." She sounded breathless, panicked. "I just got off the phone with Mick."

"Mick, the short guy with the brown hair?" One of the tougher wolves in Carl's pack.

"Yeah, yeah. He says Carl's on the hunt. He's called in everybody, he's going after you."

I sat on the edge of the sofa. "Here? He's coming here?" That would be best. If he was going to go after anyone, I wanted it to be me. I was ready for him.

"No," Becky said, and I could imagine her shaking her head vehemently. "He—Mick I mean—said Carl wants to hit you where it'll hurt the most. It's like he's not even pissed off at you, he's pissed off at what started this whole thing."

"Where?" I asked anyway.

"The radio station. He's going after KNOB."

"When?"

"Now, he's headed over there right now!"

chapter 12

What does he think he's going to do? Kill everyone there? Does he really think he'd get away with that? Or maybe he just wants to pee on the rugs," I grumbled at Ben as we got in the car. He didn't answer, just wore his smirk and gave me his hawk's stare. His courtroom lawyer, moving in for the kill hawk stare. He almost seemed to be enjoying himself.

He drove, and I let him because I had things to do. I'd signed off with Becky, after asking her to call Shaun and whoever else she could get to meet us there. We could have ourselves a regular rumble. I ought to decide whether I wanted to be the Sharks or the Jets.

I had an advantage over Carl: an in with the Denver police. I called Hardin.

"Hardin here."

"It's Kitty, I need your help."

"What's wrong?" She sounded serious and business-like, which heartened me.

"I think I'm in trouble. It's the werewolves, they're after me."

"This has something to do with your little gang war, doesn't it? I'm not going to pick sides."

"*My* little gang war? I didn't start it, I'm just trying to clean it up!"

"So you admit you're involved?"

I couldn't say anything right, could I? "I think these are the werewolves involved in those murders at the warehouse."

"Are you sure?"

Then I realized that while I trusted Becky, we had no reason to believe that Mick was telling her the truth. Mick might not really be on our side. Carl might have told him to feed us the information, give us a false lead while he struck at another target.

At least, I might think that if I believed Carl had a clever cell in his entire brain.

"Yes."

"Where?"

"At the station. At KNOB."

"I suppose you're headed there now?" I told her yes, and she said, "I'll meet you." And hung up.

Looked like we were going to have us a rumble.

"You ready for this?" Ben said.

"I don't know."

"How many people you think he'll have with him?"

"Six, seven maybe. More if Meg is with him, too."

"And we've got the Denver PD. Not bad. What happens if Hardin and her people are late? Three of us can't fight seven of them. Four if Shaun gets there in time."

"Maybe I can talk to Carl. Talk him out of this."

"Like Gabe did? You bring the gun?"

"No," I said softly, knowing what he'd say to that. I was

being weak. I was in denial. "Maybe I can claw him to death."

"No worries. I've got the extras in the trunk."

Extras. Plural. The more tired I got the more ludicrous this plan sounded.

"I don't want to face him again."

"You only have to face him until the police show up. Remember this isn't about you. It's for Jenny."

That got me angry all over again. That, and the fact that Carl, predictably, hadn't gone after me directly, but after something close to me. The part of me he'd never been able to touch—my job. What a jerk.

Far too quickly, Ben's car roared into the station's parking lot. Becky was already there, and Shaun pulled in right behind us. They were hunched and wary, in defensive fighting stances. They looked like they might spring into battle, or leap back in the car and drive off at the slightest hint of danger. I couldn't decide which.

I jumped out of Ben's car before it stopped completely. "Is he here yet?"

Before they could answer, a truck pulled up to the curb, tires squealing, not even bothering to take the few extra seconds to swing into the parking lot. Carl and another man climbed out. He was another werewolf. A breath of musk and wild came with them, fur and skin, and something foreign. An enemy, an intruder. Opposing pack. Another truck and three more followed them. No Meg. Somehow, this was a relief.

I didn't have time to go for the weapons in the trunk. They spotted us. Without hesitating, Carl stalked toward the door. He was huge, tall and muscular—a monster even if I didn't know his other nature. His brown hair and beard needed trimming, and his whole manner was as animal as it could be without him shape-shifting completely. His pack held back, wary, watching what we would do.

Near the doors, I moved to intercept him, trusting that Ben would watch my back.

"Stop!" I called at him.

Carl didn't slow. "Who told you I was coming here? Who warned you?"

"You can't be here, Carl. You need to leave." Brave words. Stupid brave. I braced like my slight body could actually stop him, or even give him pause.

He bent his arms, cocked his fists, and I knew the move he'd throw at me. He'd punch up with one, drive down with the other, trapping me and smashing me into the ground. His lips drew back in a snarl.

I waited for him. I knew what was coming, and I waited. When the blow came, double fists moving like I knew they would because I'd seen this before, I ducked. I wasn't there, and when he lurched into the space I used to be, I shoved. Planted my shoulder in the soft space under his rib cage and pushed.

He stumbled but kept his feet, and for a moment we both froze, staring at each other, panting though our expended effort so far had been slight.

After all this time, something still bound us. Because of that, we couldn't tear each other apart like animals. The thought came to me, incongruous: *I used to have sex with this man.* I almost laughed. I couldn't remember what he tasted like.

"Stay back!" Ben shouted. I didn't look away from Carl, but in the corner of my vision I saw Ben move forward, holding a gun out and ready to fire. Carl's followers had spread out, arranging themselves in a line to move in on us—a wolf pack surrounding weak and injured prey. Ben halted their advance.

"You got silver?" one of them said.

"You bet your ass," Ben answered. "Now let these two have their little chat."

The wolves stayed back.

That left me and Carl to hash it out.

"What did you think you could do here?" I said.

"You invade my territory, I can do the same. I can tear you apart."

"The police are coming. They'll arrest you. It won't take them long to figure out what you did to Rick's people."

"That's none of their business." A tacit confession. He didn't even try to deny it, or pretend that he didn't know what I was talking about.

"You're a murderer! That is their business!"

He donned a thin smile. "You shouldn't have come back. You shouldn't have gotten involved."

"Yeah," I said. "Sucks to be me."

"Now, I attack you, and your boyfriend shoots me. Is that your plan?"

It would be so easy. End it—or at least this half of it—right here. Then Hardin would drive up, see Ben with a smoking gun, and throw him in jail. I didn't think I could handle that. Not again.

The plan was to hold Carl here long enough for Hardin to come get him. We'd come out of this with our hands clean.

"Only if he has to," I said.

"You should have quit when I told you to. None of this would have happened, not Washington, not this. The police shouldn't be involved in this—they wouldn't be, if you'd just shut up. If you'd done what I told you to, I would have kept you safe."

"Like you kept Jenny safe?"

Something changed in his expression. I'd managed to calm him—he'd stayed in one place, I'd kept him talking. But a rage burned in his eyes now. His skin flushed. The snarl returned.

"She left me."

"You should have let her go."

"She belonged to me—"

"She didn't belong to you! She didn't belong to anybody!"

Roaring, he lunged. Startled, I rushed backward, almost tripping on my own feet. He sparked the flight instinct— the two-legged, human version of it. I put up my arms to protect myself from the coming blow. Not very effective.

He grabbed my arm, swung me, and slammed me against the brick wall of the building. Stars burst in my head and my vision went dark for a second. Wolf sprang to life—*run, claw, fight, rip, run*—torn between fear and anger. I felt her in my bones.

"Kitty!" That was Ben. *Don't shoot*, I wanted to say, but couldn't. As soon as he turned from the henchmen to shoot Carl, they'd spring on him. He had to hold them back; he couldn't fight them all. Becky and Shaun didn't have guns, and I didn't think they could take them all on.

I couldn't speak, because Carl had his hands—thick, powerful hands—around my throat and had lifted. My feet kicked at air. Lungs fought for nonexistent breath. I gripped his wrist, dug in my nails, tried to pull his hand away, to flail at him, but he pinned me to the wall without effort. I couldn't even look at him. He forced my face up to a fading sky.

Just when I wanted to ask where the hell Hardin was, police sirens wailed. Tires squealed. Doors slammed. Impeccable timing.

No, not timing. Intent. She'd probably waited right around the corner, out of sight, until Carl did something that they could arrest him for. Get him for assault now, prove the warehouse murders later, after they already had him in custody. I thought I was using her for muscle, but she was using me for bait. Wonderful.

"Put your hands up! Move away from her! Let her go and step away!" Five or six voices screamed that at once.

Carl's hand tightened around my neck, and I felt the vibration of his growl.

Please, please...

I recognized Hardin's voice, "Mr. O'Farrell, put down your weapon! Let us handle this!"

Then handle it, goddammit!

The voices were still shouting at Carl to let me go. We could all get shot to pieces right here. I had to assume that Hardin had issued silver bullets to her people.

Then, my back slid against the wall and my feet touched ground. Air flooded my lungs, which rattled as I gasped. But he didn't let me go. I looked at his eyes, which were fire, bestial. His body was all sweat and musk. The fur, his wolf were close. If he sprouted claws right now, he could rip out my throat. Slash the jugular and I'd bleed out before I hit the ground.

"Don't do it," I whispered. "You'll die here if you do it."

The cops were still shouting, "Step away now, *now*!"

And I thought he was going to do it, silver bullet in the back or no, I thought he was going to rip my throat out.

What happened next happened very quickly. Carl made

one of those sudden moves—the ones you're not supposed to make around the police when they're pointing guns at you. I couldn't guess what he planned—if he wanted to get shot, if he thought he could move faster than bullets. Or if he simply took a chance in the hopes that it just might work.

He grabbed my wrist and yanked. I flew from the wall and into the open—between him and the cops.

A gun fired.

A punch nailed into my back. I stepped forward to keep my balance. Then, fire. Fierce pain through my chest dropped me. Like something had exploded inside me. My knees cracked on the sidewalk.

Carl ran around the corner and away, defended by his shield.

"Sawyer, hold fire, hold!" That was Hardin, sounding fierce.

The world stopped for a moment. I couldn't see anything outside of myself, I couldn't hear anything but my blood in my ears. I was breathing fast but wasn't getting any oxygen. Blood covered my hands—it was all over my chest, soaking my shirt, slick and red.

Shot, I'd been shot. My next breath squeaked. I ought to do something, I thought vaguely. I ought to scream or cry or something. I ought to fall down and die already.

But I stayed kneeling, staring at my own blood on my hands like it was part of a movie. Just art, or ketchup, or something. My breathing slowed, and with the fresh oxygen my vision cleared. And I realized the burst of pain had faded to an ache.

I pulled down my collar, wiped away blood, tried to find the hole—the bullet had gone all the way through between my heart and my collarbone; there was the wound, covered in caked blood. Already clotted. Already healing.

Someone's hands touched my face and forced me to look up. I flinched, startled, because I hadn't known anyone was there. Ben held my face and studied me with a wild gaze. His heart was racing. I could hear it.

"Kitty," he said roughly.

I slumped, gripping his arms to keep myself upright. Every muscle had turned to molasses. My laugh sounded more like a gasp. "It wasn't silver."

He slumped, too. We were in danger of melting into the ground. "Not silver."

I nodded quickly, and he pressed his face to mine. "Oh, my God," he sighed near my ear, then kissed my cheek. I clung to him.

Hardin barked a question. "Officer Sawyer—you're not packing silver?"

"Uh...no, ma'am. Didn't have time to file the requisition form." He sounded sheepish.

Thank God. Thank you thank you thank you...

"Next time, get those bullets. And don't fucking shoot the informant!"

This wasn't over. I felt a new pain—not from the wound, which had faded. Something else tore at my gut. Wolf. We'd been attacked. We'd been hurt. Now, it was up to her to protect us. She surged through my blood, took hold of my eyes, my senses. My whole body tensed as she seized me.

"Ben." My voice grated through my clenched jaw. I was Changing; it was coming so fast.

He knew what was happening. He pulled me to him, held me tight, and hissed in my ear. "Keep it together. Deep breaths, Kitty. Hold it in."

My skin was sliding, my bones melting, I thrashed at my clothes, had to get them off, had to get away—

"Hardin, get your people out of here!" Ben shouted. Finally giving in to what was happening, he ripped off my shirt and tugged at my bra.

Wrenching out of Ben's grip, I screamed.

*D*izzy, *angry. Can't see straight. Chest aches—injured. Not for long, already healing, but the pain lingers. So does the anger.*

She kicks at the ropes that trap her, tangle her legs— remnants of the old shape. Hadn't gotten rid of that false skin in time. It's come so quickly, so unexpectedly. But she is in danger. She has to protect herself, and she can run faster on four legs than on two.

An attack, hunters on all sides of her, cornering her— Her other half recognizes the two-legged hunters with their handheld burning deaths. Must defend herself. There—the one whose hand smells hot, burns with the scent of sulfur and oil. He's the one who hurt her.

She lowers her head and growls.

"Oh, my God," the voice behind her says. "Becky, Shaun, stop her!"

Nothing can stop her. Her body is wind, her claws are blades, her voice is thunder.

Now her target smells like fear. Sweat has broken out on his skin. When he takes a step back, she knows she has him. She will rip his flesh and taste his blood. Her lips draw back from fierce teeth and a salivating mouth as she launches herself toward her victim. She runs, her claws scraping on the pavement. Digs into the ground, leaps, stretching for him, and his scream thrills her blood. Her paws are on him, her rough pads scraping his false skin, and he falls—

A body intercepts her, knocking her away from her prey. She lands on her feet and looks. The attacker crouches, facing her, staring her down. Daring to stare her down. She pants and takes the scent of the intruder— one of her kind, one of her pack. The new female.

And before she can strike at her, to put her in her place, hands—human, naked hands—grab her from behind, pull at her, hold her. She snarls, fights, twists, slashes with claws, with teeth. Two of them hold her back. They are pack. They can't do this, she'll show them, she'll show them who's strongest—

The place is chaos. There is running and shouting. Still can't see straight for all the chaos.

"Kitty! Hold still, just hold still!"

Even as the growl rattles her lungs, a hand on her chest and a voice by her ear make her pause.

"Sh, Kitty. It's okay, you're safe. You're safe."

She stops struggling; the two-legged wolf holds her back.

This is her mate who holds her, who soothes her. Whining softly, she turns to him, licks his hand. He tastes like home.

"Sh," he keeps murmuring. "We're okay. We're going to be okay."

He radiates calm and she believes him.

Then the whole pack is there. Her little pack, all of them with her, all of them safe. She leans close to her mate, presses her body full against him, panting shallow breaths because she's still nervous. Still waiting for an attack. Have to trust the pack to take care of each other. She trusts

her mate with all her being. Letting her muscles relax, let-
ting the anger seep away, she settles into his arms.

"I don't know enough about this," he says, his voice
strained. "I don't know if she's going to be okay."

"She'll be okay," says the other. "Once she sleeps she'll
be fine. Try to get her to sleep."

So the voice continues, close to her ear, breathing
comfort into the fur of her neck. Furless, clawless hands
stroke her flanks, a strange and soothing touch.

And because he smells and sounds and feels like home,
she settles with him and closes her eyes.

I remembered being shot and started awake.

I lurched up onto an elbow and looked around. I was in
a corner of the KNOB lobby, wrapped in a scratchy wool
blanket, and curled up on the cold tile floor. Underneath,
I was naked.

Ben was standing nearby, talking to Detective Hardin and a couple of other cops. Ozzie was there, too, and
some other KNOB staffers. The station manager wore a
worried frown and rubbed a hand through his thinning
hair. Some of the cops were taking statements. Red and
blue lights flashed against the front windows.

Ben turned around before I could draw breath to speak.
Quickly he came over and knelt beside me. I screwed up
my face and felt vaguely ashamed. I pulled the blanket
tightly around my shoulders.

"What happened?" I said, my voice scratching.

"You got shot," he said.

"I remember that. What about after?"

"You didn't hurt anyone."

I gave a thin laugh. "Thank God for small favors." In truth, this relieved me immensely. I felt lighter.

Idly, he tucked a strand of hair behind my ear. Bloodstains covered his shirt, complete with handprints and streaks from where I'd grabbed his arms. "How do you feel?"

"Crappy. I didn't want to hurt anyone." The horror of it took a long time to settle over me. Injured and frightened, I'd shifted in the middle of a crowd of people I'd have done it and not thought twice. I'd have just been defending myself. "I can't believe I got shot."

"Tell me about it." He sat beside me and tucked me under his shoulder, wrapping his arm around me. I snuggled in closer. "Hardin sent a couple of cars after Carl. They're cordoning off the neighborhood to look for him."

"They won't find him."

"I know. She took the rest of his guys into custody. She thinks she'll find forensic evidence linking them to the warehouse. She seems to be having a good time with all this."

"She wants to try out her silver-lined jail cell."

"Well, more power to her."

The woman herself came over then, looking tired but smug. I had an impulse to stand—I didn't want to have to look up at her. From wolf eye level no less. But I was too tired, and Ben was too comfortable. Blearily, I stared up at her.

Wary, she studied me, edging toward me like she might toward a wild animal. Which I supposed I was. She'd seen me shift—seen both halves of my being. I'd attacked one of her people, though the specific memory was fuzzy. But she seemed to have the intention of treating me like a human being. However much of a struggle that would be. She visibly gathered herself.

"How are you?" she said. The concern was touching.

I shrugged, then winced, because I still hurt some. My ribs felt bruised, and my whole body felt pounded. "I've been worse."

"For what it's worth, I apologize. Officer Sawyer's going to get a reprimand. Just because you weren't permanently hurt doesn't mean he gets away with shooting a civilian."

"And if he'd had silver bullets?" I said. Both Ben and I stared up at her, waiting for the answer.

"Just be glad that he didn't." She walked back to her people and the cleanup.

I didn't even want to think about it. "I need my clothes."

"They kind of got trashed. You ready to get out of here?"

I propped myself against Ben and braced against the wall to get myself to my feet. My muscles popped, and my bones creaked. Ben pulled me to my feet without effort. I let him hold me up. I'd turned Wolf twice in the last twenty-four hours. I'd never done that before, never turned a second time so soon after the first. Almost, it seemed the pieces hadn't come back together quite right. Fur still peeked between the cracks. Wolf still looked out of my eyes. My brain felt fuzzy, the world looked strange; the shadows seemed to loom.

He must have noticed me craning my neck and squinting, trying to focus.

"You're going to have to sleep a week when this is all over," he said.

God, that sounded so nice... "I could just let Carl kill me. Sleep all I want then."

He gave me an odd sideways look.

"Kitty! Are you all right?" Ozzie intercepted us. He was actually wringing his hands.

"I'll be fine," I said. Though I must have looked awful, all tangled hair and bloodstains. "So, are you worried about me, or are you really worried about your cash cow?"

He gave me a look that was half hurt, half admonishing. "Geez, Kitty, give it a rest. When I heard the gun and they told me who got shot I about had a heart attack. Don't ever do that again."

I smiled tiredly. "I'll try not to. Ozzie, have you met Ben?"

Ben said, "He introduced himself while you were asleep."

Ozzie pointed at him. "Don't let her get shot again."

"I think we'd better get home and cleaned up," he replied.

Ozzie found me a T-shirt and sweats from the stash of KNOB giveaways. I could add them to the million KNOB T-shirts I already had. I was just grateful not to have to drive home naked.

During the ride home, Ben kept asking if I was okay. Huddling in the passenger seat, I kept muttering that I was fine.

Finally, he gave a frustrated sigh. "You're damned lucky, you know that?"

Yeah, I was. I had to remember that. I smiled at him. "Thanks. For taking care of me."

"We're pack."

I wished he would stop saying that. I wasn't sure why it was starting to piss me off. He wasn't saying anything that wasn't true. Maybe because it sounded like a cop-out. Like if we weren't pack, he'd have been out of here a long time ago.

chapter 13

The car's tires squealed as Ben swung into the parking lot of his building. With his help, I stumbled out of the passenger seat and limped toward the front door. I hurt all over. The bullet wound itself had faded to an ache, but the shock of it, the shape-shifting, and waking up on the hard floor had wracked my whole body. I wanted a very hot shower.

Ben stopped before we reached the front of the building, and I lurched to a halt beside him. I started to ask why—I wasn't really paying attention, not like I should have been. I was lulled into a false sense of security, tucked snugly under Ben's arm. But then I saw Cheryl marching toward us on the sidewalk. She wore her usual T-shirt and jeans, and a furious expression. I hadn't seen that expression since she caught me borrowing her Metallic Mayhem nail polish when I was eleven.

Out of all the trouble I was currently facing, I hadn't expected this.

"What's she doing here?" I muttered.

"She's your sister," Ben said. "You tell me."

I'd done something. Something so horribly wrong and sinister she had to come in person to chew me out. And I thought I knew what it was. "Mom went in for surgery yesterday," I said. "I wasn't there." No, I was at the shooting range, learning how to be a killer.

A sudden cold washed through me, and I tried to dismiss it. If something had gone wrong with the surgery, someone would have called me right away, not waited a day.

"Cheryl, what's wrong?" I said when she was close enough.

She put her hands on her hips. "I've been waiting for you to get back. I'm taking you to the hospital to see Mom since you can't seem to be bothered to get yourself over there." Then her eyes grew wide, and the color left her face. She was staring at Ben's bloody shirt. The blood had turned dry and crunchy. My own shirt had a sizable spot of blood on the upper chest, where the wound was still leaking.

"Holy crap, what happened to you guys?" She started to look a bit green.

"I got shot," I said.

"You *what*? Oh, my God. Why aren't you in a hospital?" Her voice was going shrieky.

I was so not in the mood for any of this.

"Because I'm a werewolf and it wasn't a silver bullet."

"Oh my God... what... what have you gotten yourself into?"

I only sighed. This would take way too long to explain. In my silence, Cheryl kept going, and I realized that this whole talking too much thing wasn't just me. It ran in the family.

"Kitty, *what* is going on? Are you in some kind of trouble? Is that why you couldn't go to the hospital? And you—" She pointed at Ben. "This all started when she met you. This is your fault, isn't it?"

"Actually, no," Ben said, full of mock cheerfulness. "Kitty made this mess pretty much on her own."

Please, let me pass out now. I didn't want to have to talk to either of them anymore.

"Listen, Cheryl, can you not tell Mom and Dad about this?" I could imagine Mom's reaction exceeding Cheryl's level of hysteria.

"*Not* tell Mom and Dad? Are you *crazy*?"

"Oh, come on, what about all those times you snuck out of the house and told me not to tell? And that time Todd came over—"

"But you *did* tell!" she screeched.

"No I didn't, they figured it out on their own because you were an *idiot*!"

Ben was rubbing his forehead like he had a headache.

I took a deep breath and tried to start over. "I'm trying to keep you guys out of this."

"Kitty!" Cheryl said, making the word part demand, part reprimand, part plea. She was four years older than me. Our relationship had started on a foundation of years of forced babysitting and commands from our parents that were all some variation of "Cheryl, look after your sister." After she left for college, my teenage years continued in pure, unsupervised bliss. Our lives diverged radically after that, but we loved each other. We were family. And the tone of voice she was using now evoked a long history of responsibility and authority.

I spoke as calmly as I could. "Cheryl, I'm sorry I haven't been to the hospital yet. I'm sorry I can't explain everything. I'm okay. I got shot, but I'm okay. I—I think you should go home, or go back to Mom, or whatever. I'll call later. I really need to take a shower."

"No," she said. "No, enough of this, you haven't been straight with any of us since this happened to you. You know those old lists, how to tell if someone's a drug addict? The secrecy, the lies, the weird behavior—that's you! That's totally you!"

Wow. She had a point. Now if I could just *quit* being a lycanthrope. "What the hell are you going to do about it—run an intervention?" God, this wasn't going well. I had to get her out of here.

Beside me, Ben stiffened, his attention suddenly drawn elsewhere. He turned, his nose flaring, taking in a scent. He started to unzip my backpack, where he'd stashed a handgun.

"What is it?" I said.

"Do you smell that?"

I took a deep breath to taste the air.

"Kitty, what is it, what's going on?"

"Be quiet," I said, straining my ears.

Then I caught it. Ben had only been a werewolf for a few months, but he had a better nose than I did. Something was out there, something wrong. An alien touch in the air. Wolf, but not pack. No. Oh, no. Hardin hadn't found Carl. Single-minded, brutal Carl who probably only had one thought in his pea brain right now: me. He'd tracked us here, we were all doomed.

But this smelled female. This smelled familiar.

Ben drew the handgun from the backpack.

"Holy *shit*! You have a *gun*!" Cheryl cried.

"Cheryl, can you go back to your car and get out of here, please?"

"What's happening? I'm not leaving until you tell me what's happening!"

The figure, the intruder, finally appeared, coming around the corner behind Cheryl, moving toward us. Keeping Cheryl between us.

"Cheryl, move, please," I begged. My sister finally turned, to see what we were staring at—to see what was behind her.

"He wanted me to check if you were still alive," Meg said.

Ben dropped the bag and aimed at her, arms and gaze steady. Meg stopped and looked startled for a moment, like she was about to turn and flee, like she thought he might shoot. She wore jeans, a tank top, and sandals, and her long black hair draped over her shoulders. Her skin was tanned brown, her features were fine, exotic. I'd always thought she was beautiful.

Ben didn't shoot her outright. He was a lawyer, he was rational. He knew what this would look like when the cops arrived. Once she realized that, Meg relaxed a little and crossed her arms.

She kept talking. "He said, 'Don't confront her. Don't let her see you. Her bad-ass alpha male's got a gun. Don't push them,' he said. I think he's afraid of you."

"That warms my heart," I said flatly. "What about you?"

She didn't come any closer, which was sort of an answer. "You were smarter than me, picking somebody to turn," she said. "But how did you convince a sane man to let you bite him?" She talked like he wasn't even here. Ben didn't flinch.

A year or so ago, she'd made a bid for Carl's place by picking an alpha male to replace him. By *making* an alpha male to replace him. The plan had backfired horribly. The guy had been psychotic and couldn't handle the lycanthropy. A lot of people died.

"I didn't bite him. I didn't turn him. I just happened to be there to pick up the pieces. That's why we're together." And I liked him. I'd picked up the pieces because I liked him. Couldn't lose sight of that detail. I ought to tell him. I let my hand brush his leg. His whole body was tense. I wasn't sure he even felt me.

"Whatever you say," she said with a smirk, like she didn't believe me. Like she didn't respect me. We weren't equals in her eyes, but her body language spoke differently. She kept her distance. She looked Ben up and down like he was a piece of meat.

"What do you want, Meg?" I sounded exhausted.

"I don't suppose you'd tell me where Rick is?"

"You were never very good at subtlety and intrigue, were you?"

"You give us Rick, we'll let you leave Denver again. You and your mate both."

"Don't you get it? I don't want to leave. I can't leave. Everything I have is here, and if you won't leave me alone, then I'll fight."

Then she looked at Cheryl. She had to guess who she was to me—the same blond hair, short and tucked behind her ears. Same face. Even a little of the same smell—our human family.

"You have a lot to lose," Meg said. She took a step toward my sister, reaching out like she wanted to touch her. I almost grabbed the gun from Ben's hand and shot her myself. No one was going to touch my family. Cheryl had the sense to step back.

"Get away from her," Ben said, holding her in the gun's sights.

I kept myself from rushing at Meg, claws outstretched. Calmly, I said, "All the more reason to fight."

That raised her hackles. "You think just because you're famous that protects you? That you can waltz in here and take over? That we'll just bow down to you? It takes more than that to be an alpha. You don't know anything. You may have fooled the people who listen to your show, but you don't know *anything*!" She started to march off.

"Meg?" She halted, apparently willing to listen.

We were just posturing. This was the growling stage. She wouldn't start a fight without backup. I began to relax. The old fears started to fade. She was all bluster. More than that, though, she was just wrong.

"Have you ever been pregnant?" I asked it on an impulse, out of curiosity. I just wanted to know.

She almost chuckled. "Werewolves don't get pregnant. *We* can't get pregnant." She said this with an air of triumph, as if I had just demonstrated my lack of knowledge, and she was happy to rub my face in it.

I smiled sadly. I remembered Dr. Shumacher's words, that most women lycanthropes simply might never realize if they got pregnant. Maybe Meg just didn't know.

"You're wrong. We can get pregnant. The pregnancy doesn't survive shape-shifting. You might never even know it."

She gaped at me, astonished, like I'd slapped her. How many woozy, crampy mornings was she looking back on? How many times had she just written it off to an odd cycle? I didn't want to know.

"Meg, you're ignorant, you're a blockhead, and me

waltzing in here and taking over has got nothing to do with me being famous and everything to do with you being completely useless. You and Carl both." I managed to say that whole thing without raising my voice.

Snarling, she resumed her retreat.

Only after we heard her car door slam, the engine start, and the tires peel out of the parking lot, did Ben blow out a breath and lower his gun. I sat down right there on the sidewalk because my legs had turned to goo. Sheer will-power had been keeping me on my feet, but blood loss and nerves finally got the better of me.

Ben knelt and put his hand on my shoulder. "You okay?"

I leaned into him. "That thing I said, about picking up the pieces and that's why we're together—that's not just it. I mean, there's more than that, right?"

"We should have this conversation later," he said, glancing at my sister, who was standing over us, looking down with bugged-out eyes.

"What was all that about?" Cheryl said, even more hysterically, though it didn't seem possible.

"I said it was a long story," I sighed as Ben hauled me to my feet.

"No, not the mess. Not just the mess. I mean about the pregnant part."

I figured Mom had told her, but apparently not. I couldn't even look at her. Ben pulled me close and put a kiss on my hair, over my ear.

"Are you pregnant?" she said.

I smiled thinly. "Not anymore."

"Oh, geez. I'm sorry." She said it to both of us, and she looked sad.

I took her hand and squeezed it. She squeezed back,

and our argument disappeared. "Cheryl, there's kind of a war going on. I need you to go home, stay inside. Keep everyone inside. Don't let anyone in unless you know them really well. If you see anyone outside the house, if you see anything odd—if anything even feels odd—call 911 and tell them you have an intruder in the house. Don't even hesitate."

"What—"

I held up my hand to stop her. She was going to ask, again, what was going on. "That woman and some other people would happily kill me if they got the chance. We're not going to let that happen."

"Kitty—"

"Where's Dad? Is he at the house?"

"No, he's staying with us while Mom's in the hospital."

"Good. It's going to be okay. I'll call you later. I'll see Mom as soon as I can."

"Okay," she said, and sounded young. Then she hugged me, bloodstains and all. "Be careful."

"You, too."

We watched her return to her car and drive away. Ben kept hold of the gun the whole time, in case something else lurked in the shadows. Without a word, we made it inside. I made it into the shower. My upper chest had a puckered spot of skin where the bullet hole had been. That was it. I kept picking at it; it was healing, almost smoothing out under my touch.

I didn't want to leave the stream of water. I didn't want to go back to the war. But I did.

I asked Ben, who was making food, "Any word?"

"Nope."

"Are you sure?"

"Yes."

Evening came, and we didn't get any calls. No one had spotted Carl after the KNOB attack. Hardin said she'd put a stakeout at his and Meg's house, but the place seemed to be empty. That meant Carl and Meg had run for the hills. They could be anywhere now. Arturo and Rick would be waking soon. Arturo would do something—he wouldn't sit back while Rick challenged him. The trouble was, I couldn't guess what he'd do, where he'd send his people, who he'd attack first. I had to wait for a call.

I was becoming a control freak. It was part of leading a pack.

Ben made chicken and pasta for supper. He was a decent cook—yet another reason to keep him around. But I couldn't eat. I stood by the door to the balcony, staring out. From the table, where two sets of plates and utensils were set out with a ceramic bowl of food in the middle, he pestered. "You need to eat."

"I can't."

"You should."

Pouting, I sounded like a spoiled child. "I just can't."

He dropped his fork on his plate, making a ringing noise. The silence after was rigid with tension. After a long moment he said, "I wish I could fix everything. I wish I could make it all go away. But I can't. So I thought, I'll make dinner. Maybe that'll help. But I guess not."

He wore a white T-shirt, jeans. His light brown hair was a bit too long, rumpled from him running his hands through it. His face was lined, tired. Full of character. He looked like a freaking rock star. I couldn't take my eyes off him. I wanted to cling to him like a leech.

"Thank you," I said, on impulse. "Thanks for standing by me."

The smile grew wider, and he bowed his head. "Well, you know. We're—"

I held up a hand to stop him. "Don't . . . say it. Just don't."

"I don't know what else to say." Roughly, he stood from the table. Grabbed the bowl of pasta and shoved it into the fridge. The whole appliance rattled. I was relieved, though; for a moment I thought he was going to throw it.

"You don't have to say anything."

But he kept going, coming out to the living room. "Maybe you're right, maybe you've been right all along, that if we weren't both werewolves we wouldn't be together. That we'd have no reason to be together."

"I never—"

He waved me off with a frustrated brush of his arm. "No, I know you've never said it. But you've been thinking it right from the start. And I wanted you to be wrong. I wanted to prove you wrong. But hey—you're never wrong."

"Ben!"

But he was already marching back to the bedroom, where he slammed the door behind him. I curled up on the sofa and covered my face with my hands. What happened if I won this war, yet lost everything I was trying to save?

When my cell phone, sitting on the coffee table, rang, my brain rattled. All my nerves twitched. It was like I forgot what to do with it, then I rushed to answer.

"Good morning," said Rick.

And so it starts. "Hi."

"What's been happening? Anything from Carl?"

"He went after KNOB," I said.

"And?"

This was actually almost working. I ought to be pleased. "Hardin has four of his wolves in custody. Carl got away. Hardin has people looking but they haven't found him." I'm not sure I wanted them to. I wasn't sure they could handle a cornered wolf.

"And you're all right? Your people are all right?"

I hesitated, then decided there'd be time for the long version later. "I'm fine. We're all fine. Anything happening on your end?"

"Yes. Charlie and Violet saw Arturo leave Obsidian. I want to move in while he's gone," he said, and his voice was too calm. Vampiric, I realized. The city could be crumbling around him and his tone wouldn't change.

This felt like a trap. I could see it. We were supposed to draw Arturo out, not race into the heart of his territory. "You can't take his stronghold. He'll have people protecting it—"

"It's his stronghold, which means he'll have to come back. I'll wait for him, then take him."

"But Rick, where is he? Where'd he go?"

"I was hoping one of your people had spotted him."

"I haven't heard anything." I gripped the phone and gritted my teeth. My spike in anxiety seemed to be making up for his calm. "This could be a trap. He leaves, makes it real obvious so you know about it, and as soon as you show up he busts your ass."

"That's why I'd like you and Ben to come help me. And any of the other werewolves you can call on."

My first impulse was to yell at him. Did he think we were his lackeys? Did he expect to be able to call on us the way Arturo called on Carl? But that had been the arrangement—an alliance to help each other. My getting cold feet didn't change that.

"What about Carl and Meg? Where are they?" I said.

"Again, I was hoping you'd have heard something."

"Geez, Rick, what do you expect me to be able to do? I can't battle a lair full of vampires. I can't ask anyone else to do that."

Ben had emerged and was leaning on the wall by the sofa, watching me, brow raised in a question. I found I couldn't look at him. But I could feel him, smell his presence washing over me.

The flavor of Rick's calm changed, taking on an edge—tension, held tightly in check. "You can't quit now, Kitty. You're way beyond being able to back out of this. I'm moving on Obsidian, and you'll help me because you can't let Arturo win this."

He was right. I'd set this series of events in motion. Backing out now would mean losing. This wasn't a game where I could pick up my pieces and go home. But I still didn't like it. "Have you given any more thought about who your spy is?"

"I'm not convinced there is one. I think Arturo had one of us followed and got lucky with the warehouse. Listen to me. We trap Arturo—I only need to get him alone for a few minutes, and I need you to watch my back. Dack, Violet, and Charlie are already here. When Arturo's gone, he won't be able to help Carl and Meg. *Then* we can take them out."

"Or we can take them out first—they're scared, we riled them up."

"You've seen them, then? You've confronted them?"

I hesitated. "Yes."

"And they're still alive?"

"The cops were there, there were too many people, I couldn't just—"

"But you see, Kitty: I can. You've taken us this far. Let me carry us the rest of the way."

I covered the phone and stared at the ceiling. Point of no return. I'd sped by it without even noticing.

Ben went to the door and picked up my backpack. He stayed there, waiting. He had a trunk full of gear that said we could do this. Damn Cormac and his armory.

I turned back to the phone. "When should we be there?"

"Now."

I hissed out a breath. "Okay. Fine. We're on the way. I'm going to make some calls. You'd better keep your phone handy in case I find out this is all some horrible trick."

"Will do. Park a block south of the building and I'll meet you."

I shoved the phone in my pocket. When I reached the door, Ben handed me my bag.

"We're going to Obsidian?" he said.

"Yeah."

"Then let's go." He was outside before I could say anything. Like *I'm sorry*.

In five minutes, we were on the road. Ben drove, his attention focused. Not looking at me, not saying a word. I wanted to cry. But I had those calls to make.

"Shaun, it's Kitty."

"What's happening?" he said, his voice urgent. We'd all been waiting by our phones.

"Rick's moving, but I need some eyes. Any word where Carl and Meg are?"

"Someone's watching the house. I'll find out."

"And if anybody spots Arturo, I want to know about it."

"Got it. I'll call back in a minute."

He was straightforward. Reliable. A good lieutenant. I'd been lucky, finding him when I did. Or maybe my instincts were better than I thought they were. Some of my instincts, anyway.

I was torn between wanting to make more calls, and wanting to leave the line open for Shaun and Rick. I risked one. Cheryl answered the phone.

"Hi, Cheryl?"

"Kitty, oh my God, are you okay? Is everything okay?"

"I was going to ask you the same thing." I couldn't tell anything by her voice. She still had the hysterical edge going.

"Everything's fine here. Dad left the hospital after dinner. Mom was asleep. They've still got her doped up pretty good. But everyone's fine. We haven't seen anything."

Good. "That's what I wanted to hear. I have to get off the line, but I'll call again. Maybe I'll wait until morning if everything's okay."

"Be careful."

"Thanks."

I clicked the line off and waited for Shaun to call back.

Ben kept looking in the rearview mirror, repeatedly, more than the average driving maneuver warranted.

"What is it?"

"I think we're being followed."

Oh, that was almost funny. I twisted around to look out the back window. "Are you serious?"

"Could you be a little less obvious?" Ben said.

"But this is hilarious. We're being followed? Really? Do I get to shoot out the window next?"

"Kitty, sit down."

I faced front and sat. By then, we'd pulled off the freeway at Colfax and turned east.

That was when the red and blue flashing lights started.

"Great," Ben muttered, shifting the wheel to pull us over to the curb. "Unmarked police car." Sure enough, a dark sedan, unmarked and unremarkable, pulled up behind us. The lights flashed from a panel on the back of the sun visor, behind the windshield.

"I, uh, don't suppose we could outrun 'em?"

Ben gave me another look. The annoyed look that had become so common. He said, "No situation has ever been improved by trying to outrun the cops."

The sedan's driver side door opened. Somehow, I was unsurprised when Detective Hardin stepped out.

I put my hand on the door handle, preparing to pile out to confront her, but Ben said, "Don't. We've been pulled over, we're going to sit and wait like good little citizens."

He helpfully rolled down the window. When Hardin leaned in, she was smiling.

"Hi," she said.

She was supposed to be one of the good guys. She may not have believed it, but we were all on the same side. I couldn't let her hold us here. So I did the only thing I could—I let my big mouth get the better of me.

"Detective—what the hell are you doing here? Are you *still* following me?"

I should have guessed that she was used to me by now. Her expression didn't flicker. "Yep. You seem to know where all the interesting people are."

Great. Just great.

She went on. "Those guys we caught today seem perfectly

willing to rat out everyone involved. They just want to be let out before Tuesday. What's Tuesday?"

"Next full moon," I said.

Hardin winced. "Right. Got it. So. Who are you going to see now?"

Then my phone rang. I swore, as soon as this night was over I was going to shove it down the garbage disposal.

"Yeah?"

"Kitty, it's Shaun. Becky tried to call Mick—he was watching Carl and Meg's place. But we can't get a hold of him. Something happened, they may be on to us."

"Mick was out at their place?"

"He was supposed to be."

"Look, the cops have someone staking out their place and haven't seen anything. Would Mick have followed them into the hills?"

"Maybe."

"Someone should go check on him. We need to know what they're doing out there."

"Becky and Wes are on it."

"What about Arturo?"

"No sign."

I groaned. "I don't like this."

"Can I help?" he said.

"Keep looking out at my sister's, but have your phone handy. We may need some ass-saving later on."

Hardin was staring at me. "Arturo? Denver's Master vampire? The one I want to pin those murders on?"

"Uh, yeah." Ben could jump in to save me anytime, but he seemed happy to sit back and watch me dig my own hole.

"You going after him?" the detective asked.

"It's more like we're trying to keep him from coming after us."

"I thought the best way to do that was to stay home and not invite them in."

"Um, yeah. Usually."

"I want this guy, Kitty. Help me get him."

"Can you handle him? Can you really handle him?"

"A trunk full of stakes and holy water says I can," she said. "I've been doing my homework."

"You have no idea what you're getting into," Ben said.

"I'm looking forward to finding out," she said.

My phone chose that opportune moment to ring. Again. It couldn't possibly be anything good.

"What!" I said.

"I'd like a word with you, Katherine. We need to end this, before we see another bloodbath." Arturo, as refined as ever. My skin pricked; the hair on my neck prickled. Where was he? And what was he doing? How badly were we all screwed this time?

I hoped my voice didn't shake too badly. "A word with me? Why not Rick?"

"You'll see. I want to deal with you and you alone."

"I think this is a trick. I think it's a trap. No, I won't do it."

"Oh, you'll come speak with me."

I laughed. "I will?"

"Yes. Because I'm standing next to your mother's hospital bed."

The phone clicked off.

A sickly, hot/cold fever washed over me, and my gut melted into my feet. My lips went numb. I couldn't feel anything. I leaned back against the headrest.

"Kitty?" Ben said. "What's wrong?"

"What is it?" Hardin echoed.

My voice didn't work. This was Rick's fault, I wanted to scream. Wanted to growl. Wolf started thrashing—pack was in danger. My human pack, but still. Had to run, had to fight. I swallowed, counted, coiled the fear deep inside. Kept it together.

"Kitty," Ben said in a low voice, drawing me back to myself. His hand clamped over my arm, a steadying pressure.

"That was Arturo." I gestured with my still-on phone. My hand was shaking. "He's got my mom."

The pause only lasted a beat. "Do you know where?" Hardin said. She had her radio in her hand.

I nodded and told her the hospital. "She just had surgery."

Hardin was talking into her radio, calling for backup.

"Ben, we have to go help my mom," I said, and at the same time more thoughts slammed into me. More implications. This wasn't an accident. This was a setup. "Arturo knows Rick'll go after Obsidian. It's a trap."

Quickly I dialed Rick's number. It rang. And rang, and rang. "Shit."

"I'll go," Ben said. "I'll get to Obsidian to help Rick. You go with Hardin to the hospital."

I looked at Hardin. "Is that okay?"

"Sure. Come on." She headed back to her car.

Squeezing Ben's hand, I said, "Be careful."

"You, too."

I jumped out of the car to follow Hardin. I only got about halfway when I heard, "Kitty!"

Ben left the car and trotted toward me, hefting my backpack. I met him halfway, the late-night traffic roaring past us. Over us, the dark sky was washed out by city lights.

"Don't forget this." Ben handed me the bag. It had a weight snugged firmly inside that had become familiar. The handgun. "I put some stakes in there, too."

"Cool. Good."

Then he kissed me. Hand on my cheek, holding me steady, he covered my lips with his and urged open my mouth. I responded, melting against him. The movement lingered, passionate, flushing through my whole body. The touch was fire. I wanted to fall against him and keep him that close to me forever. My hands clenched on his arms.

He pulled away. "Be careful," he said, his voice tight. Then he retreated to his car. His jaw was taut, lips frowning, determined and driven.

That kiss was almost like saying goodbye.

"Kitty, come on!" Hardin called from inside her car.

Then we were back to the gangster movie. Ben drove off.

He'd be all right, I knew he would.

I climbed into the passenger seat of Hardin's car, and we peeled back onto the road.

"Lucky girl," she observed, her smile amused.

"Yeah," I said, still breathless. Yeah, I was.

chapter 14

She switched on all the sirens and lights, and we sped off at superspeed. I had calculated twenty minutes to get to the hospital. We might make it in ten.

"Tell me about Arturo," Hardin said, totally calm, not at all like she was speeding down Denver's streets at eighty miles an hour.

Where to start? "He's a vampire. I don't know how old. Maybe two or three hundred years—"

"You know, I can't even comprehend that," she said, giving a short laugh. "He was alive when George Washington was alive. What does that mean? How does this guy look at the world?"

"It means we don't matter to him," I said. "We're just a flash in the pan."

"What else?"

"He has flunkies, followers. I don't know if he'll have any of them here. I'm guessing he left them to guard the homestead. But if they are here, they'll protect him."

Her expression pursed, contemplating the dilemma: they were vampires, monsters, and she could plow right through them to get to her quarry. But they were also individuals who were entitled to due process.

"If we do run into them, how do I stop them? Can I do it without killing them?"

"I don't know. Lots of things'll hurt them: sunlight, holy water. Maybe even garlic. Staking's what kills them."

"So those stories are true."

"A lot of them, yeah."

"Good." She reached to her collar and pulled a chain with a cross pendant from under her shirt. She left it hanging over her collar.

We arrived at the hospital. After hours, the place seemed almost calm.

"All right, where's my backup," she muttered as she pulled up to the curb along the emergency drive. At this hour, that was probably the only entrance that would be open. I was out of the car and running for the doors before Hardin even stopped the car. "Kitty, wait!"

I didn't. Incongruously, the place was brightly lit, like a beacon. The rest of the world was so dark right now.

Inside, I hit the linoleum and didn't stop. I looked for a sign that would tell me how to get to the main part of the hospital, and where I could find Mom's room. I must have looked dangerous because a uniformed security guard, hand on his belt, moved to intercept me.

I realized: I could knock him over. Let out a little bit of Wolf and knock him aside. But I didn't. I begged.

"I need to get in, one of your patients may be in danger! Please!"

Hardin had followed close behind me and flashed her badge. "Let her through."

The guard stepped aside, and I ran past him. Vaguely,

I was aware of Hardin following. I didn't wait for her. I only had one thought in my head: *Please, let her be safe.*

Up some stairs, through a door, down a hall, and around a corner, we came to her room. I smelled her. The door was open, and it was dark. The bed and its occupant were visible only by pale light bleeding from the hallway. Mom was asleep, her head tilted slightly on the pillow, arms resting on the blanket, tangled in a mess of IV tubes and wires. Around the odors of illness and medication, I smelled her. She was breathing, her heart pounded steadily, she was alive. But pale. Her face was lined, even in sleep.

Sitting in a chair by her bedside, tilted with a view toward the door, watching her sleep, was Arturo.

Blood throbbed in my skull, and I thought I might faint.

"How did you get in here?" I said, my voice shaky. This could go very badly. "What are you doing?" I'd been told that the prohibition against vampires entering without invitation didn't apply to public, commercial property. Apparently, the hospital room was public space.

His gaze shifted to me almost lazily, unconcerned. He struck such an incongruous picture: he sprawled in the plastic chair like it was a throne, one leg stretched before him, both elbows resting on the thin arms. He wore tailored slacks, a white shirt buttoned at the collar, and a suit jacket. On him, the ensemble looked formal, elegant. He was a Victorian gentleman landed in the modern age.

Hardin joined me, blocking light as she stood in the doorway. She held her gun aimed at the vampire. No, it wasn't a gun. It was a hand-sized crossbow, with a wooden shaft loaded.

"Don't move. I'll shoot," Hardin said, authoritative and coplike. Arturo appeared unconcerned.

"Detective Hardin, I'd like you to rest for a moment," Arturo said. He spoke slowly, with an almost musical tone. He'd caught her gaze. The two were looking into each other's eyes like they were the only people in the world.

I knew she wouldn't be able to handle the vampires.

"Lower your weapon, please," he said. And she did. She looked relaxed, but her face held a quizzical expression, her brow slightly furrowed, like some part of her wondered why she was obeying him. Some part of her still held on to herself. Nonetheless, she'd fallen under his spell.

"Arturo, stop it," I said.

"Detective Hardin, step into the hallway for a moment. Lean against the wall and rest. Thank you."

Hardin slipped out the door, slumping against the wall as if she really had decided to rest there a moment.

I was all alone with him. My ill mother and him. Quickly I wiped a tear away. It was all over. All of it was for nothing.

"What do you want?" I whispered.

"I only want to talk," he said. "We're both safe here. We can't do battle here."

"You—you won't hurt her?" I was crying anxious, silent tears, and I hated that I was doing it. I felt so weak and helpless.

Slowly, absently almost, he shook his head. "I could save her, if you like."

He could drain her, turn her, and in three days she'd become like him. Invincible, immortal, cured.

"So could I. I offered. She refused."

"She's a wise woman."

"Yes, she is."

"Carl has to go. I see that. I told him not to strike at you. I told him that stunt last night was a ploy to draw us out. That if we stayed calm, you couldn't touch us. I'm not surprised he didn't listen to me."

"He's predictable," I said.

"Are you ready to replace him?"

"Yes."

"I could help you."

He could. In a word, a gesture, he could destroy Carl and Meg. All I'd have to do was step into the vacancy. That, and sell my soul to Arturo.

"I can't owe you anything, Arturo. I don't want to be in your debt for this."

"I thought so. I had to try, though. Carl didn't have your scruples when he took me up on that offer."

I hadn't heard that story. I hadn't ever thought about the alpha male Carl must have had to fight to replace. When I'd been attacked, infected, when I'd joined the pack, Carl had seemed like a god, enduring and eternal.

Arturo stood in a fluid movement, incomprehensibly graceful. He was sitting, then he was standing, his hands curled behind his back. He neared my mother's bed and leaned over it.

"They didn't remove it all," he said, scrutinizing her, studying her with a narrowed gaze. "She'll have months of chemotherapy ahead of her. Even after that it could come back anytime, anyplace. Her bones. Her blood. Her brain."

"How do you know that? You don't know that."

"I feel it in her blood. I feel it traveling." He held a hand, spread flat, a few inches over her chest, like he really could feel tiny cells of cancer wreaking havoc. "Her blood is sick."

I choked on a sob. My voice scraped like sandpaper. "Please, Arturo. Leave her alone."

When he touched Mom's face, a light brush of fingers along her chin, I almost screamed.

"What would you do to keep her safe, Katherine?"

Arturo had never been able to bring himself to call me Kitty. The name was beneath his dignity. Now when he said my full name, it felt like fingers curling around my throat, squeezing.

"Anything," I whispered.

His hand rested on my mother's throat, where he could squeeze and strangle her. "You'll take Carl's place. You'll answer to me."

"You can't do this." An empty, unconvincing denial.

"But I have done ever so much worse to get where I am."

I flashed on the memory of him dropping Carl with a twist of his arm. He'd incapacitated Hardin with a word. He was too strong, I couldn't stop him.

I wished I had telekinesis, to throw him across the room. I wished to bring down lightning bolts from the sky. I wished for a bag of garlic and a bottle of holy water. I wished I was religious and wore a cross around my neck.

I considered. I took a step backward, into the doorway, where I could see Detective Hardin leaning just outside. Her cross would hurt him, but it had to touch him.

"Katherine," Arturo said. "You shouldn't have to think about this. I can feel her pulse under my hand. I can stop it."

I needed another few seconds.

"Ben, too," I said, stalling. I turned my back to him, feigning despair, to hide what I was doing when I shifted aside the collar of Hardin's shirt. "Don't hurt him. Ben and I for Carl and Meg."

"Of course. I assumed as much."

Hardin didn't move, didn't so much as blink. Her eyes were half-lidded, staring at nothing. I touched the chain, and my fingers started to itch. It was silver. Damn.

Oh, well. I'd just have to cope. Gritting my teeth against the sting, I gripped the silver cross and chain and yanked. The latch broke, the necklace fell into my hand. The itch of the silver against my skin turned into a burn.

"What are you doing?"

"Making sure Hardin's all right. You'll let her go, too? She doesn't know what she's dealing with."

"She won't even remember what happened."

"I don't want to be your lackey."

"I don't want a lackey, I want a partner I can trust."

Hands at my sides, clenched into fists, gritting my teeth against the searing pain of the silver, I moved toward the bed, my gaze downcast. I would not look into his eyes.

My mother still slept. Arturo's touch was so light, he didn't wake her. I stared at that hand. I put my own on the edge of the bed, like I was preparing to surrender, to hand myself over to him. This had to work.

"I think," I said slowly. "I think you should leave my mother alone."

I put the cross on his hand.

Like a snake had bitten him, he flinched away, jerking his hand back and cradling it to his chest. The cross spilled onto the sheet covering Mom's chest. I picked it up and let it dangle, so he could see what it was, ignoring the pain it caused.

"Get out," I said, still not looking at his face, those

eyes. I had to assume he was glaring at me. When he didn't move, a rage bubbled within me. Weeks of frustration, fear, and pain boiled. Damn the ones who had made me live in fear.

"Get out! Get out of here!" This came out as a growl, and Wolf stared out of my eyes, flexed inside my hands, my fingers curling like claws. I would Change right now and leap on him. Maybe he'd be able to stop me. And maybe he wouldn't.

He moved toward the doorway, and I followed. I watched his shoulder, not his face. A rumbling in my chest felt like the start of a growl. I wanted to rip his throat out. My mouth hurt from wanting to grow fangs.

His lips turned in a careful smile. Lowering his gaze, he gave a small bow, his hand still clenched to his chest. The gesture was courtly.

Then he fled before me, like anyone would before a ravening wolf.

Actually, as much as I would have liked to see him run from me, he merely turned to the doorway and vanished with a breath. I shook my head, convinced I'd seen it wrong. He'd managed a vampire's exit, the moment of shadow and the disappearance.

I clutched my stomach and felt like the luckiest girl in the world. He'd left me and Mom alone.

And my hand felt like it was going to fall off.

"Gah!" I dropped the cross and chain onto Mom's bed. That was where I wanted to leave it, with her, in case he came back. I stretched my hand—a rash severe enough to show raised welts covered my palm. "Shit," I muttered.

"Kitty? Hm...what time is it? It's dark." Mom turned her head and mumbled, sounding very small and lost.

"Sh, Mom. It's okay. Everything's okay. Go back to sleep." I touched her hand, her forehead, brushing aside strands of ash-colored hair. I tried to sound soothing and not rattled. "Just go back to sleep. I'll come see you later."

"All right."

"I love you."

She smiled briefly as she drifted back to sleep. Still drugged out on painkillers, she'd never really woken up.

Relieved, I sighed. She was safe. She'd be safe. Could I collapse yet?

"Where is he? Where'd he go?" Hardin appeared in the doorway again, crossbow in hand, her gaze wild.

"He's gone. You still want to arrest Denver's Master vampire?"

"Jesus Christ," she hissed. She rubbed the back of her neck, where the chain had broken off.

"Detective, could you do something for me?"

She joined me by the bed. "Is she all right?"

"Yeah. Could you tie this chain around her somehow? I don't want to touch it if I don't have to." I showed her my injured palm.

"That's my cross," she said.

"I had to borrow it."

She considered me a moment, then shook her head. Her taut expression managed to convey both trepidation and annoyance. But she did get the chain tied around Mom's neck.

"The silver did that to you?"

Wincing, I nodded. "With silver bullets, it's not the bullet that kills a werewolf. It's the silver poisoning the blood."

"Not very pretty I bet."

"No, I imagine not."

Straightening, Hardin regarded me. The trepidation was fading, losing to a severe look of aggravation. "You're going to have to explain what that bastard did to me."

"The vampire hypnotic voodoo."

"Uh. Yeah."

"How do you think they get people to stay still while they drink their blood?"

She scowled. "I hate it when this crap actually makes sense."

"Don't look at his eyes next time, okay?"

"Let's get going."

I touched Mom's hand one more time. She was sleeping, and the cross was visible, lying at the hollow of her throat. She was as safe as I could make her. Which wasn't very. I hated to leave.

"She'll be okay," Hardin said, touching my arm. "I'll make sure security is watching her room."

Like that would help. Arturo would just work his wiles on them.

"I'll have them string garlic in the doorway." She grinned, but it wasn't much of a joke.

We heard pounding footsteps ahead of us. Four cops, running down the corridor. Hardin's backup.

"Took you guys long enough!" she barked at them. "Come on, we're heading out."

They shrugged and mumbled excuses. But I looked at the clock—the whole exchange with Arturo had only taken a couple of minutes. We hadn't been here that long. Time had stretched to make it seem so.

After Hardin had a word with security, we walked out

of the hospital together. "Your boyfriend was going to this guy's home base. Where?"

"You know Obsidian? That art gallery on fourteenth? He's in the basement."

"How many people has he got with him?"

"I don't know. I've seen as many as twelve or fourteen. All vampires."

"Well, this ought to be fun. Sawyer, you got that surveillance file on Mercedes Cook? She's a known associate. We might get some idea of what we'll find there."

"Yeah, it's in the car."

"Sawyer," I muttered. "Isn't that the guy who shot me?" The cop in question ducked and ran ahead of us. Avoiding me. Oh, it *was* him.

"Let it go, Kitty," Hardin said. Then, "Sunglasses."

"What?"

"You think sunglasses would work against that hypnotic crap?" She pulled a pack of cigarettes and a lighter out of her pocket and went through the ritual of lighting up. Her gestures were manic, determined.

"I don't know."

Officer Sawyer handed her a manila folder, which she handed to me. Then she gathered her people around her: four uniformed officers who looked ready for war. I was frankly dumbstruck.

Nodding at the four officers, all men, all tough-looking, she said, "Tell them what you told me. Everything you know about what to expect from the vampires."

I repeated it all, every bit of vampire lore I knew, everything I had seen with my own eyes. They were strong, they could drop grown men without effort, they could control your will simply by looking into your eyes. They were hard to kill. They had the experience of decades. Arturo had centuries behind him. How could I make them understand that?

The officers stared back at me, just as eager, just as ready. They'd heard what I'd said, but I wasn't sure they understood it. This must have looked like some kind of video game to them. I was sending them to their doom.

Hardin followed up with instructions. "Don't get separated. Stick with your partner, keep your eyes on each other. You see someone in trouble, call for backup. I don't want big heroics on this. We're dealing with unknowns here."

We'd go in three cars. Hardin directed one of the patrol cars to stop in front, while hers and another parked in back. No flashing lights or sirens. We'd sneak in.

"They'll know," I said. "Before we even get out of the car."

"Then we'll be ready for them," she said, confident.

We're all gonna die, a voice in me wailed. Not the Wolf. I could tell, because the Wolf was urging me on. *We must destroy those who harm us. We must do battle.*

I didn't know which instincts to listen to anymore.

chapter 15

During the drive, I flipped through the file folder containing the information about Mercedes Cook. The police had managed to cull a handful of photos from the hotel's security cameras—digital images printed out on plain paper. They showed her in the hotel, mostly, interacting with the staff, entertaining visitors, many of them recognizable local celebrities. Some of the pictures were blurry—like the closed-circuit footage from the convenience store robberies. Vampires, not wanting to be seen. Maybe Arturo.

One of them stopped me cold. In it, I recognized the hallway outside Mercedes's suite at the Brown Palace. A man was entering the room, his head up, his face clear. He held himself with a confidence that showed he belonged there. He knew what he was doing, and he had a plan. The man was deeply tanned, with sun-burnished blond hair and rugged, windblown skin.

It was Dack. I remembered now what he'd said: *It's a good thing, having a vampire owe you a favor. You want to be with the strongest.* And he hadn't answered when I asked if that was Rick. Evidently, he didn't think so. With a sinking feeling, I realized that we'd found the spy in Rick's camp. And I had no way to reach Rick to tell him, not if he wasn't answering his phone. Dack was there, with him now, no doubt preparing to stab him in the back. And Ben was there, too.

The whole thing had fallen apart. I wondered if it was too late to grab Ben and run away.

"You recognize that guy," Hardin said, glancing over.

"Yeah. I think we're all screwed."

"We'll see about that. He a vampire, too?"

"No. He's a lycanthrope."

"Everyone's got silver bullets this time. I checked."

"Great. I'll make sure I'm standing behind you all."

"Probably a good idea."

This was insane.

I called Rick again, to tell him about Dack, but he still didn't answer. Then I called Ben. Who didn't answer.

Obsidian was in a nicer part of downtown, a street filled with chic restaurants and funky boutiques, halfway between artsy and gentrified. The art gallery was a front; the interesting bit was the basement. Stairs around back led to the heart of Arturo's empire.

I checked where Rick had told us to park, and Ben's car wasn't there. Ben wasn't there. Maybe that was a good thing. Maybe it was all already over. Maybe they were okay.

Hardin distributed equipment from the trunk of her car to her people: crosses, stakes, hand crossbows with wooden bolts, spray bottles of what I assumed was holy water. I took a handful of stakes and a cross, steel, the size of my hand. I decided that if all else failed, I would depend on my ability to run like hell. I slung my backpack over my shoulders.

Thus armed and prepared, we approached the building. I couldn't imagine what this must look like from the outside. Five cops, stalking purposefully toward a dark building, carrying crossbows and crosses—they could only be hunting vampires.

The place was an isolated box surrounded by parking lots. I hesitated, hoping to smell something, sense something. But the street was silent, and the building looked dead.

Hardin pointed at her officers. "You two, watch the front. Don't let anyone leave."

The rest of us headed for the stairs in back.

She said, "You're a civilian. I'm not going to ask you to do this if you don't want to. But if you think you can help—"

"Maybe I can, maybe I can't. But I'll go." I'd started this thing, I had to see it through.

Rick's Beamer was parked in back. He was here, somewhere, fighting for his life or already dead. A couple of other cars were here. Not Ben's.

Hardin repeated instructions to the remaining officers. "Don't let anyone down those stairs, don't let anyone leave."

The last two cops—our rear guard as well as our backup—stayed behind, while Hardin and I made our way into the pit.

"You've been here before, right?" For all her efforts with the anti-vampire gear, she'd reverted to habit and held her gun at the ready. Shocking myself, I recognized the type—a nine-millimeter semiautomatic.

"Yeah," I said. "But it's been a while."

"Tell me what to expect."

"There's a metal door at the bottom of the stairs. It opens on a hallway. There's a closed door on each side. I don't know what's behind them. There's another door at the end of the hall. It leads to what I guess you'd call his living room."

Actually, it was more like a throne room, or a receiving hall—a holdover from an age of palaces and courts. There wasn't a modern equivalent. This was where Arturo held court, and where Carl would come to pay his respects, negotiate a dispute, or do what he needed to do to keep peace between our kinds. Usually, Carl would bring his own retinue, enough of his pack to make a show of strength, to balance the dozen or so vampires Arturo displayed on his side. Sometimes, he'd bring me, when he needed a pretty young thing at his side to boost his own ego. An alpha could increase his standing by showing off how many helpless cubs he could protect. That was what I'd been to him—a helpless child. I'd hated those outings. I'd hated being put out for show.

One of those times, I'd met Rick. I'd been young—both age wise and wolf wise. I'd only been a werewolf for a year. Rick had been standing watch at the basement door, and I'd sneaked out when Carl wasn't paying attention. I couldn't leave without Carl entirely, so I stuck around, sitting on the concrete steps, and chatted with Rick. He was the first vampire who ever deigned to speak to me at all. He could tell I was new to it all, and he was kind to me. After that, the whole place had seemed a little more real. More believable. Vampires became a little less scary.

If Arturo had returned from the hospital before us, I'd expect to find him in that room, surrounded by his minions. I had no idea where Rick might be. Almost, I expected him to still be standing guard at the door at the bottom of the steps. I'd sit down again and have a nice chat. He'd tell stories about Denver during the gold rush: The displacement in time, the sense of déjà vu, was visceral.

Hardin led the way down the stairs. I followed, continually looking over my shoulder.

At the base of the stairs, the metal door stood open.

Behind us, in the alley we'd just left, a man screamed.

Then another voice: "Officer down!"

Two shots fired. Hardin charged back up the stairs. I charged after her. I didn't even get a chance to look through the door to see what might follow us.

At the top of the stairs, Hardin shouted, "Freeze! Freeze right there!" Then, "Dammit!"

She'd pressed herself to the wall and looked out at the alley. I crouched beside her, using the stairwell for shelter.

One of the two cops—I recognized Sawyer—turned back and forth, as if searching for quarry that was no longer visible. He held a gun in one hand and a spray bottle in the other. His arms were trembling. Nearby, the other cop lay still, facedown on the ground. I didn't see any blood on him, no wounds. That didn't mean anything. I looked up, back and forth, all around. Vampires could fall on us from above.

"Sawyer, where'd he go?"

"I don't know, he just . . . just disappeared. Vanished."

I closed my eyes and took a deep, steady breath. The air was still tonight, all the summer heat leached away leaving a calm, damp chill. Good. Without a breeze, the assailant couldn't stay downwind.

Vampires smelled dead, but only partly. They were dead without the decay, the rot. They lacked heartbeats;

they were cold. Any blood and warmth they had was stolen from a living body. They smelled out of place in the world, like they'd stepped out of it somehow.

I searched for that now, tasting the air, letting that little bit of the Wolf into my conscious mind so I could use those senses. I only needed a location, a direction where I could point Hardin and Sawyer.

I smelled vampires everywhere.

My heart racing, I pushed myself against the side of the concrete stairwell. Until something moved, until we spotted one of them, we couldn't do anything. We'd be wasting what pathetic ammunition we brought by shooting at shadows. Firing blasts of holy water at nothing.

Sawyer knelt by his partner and touched his neck. He had to set down one of his weapons to do it, and to my dismay he set down the spray bottle. Not that I had faith in the spray bottles, notwithstanding the holy water in them. But the gun probably wouldn't do any good.

"He's alive," Sawyer called to us. "Just knocked out, I think."

"Can vampires do that?" Hardin whispered to me. "Just knock someone out?"

I didn't answer because I saw a flicker of something dodging from one shadow to the next. "Sawyer, behind you!"

He whirled, saw the figure who had appeared instantly and silently behind him. The assailant, a pale man dressed simply in dark slacks and a shirt, raised his arm in preparation of delivering a blow. Sawyer reacted instinctively, driven by panic, bringing his gun to bear and firing. Trigger-happy bugger, wasn't he?

Caught in the chest by the shot, the vampire staggered

back a step. But he didn't fall. I didn't smell blood. He didn't react again, except to square his shoulders and focus his gaze on Sawyer. He closed the distance between them in a second. He was a flash of movement.

"Shit," Sawyer murmured as the vampire drew back his fist and finished the interrupted strike. He backhanded Sawyer with little effort. The vampire barely moved. I wouldn't have guessed the force of it would be enough to bruise him, but Sawyer left the ground entirely and crunched on the asphalt a few feet away.

After a heart-wrenching moment, Sawyer moved. Not quickly, but he moved. He started to push himself up with his arms, but only managed to roll himself onto his back. He lay there, gasping.

"You are under arrest!" Hardin screamed at the vampire. She aimed her gun at him, no matter how little good it would do.

"Hardin, use your crossbow," I muttered. In response, she fumbled between the weapons. I approached the vampire cautiously, cross raised, like I could coax him away from the fallen man.

The vampire looked at us and smiled. Then, he ignored us and continued after Sawyer.

Hardin's belt radio cackled to life, but the voice speaking through it was muffled. It sounded like one of the other cops who'd come with Hardin. Shots fired at the front of the building. She muttered an expletive, but didn't otherwise respond. We couldn't do anything about it right now.

Two more vampires ran at us from the side of the building. Both youngish, one dark-haired, one tall and blond. With a gasp and an unhealthy dose of fatalism, I cut to intercept them, holding the cross like a shield.

Sawyer was moving, trying to sit up. He didn't see the threat behind him. Hardin fired her crossbow. The vampire flinched, brushing at his arm. The bolt fell; it hadn't stuck.

Hardin cursed and grabbed at her belt for the pouch that held more bolts.

I put myself between the newcomers and Hardin, misting the air around me with holy water. That slowed them. It kept them from doing that thing where they moved too quickly to track. But it wouldn't last. I fumbled for the stakes Ben had stashed in the backpack.

When the blond one swatted at me, I let loose another volley from the spray bottle. Water squirted out and caught his hand. He rubbed it absently, not at all incapacitated. It might as well have been a swarm of gnats. Then he backhanded me out of the way. I didn't even see him coming. I was sure I'd been out of range. I was standing, then the next moment I was facedown on the asphalt, spitting out grit. The stakes spilled out of the backpack.

In front of me, the first vampire stepped on Sawyer's chest, shoving him to the ground, then twisted his head. It was an inhuman move, requiring inhuman strength. And inhuman sensibilities. I heard the crack. Saw Sawyer's head flop back down, unsupported. Heard the beat of his heart go out. The vampire dropped Sawyer to the pavement.

"No!" Hardin screamed, then fired her crossbow again. And again. A bolt struck the vampire's shoulder, another his thigh.

She didn't see the vampire standing behind her.

The blond one was standing over me.

I grabbed a stake and slammed it into his foot. Sharpened hardwood, it went right through that shiny leather shoe. Snarling, he pulled his foot away and kicked, but I had a little superhuman speed of my own, and I was ready for him. I rolled, another stake in hand. Angry now, he rushed me. I let him. I ducked. Bracing my arms, I held the stake up and prayed.

I felt his chest give out on top of me. Then, his weight shoved me to the ground, pinning me. He was a newer vampire—mere decades old. He didn't turn to ash, a hundred years of decomposition catching up to him. When I shoved him away and looked, he was desiccated—gray flesh, sunken cheeks, hollow body. His clothes hung on him in tatters, and the stake remained poking out between ribs. His clouded eyes stared at me.

Swallowing back a scream, I looked away.

The second vampire had closed Hardin in an embrace from behind and touched her neck with his lips. A wicked smile on his lips, the first one launched himself into a run toward her. Even restrained, she still held the crossbow and managed to get one more shot off. This one landed true and buried itself in his chest, in his heart.

He halted sharply and touched his shirt, picking at it, like he was trying to pull it out. Snarling, he looked at Hardin, stepped forward like he might attack. Then he started disintegrating, before he even fell over. Bit by bit, he turned to the ash of the grave. He fell to his knees, then his knees weren't there anymore. He never took his rabid gaze off Hardin, until he was lying flat on the pavement, and his face itself disappeared into dust. Nothing left but ash.

Giving a shout, Hardin struggled, trying to twist out of the second vampire's grip, but his hold was too strong. Blood trickled from his mouth, down her neck.

I moved as fast as I could, which turned out to be pretty fast, and grabbed two stakes, just to be sure. Putting all my speed behind the blow, I crunched both stakes into his back.

He dropped Hardin, who stumbled away. Arcing his back, he fell to his knees. Didn't make a sound. Like the blond one, he was new. He didn't turn to ash, instead becoming a corpse before our eyes. Flesh and clothing dissolved, hanging on bleached bones. He smelled like mold.

"Jesus Christ!" Hardin pressed a hand to her neck and stared at her attacker. "Am I— Oh, God, am I going to turn into one of those?" She looked at the blood on her hands.

"No," I said, panting. "They have to drain you. If they only take a little you're okay."

She didn't look okay. Panic burned in her eyes and she was almost hyperventilating.

"Detective," I said, catching her attention. "Breathe."

She nodded quickly and took a deep breath. That slowed her down. She found a handkerchief in a pocket and held it to the wound on her neck.

I knew, but I had to do it anyway. I touched Sawyer's neck, feeling for a pulse that wasn't there. His neck was twisted at a strange angle, and his eyes were open, staring. He didn't deserve this.

"Sawyer?" Hardin called. I shook my head.

I looked for the others I knew must be out there. And there she was: a pale, svelte woman at the top of the stairs, blocking our way down. She had white hair and an icy expression.

"Stella," I murmured. "What's the deal? Where's Rick? Where's Ben? They're supposed to be here."

"None of you are *supposed* to be here." She stalked toward me.

"Detective?" I murmured.

"Out of ammo," she said as she went to retrieve the bolts she'd already fired.

Great. I'd dropped the cross to do the stake thing. I didn't think I could stake her by surprise—she was ready for me. I quickly retrieved what I could, shoving everything back in the pack. The spray bottle still had some holy water in it.

I met Stella face-to-face. Or as face-to-face as possible, considering how tall she was.

"Just a hint," I said, letting my mouth do what it did best—run away with me. "Did you get Rick? At least tell me whether or not you killed him. I'm sure you'd love to tell me how completely we screwed up." But she didn't tell me that we screwed up. She didn't tell me where Rick was. Maybe because she didn't know.

I hadn't noticed any other evidence of dead vampires apart from what we'd just made. I was willing to hope Arturo's gang hadn't killed Rick before he got inside. He'd evaded them. This wasn't over. I let her come closer. Let her think she didn't have to work for this one.

"Come on, you can tell me. I'll beg for it, will that make you happy? What's going on? Is Arturo here? Is Rick?" And Ben, where was Ben, goddammit?

"Oh, you haven't completely screwed up," she said, wearing a pained smile. "You're in the process of completely screwing up."

She was within arm's reach and still talking when I let loose with the spray bottle.

The mist caught her in her pretty marble face. She hesitated, blinking, confused, like she didn't know what had just happened. A rash broke out, red spots appearing on her mouth and cheeks and radiating outward. Then, she sneezed, then started coughing. Her eyes widened in shock, and she clutched her throat.

Vampires only draw air in order to speak. I'd certainly never heard one sneeze. But she'd been opening her mouth to say something, had just happened to draw a breath, and thereby inhaled a fine mist of holy water, which had gotten into her nose, sinuses, and throat. From what I'd observed, holy water had a similar effect on vampires that silver had on lycanthropes—it produced an allergic reaction on the skin, rashes, hives, that sort of thing.

I tried to imagine breaking out in hives in my sinuses and down my throat. And I thought, Oh, *yuck*.

She didn't stop coughing. She dropped to her knees, and the rash erupting over her face turned fiery.

By that time, Hardin had returned, her newly loaded crossbow trained on the incapacitated vampire.

"She out of commission?" Hardin asked. I nodded quickly. Stella didn't seem concerned with much of anything at the moment but her own discomfort.

The radio at Hardin's belt was calling again. She ran for the front of the building, and I chased after her.

"Lopez, talk to me!" Hardin called.

Sneaking a look around the corner, I could see the two officers, back to back, weapons out—one had a gun, the other a crossbow. Both of them looked wild-eyed and on the verge of panic, waiting for an imminent attack.

"I don't know!" Lopez, the one with the gun, called back. "There were three—"

"—four," the other cop said. "Four of them."

"I don't know, three or four of them, I thought we were finished. But they just disappeared."

I still hated when vampires did that. Reflexively, I looked behind, up, all around, waiting for another shadow to move and strike.

"They won't have gone far," Hardin said. "Keep watching."

Again, I turned my nose to the air. I had other ways of watching. They were here. I could smell them, even differentiate individuals. They had different flavors to their scents, but I couldn't quite identify them. Part of it was the nature of the place—it all belonged to vampires. We could get rid of them all, bulldoze the building and plant a garden, and some of that undeadness would still linger.

We stayed like that, stalled in place, waiting for shadows to strike.

Finally, Hardin said, "Well? We scare them off or what?" She smelled of nervous sweat, but her manner was calm. Lopez and his partner didn't believe it—they remained back-to-back, tense and ready.

I wasn't willing to make any guesses. The street was quiet. Nothing could possibly happen on a street this quiet.

"I'm going to go back to check on Kramer," Hardin said. "Call me—"

Lopez fired another shot.

"Would you stop doing that!" And there was Charlie, yelling at the officer and rubbing at a smoking bullet hole in his T-shirt. He came around the corner and dropped a body—vampiric, male, built like a fighter—in front of us. He looked me up and down. "What are you doing here?"

Hardin's cops trailed after him, still tense to the point of quivering.

"Where's Rick?" I shot back. "Where's Ben? Ben was coming to help but I don't see his car—"

·"Rick's downstairs. I need your help, Violet's hurt."

"Wait a minute, is this another vampire or what?" Hardin said.

"He's one of the good guys." I think. "Charlie, Detective Hardin, Detective, Charlie. So is that guy dead or what?" A dead vampire decomposed. This one hadn't, so what was he, knocked out?

How do you knock out a vampire?

But Charlie didn't answer. He grabbed my shoulder and pulled me around the opposite corner.

Lopez pleaded with Hardin, "What the hell is going on?"

"I don't know. Follow Kitty's lead, keep your eyes open."

Propped against the wall, safe in a shadow, lay Violet. A glistening trail streaked the front of her black shirt—blood, streaming from a gash in her neck. Something had ripped half her throat out—vertebrae were visible. The shredded wound wasn't bleeding anymore—all the blood had drained out. Lopez turned away, a hand covering his mouth.

Her eyes were closed; she didn't move. I couldn't tell if she was dead. More dead. All vampires smelled dead. It looked like all the blood she'd borrowed—that was why vampires drank, to replace the blood they'd lost when they were turned—had spilled out, and maybe she was gone forever this time.

Charlie knelt by her and tenderly cradled her in his lap. "Violet, Violet baby, I brought help. Stay with me now, okay?" He stroked her cheeks, her hair, clutched her hand, and she didn't respond. "Kitty's going to help, okay? Hang on for me, baby."

"What can I do?" I murmured, my heart breaking over the scene.

Charlie looked at me. "She needs blood so she can heal. Strong blood."

Of course she did. She didn't even need much, a mouthful or so. I'd seen how this worked.

"Do I have to?" I said, wincing.

"Please. Just a little." I'd never seen such a look of pleading on anyone's face, much less a vampire's.

I nodded. "Detective Hardin, do you have a jackknife or something?"

She stared. "You can't be serious."

"Yes, please," I said softly. "And you might want to pay attention. This gets pretty interesting."

She didn't have one, but Lopez did, a thin penknife on a keychain. It would have to do.

I knelt by Violet, pulled open the blade, and before I could flinch or change my mind, I drew it across my left forearm. It cut deep. I didn't look at it. Almost, it didn't hurt—until my blood hit the air. Then it stung viciously. I gritted my teeth and held my arm over her lips.

Charlie tilted Violet's head back, holding her jaw in order to ease open her mouth. The first drops that fell from the wound hit her cheek, drizzling a scarlet line to her jaw. But by the time the dripping blood became a steady stream, it fell straight into her mouth. Like giving water to someone dying of thirst.

Because of my rapid healing, the stream of blood didn't last long before clotting, and the cut scabbed over as we watched. But Violet didn't need much. After the first few drops, she closed her mouth by herself. Her throat moved, swallowing. We could see the exposed muscles and tendons of her neck working. Then, her throat started healing. I healed quickly, but this was faster, skin creeping, stretching to cover flesh and blood that now glowed with life. Hardin murmured an expletive.

Violet licked her lips, catching the stray drops, straining forward for more. She winced in pain, then leaned back, settling into Charlie's lap.

"Charlie?" Her voice was small, childlike.

"Yeah, baby?"

"It hurts."

"It won't, in a minute."

Her skin flushed, gaining some color as my blood took effect. Her fingers moved, then her hands, then she stretched her arms to grip Charlie.

He helped her sit up, and all at once she seemed like she'd only been sick, maybe hungover, not drained of blood and near death—or what meant death to vampires.

"Shit," she muttered. She picked at the blood on her clothing and grimaced. "All this good stuff gone to waste."

"Feeling better?" Charlie said.

Her answer sounded tired. "Yeah."

"You're welcome," I said, rubbing the newly healed cut on my arm. It had already turned to a closed, pink scab.

I noticed two stretched-out piles of ash on the concrete nearby. The ones who got Violet, I was guessing. Charlie hadn't let them survive.

So. Had we gotten them all?

"How many more are there?" I said.

"I don't know," Charlie said. "Three, maybe four. Maybe more downstairs. Rick wanted them all alive. He wanted everyone alive."

"Kitty, are these good guys or what?" Hardin demanded.

Violet purred, "Ooh, I wouldn't say *good* guys."

Hardin opened her mouth for a retort, but then narrowed her eyes. "Do I know you two? Have I seen you before?"

Charlie and Violet glanced at each other, then back at her.

"I don't think so," Charlie said. Violet giggled. Right, so Bonnie and Clyde were back to normal.

I wanted to grab them both by their necks and shake them. "Is Rick downstairs?"

"Yeah."

"What about Ben? And Dack, we have to find Dack, he's working for Mercedes."

Charlie's smile fell. "Shit."

"We have to tell Rick."

Hardin pointed at Lopez. "You two, call for backup, check on Kramer out back."

"Where's Sawyer?" Lopez asked. Hardin just shook her head.

"There's another one of those things down out back, keep an eye on her." She fired off the patter of instructions.

"Things?" Charlie said. "She calls us things?"

Then Violet jumped to her feet and braced, preparing for a fight. "They're still out there."

I didn't see anything but shadows, and they were everywhere.

Charlie grabbed my arm. "Go downstairs. Tell Rick what's happening. Go!" He shoved me on my way.

Hardin and I ran to the back, passing Lopez, who was talking into his radio. Calling for backup. Lopez's partner had a crossbow trained on Stella, but she was doubled over and croaking. Hardin led with the crossbow, moving cautiously along the wall. The basement door still stood open. I couldn't hear anything from inside. Slowly, Hardin leaned around the doorway for a look, then slipped into the hallway. I followed.

The hall was carpeted with a dark-colored berber. The lighting was muted, atmospheric even.

Two figures lay shoved up against the wall, appearing dead. The two side doors stood open; the rooms inside were dark.

"More vampires?" Hardin said. I nodded. An unconscious vampire might as well have been a body—pale, waxen, not breathing.

And once again, how the *hell* did you knock a vampire unconscious? I'd have to talk to Rick about that later.

We hurried down the hallway. Hardin kept the weapon trained on the bodies the whole time.

I said, "Remember, don't look—"

"At their eyes, I know."

The door at the end of the hall was already open, into a room that looked like it came from another world. We inched forward and peered in.

The place was marvelous, with low ceilings and brocade fabrics draping the walls. Bronze lamps gave out soft light, and the carpet was thick and lush under our feet. The colors were luscious to the eyes, the furnishing opulent, and at one end stood an actual dais, a raised platform decked with Persian rugs and antique furniture. The central piece was a throne, upholstered in red plush with gilt carvings on all surfaces.

Rick sat on the throne, gripping the scrolled edges of the armrests, and leaning forward. Arturo stood before him, a look of fury twisting his face. Rick had done exactly what he said he'd do: come here to wait for Arturo.

Rick said he only needed a few minutes alone with him. He should be leaping, attacking. Why was he hesitating? The longer he gave Arturo, the more chances Arturo had to speak, to act, the better chance he had of winning.

"It takes more than sitting in that chair to take my place," Arturo said.

Rick looked to the doorway, where we were standing. Hardin had her crossbow ready, but moved it back and forth between them, like she didn't know who to shoot first.

"Stand down, Detective," he said. "I'm going to do this right, and that means not staking him."

Hardin shook her head. "You—" she spoke to Arturo, "are under arrest for assault."

Arturo spared a quick glance over his shoulder. "Katherine, have you changed your mind? My offer still stands."

I couldn't answer, not even to shake my head. Hardin and I needed to get out of here. This was more of a window into vampire politics in action than most people outside their world ever got. I was strangely fascinated. At the same time, I wanted to be anywhere but here. This was going to get very, very messy.

Rick spoke, his voice even. "The fact that I'm here, that you haven't been able to stop me, shows that you're weak. It's time for you to step aside."

"Are you giving me a chance to concede?" Arturo said, laughing.

"Yes."

Still smiling as if deeply amused, Arturo shook his

head. "You are too soft for this, Ricardo. You're too weak to sit on that chair."

"Actually, I plan on replacing *this* chair with something a little more practical."

"Why is everyone ignoring me?" Hardin said.

"Because they think we're bugs," I reminded her. Rather than being frustrated, though, I wanted a bucket of popcorn.

Arturo said to Rick, "You don't have the years to do that. You don't have the time stretching behind you, supporting you. You need age to take my place."

"Oh, that's the game, is it? You have no idea how old I am." He was calm. Relentlessly calm.

Arturo's expression fell, and he said, angrily, "How old, then?"

I had pegged them both at about two or three hundred years old, by inference and rumor. Rick had controlled those rumors, evidently. With age came strength and power. He'd kept his hidden.

Rick—Ricardo, I suddenly saw the difference—studied his rival, as if he could peel back the skin, yank out the secrets he wanted simply by looking. When Arturo took a step back, his hand touching his cheek, rubbing it almost like it hurt, I missed what had happened, if anything had actually happened. Then I smelled it: blood in the air. Arturo looked at his hand, which was covered by a sheen of red. A film also covered his cheek, his jaw—all his exposed skin. He was sweating blood.

Teeth bared, fangs showing, Arturo stared at Rick in a panic. Was Rick doing this? Making Arturo sweat blood? Drawing the substance out of his body?

When Arturo glared back at Rick, attempting to stun

him, or hypnotize him, or knock him unconscious like those vampires in the hallway, or draw blood through his pores—he couldn't. It didn't work. He didn't have the years, the power.

"I followed Coronado into this country, Arturo. I have age," Rick said.

Five hundred years old. He was over five hundred fucking years old. Arturo gaped at him. Arturo, who was only two or three hundred years old. Only.

Rick carried his five centuries well. He didn't let on that the weight of those years pressed on him. The old ones tended to get smug, becoming bored and arrogant as they grew powerful and isolated. Not him. He acted like he still had discoveries to make. Like the world was still fresh to him. He'd misled us all.

"You don't," Arturo said in a breathless tone that betrayed his belief—and his fear. He wiped his cheeks, rubbed his hands, smearing red over his skin, but he couldn't wipe it off.

When Rick stood and stepped toward the younger vampire, Arturo stumbled back, losing all his grace, almost falling. Rick pressed forward, grabbing hold of Arturo's collar, hoisting him upright, trapping him. He locked gazes with the other vampire, and Arturo froze. Like he was only mortal, a vulnerable human trapped in a vampire's stare.

Rick had intimidated him into submission. Holy cow.

"Ricardo. Step away from him, please."

A curve of color that had seemed just another part of a tapestry moved forward. Mercedes Cook, emerging from the shadows. Wearing a tailored jacket, long skirt, and heeled boots, she walked with confidence, head high, eyes half-lidded, like she was onstage, on show. And she left no doubt as to who was really in control here.

Of course she hadn't left Denver, not with the situation still unresolved.

"Mercedes," Rick said, grimacing. He didn't turn away from his quarry. "What's her price? How much are you paying for her to keep you in power?"

"Price? I'm not paying anything! She has no power here!" But he glanced at her, uncertain.

"Mercedes?" Rick said again, this time questioning the woman.

Her poise was deeply practiced, unflappable. The end of the world would not shake her. Humanity would destroy itself with nuclear bombs or rampant plagues, and vampires like her would stand among the ashes, imperious.

"Arturo and I haven't made a deal. Yet. Arturo? It's not too late."

Still dangling in Rick's grip, Arturo stared, his eyes widening. "It was you. All along, it was you."

And I saw it then myself: the nightclub attacks, the bodies left in the warehouse for the police to find, all of it giving the impression that Arturo was losing control. Indirectly, she'd inspired Rick to rebel. She'd made Arturo seem—and maybe even feel—weak. All so she could stroll in here and offer to rescue him.

"Kitty, what's going on?" Hardin whispered.

I shook my head. I'd have to explain it later.

Rick stared, like the same realization had just dawned on him as well. He said, "Why? Why back him?"

"The known quantity is always to be preferred," she said. "Always maintain status quo, when the status quo in question is sufficiently under control."

"Under control!" Arturo said. He kept looking around for followers who were all unconscious or dead. "Whose control? No one controls me!"

"The Long Game put you here, Arturo, and the Long Game will keep you here because you are weak."

Arturo's expression turned cold. Frozen and disbelieving.

For my part, I wished I could hit pause and rewind to play that bit over. The Long Game?

"What interest do they have in Denver?" Arturo said, his voice fallen to almost a whisper. "Denver is nothing to them."

"Even a pawn may threaten the king."

She glanced at me, then, and I almost squeaked. I had nothing to do with any of this, I was an innocent bystander, an accidental witness who wanted nothing more than to flee.

Her attention on me lasted less than a second, less than the blink of an eye. How had she put so much meaning in that short a space of time? Then she was regarding Arturo again.

"You've reveled in your power here for quite some time by local standards. As long as Denver's been a city, you've been here. You've grown comfortable, complacent. You've lost sight. You've forgotten that this isn't about you." She approached them step by step, like a lion. No, a jackal waiting to clean up the pieces.

"You—" he spoke to Rick, "you're fighting them. You've always been fighting them, haven't you? You'll keep this city out of their hands."

"I will."

Arturo's smile changed, thinned, turned sly. It became

the familiar smug expression he usually wore. "Then I concede. Denver is yours. I'll leave here forever."

Rick said, "Mercedes, you're here as a witness. Is that enough? Do you accept that I am now Master of Denver?"

Mercedes's voice chimed with hidden laughter. "Where will you go, Arturo?"

"Back to Philadelphia. I have friends there."

"Friends like me?" she said. "Friends who are also playing the game? Will they want you back?" Arturo's expression turned stricken.

She was two strides away from Rick. She'd never said her age. I'd guessed that it was young, less than a hundred years. But she was an actress, and she had disguised herself. She carried herself with a confidence that exceeded even Rick's. Having seen what Rick could do to Arturo, I could almost imagine what she could do to Rick.

I was way out of my league here. I knew that, I accepted that. But I also knew that I absolutely did not want this woman poking her sticky undead fingers into my city.

I sprang forward, spray bottle in one hand, cross in the other, both stuck out in front of me, braced in my grip like they were Ben's gun. "Stop."

Mercedes arched a perfect, questioning brow at me. She almost seemed amused.

"It's holy water," I said.

"Oh my." She smiled, but she didn't move.

What the hell good was a spray bottle of holy water going to do? She could bat it out of my hand in a second.

Hardin stepped up beside me. "Stop! All of you, put your hands up!"

Mercedes smiled at Rick. "You have minions. That's so sweet."

Rick said, "Mercedes, yes or no: Do you accept that I am now Master of Denver?"

"What does it matter if she accepts it or not?" I said, losing patience. "She's not even from here!"

"Do *not* ignore me! I said hands up!" Hardin sounded flustered.

Something happened. Rick moved, then a shadow fell over Hardin, and her crossbow disappeared. He broke the weapon over his knee and tossed the pieces aside like they were nothing.

"Hey!" she said.

"Both of you stay out of this," Rick said roughly. "You have no idea what's happening here."

"Explain this to me, Kitty," Hardin said.

"Rick wants to be the new Master of Denver. Mercedes wants to stop him."

"I'm here to arrest that guy." She nodded at Arturo. "That's all I want."

Rick never took his eyes off the other vampires. "If anyone but me removes Arturo, my authority here will be suspect. Your answer, Mercedes."

"Why are you even asking her?" I said. "Just kick her butt!"

Rick said, cutting, "I can't do anything to her if I want the city."

"Diplomatic immunity," Mercedes said.

"But she isn't exactly being neutral here—"

"Kitty, be quiet, please," Rick said, ice cold. "Mercedes?"

"No," Mercedes said. "I will carry word that Denver is

torn between two Masters and ripe for the taking." When she reached for him, Rick stepped back. If I didn't know better, I'd have said he looked afraid.

Enough. I shot her. Sprayed her. Whatever.

My hand was shaking, and she twisted out of the way. Somehow, she'd seen it coming, anticipated me in the protracted way vampires saw time. The arc of water only caught her arm.

She didn't make a sound, not so much as a hiss of pain or anger. Splotches of water marred the sleeve of her jacket. The water probably hadn't even soaked through.

Something hit me. The water bottle went flying in one direction, smacking against the wall behind me, and I couldn't breathe. A weight slammed into me, and I crashed to my knees. Mercedes grabbed my throat and squeezed, holding me still. I clutched her wrist, scratched at her arm, trying to free myself. I gasped for air. She could kill me with one hand.

She said, "And you have *both* let the wolves here become unruly. You ought to be ashamed of yourselves."

"Right," Hardin said. "That's it. I've heard enough. You're all under arrest!" She'd retrieved the spray bottle and held it trained firmly on Mercedes. Not that that had done me any good.

With her other hand, Mercedes batted the spray bottle out of Hardin's grip. The cop stumbled back.

"Mercedes, let her go," Rick said.

She didn't. My vision started to go splotchy, and a growl forced its way out of my throat. Inside, Wolf was thrashing. *We could claw her, we could run—*

Somehow I knew that I could turn Wolf, and Mercedes

would keep her grip on my throat and still be able to strangle me.

"Mercedes!" Rick lunged at her.

"No!" Arturo grabbed his arm and stopped him. He took Rick's wrists, then placed Rick's hands back on his own collar. "Do it. You planned it this way all along, so get it over with." Then he became calm. Almost pulled himself into Rick's embrace. For a moment, he was still the Master.

"Arturo—"

"I am not their pawn. I've not lived for three hundred years to be their pawn. You'll stand against them."

"I didn't want this."

"Oh, yes you did. Ricardo, do not waste my blood."

Mercedes let me go. I collapsed, clutching my neck and coughing. I could feel bruises where she'd squeezed. Hardin touched my shoulder.

For the first time that evening, desperation touched the singer's voice. "Arturo. Three hundred years on this earth and you won't even fight for your life? I don't believe you."

Arturo let out a bitter chuckle. "Three hundred years on this earth and I was never once my own man. I see it so clearly now. And I thought I had nothing left to learn."

A look passed between him and Rick. Then, Rick struck.

I flinched at the speed of it. This wasn't happening. I kept telling myself this wasn't happening.

Rick struck at Arturo's neck, biting into his throat. Arturo's head whipped back. His teeth bared in pain, and his hands dug into Rick's arms, the tendons of his fingers taut against his skin. One of his legs kicked out, but Rick braced him to hold him in place, to keep him upright. Rick's mouth stayed pressed to his throat, lips working as they sucked, for what seemed a long time.

Mercedes looked away.

I noticed it in Arturo's shirt first—the fabric of the sleeves collapsed. The effect spread to his pants. The clothing wilted, withered, then the fabric itself blackened and crumbled, turning to ash. The body within decayed—three hundred years in a few minutes—shriveling, desiccating, turning black, turning to ash. It spread to his neck, his head, his golden hair turning white, then to powder. And still Rick pressed his face to it. He dropped to his knees, supporting Arturo—what remained of Arturo—as he disintegrated.

Finally, when nothing was left, Rick straightened, sifting gray ash through his fingers and wiping it from his face. The dust smudged the front of his clothing and streaked his sleeves, which also showed stains of blood.

Arturo wasn't an evil person. An ambiguous person, maybe, who'd done some pretty bad things. But I hadn't wanted to watch him die. It was him or Rick, I kept telling myself. Him or Rick.

Rick turned to Mercedes. "I have his blood. Blood is all, and all that was his is mine. His land, his people, his power. Mercedes, you go, you tell them that this city is mine, and that it is well defended."

"I should arrest you. For murder. Both of you," Hardin whispered. Her eyes had gone wide, shocky almost.

"He died three hundred years ago," I whispered. Was it still murder? Semantics, at this point.

"You have no jurisdiction here, Detective," Rick said.

Mercedes had to collect herself. Her expression froze

in an indifferent mask, and she smoothed out her skirt and jacket.

Before she moved away, she said, "Kitty, you kept asking about my age. You should know, because I want you to, that I am older than them both." She indicated Rick, and the dust on the floor that had been Arturo. Then, she walked away, through the door, vanishing into shadow.

Hardin was staring at that dust. To Rick she said, her voice hushed, "Tell me you play by a different set of rules than he did. That I won't find warehouses filled with ripped-up bodies. Tell me I won't regret helping you."

"You won't," Rick said.

It couldn't be that simple. *The Long Game,* she'd said. I wondered who Rick would have to defend his place against, and what he would have to do against them.

"This is so Twilight Zone. I need to go check on my guys," Hardin said, running a hand through her hair. "I'm going outside for a cigarette." She reached into her pocket and went out the door.

Rick slouched, like he was tired. "It's over."

"But she's still out there," I said. My voice cracked, still injured. "Mercedes. What if she comes back? You could have stopped her."

"No, I couldn't. Her status protects her. I'd forfeit everything I've won if I destroyed her."

Vampire politics. I didn't care anymore. I had work to do. "Rick, there's a problem. Detective Hardin's people have pictures of Dack at the Brown Palace—"

"What?" Rick said. He still had Arturo's ashes smudged all over him. My stomach turned, and I swallowed back bile.

I said, "They went over security footage from the hotel

and found pictures of Dack going to see her. I think he's been telling her and Arturo everything. He's your spy. It makes total sense—she knew your people were at the warehouse and told Arturo, she told Dack to call 911 so when the police came breathing down Arturo's neck he'd need her help to get the situation back under control. He even saved you because she wanted you alive to put more pressure on Arturo."

Rick didn't react right away. His gaze turned to Arturo's chair. His expression was impassive. Then, all he did was whisper, "Not Dack. I don't believe it."

"You want me to go get the pictures? What else would he be doing there?"

He turned away, giving his head a shake, a harsh movement when I was used to seeing nothing but grace from him. "Damn," he murmured.

"Where is he?" I asked. "Is he here? How much does he know about what we planned? And Ben was supposed to come find you—"

He pursed his lips in a wry smile. "Dack's not here."

"Then where is he?"

"I sent him and Ben to go after Carl and Meg." His voice was bitter. He lowered his gaze.

I could only stare at him, frozen. More than numb. The words he'd spoken sent the world crumbling apart around me, and my blood hummed in my ears.

"You've killed him," I said starkly. "Dack's taking him into a trap. They'll tear him apart." Unless Shaun and Becky's friend Mick was out there, and if anyone else was out there who could save him, and if Carl and Meg hadn't already killed them all. Too many ifs. They might all be dead.

"I knew—I believed you wouldn't be able to face Carl and Meg. Part of you still sees them as dominant over you. There's too much history between you. Ben agreed with me. So he and Dack went after Carl and Meg without you. It seemed like the right thing to do. They were supposed to take care of it while I faced Arturo. We'd finish it all in a night." He'd become emotionless, his voice monotone. If I punched him now he'd probably stand there and take it.

He didn't have that right, to decide I couldn't face my old alphas. He didn't know me, didn't know what drove me. Neither he nor Ben had the right to make that decision. To take that away from me. The mess they'd created because of that might very well be irreparable. I didn't know which of them I was more angry at.

Time enough for getting pissed off later.

"Rick. We have to go after them. Now."

"It's almost dawn. I can't. Kitty, Ben's strong, he's resourceful. Maybe he's okay—"

"Like hell! One man against the three of them? When it's probably a trap?"

"I'm sorry," he said, sounding small, surprisingly young.

"Give me your keys." I held out my hand. "Your car, give me the keys now."

"It's too dangerous by yourself. Find someone to go with you—"

All I could think about was finding Ben. "Just give me the keys."

He did, pulling them out of his pocket and tossing them to me. I was on my way to the door as soon as I caught them. I still had my backpack, which had everything I needed.

"Kitty—"

I didn't turn around.

In the corridor, I nearly ran into Charlie and Violet. They were carrying inert vampires into the lair. Stella, unconscious, her face thick with hives, was among them. Charlie said Rick hadn't wanted any of the vampires killed. I understood now: they had been Arturo's. Rick had taken Arturo into himself, and now they were Rick's, and Charlie and Violet were bringing them underground before dawn. Rick hadn't wanted to waste any of his potential followers.

Right now, it would be easy to see him as conniving and selfish as the rest, ready to sacrifice anyone.

"Hey, Kitty, a little help here?" Charlie said. I walked right past him. "Hey!"

I ignored him. I could only think of the car, the road, the route to Meg and Carl's house, where Dack must have taken Ben. My Ben.

Outside, the sky was lightening—twilit blue on the edge of gray. Rick was right—dawn was close. I hadn't realized how much time had passed. How much time had passed since Dack and Ben went after Carl and Meg? How long ago had they killed him?

The alley behind Obsidian was broken by many sets of flashing red and blue lights. Ambulances, police cars. EMTs were checking out Kramer. A couple of cops were putting up yellow tape around the whole parking lot. A couple, wearing latex gloves and carrying crime scene equipment, crouched by Sawyer. Investigating. Hardin was near one of the ambulances, nursing a cigarette and talking on a phone.

I walked past them all.

"Kitty!" Hardin called. "Hey, Kitty—"

I jumped into Rick's car and drove. Had to drive fast, focused. I knew the route, I knew what waited for me.

The sports car was unlike anything I'd ever driven. Little seemed to separate me from the pavement; the car was low, the tires humming, and it responded to the tiniest touch. A hair-thin turn of the steering wheel had me zipping around corners. The barest press of the gas pedal made the car shoot ahead. I never even looked at the speedometer to see how fast I was going. The world scrolled past me. This time of night—of morning—I had no traffic to contend with. The feeling was close to running free, on four legs, over open, unbroken country, the wind drawing fingers through the fur on my body.

I am a hunter. I will stalk them and strike.

I shook my head and refocused, because for a moment my vision had wavered and gone gray. For a moment I'd seen the world in wolf tones. Had to stay human. Wolf couldn't drive the freaking car.

Or hold the gun.

chapter **16**

The sky was pale now. Take care of him, Cormac had said. Keep him out of trouble. How would I ever be able to face him again? What would I say? I'd gotten Ben killed. I wiped tears from my face.

How was I going to keep going without Ben?

No time for that. I am a hunter. I can already taste their blood. My mouth waters for it. I let that part of Wolf edge into my mind. Our territory, our mate, they can't do this to us.

We've learned to fight. We'll show them. Or die trying.

They lived at the edge of town, near the foothills, on a chunk of land with a backyard that opened to wilderness. This was the heart of their territory. The pack came here to run on full moon nights. Even if they weren't at their house, they'd be around here. I was betting Dack knew exactly where. Ben and Dack would have gone here to find Carl and Meg, and Carl and Meg would draw Ben here to kill him. I knew this as if I had smelled their trail the whole way.

Carl's truck was in the driveway, but the house was

dark, like no one was home. But it was also the crack of dawn, so who knew. An unmarked sedan sat half a block away; someone in the front seat was sipping coffee and looking bored—Hardin's stakeout. I drove another couple of blocks. There, on the street outside a state park trailhead, Ben's car was parked.

My heart lurched and a new wave of nausea struck me. Like morning sickness, like a miscarriage. Impending death, settling in my gut.

I passed Ben's car and drove a few yards farther, peering through the cottonwoods to the open field beyond, hoping to spot something, looking for signs that they were near. Couldn't see anything. I'd have to go looking for them. I stopped, shut off the car, and reached for my bag.

If you need to kill someone, make sure the thing's loaded. That was what he'd said. I remembered all his instructions, like he was standing behind my shoulder, whispering to me. I could feel his arms around me, guiding my own.

I popped the clip. Full up, bullets gleaming silver. Slid it back into place and chambered a round.

Sure didn't take long to get into this gun thing, did it? I wished it were over so I could curl up and be sick. But the Wolf whispered, *I am a hunter.*

The world wavered to gray again. It was the dawn, it was the Wolf's sight. It drove me on. Steadied me. Could only think of one thing now: them, and death.

"Rick? Rick, what are you doing here?" Dack came through the stand of cottonwoods, walking toward the street. He saw the BMW, recognized it, assumed.

My first catch.

I stepped out of the car. Thank God the BMW was

low to the ground—I could actually look over it without appearing ridiculous.

"Rick's not a morning person. You know that," I said.

Dack froze, and his eyes grew round. He hadn't expected to see me. Absolutely hadn't expected to see me.

"Where's Rick?" he said carefully.

"The basement of Obsidian."

"What—"

"Arturo's gone. Rick's ordered Mercedes out of town. And we know all about you." I rested the gun on the roof of the car. "You should have sided with the strongest vampire."

He ran. Didn't even hesitate. Flat out sprinted toward Ben's car. Quickly—belatedly—I raised the gun and fired. Squeezed the trigger, and again, and both times the weapon jumped in my hand. Forgot Ben's whispering voice, everything he taught me. Didn't hit Dack—one of the trees shredded splinters, where I accidentally shot it instead. By then Dack had safely climbed into Ben's car and had lurched it around in a U-turn to drive away.

Son of a bitch had stolen Ben's keys.

Ben.

I let Dack go and ran to the trees. Did some quick math—fired twice, fifteen rounds, thirteen left. Should be enough. If I could keep my aim straight, I only needed two. I followed my nose.

There they stood, in a field on the other side of the cottonwoods, out of view of the street. All three of them. Ben was on his feet—but Carl was holding him there, standing behind him, wrenching both his arms back and pinning him immobile so Meg could torture him. Blood covered her, spattering her face and soaking her clothing. She was letting her wolf slide to the fore, and her hands had turned to claws. She had been slashing at Ben. I was twenty paces away, but I could make out wounds. He had cuts, parallel lines across his cheeks and across his neck as if someone with claws had grabbed him there and squeezed. His shirt was shredded, dripping with blood.

She had been taking him apart, piece by piece, while Carl held him still.

I painted this scene by inference, because they had paused. Meg had taken a few steps away from Ben—probably drawn by the sound of gunfire, trying to decide whether to go see what was wrong.

I wanted to watch Ben, find some sign that he was moving, that he was going to be all right, that they hadn't gone too far and that his injuries wouldn't kill him. We were less than a mile from where T. J. had died, after Carl ripped out his heart. I couldn't watch that again. I couldn't take that happening again. It was all I could do not to scream in agony.

Meg saw me and snarled. Beyond words.

Dack had delivered him, and they were dealing with him. Then, Ben's keys in hand, Dack was probably leaving to go get me, lure me out here on some pretense. Maybe he'd say he'd help me rescue Ben. That had probably been part of their deal with Arturo—Carl and Meg could keep the pack, but they had to get rid of me and Ben. Or maybe it had been Mercedes's idea. Like Rick, we were too independent, too much trouble. She sent her minion to get rid of us.

They'd planned on killing the three of us—me, Ben, and Rick—the same night we planned on killing them. It had all come down to who got there first.

I had a flash: all the things I could say to Meg, all the mercy I could show her—stop, get away from him, don't make me do this. Get out of Denver, you get the same deal Carl gave me, go away and never return.

She moved toward me, her bloodied hands clenched, shoulders tight like hackles, and I sensed the attack she was about to make—the tensing muscles, the quickening stride. I stood my ground. She was so fixated, so high on adrenaline and victory, she didn't see the gun I held at my side, behind my thigh, out of sight.

She thought she had the power here, but she didn't. That knowledge gave me strength.

This time, I was calm, and Ben's instructions whispered at me. Take a breath. Hold the gun in both hands. Aim. Exhale slowly. It only took a second. Her eyes registered a moment of surprise. She hadn't expected to see a weapon.

I aimed for her head. Fired. Fired again.

One bullet hit her shoulder, another her chest, sending out sprays of blood. She spun back and fell. Didn't even cry out.

Carl ducked, flattening himself on the ground. Released, Ben fell beside him— not moving. I choked on a cry.

Meg writhed on the ground. I kept my distance. The gun was warm in my hand. I held it straight before me, sighting down the barrel. The wounds hadn't killed her. I'd have to finish it. I didn't want to have to do this, please, God, don't make me do this . . .

Then, she wailed. Seized by pain, she arced her back, flung out her arms, clutching at the grass. Her head tipped back, and her mouth opened wide, screaming. I smelled something—ill and rotten, it came from her, growing until it vied with her normal human-wolf scents. The wounds didn't smell just of blood. Sickness oozed there, too, something sour and burning, growing to be overpowering.

I stepped closer.

Meg didn't notice. All her muscles clenched, pulling her body into a trembling, fetal form. The wounds, marked by bloody splatters, had blackened. The veins in her neck had blackened, showing the trail of poison carried from the wounds by her bloodstream. In another moment the searing trails of silver poisoning traced down both her arms, into her face. Under her clothing, they would soon mark out her whole body.

She stopped shaking. Her eyes and mouth had frozen open, and her fingers remained tensed in the shape of claws. They were only fingers now, harmless, and covered with blood.

"Oh, my God," breathed Carl. I turned to look at him, and he scuttled away from me. Afraid of me. I wasn't even pointing the gun at him.

Oh, this moment was a long time coming.

Moving toward him, I raised the gun, aimed it. I forced myself to step slowly, exhibiting calm, exhibiting power, when all I really wanted to do was throw myself to the ground at Ben's side. Or let Wolf come out and rip into Carl. I could almost feel his blood on my tongue.

Ben moved, starting to sit up—alive. He was alive. He clenched his jaw, grit his teeth, bent over in the wracked pose that meant he was fighting his wolf, trying to keep from shifting. All that pain and anger called his wolf up, and he was fighting it. I couldn't go help him yet.

On his feet now, Carl was still backing away.

"Kitty," he said, his voice sounding different than I'd

ever heard it. Tighter. Higher. Fearful. Close to panic. "Don't...don't do this. I know you don't want to do this. Kitty."

Behind him, something moved in the scrub, where trees started growing at the base of the hills. A wolf, moving in from the wild, trotted toward us. Then another. These were large—too big to be wild wolves. These were wolves that conserved the mass of their human halves—a hundred fifty, two hundred pounds maybe. Big, but still lithe, trotting smoothly and with purpose.

Behind them came a person—a woman, naked, flexing her muscles, her arms and hands, in a familiar gesture. She was about to shift.

I took a deep breath, trying to scent a nonexistent breeze, catching what odors the morning air carried. The pack. This place always smelled like pack—this is where they gathered, where they made their home. But this smell was alive, not a passive scent left behind on a place. The pack was here, now.

I ventured a look around. On all sides of us, people approached. I counted four, then six, then nine, and more. Shaun was one of them, coming from the street. He gave me a nod of acknowledgment. They weren't all dead. They'd found us.

Carl saw them, then. For just a moment, a hairbreadth of a moment, he smiled, almost relaxed—he thought he was saved, that his pack would rescue him.

But they weren't his pack anymore, and they all moved toward him. Their glares held malice. In return for the abuse he'd handed out, on behalf of the ones he had killed, they wanted blood.

Carl's expression turned to panic.

He raised his hands in a pleading gesture. "Kitty, no, no, please! I'll leave. I'll leave Denver, I won't come back. It'll be yours, it'll all be yours."

"It's already mine," I said.

His face went slack, as if the muscles gave out. The wolves, on two and four feet, came closer.

"Please let me go, Kitty." He sounded like a little boy. "I'll never bother you again."

My mouth was dry. But I had to see this through. I couldn't turn away. "You'll leave Denver, never come back?" I said. "Same deal you gave me?"

He nodded quickly. "Yes, yes!"

A dozen monsters wanted his blood.

"I'm sorry, Carl. That's not for me to decide."

The pack closed the circle around him. A wolf clamped teeth around his waist, another raked claws down his back.

Carl screamed and started to Change. His wolf had sensed the danger and had clawed its way to the surface. His face stretched, growing a snout. His reaching arms bore claws, his skin shone with fur. But it was too late. The others were too many and too strong. They overwhelmed him, swallowed him in their crowd. I lost sight of him, but still heard him. His screams came fast and desperate, turning high-pitched and squealing, like the wailing of a dog, then gurgled to silence. They tore him apart.

I dropped the gun and ran to Ben.

"Ben! Ben, hold on, please—"

"Kitty!"

Already sitting up, he fell into my arms. We clung to each other, as if afraid of drowning.

My arms tight around him, his blood soaking into my

clothes, smearing on my face, I kept saying, sobbing, over and over, "Don't die, don't leave me, don't ever leave me."

For all his injuries, he squeezed back just as tight. I couldn't breathe, and that was okay.

"I'm all right," he said, his voice weak. "I'll be all right. I won't go."

"I love you. I love you, Ben."

He kissed me. He could only find my ear because I pressed myself so tightly to him, my face against his neck. I responded, turning so my lips met his. He held my head, his fingers digging in my hair, and we kissed. I could taste the blood on his lips and face. I didn't want to come up for air.

Ben slumped against me, and I had a moment of panic. Maybe he wasn't all right after all, maybe he was dying, maybe—

He rested his head on my shoulder. He'd let himself relax, settling into my embrace. He wasn't going to shift, he wasn't going to die.

He murmured, "She kept saying, 'We'll give you back to her in pieces. We'll show you to her in pieces, before we take her apart.' And all I could think was, Don't hurt her. Please don't hurt her."

Together, we sighed. The world had paused for a moment, and we took advantage of it.

"Are you sure you're okay?" I tried to get a look at him, at his injuries. But I didn't want to move. I wanted to keep him close.

"I feel like shit," he said, and chuckled. "Dack's with them, he's one of the bad guys."

"I know. He's gone, he went away."

"Did we win? Did the good guys win?"

"Yeah, the good guys won. Let's take a look at you."

He winced as he straightened, and we surveyed the damage: bruises everywhere, cuts on his arms. His shirt was so torn it practically fell off him. Slash marks covered most of his body. Face, neck, chest, stomach. They looked deep and oozed red. The skin around the wounds separated when he breathed. She'd wanted to make it slow, which I supposed I ought to be grateful for. It kept him alive for me.

"Oh my God," I whispered, wincing in sympathy.

He shook his head. "It's already better. Now that she's stopped, it's better."

"You should lie still for a while."

"As long as you keep me company."

I smiled. "Okay."

The noise from the pack—ugly, wet noises—had stopped. The wolves remained. Most had Changed to their four-legged selves, pushed over the edge by the blood and violence. But they were all calm now, lying down, licking their paws, or each other's muzzles. A couple of human forms sat among them, watching them. Their arms were bloody.

There was no sign of Carl.

The wolves gathered around me and Ben. The whole crowd of them, over a dozen, formed a circle around us. When they noticed me looking at them, they glanced away, bowed their heads, lay back their ears, lowered their tails. All signs of submission. All body language that said, *You are the leader now.*

"I'm not ready for this," I whispered into Ben's neck.

"Didn't you say you wanted kids?"

Not like this. One kid, maybe. A child of my own flesh

and blood. Not…not a dozen killers. Still, I giggled, high-pitched and nervous.

"O alpha, my alpha," Ben said, and I punched his arm—very gently. He kissed my forehead.

Shaun hadn't joined the others in the kill. He'd stayed back, near me. Watching over us.

"You okay, Ben?" he asked.

"Getting there." He showed no inclination to try the next step of struggling to his feet, but that was fine. We could stay here awhile. We were safe now.

"What are you doing here?" I said, choking on the lump in my throat. "All of you." A couple of the wolves had perked up their ears, listening to us.

"Mick was watching the house, but when the cop got there he went into the hills. Lost phone reception, so Becky and Wes came looking for him. They caught Carl and Meg's scent and followed them. Then Rick called me about Ben and Dack. He said he sent the cops here as well. They should be here any minute."

I let out a bitter laugh. Rick probably thought calling the cavalry made up for sending Ben into danger in the first place.

"Thank you," I said, instead of swearing a blue streak.

"You looked like you were doing just fine," Shaun said.

I shrugged. To be honest, I was glad to not have to shoot Carl in the end. I didn't regret not being the one to pull the trigger on him.

"Wolves hunt in packs," I said, and left it at that.

Police sirens howled, far at first, but quickly growing closer. Sounded like three or four cars.

I sighed, resigned. I didn't know how I was going to explain all this.

"Wes!" Shaun called out to one of the pack who was still human. The man stood, displacing a couple of wolves who'd settled in near him. Wes trotted over. "Help me clean up."

Before moving off to where Meg lay, Shaun said to me, "We'll take care of it."

The two men pulled Meg's body off the ground, hoisting its arms over their shoulders. Meg's long, dark hair fell forward, masking her face. Quickly they dragged her into the hills, out of sight. There were places they could make bodies disappear. The pack cleaned up its messes. I watched her go, surprised at the hate still welling in me at the sight of her. Gone, she was gone, I had to remind myself. She couldn't hurt us anymore.

Ben brought me back to earth.

"Nice of them to give us some warning," Ben said. "It's Detective Hardin, isn't it?"

"Oh, probably."

"Should we go meet her? Where'd you put the gun? Ergh—" He tried to get to his feet, then slumped back, halted by pain.

"I dropped it. I'll look for it in a minute. Hardin'll take care of herself."

Sure enough, five minutes later, Hardin and a half-dozen officers came from the street, emerging around the cottonwoods. They fanned out, like they expected resistance in force, and they all had weapons drawn.

The wolves, the pack, had gone, fading into the hills. Only Ben and I remained, covered in drying blood, sitting in the dry summer grass, drenched in the morning light.

I put my hands harmlessly in the air and tried not to look like a target. "Hi, Detective."

"Kitty? What's going on here? Is everything okay? Oh, my God!"

She'd gotten her first look at us. We were a mess.

"It's over. It's all over," I said.

She hesitated, clearly at a loss for words. Not that I could blame her. Frankly, I didn't much care what she made of all this anymore. She could figure it out on her own.

"Do you need to go to a hospital?" she said finally, picking what seemed to be the most immediate problem.

Ben wore a punchy grin. Either he was feeling better or he'd completely lost it. "Naw. I just need to spend a day in bed with my girlfriend taking care of me."

Awe, he was so cute. A day in bed...sounded great. I wondered—was he too hurt to cuddle?

I asked, "Do you need us for statements or anything or can we go?"

"I ought to lock you both up," she said.

I batted my eyelashes innocently. Please, no more, just let me sleep...

She sighed. "Go. But I'll call you later."

"Thanks. Oh— and Dack's still loose," I said.

Hardin shook her head and smiled. "My guy staking out the house caught him speeding in a car I suspect is stolen. We've taken him into custody."

"Silver-painted cell?"

"You got it."

"And everyone lived happily ever after," Ben said, smiling vacantly.

Wow, I needed to get him home before he really did lose it. "Come on, Prince Charming." He had to lean on me and move very slowly, but he managed to stand. He was creaking like an old man.

"Don't forget the gun," Ben said.

Hardin looked at me. Watched me the whole time while I hunted around in the grass. I finally found it by the smell of spent powder.

"Do you have a permit for that?" she demanded.

"Yes, I do," I said quickly, returning to Ben's side.

She opened her mouth, pointed at me like she was going to say one thing. Then she shook her head. "You stay out of trouble. *Try* to stay out of trouble."

I smiled. "Thanks, Detective." I pulled Ben's arm around my shoulder and encouraged him to lean on me as we walked.

I couldn't guess what Hardin and her people would make of this. They'd find a lot of blood on the ground. A few shell casings. But no bodies. Nothing else to pursue. It ended here. Maybe, finally, it ended here.

Ben and I traveled to the street by the trailhead, and I walked him toward the BMW.

"Wow. You upgraded," Ben said.

"It's a loan."

"I hate to get blood all over that nice leather seat."

Too late. I'd already opened the door and lowered him into the passenger seat. "It's Rick's car. He'll appreciate it."

As we pulled out to the road and headed for home, Ben murmured, "The world looks better in the light, doesn't it?"

Morning was progressing nicely. In the east, the sun had risen fully, and the sky had finally turned blue. I glanced at him—he'd closed his eyes, and his breathing had turned deep and regular. He'd fallen asleep.

I smiled. "Yeah, it does."

Epilogue

About a week later, at twilight, I went to Carl and Meg's house. The place had an empty, haunted air to it. I wasn't sure what would happen to it. Ben said the bank would probably foreclose when the next couple of payments didn't come in. They'd discover it was abandoned. Maybe Carl and Meg would be reported as missing, if they hadn't already, and if they had a will or next of kin the house would go to them. If not, everything would go up for sale, and that would be that.

I had decided to move the pack to a different den. I wasn't sure where, yet. A few days ago we'd spent the last full moon—our first under the new management—in national forest land due west of Denver, along I-70. New territory for us. Untainted, I thought of it. The night went smoothly. The pack fed well on deer, slept and woke calmly. I was still getting used to the way they all slouched and ducked their gazes around me.

I was relieved that I'd managed to keep everyone safe. That was my job now: keeping them safe, keeping the peace.

I wasn't sure I wanted to do what Carl and Meg had buy a house and make the place home for both halves of my being. Or if I wanted to find an even wilder place and save it for the wolves. For the pack. Maybe I'd put it to a vote.

In the meantime, I had to come here one last time. I'd picked up some flowers on the way over—a mixed bouquet, not too big. Lilies, daisies, baby's breath. Happy, colorful flowers.

T. J. hadn't had a funeral. He didn't have a grave. But I remembered the spot where he'd died, thirty yards or so from the house, toward the hills, among the prairie grass and a smattering of pine trees. At least, I thought I remembered the exact spot. I wanted desperately to remember where that was, but I hadn't been thinking clearly that evening.

Walking out, I found the place where the shape of the ground looked right, along with the placement of the trees, the distance from the house, and the line of the hills. T. J.'s blood and scent had been washed away by a winter full of snow and spring full of rain. I smelled the pack, all the other werewolves running and breathing. But not him.

I sat on the ground and lay the flowers on the spot.

"Hi, T. J."

It hadn't even been a year since he died, but sometimes it felt like forever. He felt like a distant memory. Then, suddenly, I'd feel a stab through my heart all over again. I'd hear a sad song, drink bad coffee in an all-night diner like T. J. and I used to do after I got off my shift at KNOB, and all over again I'd be so angry that he wasn't still here.

It was a beautiful summer evening, the sky darkening

to a deep shade of blue, a cool wind washing away the day's heat. The scent of the hills swept over me.

I kept talking. Explaining. "Well. We got them for you. Revenge and all that. I feel bad because I didn't mean to. I didn't want to shoot her, I—"

I stopped, swallowed, shut my eyes. I'd killed her. And those two vampires, couldn't forget them, however easy it would be to call them monsters, inhuman, inconsequential. They'd been people, too. This wasn't the first time I'd killed someone, but the first time it had been Wolf who did it, out of instinct and self-defense, and he'd been a wolf and deranged to boot. It had seemed like a dream. And Arturo's two vampires had been to save myself and Hardin. It had happened so fast, it hardly seemed real. But Meg had been all me, wide awake, pulling the trigger. As much as I hated her, it still left a hollow spot inside me. I'd done something a normal, civilized person wasn't supposed to be able to do. I could still see the look on her face.

I wondered if I was ever going to have to do this again. The thought left me drained.

I tried again. I had to talk to T.J. "I didn't come back here wanting revenge. But maybe I should have. Maybe I should have been trying to get back at them all along, and—" I wiped my eyes. I'd never stop crying, would I? "So here I am. Back where I started. I just wish you were here, too. I don't think I can do this. Even with Ben, I'm just not sure."

Then, the wind stopped for a moment, and the world became very still. Quiet, like the pause before a sigh. A while back, a medium—a channeler, the real deal, not a fraud—told me that T.J. was looking out for me. That some part of him was watching — not a ghost, not an angel, nothing like that. Just…a presence. A voice. It sounded like my own conscience reminding me. Straightening out my path a little. I heard it now.

I'm proud of you, Kitty. You'll do fine.

Or maybe I imagined it. Not that it mattered. It sounded like what he'd have said, if he'd been here.

I smiled. "Thanks."

I returned to the street, to my car, and drove away.

Detective Hardin took me out to lunch. Nothing fancy, just a hamburger place near the police station. But it made me nervous. I wondered what she wanted.

After we ordered and the server moved out of earshot, she pulled a manila folder out of her attaché case. I *knew* it. Please, no bodies, no blood, no mauling, no death. I didn't want to help on any more cases.

"There's been another robbery," she said.

I needed a minute to think about that. I was expecting death and mayhem and she was talking a robbery? Oh, yeah—last month, the case she was working on before all the other crap happened.

"Any new leads?"

"Oh, I think so." She handed me the folder.

I opened it and found a couple of photos. They had the familiar, low-res, black and white appearance of security footage. The setting was your average, soda and cigarettes stuffed convenience store. The site of Hardin's robberies maybe? Instead of a blur at the counter this time, a very clear, very familiar figure stood collecting the goods.

Male, dark hair, sunglasses. His partner, a woman with a big ponytail, looked straight at the camera and waved. Charlie and Violet.

I couldn't help it. I covered my mouth to stifle a laugh. All a trick of the light.

Hardin jabbed her finger at the picture. "I knew I recognized them. We never got a clear shot before, but I just *knew*. I'm gonna get those two. Do you know I'm about to write a memo recommending that twenty-four-hour convenience stores put garlic and crosses in their doorways? I can't believe I'm going to do that."

"If it makes you feel better, robbery is beneath most vampires. I think those two do it because it's fun. For them," I quickly added. Actually, the more I thought about it, the funnier the whole thing got. Vampire crooks? Perfect. Just perfect.

"I'm still going to get them." She put away the folder. "I don't know how, but I'm going to do it."

That was next on her list—she'd gotten werewolves into custody. Now she had to figure out vampires. And if anyone could do it...

That made me wonder. "Last full moon. What happened with those werewolves you arrested?"

She blew out a sigh. "I commandeered a whole row of cells at county. Put silver paint in them, put each one in a separate cell. Got all my people out and watched the whole thing on closed circuit TV. Never seen anything like it." She shook her head, and her gaze turned vague, sliding to a different place, like she was recalling a nightmare. I supposed she was. "One of them kept throwing himself against the bars. I thought he was going to kill himself. In the morning he had welts all over his body—from the silver, not from bruising. The others snarled at each other for twenty minutes, then paced back and forth all night. We had our own zoo. But it worked. I think we can hold them as long as we need to."

"Give them something to eat next time. Raw meat. It might settle them down."

"Okay. Thanks."

I was curious. "What did you think of Dack?"

"I had to look in an encyclopedia to figure out what he even was. African wild dog? Where do they come up with this shit?"

I shrugged. Who knew? It only demonstrated that just when you thought you'd come to the end of what could possibly surprise you, something did.

"I'm in over my head," Hardin said. "I keep wondering which one of these things is going to get me. I keep going like this, something is going to get me."

I couldn't argue. She was like me. When this happened to me, I'd started reading. Delving. And that only touched the surface of what might be out there.

"Do you remember Cormac?" I said.

"The assassin? The one that went after you? Yeah."

"You should talk to him. He's in Cañon City, in prison—"

She snorted, interrupting. "About time. That guy's a menace."

Yeah, well… "His family's been doing this sort of thing for generations. He knows things that aren't in the books. He can help you. Give you some advice, maybe."

"So, I go talk to him, pick up some pointers, maybe get a few months shaved off his sentence for helping out?"

I perked up. "Can you do that?"

Now she sounded frustrated. "I'll consider it."

Which was something. For once, I felt better after a meeting with Hardin, rather than worse.

And this seemed as good a time as any to ask the big question. "Do you want to come on the show? I'd love to interview you. One of the first paranatural cops in the country—"

"No," she said, glaring and stabbing into her newly arrived plate of french fries with her fork.

Ah well. I couldn't have it all.

Mercedes Cook resumed her concert tour. The fallout from the public announcement of her vampirism was mixed. She was taken off the cast of the *Anything Goes* revival. The producers were fairly blunt about not wanting to be a party to the potential irony of having a vampire play the role of evangelizing chanteuse Reno Sweeney.

But her concerts sold out for the remainder of her tour. She added another dozen shows, and those sold out. She was in demand.

I had a feeling the whole performance gig was a sideline for her, and she didn't much care about getting kicked off the musical, or that her concert popularity was skyrocketing. For her, it was all a means to an end.

I wondered: In how many of those cities on her tour did she inspire mayhem? How many revolutions did she leave in her wake?

And how many others like her moved from place to place for the purpose of manipulating the players on their own personal game boards?

*   *   *

And finally, at long last, the book came out.

Check another one off the "dream come true" list. I got to sign books at the Tattered Cover Bookstore. Awesome.

The late-evening event was totally last minute. I hadn't planned on it—because I hadn't planned on being in Denver when we were setting up all the publicity. But, as they often do, the plans changed. And there was the book, in hardcover, with the title blazoned across it: *Underneath the Skin*. With a cheesy subtitle, "Life and Lycanthropy," which explained it all, really. The picture was from my trip to D.C. last fall, me walking through the crowd on the last day of the Senate hearings, my face looking up, determined, ready for the battles ahead. I hadn't felt like that when the picture was taken. I'd felt like I was drowning. Ben in his polished lawyer guise was at my side, calm and ready for anything. He'd helped me get through it.

Better yet, people even showed up. A whole line of them. How cool was that? The line even stretched to the end of the room. A really interesting mix of people made up the gathering. Some of them I expected: a couple of clusters of folks dressed all in black, with stripy stockings, corsets, dyed hair, eyebrow rings, the whole nine yards. They stood right next to people who would have been at home at my parents' country club. And everyone in between.

I even smelled a couple of vampires and lycanthropes.

Because of that, I wasn't surprised when the line moved forward and Rick appeared in front of me.

We regarded each other for a long moment.

I spoke first. "Did you get the car back okay?"

"Yes. I even refrained from sending you the cleaning bill for the interior."

"You mean you didn't just—"

"Ah, no. I have some dignity left."

I grinned at him. I had to appreciate a vampire with a sense of humor.

"I wanted to thank you," he said. "I couldn't have done it without your help. I'm glad everything worked out." Meaning: he was glad he didn't get Ben killed. Me, too.

"So you owe me big-time, right?" He only smiled. "Can I ask you a question?"

"You can ask."

"What's the Long Game?"

He considered a moment, glancing briefly around at the line of people waiting to get their books signed, at others who might be listening. I didn't expect him to actually speak. But he did, his voice low.

"Vampires have long lives. Long memories. Their strategies aren't planned in terms of years or decades, but in centuries. From the start, they've asked the question, how much power can they get? How much can they control—how many lives, how many cities? Can anyone control it all? What would happen if one person—one being—could control it all? That's the Long Game."

"Control it all," I said, baffled at the concept of trying to plan anything past next week. And here we were talking about centuries. "Why? Who'd want to?"

"That is a question I hope I never learn the answer to." He seemed tired. Sad, maybe. The smile hid pain. "Some of us refuse to be a party to it. We keep our pockets of chaos operating."

"This isn't over, is it?"

He shook his head. "We'll always have to watch."

For usurpers, for invaders, for the ultimate evil descending upon us and stealing our souls. All of the above. I didn't want to know.

I changed the subject. "Someday you have to tell me about Coronado. I want you to tell me where you came from and how you got here. The whole story. No dodging."

"All right. I will, someday."

Then he produced a copy of the book, which he'd been hiding behind his back. He gave me a *gotcha* look. "Can I get mine signed, too?"

Happily I took it and wrote with the most flourishing handwriting I could manage: *To Rick: Always look on the sunny side of life. Love, Kitty.*

Then Ben and I got this great idea. Well, I had the idea— borrowed it from Ahmed, the werewolf I'd met in Washington, D.C., who didn't hold with packs and fighting. But Ben made it happen. Found the place and did the paperwork to set up the business.

He let me tell Shaun about it.

I picked up Shaun after he got off work and took him to the storefront on the east side of downtown. It had been a bar and grill until a few months ago, and would be again, or something like it, maybe, with luck. Shaun knew the place. He gave me a startled look when I pulled out the keys for the front door.

"It's yours?" Shaun asked.

"Ben and I picked up the lease." I led Shaun inside.

The fixtures had been gutted, which was fine, because I hoped we could redo it all. The bar and shelves behind it were intact, but everything else was a wide open expanse of hardwood floor. Potential incarnate.

I told him about D.C. "There's this place run by a wolf named Ahmed. It isn't anybody's territory. Anyone's welcome there, as long as they keep the peace. Wolves, foxes, jaguars, lions, anybody. People come there to talk, visit, drink, play music, relax. No pressure, no danger. You understand?"

He nodded, donning a slow smile. "Rick's Café."

I shook my head. "No, it's got nothing to do—"

His grin broke full force. "Not that Rick. *Casablanca*."

Oh, that Rick. "Yes. Exactly. Ahmed subsidized his place with a restaurant, but this has to be a real business. It has to support itself, and there aren't enough lycanthropes around here to do that. So it has to be real, open to the public, everything, and still be a haven for people like us. And we need someone to run it. Do you think you can handle it?"

"Totally," he said, not even a spot of hesitation, which gave me confidence. "Absolutely. There—that's where the stage goes, for live music." He marched to a corner and turned, sweeping a circle with his arms. His eyes lit up with plans. "And no TVs. I hate TVs in bars. And maybe we can have a private room in back for the pack."

His enthusiasm was infectious. This was going to be good, I could feel it.

He said, "You know what you want to call the place?"

"I've had some ideas. Do you have any suggestions?"

He was still looking around, gazing in every corner, studying every wall. "New Moon," he said.

I could already hear Billie Holiday playing on the sound system. I could smell beer and fresh appetizers, hear an espresso machine hissing away in the corner. Sense the press of bodies around me, all of them smiling. Nobody fighting.

"I like it," I said.

"We'll stay open all night," he continued. "Feed the nightclub crowd on weekends. We'll need a liquor license, and—"

He kept going, spinning out plans, and I happily basked in the knowledge that I had chosen my minion well.

In the end, Mom was right. She'd been right the whole time, every single phone call she made to me when I was on the road, asking me when I was going to come home, making all those pleas. She knew, and I should have known, that I'd come back eventually.

For Mom's birthday, we had a big party at their house. The spirit of celebration was headier than usual. After facing the possibility that one of these birthdays we wouldn't have her anymore, we were determined to make a production of it. Cheryl had decorated the living room with streamers and balloons—which the kids couldn't keep their hands off. Then Jeffy started crying when Nicky popped one in his face, and well...Cheryl stuffed all the balloons in a closet after that, and Dad distracted the kids with wrapping paper and boxes, the best toys ever. I'd brought a huge ice cream cake. The whole family was there, relatives I hadn't seen in years stopped by, and with all the cake, snacks, and sodas, the whole place smelled like too much sugar.

The medical gurus decided Mom's cancer was Stage II. The prognosis was still good, as she kept saying. She was recovering from her second chemotherapy treatment. We'd tried to schedule the party so she'd be mostly over the effects, and the plan seemed to have worked. She was up, well, and smiling. She still had her hair, but not her appetite. We'd filled the house with her favorite foods, and she couldn't eat any of it. But she didn't complain. She was determined to put on a good show for our guests.

I felt a shadow over her, from what Arturo had said at the hospital. That she was still sick, the cancer was still there, waiting to strike. I thought about telling her, with the idea that she could do something about it, we could attack it, really stop it. But I didn't tell her. No matter what we did, we couldn't know if the cancer was all gone. And Arturo could have been lying about it. All we could do was wait, which we'd have had to do anyway.

Cheryl and I were friends again. Not that we'd ever stopped being friends. But we were sisters, and sometimes that was different. We could take each other for granted.

We sat on the sofa together, kvetching.

"It was *cool* having a DJ for a sister," Cheryl said, pouting a little. "I miss you just playing music all the time. You used to dig up the best stuff."

"Like you ever listened," I said. "I always did graveyards."

"What do you think I listened to when I was up with the babies at midnight?"

She had a point. I let the warm glow of the compliment settle over me. My sister, my big sister, listened to *my* shift. "I used to think you had the best stuff. I think you're the one who got me started on the whole music thing."

She narrowed her gaze. "Did you ever give me back that Smiths tape?"

"Oh no, we are *not* starting that again—"

Mom, as usual, intervened. "What about you, Ben—what kind of music do you listen to?"

"He doesn't like music," I said, glaring.

Ben occupied a nearby armchair, nibbling at a piece of cake and trying to be unobtrusive. He looked at me, feigning shock and hurt. At least I thought he was feigning.

"I never said that," he said. "I grew up watching MTV just like everyone else."

Cheryl said, "And he's old enough to remember when MTV played music."

I rolled my eyes. "Ah yes, the battle cry of Generation X." Now I had them both glaring at me. I gave up. I stood and headed toward the kitchen. "Anyone else want a soda?"

Mom watched all this, beaming, queen of all she surveyed. I stopped to hug her as I passed her chair. She was still sore, but her returning hug was strong. She'd make it, I knew she would, no matter what Arturo had said.

When I closed the fridge, I looked up to find that Ben had followed me into the kitchen.

"Can I talk to you a minute?" he said.

"What is it?" Something serious, I thought. Had to be. He had this look on his face, this too-somber and intent expression, like he was getting ready to do something difficult. To defend a client he knew was guilty. To break up with a girlfriend.

We stood for a moment, regarding each other, leaning side by side against the counter. My arms were crossed, his hands were shoved in his pockets. He was working up to saying something, and I wish he would just come out with it. I was starting to get nervous.

"Can I ask you a question?" he said.

"I think I already said yes, didn't I?"

He pulled his hand out of his pocket and held it out to me. It was cupping a box. One of those little black velvet boxes from jewelry stores. I stopped breathing. Honest to God, I stopped breathing.

"I thought since we seem to have gotten the wolf side all straightened out, if maybe you'd want to make it official on the human side." He opened the box, which was good, since all I could do was stare at it, completely dumbstruck. Sure enough, there it was. A diamond ring.

I looked at him. "You—you're joking."

"Oh, come on, even I'm not that big of a jerk. No, I'm not joking. Kitty—marry me."

And I still couldn't breathe. My eyes were stinging. I knew what to say. A shrill, obnoxious voice inside me— the DJ voice, I'd always thought of it—was screaming, *Say yes, you idiot! Yes!*

This was the most surreal thing that had ever happened to me. Then I realized—it was also one of the coolest things that had ever happened to me. I was about to burst, and that was why I couldn't speak.

But something was wrong. I swallowed, thinking there must be some kind of mistake. "It's silver."

"Ah, no. White gold. I thought it'd be funny." He shrugged and gave me the most sheepish, adorable grin I'd ever seen.

And it was funny, and I laughed, and threw myself at him, clinging to him, and he held me tight enough to break ribs, and I said it, "Yes, yes, yes."

"What the hell's going on in here?"

Ben and I pulled apart. My sister stood in the doorway. I was surprised to notice I didn't feel at all like she'd caught me at something, like I usually did. No, I felt very, very smug.

Cheryl continued giving us her demanding big sister glare. Ben regarded her a moment. Then, with an obvious and dramatic flourish, he took the ring from the box, held it up to show her, lifted my left hand, and slipped on the ring. He looked back at her with a smug glare. I was grinning like an idiot.

She shrieked loud enough to crack glass. Ben cringed.

"Oh my God!" Then she ran to the next room and shrieked again. "Oh my God! Guess what guess what guess what—"

At least she'd left Ben and me alone again. I pressed myself close to him and nestled happily in his arms. He held me like he wasn't going to let go anytime soon, which was just fine.

I felt him breathe out a long sigh. I could almost guess what he was thinking: *That's* going to be my sister-in-law? He said, "You have too much family, you know that?"

"Impossible," I said. "You can never have too much family."

NEW GIRL.
NEW SCHOOL.
SAME OLD MONSTERS.

As the new girl at the elite St. Sophia's boarding school,
Lily Parker thinks her classmates are the most monstrous things
she'll have to face. When a prank leaves Lily trapped in the catacombs
beneath the school, she finds herself running from a real monster.
This is a world of magic, vampires, demons and secrets.
Get ready to join the Dark Elite.

For more information, proof giveaways, exclusive competitions and
updates please visit: www.orionbooks.co.uk/gollanczya

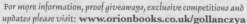

Philip K. Dick • Alastair Reynolds • H.G. Wells • Joe Abercrombie • Arthur C. Clarke • Charlaine Harris • Ursula Le Guin • Holly Black • Richard Matheson • Patrick Rothfuss • Kurt Vonnegut • Stephen Donaldson • Scott Lynch • Steph Swainston • Richard Morgan • Alfred Bester • Chris Wooding • Ray Bradbury • Carrie Ryan • Jacqueline Carey • Joe Haldeman • Kristin Cashore • Samuel R. Delany • Nalini Singh • Tom Lloyd • Ian McDonald • Chloe Neill • Stephen Deas • Pierre Pevel • David Moody • L.A. Banks • Suzanne McLeod • Sarah Pinborough • M.D. Lachlan • Gavin Smith • Graham Joyce • Sam Sykes • Jon Sprunk • Rob Scott • Adam Roberts • Hannu Rajaniemi • Mia James • Jonathan Maberry • Lynsay Sands • Mary Gentle • Paul McAuley • Geoff Ryman • Robert Rankin • Greg Egan • Beth Vaughan • Sheri Tepper • Gwyneth Jones • Carrie Vaughn • Sophia McDougall • Robert Holdstock • Justina Robson • Robert J. Sawyer • Ann Aguirre • Sarah Silverwood • Anna Kendall • Philip K. Dick • Alastair Reynolds • H.G. Wells • Joe Abercrombie • Arthur C. Clarke • Charlaine Harris • Ursula Le Guin • Holly Black • Richard Matheson • Patrick Rothfuss • Kurt Vonnegut • Stephen Donaldson • Scott Lynch • Steph Swainston • Richard Morgan • Alfred Bester • Chris Wooding • Ray Bradbury • Carrie Ryan • Jacqueline Carey • Joe Haldeman • Kristin Cashore • Samuel R. Delany • Nalini Singh • Tom Lloyd • Ian McDonald • Chloe Neill • Stephen Deas • Pierre Pevel • David Moody • L.A. Banks • Suzanne McLeod • Sarah Pinborough • M.D. Lachlan • Gavin Smith • Graham Joyce • Sam Sykes • Jon Sprunk • Rob Scott • Adam Roberts • Hannu Rajaniemi • Mia James • Jonathan Maberry • Lynsay Sands • Mary Gentle • Paul McAuley • Geoff Ryman • Robert Rankin • Greg Egan • Beth Vaughan • Sheri Tepper • Gwyneth Jones • Carrie Vaughn • Sophia McDougall • Robert Holdstock • Justina Robson • Robert J. Sawyer • Ann Aguirre • Sarah Silverwood • Anna Kendall •

Old Masters. Future Classics.

GOLLANCZ ADVANCE
BRINGING OUR WORLDS TO YOURS

Sign up to the Gollancz Newsletter
www.orionbooks.co.uk/newsletters